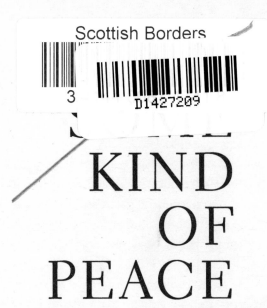

KIND
OF
PEACE

About the Authors

Camilla Grebe (b. 1968) is a graduate of the Stockholm School of Economics and has had several entrepreneurial successes. She was a cofounder of Storyside, a Swedish audiobook publisher, where she was both CEO and publisher during the early 2000s. She lives in Stockholm, Sweden.

Åsa Träff (b. 1970) is a psychologist specializing in cognitive behavioral therapy. She runs a private practice with her husband, also a psychologist. She primarily diagnoses and treats neuropsychiatric disorders and anxiety disorders. She lives in Älvsjö, Sweden.

SOME KIND OF PEACE

Camilla Grebe & Åsa Träff

Translated from the Swedish by Paul Norlen

**SIMON &
SCHUSTER**

London · New York · Sydney · Toronto · New Delhi

A CBS COMPANY

First published in Sweden by Wahlström & Widstrand under the title *Någon sorts frid*, 2009
First published in Great Britain by Simon & Schuster UK Ltd, 2012
A CBS COMPANY

1 3 5 7 9 10 8 6 4 2

Simon & Schuster UK Ltd
1st Floor
222 Gray's Inn Road
London WC1X 8HB

www.simonandschuster.co.uk

Simon & Schuster Australia, Sydney
Simon & Schuster India, New Delhi

A CIP catalogue record for this book is available from the British Library

Trade Paperback ISBN 978-0-85720-946-7
Ebook ISBN 978-0-85720-948-1

Poem © Erik Blomberg, translated by Paul Norlen. Permission granted by ALIS, Sweden.

Printed and bound by CPI Group (UK) Ltd, Croydon, CR0 4YY

TO MUM AND DAD

Don't be afraid of darkness,
for in darkness rests the light.
We see no stars or planets
without the dark of night.
The darkness of the pupil
is in the iris round,
for all light's fearful longing
has darkness at its ground.
Don't be afraid of darkness,
for in it rests the light.
Don't be afraid of darkness;
it holds the heart of light.
—Erik Blomberg

SOME
KIND
OF
PEACE

It seems so idyllic.

An insidiously calm, dew-damp morning. The rays of the sun slowly but relentlessly take possession of the art nouveau building's clean plaster façade, triumphantly embracing it with their indifferent heat and giving it a sheen the night had hidden.

As if nothing had happened.

As if this summer morning heralded a day like any other. A day full of life: sweaty bodies on bicycles; suppressed giggles in front of the ice cream stand by the harbor; steaming, sunburned shoulders; clumsy summer sex as light-blue twilight seamlessly turns to daybreak; the nauseating smell of white wine and lemonade in the pine needle–carpeted edge of the forest north of the pizzeria; the cold water of the lake against skinny child bodies with ribs that seem ready to burst out of their cages, through the soft, paper-thin, milk-white skin.

Gawky teenage boys swim races to the island and back, outlined like pale frog people, amphibious sailing vessels, against the water's saturated blue-brown darkness. They howl as they jump off the rock. The air is filled with the aroma of grilled meat and the sound of distant motorboats.

Mosquitoes. Wasps. Insects with no name: in your hair, in your mouth, on bodies, itchy, sweaty bodies.

As Swedish as it gets.

A summer without end.

As if nothing had happened.

Even the building appears indifferent. Heavy and listless, it sits in the lush garden, bedded in leafy, dew-covered greenery. Its massive three-story-high body reaches toward the blue of the brightening summer sky.

The plaster has not flaked in a single spot. The gray-green paint that covers the windowsills and doors is fresh and still glossy. There are no cracks or dust in the leaded, stained windowpanes with their coiling organic flower patterns. The roof is covered with old emerald-green copper plate, the kind roofers no longer use.

It seems so idyllic.

But something is out of place.

In the neatly raked gravel parking area is a dazzlingly clean black Jeep. The paint of the Jeep reflects a clematis with large pure white blossoms climbing up a knotted old apple tree. Someone is lying under the low trunk and crooked branches of the tree.

A young woman, a girl.

She is curled up in the grass like a bird, her red hair covered by a thin film of dew. Her slender, pale arms are thrown out along her sides, her palms turned upward in a gesture of resignation. The blood that has seeped from her body is congealed in reddish-brown patches on her jeans and in the grass. Her open eyes seem to be inspecting the crown of the apple tree.

Up there, in the branches, there are small green apples. There are many: The tree will bear plenty of fruit in just a few months. Above the apple tree the swifts and gulls fly unaffected—what do they care about a dead human child?

Under the body, the smallest inhabitants of the garden have already discovered what no person has yet seen. A small black beetle creeps between the waistband and the cold, pale skin in search of something edible; flies have set up camp in the lush red forest of hair; and microscopic creatures are moving slowly but steadily deeper and deeper into the windings of the ear.

In a little while, the inhabitants of the house will wake up and look for the girl. When they don't find her, they will search for her in the garden, where they will see her in the grass under the tree, her eyes gazing toward the sky.

They will shake her as if trying to wake her from a deep sleep, and when that doesn't work, one of them will slap her hard across the cheek, staining her face red with her own uncoagulated blood on his hand.

They will take her in their arms and slowly rock her back and forth. One of them will whisper something in her ear, while the other one buries his face in her hair.

Later, the men who never knew her, who don't even know her name, will come to get her. They will put their calloused hands around her slender, rigid wrists and ankles and lift her effortlessly onto a cold stretcher, cover her with plastic, and drive her far, far from home.

She will be placed on a metal table, alongside the surgical instruments that will open her up and—hopefully—solve the mystery, explain the unexplainable, restore balance. Bring clarity to something no one understands.

Create closure and perhaps peace as well.

Some kind of peace.

AUGUST

Date: August 14
Time: 3:00 p.m.
Place: Green Room, the practice
Patient: Sara Matteus

"So, how's your summer been?"

"Is it okay if I smoke?"

"Sure."

Sara roots around in her camouflage-pattern cloth bag and pulls out a red pack of Prince cigarettes and a lighter. With chapped, trembling fingers she lights a cigarette and takes two deep puffs before she fixes her gaze on me. She inspects me awhile in silence before blowing out a cloud of smoke between us—a carcinogenic smoke screen—which for a moment conceals her heavily mascaraed eyes. There is something demonstrative about the gesture, something both playful and provocative that makes me decide not to release her gaze.

"Well?" Sara says slowly.

"Summer?"

"Oh, right. Summer. It was good. I worked at that bar in Gamla Stan, you know, by Järntorget."

"I know. How have you been feeling?"

"Good, really good. Just great. No problems."

Sara falls silent and looks at me with an inscrutable expression. She is twenty-five but doesn't look a day over seventeen. Bleached-blond hair in various shades of white and butter-yellow curls down her slender shoulders, forming tangled ringlets along the way. Ringlets. She twists them with her fingers when she gets bored and sometimes slides them in and out of her mouth as she bites or chews on them. When she's not chewing on her hair, she smokes. She seems to always have a cigarette ready in her chapped fingers.

"No anxiety?"

"Nah. Well, maybe a *little* . . . at times. I mean, Midsummer and that kind of shit. Doesn't everybody get anxiety then? Who doesn't get anxious at Midsummer?"

She looks searchingly at me in silence. A smile plays at the edge of her mouth before she continues.

"You can bet your ass I get anxious."

"And what did you do?"

"Nothing," says Sara, looking at me through the cigarette smoke with an empty stare. She seems strangely indifferent in the face of the emotions of anxiety and estrangement triggered, she claims, by the Midsummer celebrations.

"You didn't cut yourself?"

"Nah . . . Well, just a *little*. On my arms, that is. Just my arms. Had to, couldn't put up with the Midsummer thing otherwise. But. Not much. I promised you that I wouldn't cut myself anymore. I always keep my promises, really. Especially when I promise *you* something."

I notice Sara hiding her forearms in a presumably unconscious gesture.

"How many times did you cut yourself?"

"What do you mean? Like, how many cuts?"

"No, *on how many occasions?*"

"Ahh, a few. A couple, maybe three times during the summer. I can't remember . . ."

Sara's voice trails off and she puts out the cigarette in the blue flower vase that I had put on the coffee table in an attempt to make the room more inviting. I must be the only psychologist in Sweden who allows a patient to smoke, but Sara gets so restless otherwise, it's almost impossible to carry on a conversation with her.

"Sara, this is important. I want you to return to those occasions when you cut yourself. Try to remember what happened, what it was that triggered the feelings that made you do it."

"Uh . . ."

"Start with the first time. Take your time. When was it? Start by telling me when it happened."

"Must have been Midsummer Eve. At the Midsummer celebration, that is. I already said that!"

"What did you do that night? I mean, beforehand?"

"I went to see my mom. It was just her and me. She had made some food and stuff. And she bought wine."

"So you weren't at a Midsummer party?"

"Nah, that was more like a, what's it called . . . a metaphor. A metaphor for how fucked-up Midsummer is. Everyone's so happy. You have to socialize with your family and be happy. It's somehow so . . . forced."

"So the two of you weren't happy?"

Sara sits quietly for a long time without speaking and for once holds her hands calmly in her lap while she thinks. The only sound in the room is the humming of the video camera as it records our conversation. She sighs deeply, and when she starts talking again, I can sense her irritation despite the calm, expectant tone of voice.

"Nah, but I'm sure you get that. I really don't understand where this is supposed to lead. I've talked about my old lady at least a *thousand* times. You *know* she's a drunk. *Hello,* do I have to write it down for you? It was like it always was. Everything was going to be so nice . . . and then . . . she just drank, and then she started bawling. You know that's how she gets when she drinks. Sad and . . . like . . . She's, like, sorry. Like she regrets everything. Like I should sit there and forgive her because she hasn't been a good mother. Do you think I should forgive her?"

"What do you think?"

"Nah, I don't think so. I think it's unforgivable, what she did to me."

"So what did you do?"

Sara shrugs, and I can tell by her posture that she no longer wants to talk about either her mom or herself. Her voice has become shrill, and pink patches are spreading on her neck like spilled wine on a tablecloth.

"I split. I can't stand it when she's bawling."

"And then?"

Sara squirms and lights yet another cigarette.

"Home, I went home."

"And?"

"But you *KNOW* what happened then. It's the old bag's fault. It's like I can't . . . can't breathe when I've been there."

Now Sara is getting angry. That's good. I'll try to hold on to that feeling. When Sara is angry, the truth often comes out. The protective shield of self-manipulation disappears, replaced by the raw honesty of someone who doesn't have much to lose, who doesn't care what you think of her.

"You cut yourself?"

"Damn straight I *cut* myself."

"Tell me more." I say.

"But, *seriously,* you *know* what happened."

"This is important, Sara."

"I cut myself on the arm. Satisfied now?"

"Sara . . . listen to me! What you're describing, what you're feeling, it's completely understandable. It's Midsummer, you see your mom, she is drunk and asks you for forgiveness, this stirs up a lot of emotions. Can you see that?"

Sara looks down at her fingers, closely studying every fingernail. She nods, as if to confirm that she too thinks that maybe her emotions and reactions are understandable.

"The problem is that when you start feeling anxious, you want to cut yourself, which is not a good solution, especially not in the long run."

Sara nods again. She knows that the cutting, the drinking, the impulsive sexual relationships provide relief only for the moment, and that the self-loathing and pain come back with redoubled force. Her desperate attempts to try to keep the anxiety at bay only seem to increase it.

"Did you try to do what we talked about before? You know, trying to put up with the anxiety. In itself, anxiety is never dangerous. It just feels that way. That's what you have to work with, putting up with that feeling. Just for a while, because then it passes."

"I know."

"And the other times?"

"What other times?"

"That you cut yourself."

She sighs and looks pointedly out the window. Fury has partly been replaced by fatigue in her voice.

"Oh, yeah. One time I was drunk, so that doesn't really count. I'm not really myself then. It was at a party in Haninge, with a guy from work."

"Did anything in particular happen at the party that triggered those emotions?"

Sara shrugs and drops yet another cigarette butt in the vase with my by now nicotine-poisoned flowers.

"Try. Sara, this is important. And you have to help. I know it's hard."

"There was a guy there . . ."

"And?"

"And, he was a little like Göran."

"Your foster dad?"

"Yeah." Sara nods. "He touched me like Göran. Suddenly . . . you know I don't like thinking about that stuff, and when he started groping me, grabbing me with his icky hands, it all just came back. I pushed him hard, right into a table. He was really loaded, so he fell down and cut his eyebrow."

"What happened then?"

"Well, he got really mad. Started yelling and chasing me around."

Sara suddenly looks exhausted and strangely small in her chair.

"Listen, it wasn't really as bad as it sounds. He was loaded, did I already say that? He couldn't get ahold of me. I went home."

"And?"

"And then I did it, *okay*? Can we talk about *something else* now?"

"Try to describe how you felt just before you cut yourself."

"What I *felt* then? HEL-LO, you KNOW how I felt. Like I was about to fall *apart*. I thought about that disgusting guy and about his icky groping and about Göran, and then it felt like I was going to fall apart, or that I couldn't get any air. And then I did it, and then it felt better. I felt, like, cleaner. And calm. I could sleep. Okay? Can we talk about something else now? I've got to go soon anyway. I have an interview for an internship. Can we talk next time instead?"

"Until then I want you to do the homework we talked about, Sara."

"Sure. So I can leave now?"

"Go ahead. See you next week."

I turn off the video camera and sink back in my chair. As always after my sessions with Sara, I feel drained. It's not just due to all the awful things she tells me, it's also because I have to be on my guard the whole time— being Sara's therapist is like walking a tightrope.

Her background is unfortunately not all that unusual. She grew up in a seemingly normal middle-class home in Vällingby, the youngest of three siblings. The only thing that was abnormal in her family situation was that her mother had problems with alcohol, but she could still function well socially. Sara always says that she even benefited from her mother's drinking at times, when she was younger. Her mother kept silent at the parent-teacher meetings, for example, aware that she would expose herself as an alcoholic the moment she opened her mouth. She was always wasted when Sara came home, never questioned where she had been, why she came home in the middle of the night, or now and then where she got her new clothes—clothes her parents hadn't bought for her.

From an early age, Sara had difficulties concentrating and problems in school. In third grade she set fire to the curtains in the gym with a lighter she had swiped from the PE teacher (who would always sneak a smoke in the locker room while the kids jogged around the schoolyard, lap after lap in the fall rain). In middle school she rode in a police car for the first time after she was caught shoplifting at the Konsum supermarket. She started seeing older guys and paired up with Steffe, who was eighteen when she was thirteen. She got pregnant and had an abortion.

It was around then that her parents realized they had completely lost control and they went to social services to get help. An investigation by the local office resulted in Sara's being assigned a contact person and forced to submit regular urine samples. Such measures are usually pretty toothless, and they were in this case, too. Sara's contact person gave up the assignment after Sara called her obscene names and spit on her desk. The social worker claimed that she felt threatened by Sara, but perhaps the truth was that she got tired of how difficult and demanding Sara was, and that not even she could cope with her.

Aggressive? Absolutely. But I have never seen Sara hurt anyone other than herself. She has what might best be described as an unfailing, almost paranormal capacity to consistently choose the option most detrimental to her, always following the path that causes her the maximum amount of pain. She seems to have a kind of built-in, indestructible Via Dolorosa compass in her skull.

After she offended the social worker, Sara was placed in a foster home. When she was fifteen, she was raped repeatedly by her foster father, which led her to do the only—from her viewpoint—logical thing: try to run away. She almost succeeded several times but was always caught and returned to the foster home by the overzealous local police force. That was when the truly destructive behavior started—the self-injuring and sexual acting out.

When Sara was eighteen, she received a real psychiatric diagnosis for the first time: borderline personality disorder. As usual, the fact that psychiatry was finally able to put a label on what was wrong with her did not help. She got steadily worse. Shortly thereafter she was treated at a psychiatric clinic for two months for a presumably drug-induced psychosis-like condition. Sara herself usually refers to the psych clinic as "hell," and I assume that in her descent there she more or less gave up any ambition of having a normal life, a "Svensson" life, as she always called it. In Sara's case, the stint at the psychiatric institution was followed by increasingly intense drug abuse, and six months after she was discharged from the clinic, she was committed to a facility in Norrtälje for treatment with special focus on her drug problems, which at that point primarily consisted of abuse of amphetamines and synthetic hallucinogens.

Then something happened. It's not clear what. Not even Sara can explain it, other than that she decided to live. So as not to die.

And today? Drug-free for two years and living in her own apartment in Midsommarkransen. Unemployed. Single. With many friends and even more boyfriends.

Sara is truly a veteran within psychiatry. She has been analyzed from every which way: by psychiatric outpatient clinics and in institutional care. She has met more social workers, caseworkers, psychologists, and psychiatrists than I have had patients. This creates an obligation. Sometimes it feels as if she is evaluating me and my analysis, categorizing me and sorting me into a mental ranking of shrinks. She makes comments that undoubtedly are derived from conversations with my predecessors: "I see, but have you taken into account the increasing sibling rivalry that was the result of my parents' early separation?" or "I realize this sounds really Oedipal, but sometimes I actually thought Göran loved me in *that* way."

I think of Sara's thin, scarred legs and arms. They resemble a railroad yard where the tracks sometimes cross each other, sometimes run parallel. Girls who cut themselves to relieve their anxiety are often called "cutters."

But obviously Sara is much more than a psychiatric diagnosis. She is intelligent, an expert at manipulation, and, actually, pretty entertaining when she is in the right mood. Now she needs to be rehabilitated once again. To the kind of *normal* life she has never had and never expected to have.

I put my hand on her file—as thick as a Bible—complete with investigations from social service agencies, case records from the psychiatric outpatient clinic and institutional care. I browse through the documents absentmindedly. My gaze stops at the notes from St. Göran's Hospital, from the time when Sara was admitted to the psych ward.

Patient: Sara Matteus, ID no. 82 11 23–0424

Reason for admission: Pat. comes to psych. ER 6:37 p.m. via Norrmalm police after having been taken into custody for shoplifting in the Twilfit store, Gallerian. As pat. acted confused and aggressive, police brought pat. to psych. ER.

Current: Pat. is an 18-year-old woman with drug problems and anxiety disorder UNS. She has previously been in contact both with CAP and psychiatric outpatient (Vällingby outpatient clinic). Presently pat. has no psychiatric contact and is not on medication. Pat. states that she does not feel well and wants help. She is oriented for brief periods and then complains of severe anxiety and also says that she has taken drugs but cannot remember what. Otherwise aggressive and expresses paranoid compulsive ideas that she is being persecuted by social services and police. Pat. shows signs of self-injuring behavior (scars and wounds on forearms and inside of thighs).

I sigh and let go of the heavy file, causing the documents to fall on the floor with a dull thud. I've had my dose of Sara Matteus for the day. It's time to air out the office and see Ilja, the Russian mother of a small child who met her Swedish husband on the Internet. The woman who is doing so well in Sweden and already speaks fluent Swedish. The woman who is so capable and well-adjusted, and works as an OR nurse at Sophiahemmet, but who suffers from an irrepressible compulsion to hide all the knives and scissors in the family's garden shed out of fear of hurting her baby with a sharp object.

It seems so idyllic.

My small house is a stone's throw from the shore. Large French windows cover the side facing the water—the house gets a lot of light. The floors are made of old, wide, worn pine boards separated by deep cracks filled to the brim with decades of dust. In the kitchen, the original 1950s cabinets with sloping blue plywood sliding doors live awkwardly side by side with new appliances. The bedroom faces the cliffs on the one side of the point, and through the large window the sea is visible on the other even when I'm lying on the bed, which is much too wide for me. The bathroom is in a separate building, in what was once a little woodshed. To get there I have to go out the door at the front of the house and pass through flower beds of dog roses.

In front of the house is a small expanse of lawn. Undisciplined and overgrown, it makes all traditional lawn activities impossible. I have trampled down two narrow paths through the wild vegetation: one to the lopsided old pier and one to the rocks. By the shore, red-leaved sedum grows among the heather and thyme. Small wind-whipped pines border the large rocks before the forest begins. Even though I live less than an hour from Stockholm, my closest neighbor is almost half a mile away.

It was Stefan's idea to live like this, spartan and close to nature, close to diving sites. It seemed like a good idea. At the time. No dreams were too naïve, no ideas too wild for me then. Now I don't know anymore. Along with the solitude, a strange passivity has come; changing light-bulbs is suddenly a major task and repainting the woodshed feels like an unachievable enterprise, impossible to break down into manageable stages of work. But moving isn't an option either. I wouldn't know where to begin.

My friends usually observe me with a mixture of compassion and horror when they visit. They think I ought to clear out Stefan's things: the razor in the bathroom, the diving equipment in the shed, the clothes in the closet, the watch on the nightstand that I hold at night when the sense of loss is too great.

"You can't live in a mausoleum," Aina always says, gently tousling my short hair.

She's right, of course. I ought to clear out Stefan's things. I ought to clear out *Stefan*.

"You're working way too much," she says then, and sighs. "Come out with me this weekend."

I always thank her and decline. There's so much to do with the house and so many patient protocols to be written. Papers to be sorted. Upon hearing this, Aina always smiles as if she knows I'm lying, which of course I am.

Sometimes Aina stays with me instead of spending the weekend in the noisy bars of Södermalm in the company of men whose names she quickly forgets. We eat mussels cooked in wine, drink lots of cheap white wine, and talk about our patients or Aina's guys—or about nothing in particular. We jump naked from the rocks into the water and listen to David Bowie at too high a volume while the forest animals watch in horror.

After she leaves, the house feels even emptier than before, with its windows gaping like big vacant holes toward the sea, and the deafening silence. I always wake up with a hangover and, because I'm too lazy to go shopping, I often end up eating vanilla ice cream for lunch and pasta with ketchup for dinner—with a couple of glasses of wine. When evening comes, I always make sure I turn on all the lights—because I don't like darkness. It's as if the absence of light erases the boundary between me and the world around me, which frightens me more than I want to admit and brings forth the feeling I know best of all: fear.

I have dealt with fear for many years now, and without exaggeration I can say that we are close, so close that I no longer notice when he arrives in the twilight. Instead, I receive him with resignation, like an old, if unwelcome, acquaintance.

And that is why I sleep with all the lights on.

So I'm a therapist. On the door to the practice a shiny brass nameplate clearly states: SÖDERMALM PSYCHOTHERAPY PRACTICE. CERT. PSYCHOLOGIST, CERT. PSYCHOTHERAPIST. SIRI BERGMAN.

I sometimes wonder how my patients would react if they knew that the seemingly calm, competent woman they turn to with their secrets and fears cannot sleep alone in a dark house. What would they think about my inability to confront my own phobias, when I demand that they approach theirs head on? These thoughts make me feel ashamed; I'm a bad therapist, I've failed, I should have gotten over it, it's in the past.

I should have moved on.

Aina always laughs at me and attributes my worries to my need for control and my perfectionism. "You are not your profession," she says. "Being a therapist is not a stupid *calling*. You come here and see your four patients a day and then you go home and be Siri. Being a depressed, passive failure with phobias can make you a better therapist, damn it. Just as long as you aren't that way with your patients. By the way, you should have learned about this during the first semester of psychology."

And Aina ought to know, because her name appears under mine on the shiny brass plate: AINA DAVIDSSON. CERTIFIED PSYCHOLOGIST. CERTIFIED PSYCHOTHERAPIST.

Aina and Siri. A team since those first nervous weeks at Stockholm University. The strange thing is not that we're still friends but that we made our dream of starting our own practice a reality. We have one other colleague, Sven Widelius, an old fox who has worked as a therapist for more than twenty years, with whom we share the office, a receptionist, and a break room. Our collaboration with him extends no farther than this. The practice is by Medborgarplatsen, in the same building as the futuristic premises of Söderhallarna, just a few floors up.

Every weekday morning I stop and catch my breath after running up the stairs. I look at the polished nameplate, think, hesitate, and then put the key in the lock.

And today is no different from the rest. It is the middle of August. The summer has been intensely beautiful in a dangerous, slightly erotic way. The scents and odors of nature are sultry sweet and suffocating, reinforced by the oppressive heat. In the city, the metallic odor of car exhaust and air pollution blends with the scents of cooking from restaurants and hot dog stands. And in the midst of this cacophony of aromas, it's there—the unmistakable smell of decomposition.

Both in the city and out at my home, the vegetation quivers with intensity and the air is filled with thousands of flying insects. I can hear the sound of creeping, wriggling, primitive life as I walk between the bus stop and my home. The green carpet of the forest vibrates with the movements of millions of bugs, and every step I take crushes innumerable small organisms, creating new biotopes of trampled-down moss and squashed ants and beetles. For me, the fleshy sensuality of summer is the high point of the year.

But summer is also demanding. We must partake in happiness and social life, friendly gatherings and vacation. This year, my summer has consisted of a required stay at Mom and Dad's cabin in the forests of Sörmland. For one week I was forced to listen to my parents' and siblings' concerns and fretting, before they dared let me go home again. I could see the fear just behind Mom's smile and in my sisters' way of treating me, as if I were made of brittle porcelain. And there was panic right below the surface of my dad's attempts at conversation. I doubt that anyone really missed me when I finally went home.

The rest of the summer I spent sitting in my garden, looking out over the sea, thinking about taking up diving again. The equipment is here. I have the experience. I miss the feeling of immersing myself in another world—perhaps a better one. Diving doesn't frighten me, despite all that's happened, but I don't have the energy to maintain the commitment that's required. And I don't want to have to see old friends from that period of my life.

Instead I puttered aimlessly about the flowerbeds and drank wine, played with the fat farm cat, Ziggy, who made a home for himself in my house a year or so ago, and endured the endless space of time called summer.

Until now.

It is my fourth day of work. Day four. With four appointments.

Marianne is at the reception desk. A part-time secretary is a luxury we don't really need but indulge ourselves in anyway. She has only been with us for a year, but her work ethic makes the rest of us look downright lazy. She has transformed the office into a professionally run operation, where the patients always get written notices and the bills get paid on time.

Marianne. How would we manage without her? She grins as I come in, her short blond hair curling at her forehead.

"Siri! Now we're at full capacity today, too! You have a cancellation at ten o'clock."

She immediately looks regretful, as if it were her fault that Siv Malmstedt is no longer coming. If I had to guess, Siv has canceled in order to avoid being exposed to a two-hour subway ride. Marianne, who is familiar with the procedures, informs me that a bill has been sent and that Siv still wants her usual time next Thursday.

The practice is small but cozy. We have three consultation rooms, a reception desk, and a small kitchen where we make coffee. At the far end of the practice is a bathroom with a shower. My office is casually called the Green Room, because the walls are painted a soft lime-blossom color, in an effort to evoke a peaceful atmosphere. Otherwise it looks like any therapist's office: two chairs at an angle to each other, a small table with a hand-blown glass flower vase, and a box of tissues that signals that here you can open up, let go of your feelings, and cry.

A whiteboard is mounted on the wall, which is otherwise decorated with neutral lithographs by the usual suspects. What possibly distinguishes my office from most other therapy offices is the old video camera sitting on its tripod. I record the majority of my sessions. Sometimes so the patient can take a copy of the session tape home, sometimes for my own sake.

The tapes are part of the case records and are stored, locked, in a heavy green fireproof cabinet in the reception area. Aina claims that my tapes are further evidence of my need for control and complains that there is less and less space in the cabinet for her own records. I reply that she mustn't worry, since she never writes notes longer than two lines.

She leaves me alone.

I had to make her understand. That was how it all started. I had to make her understand what she had done to me. But how could I explain? That at night the pain twisted like a thousand knives in my guts, knives that work their way up through my belly and chest. As if a ravenous predator were eating me up from inside, a massive parasite with razor-sharp teeth and cold, smooth lightning-fast limbs from which it is impossible to free myself.

Would I be able to describe the emptiness and the loss? That every sunrise announced that yet another meaningless day was approaching. Meaningless hours filled with equally meaningless activities awaiting nothing. And with every day the distance increased. The distance from Her.

Would I be able to explain that my dreams were so intense and real that I wept with disappointment when I woke up, bathed in sweat like in a fever?

Can you get someone else to understand something like that anyway? And even if I succeeded, what good would it do?

Really?

Date: August 16
Time: 1:00 p.m.
Place: Green Room, the practice
Patient: Charlotte Mimer

"Charlotte, I think we should start by looking at how things have been going for you over the summer. It's been a long summer break."

"I think the summer was just fine. I'll be happy to show you my entries."

Charlotte Mimer bends over her briefcase and pulls out a folder where the pages of her food diary are in perfect order. I note that as usual she has made all her entries with the same pen and in her signature tidy handwriting. Charlotte hands over the folder to me as she pushes her well-coiffed brown hair behind one ear. I see that she is expectant and proud, and I feel happy for her sake.

"Let's start by looking at the entries from June."

This summer I had asked Charlotte to take notes about every meal: where she was, what she ate, and how much. And at the end of each meal she would assess her uneasiness and distress. For an individual with a serious eating disorder, ordinary mealtimes often give rise to strong anxiety; food is associated with fat. To avoid this feeling, certain destructive behaviors develop and may last for years: starvation, vomiting, and excessive exercise. The patient may not even be aware that all this leads to renewed bingeing, and yet the anxiety is so strong and painful that for the moment it doesn't matter. It's a vicious cycle.

I pick up Charlotte's meticulous food diary and look through the entries for June. Regular mealtimes, no high-anxiety estimates after finished meals, no overeating, no vomiting.

"Can you tell me about it?" I ask.

"I don't know . . . it just went fine. Suddenly it was . . . easy."

Charlotte is about forty years old and successful in business. She works as a marketing manager at a large international company. She has struggled with eating disorders in silence for almost twenty-five years. It was only when her dentist confronted her about the corrosion damage to her teeth that she sought help. She has been in treatment since the end of April and is something of a model patient. Just as she is a perfect marketing manager, she is also the perfect psychotherapy patient. Her major problems seem to stem from the incredibly high demands she places on herself. Charlotte is scared to death of failing. So far we have touched on this only peripherally, working on reducing her bingeing and vomiting. In contrast to Sara Matteus, Charlotte seems to spread energy around her. Her fear of being incompetent or inadequate makes me feel accomplished and capable.

We continue to study Charlotte's notes. July, August: low anxiety, no vomiting. We find ourselves laughing together, and Charlotte finally gets the praise she so desires, and that she also deserves.

"There was something else, too."

Charlotte looks hesitant. She squirms in the 1950s-style Lamino chair and, as always when she is worried, she starts wiggling one foot, today clad in a Tod's loafer. I suspect this is a type of shoe I could never afford.

"Tell me!"

"I don't know . . ."

Charlotte suddenly looks as if she is keeping a secret. A secret that she will soon tell me. You see, that's the way it works: They tell me all their secrets in the little green room.

"I don't know if it has to do with therapy exactly. I've been thinking, you know, about life."

Charlotte stops herself and a blush creeps up her neck. I realize that it takes a lot of courage for her to bring up what she now wants to say.

"I've spent . . . how many years is it really—good Lord, twenty-five, maybe?—devoting all my time to thinking about food. And about my body. And about my stomach. And about my thighs. And about going to the gym. When I wasn't doing that, I was working. Work. Body. Food.

I'm the youngest, most successful marketing manager at the whole company, but I have no life. No *real* life. No friends. No *close* friends, anyway. No husband. No children. I've been so preoccupied with making myself perfect that I've forgotten why I wanted to be perfect. I wanted . . . to be . . . loved. I want to be loved. And now it's too late."

The tears have burst forth and are running down Charlotte's blushing cheeks like little streams. She sniffs and takes several tissues from the box. Blows her nose, dries her tears, and cries some more. I push the box across the table toward her and place my hand lightly on her arm.

"Charlotte." I catch her gaze. "It's not unusual to feel this way when you're going through what you are right now . . . You've been handicapped, held back by a severe illness, and now you're starting to get healthy. Of course there will be insight into the years you've missed. It's not strange. It's good. What I want to know is why you say it's too late now."

She sits silently while inspecting the wall above my head before answering in a cracked voice.

"Old, I'm getting old. And it's as if I can't understand it, can't take it in. It's like I'm just waiting to . . . that I'll be young again."

"Young again?"

"Well, by spring maybe?" she says and smiles—a crooked, melancholy smile, filled with pain.

I smile back. The thought sounds familiar somehow, as if time were a channel, where it was possible to travel in both directions under controlled circumstances, instead of a waterfall. She shrugs slowly and fixes me with a dejected look.

"Who will want me now . . . I am . . . maybe I can't even have children now."

Charlotte's sorrow. Charlotte's fear. So close to my own. No children. Too late. No husband. No idea. Never again.

I try to collect Charlotte's thoughts and do something with them. Get her to look at them from outside. Objectively. Assess the level of truth in these assertions. We agree on an assignment for Charlotte to work on, and then her forty-five minutes are over and she takes out a brush, pulls it through her hair, and somehow manages to collect herself. When she shakes my hand and says good-bye, the sobbing little girl Charlotte Mimer is no longer there. Out of the room walks marketing manager Charlotte Mimer and I, psychotherapist Siri Bergman, stay behind.

I go to the window and look down at the street. Far below me, on the stone pavement of Medborgarplatsen, a group of preschool children walks by. The August sun is shining like it doesn't have the sense not to. No noise penetrates my office, but when I close my eyes I can imagine how the children's voices sound down there. A quiet feeling that I cannot identify fills my chest. Maybe it's sorrow, maybe it's only calm and emptiness.

Evening.

There is a ritual I have to perform every evening. Almost without exception, I bring work home with me. When it's finished, I go for a swim in the sea. When it's summer I try to take the opportunity to swim a little. Then I prepare dinner.

Dinner for one.

It's never elaborate or nutritious: spaghetti with canned tomato sauce, frozen pancakes, Frödinge brand quiche, grilled chicken from the ICA supermarket in Gustavsberg. I don't even own a cookbook. I drink wine with dinner, carefully clean up after my meal, and then go outside and walk the short stretch between the rosebushes to the bathroom in the shed; I don't want to risk needing to go outside after the onset of darkness. I call for Ziggy. Sometimes that works. Certain nights he wants to go his own way instead of warming my bed. When I've returned to the house, I go through all the rooms and turn on the lights. All the lights: ceiling lamps, bed lamp, desk lamp, even the stove light in the kitchen. I check that the big flashlight is strategically located next to my nightstand. Power outages are not unusual where I live. Then I look out into the darkness through the big windows, which at this time of evening are like empty, black holes.

I fall asleep, deeply and dreamlessly, with the help of a little more wine.

One of my earliest memories from childhood is when my sister locked me in the closet in her room because I had smeared Nutella in the hair of her Cindy doll. I hadn't planned to transform the doll's flowing locks into a poop-brown cake of oily, rancid Nutella. The idea was to make

Cindy better looking. My mom and my sisters all used face masks and hair packs when they wanted to look really good.

I clearly remember how I begged and pleaded for her to let me out as she roughly and mercilessly shoved me deeper into her closet. "You brat! I'll kill you if you touch my Cindy again!"

It was dark and stuffy in the closet, the heavy air felt like it was pressing against my face and my thin limbs, forcing me farther and farther back against my will. I remember a faint odor of wool and dust and something else, like rubber.

Haltingly, I made my way in the darkness with my hands stretched out in front of me. Clothes that had been stored away for the summer brushed against my cheeks and the steel edges of a pair of old skis struck me on the shoulder.

My heart was beating faster and faster, and a strange pressure was growing in my chest. My first feeling was surprise rather than fear; it was as if my body became afraid before my intellect understood what was happening, as if I could clearly feel and register all the physiological expressions of fear before I actually *realized* I was afraid. I heard the hangers screeching against the rod above and instinctively starting waving my arms. Down jackets, cardigans, and old ski clothes tumbled down with dull thuds around me on the floor, and to my own surprise I heard a peculiar shrill sound emerge from my throat. It sounded just like the pigs we had seen when my class went on a field trip to the farm in Flen.

"Aaauuaa," I screamed.

I then fainted, among the woolen mittens, tracksuits, and neat bundles of *My Life's Story* magazine.

Date: August 21
Time: 3:00 p.m.
Place: Green Room, the practice
Patient: Sara Matteus

"I *have* to tell you something!"

Sara is eagerly picking at a scab on her forearm with a long, green fingernail. Picks, scrapes, lifts up the scab until pus comes out.

"Of course," I say encouragingly, studying Sara more closely for the first time since our conversation began. She seems exhilarated and energetic. Manic. Drumming the lighter faster and faster against her pack of cigarettes, she opens her eyes wide. She evidently is having a hard time sitting still. My cynical brain immediately thinks uppers, but I know that's wrong. Sara is clean.

"I met a guy!"

I look discreetly down at my notebook so that my eyes will not reveal what I'm thinking, but Sara sees through me.

"I *know* what you're thinking, but this time it's different! And I know that now you're thinking that I say that *every* time, but this time it's true. *Promise!* He's much older. He has a *real* job, he's supersmart. Makes an *awful* lot of money. But that's not what matters," she adds, as if to downplay the fact that the man she has met possesses all the right conventional attributes.

She lowers her voice and whispers dramatically. "He *sees* me and understands me like no one else has. Don't be offended, but I can talk with him about the kinds of things I can't say to anyone else, not even to *you*. He listens to me for hours. Listens to my *harping*, you know."

Sara smiles, lights a cigarette, and slowly shakes her head, making her golden curls dance over her shoulders.

"He wants me to move in with him."

She says this slowly and in a contemplative tone, but there is also something triumphant in her voice.

I gather my papers together and try not to stare at her flushed cheeks and defiant expression.

"I'm happy for your sake, Sara. Truly. How long have you known this . . . man?"

Sara looks down at the carpet, resting her upper body against her knees and rocking slowly back and forth.

"Oh, a few weeks. But we've been seeing each other *a lot*. He gave me this bag," she adds, and as if to prove the legitimacy of the relationship, she holds up an oversized, monogram-patterned Gucci bag.

"He takes me out for dinner."

I say nothing.

"He's *nice* to me."

Sara shrugs and looks questioningly at me, waiting for validation.

"Sara, you're a grown-up and hardly need my approval before you start a relationship," I say, but my tone of voice reveals how worried I really am.

It doesn't seem right. A middle-aged, successful man courts a young girl with bright green nail polish, a charming borderline personality, and arms and legs zebra-striped with scars from razor blades and knives. I realize to my own surprise that I'm afraid he will exploit Sara.

After the session, I stay sitting for a long time in my green office, looking out the window. During the entire time I've been her therapist, Sara has been with one guy after another. Most often they have been her age, usually with problems that resemble hers. Rootless, beat-up young guys with scars from syringes and God knows what else. And other, much worse scars, carved into their very souls. Every time, Sara has been just as enthusiastic, just as infatuated as she is now, and every time it ended the same way: in bottomless, dark despair.

I wish I could prevent this from happening again.

I met Stefan at a party in a barn outside Eslöv in Skåne seven years ago. It was a lovely but cold midsummer evening. I remember that he had warm hands and that he generously lent me his jacket as we walked through the fields of canola. He fascinated me, which I decided afterward was due, at least in part, to the fact that we were so different. Stefan was tall and blond—I'm small and slender with short black hair and a boyish body. He was constantly happy, never gloomy, had lots of friends, and was always on his way to something. I think I was hoping that a little of his joie de vivre would rub off on me. And it did.

It feels so strange that Stefan isn't here anymore. But I really believe I have accepted his death. The complete paralysis and the panicky sense of being all alone went away long ago, making room for a gentle, melancholy sorrow and an almost physical emptiness: My body still remembers how soft his skin felt, my hands miss the feeling of touching his thick blond hair, my tongue longs for the salt of the skin on his neck.

So I'm a widow. How can you be a widow when you're only thirty-four? I always tell anyone who doesn't know me that I'm single. I don't want to end up in conversations about the diving accident, or how they know exactly how it feels because the same thing happened to them a hundred years ago, or how it would be good for me to get out more, or something else that would only make me angry anyway.

I never need to explain it to my friends, who already know everything. They let me be and don't try to fill the silence with meaningless blather. They let me sit in my cottage and sip wine instead of forcing me out to some bar.

For my patients, I am Siri the therapist, and no one ever asks about my private life, which in itself is a relief.

To them, I am a professional spiritual adviser without a past.

I'm comfortable with that.

When Stefan and I met, he was doing his residency at the hospital in Kristianstad and I worked in Stockholm. The back-and-forth between the two cities was really trying. When Stefan was in Stockholm, he stayed with me in my little studio apartment on Luntmakargatan. Then a routine took shape that we would follow for the next year: work and friends during the week, isolation in my apartment on the weekends. We spent that time wrapped up in each other, fused by our longing in my narrow, uncomfortable bed.

All my friends thought Stefan was good for me. He made me blossom and dampened my dark, brooding traits. He had an uncomplicated relationship to the big questions in life and often answered my despondency with statements along the lines of, "If you only got out more you wouldn't feel like this" or "Stop thinking about that and help me with this plank instead." He had a way of resolutely but carefully guiding my thoughts away from dark abysses, and I never missed my difficult side. I was never really happy with the way I intellectualized emotions and problems, and so I received his frank, simple manner with joy.

Then Stefan started his specialist training at the Stockholm South General Hospital. No one was surprised when he chose orthopedics. That was so very Stefan. If something was broken, he wanted to fix it, not just study it or talk about why it didn't work.

When Jenny Andersson, one of my patients, committed suicide, Stefan was a big support. I lost myself in doubt and self-examination, questioning both my choice of profession and my capacity for empathy. Stefan made me realize that it was not my responsibility. In his resolute, analytical way, he explained that if someone *truly* wanted to take her own life, then neither I nor anyone else could prevent it. I still remember our conversation that evening, as Stefan tucked me in on the couch under the patchwork quilt his grandmother had sewn out of old handkerchiefs in the 1960s.

I told Stefan that I thought I ought to have *seen* that it was about to happen.

"Why is that?" he asked, shrugging.

"If anyone should have known, it was me."

"Do you think, in retrospect, that there were signs?"

I hesitated for a moment and tried to recall my last encounters with Jenny. She had appeared both happier and a little calmer than usual. Perhaps she had already decided? Was that a sign of relief—that the understanding of the choice she had made, and its consequences, was like a weight that had been taken off her chest? Peace?

"No, not really. Not at all," I corrected myself, shaking my head. "There were no signs. I mean, of course there were signs: Jenny suffered from anxiety, she was depressed, but she denied that she was thinking about taking her own life. I asked her, asked the standard questions about thoughts of death, thoughts of taking her own life, plans . . . Jenny just laughed. She said that suicide was for the weak. The losers. I didn't ask if she saw herself as a loser."

"Would you blame her family or friends because they didn't see what was about to happen?"

"No, absolutely not."

"Then why do you blame yourself?"

"Because it's *my job* to see that kind of thing."

"Siri, dear Siri." Stefan took my hands in his, as he always did when he wanted my full attention. "You and I both know that even a trained psychologist can't read minds, can't see into someone's future, prevent her from making mistakes, or even interpret her intentions with any great certainty. There are no blood tests you can prescribe, you can't send your patients to the lab and get results the next day. You asked the questions, you got answers. You couldn't do more than that."

Actually, I knew deep down that Stefan was right, but that hopeless, suffocating, chafing feeling of guilt would still not release its grip on me. I could not say with certainty that I had *not* contributed to Jenny's death.

"Siri, *forget* Jenny now."

But I was no longer listening.

Carefully he helped me up off the couch and led me into the kitchen, as if I were a child.

"Siri, I need help with the potatoes."

I looked at him without understanding, unable to speak.

"Here." He placed the potato peeler in my hand and poured what must have been several pounds of potatoes into the sink. Slowly, almost mechanically, I started peeling potatoes. At least an hour went by, and by the time I had peeled the last one, I had actually collected myself enough so that we could talk about something other than Jenny's death.

Yet another one of Stefan's talents: meeting me halfway and healing me without words. While I was convinced that everything could be figured out, sorted, and resolved in conversation. Sometimes I felt that was all I did, talk and talk—at the practice, with my friends, and with Stefan.

"People are what they do," Stefan would always say. "Actions make us who we are." So, who did that make me?

It started as a way to pass the time.

Time: I had an ocean of it now, so why not investigate what she did when she wasn't working? I already knew what she did during the day, of course.

More and more often I made my way to the bars around Medborgarplatsen where I assumed she would hang out sometimes after work. I had no plan, didn't know what I would do if I saw her. It was more like a compulsion, an implacable need to see her.

An itch.

Then suddenly one day she was standing right in front of where I was sitting in the sun on the stairs to Forsgrénska, smoking. That is, she was standing ten yards away, looking aimlessly out over the square. I was struck by how ugly she was. Small and bony with very short brown hair. As far as I could see, she had no makeup on at all and expectantly observed the crowd with gray, expressionless, dead eyes. Her mouth was pinched, which made it look like a little pink grub. Her arms and legs were skinny and tan, with chapped, bony kneecaps and elbows. Her attire was that of the typical Södermalm intellectual: short, formless khaki skirt, flat sandals, black, loose-fitting cotton blouse (I couldn't even see a hint of breasts), and a scarf wrapped loosely several times around her neck. On her wrist she wore a bracelet with colorful beads, which made her look incredibly childish. Like the innocent preschool teacher she TRULY wasn't. I put out the cigarette in the palm of my hand and welcomed the sharp pain because it kept my other emotions in check.

It's an unusually lovely evening, even if there is a chill in the air that announces that autumn is inexorably approaching. The outdoor cafés on Medborgarplatsen are full. It is as if everyone knows that summer will soon be over and they want to take hold of the evening and sit outside awhile longer. Over the square, a lone seagull hovers in search of food scraps.

Aina and I walk through Södermalm. We pass Björn's Park, where a couple of teenagers entertain themselves on the skateboard ramp while the regulars drink out of unidentifiable bottles and serve as an enthusiastic audience. We go farther up toward Mosebacke Square and in through the gates to Mosebacke Etablissement.

It looks like there aren't any available tables outdoors at the café. A mixture of young locals, Japanese tourists, and older couples are squeezed in at every seat.

Aina peers into the crowd. "Look over there. We're in luck!"

Our colleague, Sven Widelius, is sitting at one of the tables with a cold beer and a newspaper. His wavy, graying hair falls like a curtain over his furrowed, tan forehead. If I didn't know him, I would probably think he was an attractive man. Even though he's twenty years older than I am.

There is something about the way he brushes his hair out of his face, something about his bony, well-defined cheekbones, his heavy eyelids, and the intensity of his gray eyes. Something about the way he fills a room with his presence and his nervous energy; he is constantly in motion. And he is physical: brushing my shoulder as he walks by, pressing my hand as he looks at me, giving me all his attention. And then his laugh. Not always nice—often cynical, teasing. Sometimes I feel insecure when he looks at me; he makes me feel younger, and naked.

Ignorant.

That's what his gaze is like. And he takes his time. Lets his gray eyes rest on me without shame or hesitation. As if we had a secret pact.

He and I.

Aina and I move through the sea of tables and chairs, squeeze between a group of heavy-set women with Finnish accents, and step over an enormous black dog before we finally reach Sven, who looks up and cocks his head to one side.

"Ah, my young female colleagues," he says, not without irony. "You want to keep me company? Is it me or the table you're after?"

"Stop sulking, Sven!" says Aina. "We'll treat you to a beer."

"That's no good," Sven answers. "I'm waiting for Birgitta."

Birgitta Börjesdotter Widelius is Sven's wife. She's a stocky woman with salt-and-pepper hair and sensual features who for many years has been a professor of gender studies at Uppsala University. Both Aina and I are impressed by Birgitta. Her academic career is without compare, her research significant, and her personality strong.

But, as impressed as we are by Birgitta, we are equally mystified by her relationship with Sven. He is charismatic and attractive, and aware of it. He is a charmer, and possibly also a seducer. Malicious rumors claim that his academic career was cut short due to an affair with a doctoral student, perhaps even with an undergraduate. It is hardly a secret anymore that he was unfaithful—even Birgitta must know by now. But despite all that, they're still together. And if there are cracks in their relationship, they aren't visible to the outside world. Birgitta doesn't appear to be the type to go for public demonstrations of affection anyway. She is a private person, bordering on secretive, as Aina always says. She is more than happy to talk about her work but not about her personal life. And who can blame her? Being married to Sven can't be easy.

"May we sit with you?" I ask politely.

"Be my guests," Sven replies, once again running his hand through his hair. "We're only meeting here, we're going to a concert at Katarina Church," he continues, slapping the seat beside him with the palm of his hand in a welcoming gesture.

Aina fights her way to the bar, pushing to get past an old couple and a long-haired guy with dreadlocks carrying a baby on his hip, wrapped in a kind of hand-woven shawl. Sven and I stay at the table and take in the scene.

We fall silent, look at each other, and start laughing. Embarrassed.

"If we met more often outside the office, maybe it wouldn't be so awkward."

Sven looks at me and smiles again, and for a moment it feels as if I'm on a roller-coaster ride. He is looking right into me. He sees my loneliness, I'm sure.

"Maybe we could get together, Siri, just the two of us?"

The roller-coaster ride is over and I feel anger rising, even if it's hard to tell whether or not Sven is being serious. However that may be, I don't need to have this conversation with a colleague, who is married to boot.

"Sven, *knock it off*," I say curtly.

Sven's laugh is loud and ringing, and it rolls out over the café, making me even more uncomfortable.

"If it wouldn't make me come off like an uneducated, male chauvinist pig, I would say that you need a man, Siri. Do you intend to live like a—"

I cut him off. "Here comes Birgitta. And by the way, Sven, maybe I do need a man, but not a married colleague who is twenty years older than me. Surely there are other, more suitable candidates . . ."

I smile at one of the guys at the next table.

But Sven no longer notices me and my move goes right over his head. As he gets up and hugs Birgitta, I am astonished at his ability to switch between various situations as if there were no overlap.

Everything in a separate compartment.

Birgitta greets me and Aina, who has returned with two glasses of wine. We chat for a while about an article that Aina has read, and then Sven and Birgitta wander off in the summer night, side by side.

Aina can tell immediately that I am annoyed.

"I see that our colleague has tried to seduce you again."

"It's nothing," I answer. "It's just . . ."

I pause. Usually, Sven is okay. He is easy to share a practice space with. He always pays his portion of the expenses and does so on time. He is knowledgeable and has a lot of experience that he is more than happy to share. He has helped me often with my patients when I felt I wasn't getting anywhere. But sometimes he crosses the line. And although I ought to be able to handle his flirting, it makes me uncomfortable. But maybe he's right. Maybe I am a prudish, dried-up woman who desperately needs a man. But I don't think so. What I actually need is to learn not to take everything so seriously.

This is why I say, "Forget it."

Instead, I sip my wine and listen to the latest chapter in Aina's ongoing conflict with her mother. What the disagreement is really about has long been forgotten. It has a life of its own, and neither of them seems able or willing to resolve it.

I have a hard time concentrating on Aina's story. My thoughts are constantly sliding back to my conversation with Sara Matteus earlier that day. Something bothers me more than I can explain.

Aina notices my lack of engagement, but instead of being offended she confronts me: "Do you want to tell me about it?"

"Yes, but not here."

An outdoor café is hardly the right place to discuss confidential matters. So we empty our wineglasses, leave our table, and walk aimlessly through the streets around Katarina Church as the summer sky darkens above the buildings and the air fills with the odors of the night: an indefinite, damp-saturated stench from rotting plants, the smell of frying from the crêperie around the corner, and the cigarette smoke from the customers at sidewalk cafés. And everywhere we are surrounded by that strange murmur, the buzzing sound produced collectively by the city's many inhabitants. In the distance I hear Arabic music and the sighing, far-off sound of the traffic on Folkungagatan.

"It's Sara Matteus," I begin. "Something worries me. She's met someone. A guy."

Aina interrupts me with a short, bubbling laugh.

"Sara Matteus met a guy and you're *worried*. Come on, hasn't she met guys before? What is it about this one that makes you nervous?"

Aina's teasing helps direct my train of thought.

"It's the man himself, I think. He is, according to Sara, older, established, settled. He gives her presents. And has already started talking about moving in together. What does he want with Sara? Why would an older man with money want to be with a twenty-five-year-old girl who so obviously has problems, if he doesn't—"

"If he doesn't want to *exploit* her," Anna fills in. "What does Sara herself say?"

"Oh, the usual. That it's different this time. That he *sees* her, that this is *for real*. Which also frightens me. Because it makes her vulnerable. And if she gets hurt, that increases the risk of a relapse. She has almost stopped cutting herself, she's much more stable than she was before. But if something happens . . . I'm truly afraid that she'll . . ."

I pause.

Aina looks expectantly at me.

"If something happens, *then what,* Siri? She has to live her life, and you know that. And you have to stop viewing Sara simply as a victim."

"But she *is* a victim. She is a victim of a school that could not understand, of poorly functioning child psychiatry, and of social services that couldn't help her or her family."

Aina pats my arm almost tenderly.

"Of course, Sara is partially a victim, but you know that she has resources, too. Come on, she's a smart girl. Sure, she has had some tough experiences, but she's moved on and she's done it with her own strength. How many people do you know who have stopped using drugs on their own? Just as an example. And now she's met a guy who *you* intuitively think is bad for her. If he really is, then Sara herself will be able to break up with him, with or without your help. And Sara must be able to continue to have her own experiences. Should she never again risk being hurt? Never again feel pain? Then she probably has to live the rest of her life away from other people."

Aina falls silent and gives me time to let her message sink in. I know she's right. I only wish that Sara could wait a little.

It's early. Too early.

One mild summer evening I followed the other one, her slutty colleague. I followed her the whole way from Medborgarplatsen to Hornstull Beach via Mariatorget and Fogelströmska High School, as twilight fell over Söder. I was careful to keep a distance so she wouldn't see me. But I didn't need to worry, because she never turned around, just walked as if she was in a hurry; as a matter of fact she was almost scampering, she looked a little crazy.

Like an overgrown kid.

At Hornstull, she veered off and went down toward the water, the market, and the outdoor café by the pier. I watched as she embraced a man, kissed him lightly on the mouth, and sat down with him at the café.

I was sitting on a pile of lumber at a safe distance, smoking, while I observed them through the throngs of people; she looked cheap but I have to admit, not without a certain style. She was wearing a pink T-shirt dress with a deer printed on the chest and a deep neckline that she consciously let slide down over one shoulder to reveal an angry green bra strap. Bare, tanned legs, worn Converses on her feet, her hair tied back in a careless bun.

The man across from her looked younger than her. He was wearing worn jeans, a hoodie, and something that looked like a Palestinian scarf wrapped tightly around his bearded neck. His long, frizzy hair was fastened in a ponytail at his neck.

I really wanted to know what they were talking about, but it was impossible, even though they were sitting only a few yards away, with the loud mass of people scurrying back and forth the whole time.

Then the other one leaned over toward the man and played with a lock of hair that had come loose from his ponytail. She smiled and looked at him with a gaze that could not be described in any other way than horny. The guy in the Palestinian scarf took her hand, laughed, and squeezed it. She laughed back, wriggled out of her shoes, and unabashedly put her feet on his lap.

I leaned forward to see better. The man's facial expression had frozen and he was squeezing her hand harder now. It looked white. She grinned, and as I leaned forward I could see her feet kneading, massaging, and caressing his crotch. A sudden wave of nausea and dizziness forced me to turn around and take a deep breath of the damp night air.

Suddenly everything was spinning. I wanted to get away from all this decadence, away from all the bodies, all the flesh and desire. All the emotions that I had to exert so much energy to restrain.

The filth, the sweat, and the stench of the crowd oppressed me with renewed vigor, and suddenly the people in front of me seemed to flow together to create a single large organism. A stinking, moaning, passive amoeba of human urges and desires that encircled me as I sat helplessly, with a cigarette butt between my fingers.

I got up and shakily left the place: disgusted, nauseated, and without looking back.

The evening has turned into a black, late-summer night, and the air around me is damp and raw. My house rests like a sleeping animal between softly rounded rocks and pine trees forced to their knees by the wind. I hear the sound of the sea as I jog along the narrow gravel path toward my door. I have to remember to install some kind of lighting outside.

Inside the house I follow my usual routine. I turn on the lights and make a quick visit to the bathroom. In the kitchen I pour a glass of wine, serve myself a bowl of canned soup, and sit down at the table to go through the day's mail. An electric bill, an invitation to a workshop, a statement from the bank.

Among the mail on the table is a high-quality gray envelope. I tentatively feel the thick, textured paper and let the envelope rest in my hand to feel its weight.

My name and address are printed in black ink. The handwriting is neat and regular. I have saved it for last because it looks the most intriguing. Perhaps it's an invitation, or a letter—a real letter. I slowly open the envelope. A photo falls out. For a few moments I study it with interest without grasping its content. Then I understand, and a wave of uneasiness spreads through my body.

It is a picture of me.

I am wearing my linen outfit and sandals and seem to be in a hurry as I cross Medborgarplatsen. The picture must have been taken recently.

On the back, someone has written, "*I'm watching you.*"

Date: August 24
Time: 2:00 p.m.
Place: Green Room, the practice
Patient: Peter Carlsson—first visit

"I thought I would start by informing you about how an assessment interview is done and what happens next."

"Okay. I understand."

I observe the patient in the chair before me. A handsome man approaching forty. He is well dressed and looks kind of . . . expensive. His shoes are polished and his nails manicured. He doesn't fit the description of my usual target group.

I describe the procedures, the two to three assessment interviews, the treatment structure, and information about payment. Peter Carlsson nods, listens, and appears to be concentrating. Despite his controlled manner, I sense he is nervous. I guess that he would not be here if he did not feel he absolutely had to.

Just as I inspect Peter Carlsson, I can tell that he is assessing me. Taking me in, my face and my body.

"Are you really a therapist, I mean, that is . . . you look really . . . *young.*"

I've heard that question before. My appearance is sometimes a disadvantage in my work. My patients often expect to see an older woman and are surprised when they see me. Maybe I have to work a little harder to get them to accept my relative youth, which seems to signal inexperience.

"Yes, I really am a therapist," I answer, trying not to look irritated. "But now I want to talk about you. Can you tell me what makes you want to get treatment? During our phone call you mentioned obsessive thoughts and anxiety. Can you describe them in more detail?"

"Okay." He nods again and looks out my window. "So, I guess I've always been a little prone to anxiety. Worried."

He meets my gaze to confirm that I'm listening and that I understand him.

"When I was a child, it was important for me to do things a certain way, not to step on cracks in the sidewalk, to leave my clothes in a particular order in the evening. It was nothing strange, really, I think many kids behave like that, but the difference is that I never grew out of it. Or, I grew out of that sidewalk business, but there were always new rituals."

"Did you have any thoughts about what would happen if you didn't perform these actions?"

Peter looks at his nails, inspects his manicured hands.

"Well, that something would happen to my parents maybe. Especially after my grandmother died."

"Your grandmother died?"

. "Hmm, she was . . . special . . . she was very close to us children. And she was pretty young, too, only in her sixties. She seemed so invulnerable."

Peter falls silent, and I see that he is losing himself in memories of his dead grandmother.

"What happened?"

"Cancer," he answers shortly. "And after that the world was, like, never safe again. Do you understand? Everything I believed to be fixed and anchored proved to be . . . *transitory*. My childhood changed after that. It wasn't that I grew up too quickly or something, but it was different. The conditions of my existence changed and these rituals became a way of trying to hold life in check. I became afraid that something would happen to my parents, that everything would be even more disrupted. I was worried they would get sick, or get in a car accident, or whatever. I started watching over them, always wanted to know where they were and what they were doing. I had meltdowns whenever they left the house. Although it settled down after a while, it's like those rituals are still there. Routines."

"In what way did they change? What were they replaced with?"

"Other things," Peter says hesitantly.

I try to make a quick mental summary of what Peter has told me so far. What he is describing sounds like classic compulsive actions or rituals. Fairly common in childhood, this kind of behavior is often not of clinical significance. It's part of a child's normal development. For Peter, however, the grief and fear in connection with his grandmother's death seem to have made the rituals persist into adulthood.

For many individuals, compulsive thoughts and actions are strongly associated with shame. You are ashamed of your thoughts and fears, and of your inability to control them. Many times you behave according to rituals that those around you may think strange and odd, and so you do everything you can to conceal them. Often there is a fear of losing your grip or going crazy. And I can sense this fear in Peter. I can see it in his gaze, which avoids meeting mine, and in the slight redness in his face. It is so hard for him to tell me, to break the silence and talk about what I guess he has kept hidden from others since childhood.

"Have you sought help for these difficulties before?"

Peter only shakes his head, thereby confirming my suspicions.

"Tell me about the other things that worry you."

I want to signal that what he is admitting doesn't surprise me, that I have heard similar stories before.

"There are thoughts about hurting someone."

He looks down again and slowly brushes away some invisible specks of dust from his pant leg.

"Hurting someone?"

"Uh, it started when I got my driver's license. I had thoughts that I might run someone over with my car. A child, perhaps. Some poor person who had the bad luck to cross my path."

He makes a grimace and looks profoundly sad.

"And I couldn't let go of that thought, I started thinking that I really had run over someone, without noticing it. I would drive back in my car to look. I would get out of the car and walk around searching for signs that I had injured someone: broken branches, blood on the sidewalk, a body. Sometimes I'd see a stain on the street or something—an oil stain, maybe—and I simply had to find out what it was. I'd get down on my knees and sniff the stain. Scared to death that someone would see me and think I was strange. Out of my mind. And then, when I was done searching and hadn't found anything, I still would not believe it. I was forced to go another round, and another."

Again, Peter falls silent, his face tormented and pinched.

"What did you do?"

"I stopped driving," he answers very quickly. "It was too difficult. I didn't drive for almost ten years."

"And what happened after ten years? You started driving again?"

"I had to drive Dad to the hospital. We thought he'd had a stroke. It was Christmas Eve, there were no taxis available. Chaos at nine-one-one. The ambulance was delayed. Mom was going crazy, screaming and crying. Everyone had been drinking except me. Somehow it just worked. We drove to Sankt Göran and I didn't even think about running someone over. I just wanted to get there."

"And then?"

"And then it worked. Driving, that is. The thoughts didn't come back. Although by then I had other thoughts, of course."

Again, Peter falls silent. This time there is something different about his silence, and I can tell that we are starting to approach the reason he is seeking help right here and now. I also sense what I believe is hesitation; his thoughts are circling around something he doesn't want to talk about. I glance at the clock. Our time is about to run out, and before the session is finished I want to give Peter a brief description of compulsive illness and explain that he can be helped.

I also want to give him some self-reporting scales to fill out for the next visit. If I press him too much now, he will start to open up, but we risk being forced to end the session before he is through talking—without my being able to give him adequate information on how he can work through his issues, and I don't want to subject him to that. I decide to guide the session toward more practical matters instead and wrap it up.

"Okay," I reply. "I understand. And next time we will focus more on just those thoughts. But now I would like to talk about what you've told me so far. Are you familiar with the term 'obsessive-compulsive disorder'?"

Now that the day's patients have gone, calm starts to settle over the office and I feel exhausted. The day was packed with appointments and an administrative meeting with Aina and Sven about the division of new cases and a final reminder about the practice's annual crayfish party. The fast pace didn't leave any time for my own thoughts. But now the fear and concern that I have tried to keep out of my mind since this morning come back and hit me with full force.

Who is secretly taking pictures of me? I try to think rationally and keep my anxiety in check. This is a joke, someone is playing a prank on me.

No one wishes me harm.

I'm just being paranoid.

But at the same time, there is another voice inside me, one that says that perhaps I have good reason to be worried. Several times this summer I had the unpleasant feeling of being watched while I was alone at home. Many late evenings I went up to my darkening windows and observed the garden, but it was always empty, extending peacefully and silently around my little cottage.

But what do you do when you receive an anonymous envelope with a picture of you?

Should I call the police?

Should I tell Aina?

Should I install an alarm at the house?

Lock myself in and never go out again?

I immediately reject the first idea. The police probably think this type of incident is a hair above kittens in trees on the danger scale. Putting alarms in the house and locking myself in feels like an overreaction. Only Aina remains. The problem with Aina is that I don't know how she will react. What I fear most is that she will worry too much, and I am sick and tired of wearing out my friends with my grief, my dwelling on things, and my anxiety. At the same time I realize that I would be angry with Aina if she withheld things from me just to *spare* me. So what can I do? Wait and see what happens? I decide that this is the wisest strategy. Perhaps it is only a prank after all.

I hear Marianne rummaging around at the reception desk and call to her. "Stop working, your workday is over!"

Marianne stops rustling papers, and I hear her steps as she approaches the kitchen.

"You look tired, Siri. Shall I make you a cup of coffee?" she asks in her usual caring way.

She turns her broad, sturdy back to me and takes two blue ceramic mugs out of the cupboard. I decline the coffee. The fact that I have employed a secretary is hard enough to handle. That she should make coffee for me to boot feels ridiculous. I can make my own coffee.

I watch Marianne as she stands with her back to me, arranging the instant coffee and the electric kettle. We live such different lives. Marianne is more than ten years older than me and had her children early, soon after the age of twenty. Now both sons have left home. The older has a tech company with a friend, and the younger is studying at the Royal Institute of Technology.

Marianne has had two marriages, one with the boys' father, which lasted a few years, and one with a man who is referred to only as "Patrik the Pig."

Patrik the Pig and Marianne were married for ten years before the most classic thing happened: He left her for his secretary. When Marianne first started working with us, she came across almost as a caricature of a man-hating, rejected woman. Yet behind her bitterness lay enormous sorrow. Presumably, the destruction of her second marriage was much too painful to face, but nevertheless, she ventured into a new relationship. Last spring, Marianne met a new man. She doesn't say much about him, which is not unusual considering her previous experiences. But now there is a certain Christer whom she mentions at lunch and in the break room.

Aina's theory is that Christer and Marianne live in some sort of asexual symbiosis, a partnership that is more about golf, theater, and weekend trips than passion. One morning in the break room, Marianne declared out of the blue that she had "gotten over that thing with sex," which felt "liberating." Aina rolled her eyes and smothered a giggle, whereupon Marianne sniffed, offended, "Well, maybe you ought to consider it too . . ."

My relationship with Marianne is rather unclear. I don't really know what I think about her. She is competent; keeps the patients' records, sends notices, and takes care of other practical tasks. Work at the practice has gotten easier since she started. At the same time, I can't stand her meddling and cloying mothering. I often think she treats Aina and me like two little girls who can't blow our own noses. She has a desire to dominate and take over, and sometimes, though she means well, she tries to advise me regarding various patients, which drives me crazy. If in Marianne's eyes Aina and I are little girls, then Sven on the other hand is God. As the older male, he is the king of the practice and must also be treated as such. His records are typed up the fastest and his letters are the first ones in the mailbox.

"Siri, you really ought to go home. You're running yourself ragged."

Marianne looks sincerely worried and I am immediately ashamed of my thoughts. Her consideration is genuine and I am sitting here thinking unfair, ugly, mean things about her.

"I'm just going to finish up a few preliminary notes," I answer, trying to look happier than I am.

"You know, Siri, you are important to the practice and to your patients, but you're not doing us any favors by wearing yourself out. *Go home!* Or go see a movie, or have a glass of wine with a girlfriend. Do *anything* except sit here. It's a beautiful summer evening and you're sitting here and . . . polishing your notes. *Go home!*"

She looks so stern that I start to giggle. Marianne's concern suddenly feels welcome, and a feeling of warmth spreads inside me. I get up from the chair and push it in by the small table.

"You're right, I will go home now. And you're right—I am *hopeless.* I'll go home. Rent a movie and eat candy."

"Good girl. We'll see you on Saturday," she continues. "At the crayfish party. It's going to be so nice—and I'm bringing Christer."

Marianne pats me almost tenderly on the arm with her chubby hand, which is covered in liver spots, and I wonder for a moment if I've been wrong about her.

Maybe I've just never taken the time to find out who she really is.

A boat horn cuts through the stillness, car doors open and close, and a moment later there are voices. I'm in the kitchen, looking out over the bay. It's time for one of the year's social gatherings. Like at most offices, my colleagues and I try to boost the team spirit with parties and dinners: Christmas lunch in December, summer lunch in June, and a crayfish party at the end of August. I don't know if these activities really bring us closer, or if the others, like me, see them simply as a necessary evil. Hours to be endured to please other people.

A couple of times I didn't show up, blaming a cold or a sudden onset of migraine. Tonight that's impossible, since the crayfish party tradition-ally takes place at my home. I do as I always do. Endure, despite the slight unease in my stomach. Tomorrow the party will be in the past and I will be on to the next thing.

I set the table with my old, chipped china set, napkins, and colorful paper lanterns in the twilight, as the water in the bay quiets down in the warm August evening, and think that this fits the cliché of a Swedish crayfish party.

Sven and Birgitta stand outside on the gravel drive, loaded down with bags of groceries and clinking beer bottles from the state liquor store, Systembolaget. Marianne stands behind them, with a tall, thin man with brown hair and goatee. Christer. A small bonus of work parties like this is the opportunity to meet people's significant others. And I cannot deny that I am curious about this Christer, who has gotten Marianne to take a chance, to gradually soften and become more emotionally capable of opening up to a potential partner.

Maybe I'm jealous, too.

We exchange names and pleasantries while secretly taking stock of each other. I sense that Christer is observing me much in the same way that I am observing him.

Creating an impression. Drawing conclusions.

Marianne comes up to us and Christer immediately encloses her hand in his. I feel sympathy for this man. He radiates a peculiar mixture of confidence and nervousness, and seems to be most at ease in Marianne's presence. There is something gentle and a little vulnerable about him, even though he discreetly wears all the accessories that indicate success: an expensive watch, a well-cut blazer, casual, good-looking shoes. I want him to feel welcome and try to convey this with a smile. He, in return, looks grateful, and the tension in the air slowly starts to ease. Marianne seems to pick up on this, and her slightly stiff posture changes to outright pride: He's mine!

Marianne herself is unusually beautiful this late-summer evening. Her curly hair is set in a slightly old-fashioned but becoming hairstyle that immediately makes me think of the curlers and hairpins that Mom stored in an orange terry-cloth bag that disappeared sometime in the early eighties. Does anyone under the age of seventy still use curlers? Apparently. Marianne's green dress shines against her suntanned skin, and there is a large bag from the Östermalm indoor market hanging from her arm.

"Well, here are fresh crayfish," she says in a tone between accomplishment and embarrassment. "Christer thought . . . well, it's enough for everyone . . ."

She gets appreciative looks from Birgitta and Sven, who appear uncharacteristically intimate, standing close to each other. Their solidarity with this new couple is so obvious, almost tangible, although I know that their relationship is far from uncomplicated. I suddenly feel extremely alone.

Aina is late, of course, but when she finally arrives she is in the company of a slim, ruddy guy I have never met before. This is not surprising. Aina has made it a sport to bring a different date to each and every work-related event we have ever had. I think she enjoys projecting the image of a wild femme fatale. Her date is about thirty-five years old and looks out of place in the group, with his overgrown beard and what I suspect will eventually grow into dreadlocks. He introduces himself as Robert and says that he is currently working on a doctoral dissertation in microbiology.

"And I'm a bass player in a band that will soon have a major break-through," he adds, grinning.

The crayfish party proceeds exactly according to the tradition we established several years ago. In the dusky twilight, the table is set with crayfish, bread, and traditional Västerbotten quiche. Beer bottles and wine boxes are set out. Some kind of ice-chilled aquavit is poured into the beautiful little glasses I inherited from my grandfather. I put on a record by the Swedish rock band Kent and notice Aina's Robert pretending to stick his fingers down his throat and throw up in disgust when he thinks only Aina is looking.

We embark hesitantly but adroitly on a conversation, tackling the weather, the new health-care contract with the county, and plans for next year's vacation. Gradually the general conversation breaks up into different configurations. I hear Aina and Marianne talking about yoga. Christer and Robert are discussing music, and I am surprised at how knowledgeable Christer seems to be on this subject.

Only a few drinking songs and crayfish later it happens—the conversation shifts inexorably to more sensitive topics. In reference to a book review in the newspaper, a discussion ensues about rape and its causes. Birgitta is the one who drives the debate.

"No one at this table could possibly claim that rape is a sexual act. After all, isn't it just an issue of patriarchal power?"

She looks around challengingly and licks her plump lips. Her salt-and-pepper hair sits perfectly coiffed on her head, a short pageboy with bangs. She looks like the prototype for a successful feminist. As always, her academic interest seems to be the only subject that really engages her. Otherwise, Birgitta has a tendency to position herself outside human society. She is an observer, who seems to register and analyze other people but seldom reveals her own views. Although I admire her, she also scares me a little, and on occasion I even feel nervous in her company.

"What I'm saying is that, in some respects, rape may be said to constitute our understanding of gender and gender hierarchy in society."

Birgitta, still waiting for a reaction, looks around and her gaze comes to rest on me. Is she seeking my support? She sighs and looks disappointed. Like a schoolteacher who discovers her pupils haven't done their homework.

"What I mean is that sexual assaults on women rely on the same structures whereby men have higher salaries than women—gender hierarchy."

Marianne draws on her cigarette and looks meditatively out over the bay with furrowed brow. She looks like she's trying to think of something to say. Christer glances down at his plate and then reaches for another crayfish.

"What do you think, Christer?" Aina asks. She turns toward him and in her usual physical manner places a hand on his arm and leans forward. Good Lord, I think, sometimes she goes too far. Christer's gaze meets Aina's for a moment before he turns back to his crayfish.

"I guess I don't really have an opinion," he says calmly, without letting his eyes linger over Aina's proffered breasts.

I wonder if he understands how sensitive the issue is, if he can accurately determine its weight and grasp the consequences should he give a wrong answer.

"I think you're onto something," Sven interjects, nodding meditatively as he grabs his glass and leans over to refill it.

Sven is going to get drunk this evening.

Again.

"So," Robert begins, "I'm not buying what you're saying about gender hierarchy. I think rape is about horniness combined with bad impulse control. Besides, human beings have a natural instinct for survival, which is responsible for the urge to spread one's genes as wide as possible. Maybe that's just inherited. Evolutionary theories are pretty damn interesting. Otherwise I think all men are . . . hmmm . . . animals."

Laughter erupts around the table. Robert's consciously provocative comment has broken the tension. Christer laughs loudly, and Sven snorts and his beer goes down the wrong way. Aina giggles, almost doubling over uncontrollably onto Robert's lap. The only one who doesn't look amused is Birgitta, who smiles stiffly, her lips pressed hard together.

"Yes, that's also an opinion," she says slightly sarcastically, well aware that she has been outplayed.

By a guy twenty years younger.

With dreadlocks.

I notice the look she gives Sven, distant and reproachful. Her eyes rest on him and I sense that she will have trouble forgiving him for having laughed at her, contributing consciously or not to her losing face in front of everybody. And I think that Sven knows what's up, because he suddenly goes quiet and staggers off toward the edge of the woods, his glass still in hand.

Why does it have to be so hard? All these conflicts, people who wear on each other like stones on a beach until nothing is left. It chafes and aches.

As darkness sets in, the intoxication also increases. Aina is sitting on Robert's lap at the end of the table. I notice her hand caressing his thigh and that he is touching her breasts under her sweater. Their kisses are deep and I catch myself looking away.

Christer and Marianne don't seem to be bothered by Aina and Robert. Instead they are trying to outdo each other with bawdy drinking songs. I feel slightly embarrassed for Marianne when she starts singing loudly that she's never seen anything naked, all the while smoking what must be her thirtieth cigarette of the night. Birgitta sits silently, the corners of her mouth demonstratively turned down, her fists clenched.

At this point Sven comes back through the pine trees carrying a guitar and I realize that the high point of the evening is near: Sven will play and sing. Something he never can refrain from in a state of intoxication. His repertoire consists of a number of old Mikael Wiehe and Hoola Bandoola Band songs mixed with early Ulf Lundell. I am sure I am going to throw up, for real, unlike Robert's mimicry, if I have to endure "you are the fiiinest I knooooow" in a phony Skåne dialect one more time. So I excuse myself and take my wineglass and a flashlight and start walking down toward the bay on legs that are not completely steady.

The raucous voices grow quiet and the sounds of the night emerge: waves crashing against the rocks, mixed with the humming of a distant motorboat. Behind me I hear determined footsteps, and when I turn around I see a silhouette approaching down the pier.

It is Christer.

"Did you also have enough?" He looks at me questioningly and smiles a little.

I angle the beam of the flashlight down toward the ground, covered in pine needles. The roots cast long shadows across the path. A moth flies aimlessly back and forth through the beam of light.

"Hmm, sometimes I get a little embarrassed when grown people start acting like teenagers. But actually," I continue after a brief hesitation, "actually they're just having a good time. I'm afraid I'm the one who's a hopeless bore."

Christer laughs. "Then that makes two of us. That bit with the guitar and the red wine has never really been my thing, you know, but maybe it's typical for psychologists," he continues in a mocking tone.

"Well," I answer, "I guess that depends on the psychologist. If you did your training before 1982, lived in a commune, and were part of the green movement, then maybe . . ."

"But, Siri, aren't you part of the green movement yourself?"

I don't understand what he means. "The green movement?"

"Well, you live out here all by yourself. Isn't it because you want to get closer to nature or something?"

He laughs again and I feel something heavy gathering in my chest. I can't bear to explain my reasons.

"I lived here with my husband." My curt answer signals that I don't want to expand on the subject.

"Oh," Christer says, looking thoughtful. "But you're not divorced, are you?"

"Widow," I say bluntly. "And I don't want to talk about it," I add, to be on the safe side.

"I'm sorry, I didn't want to pry, I didn't know."

Christer looks genuinely apologetic, and I make a gesture with my hand to show that I understand and that everything is all right.

"But this is a nice house you have," he continues. "Truly charming, even if you do need to repaint it and maybe replace the bargeboards, too."

I understand that he's trying to change the subject, and I am happy to help him.

"Yes, I know, but even just choosing the right type of paint feels like a drag—you know, acrylic or oil-based."

I lie.

I know exactly what kind of paint I need, but I'd much rather continue talking about something other than Stefan and the reason that I live alone in this inaccessible, wild, and beautiful place.

"Well, now, that depends on whether you're part of the green movement or not," says Christer, smiling tentatively.

I smile back and we start to discuss the pros and cons of different kinds of paint and the best time to paint houses. Christer surprises me by offering to help with the painting.

"I know how hard it is to get something done when you're all alone," he says, looking sad for a moment, and I am reminded that we all have a history that we carry with us and that determines our behavior and our lives.

I'm not the only one who has experienced loss and pain.

Suddenly the stillness is broken by agitated voices and cries coming from my house. We rush back up the narrow forest path. Sven and Aina are standing by the table, looking at each other angrily. By the door, Ziggy stands in a defensive position, his back arched, a low hissing sound coming from his throat.

"But Sven," Aina yells angrily, "you can't kick the cat, damn it! He just wanted to sit on your lap. He's an animal, understand, he hasn't come up with some kind of diabolical plan to frighten you. All you have to do, if he's bothering you, is put him down."

I can see in the light from the door that Aina is swaying.

"I just don't want it to come here," Sven says sullenly. "I . . . can't stand cats."

"You need to grow up already!"

Aina's face is red with anger and intoxication.

I carry Ziggy into the house. At the same time Robert has managed to grab hold of the guitar, without Sven noticing.

"Time to change genre," he says, grinning with glazed eyes.

"This one's dedicated to the cat-devil."

A second later he starts playing the intro to "Ziggy Stardust."

I stand in the kitchen scraping crayfish shells from the big platter into a garbage bag. The sink is full of dirty dishes. Outside, the party continues. Robert has succeeded in getting the others to join in, and now Marianne and Christer are dancing close, under the colored paper lanterns. The sky has turned coal black, adequately brightened by a large yellow August moon. It is a beautiful, melancholy reminder of summer's inexorable farewell and that darkness and cold will soon envelop us.

Suddenly I feel someone embracing me from behind, placing a hand over my right breast, a wet tongue leaving snail tracks on my neck.

"Siri, you are so damn pretty."

I push him away forcefully and turn around.

Sven is standing in front of me. He looks very drunk but is doing his best to conceal it. I don't know if I should feel violated and make a scene or just let the whole thing pass. At the same time, I am filled with disgust thinking of the unwanted intimacy he has just subjected me to. The conversation earlier about rape and the gender hierarchy further increases my unease. After a couple of beers, Sven, who is so damn politically correct in front of Birgitta, proceeds to confirm her, and possibly also Robert's, theories.

I back away and growl quietly at him. "What the hell, Sven."

My voice is faint but I know it comes across as determined.

"I like you. I like working with you, but a prerequisite for our collaboration is that you stop groping me. I'm not interested. Do you get it?"

I'm not so calm anymore, and I can hear how shrill my voice has become. Sven's face turns very red and he looks extremely ashamed. He stands in the middle of the kitchen, swaying back and forth like a buoy in a storm.

"Damn. I'm sorry, Siri. I'm really . . ."

He falls silent, searching for words, shakes his head, and looks like he's trying to collect himself. Or maybe he's just trying to regain his balance.

"I'm sorry. I don't know what got into me. I'm just drunk . . . Damn it. Can you accept my apology? I truly mean it. Damn. Stupid alcohol . . ."

Sven looks like he's about to embark on a long conversation about his relationship to all manner of drugs, something I'm really not in the mood for.

"It's okay, Sven."

I place a hand on his arm to underscore that I mean what I say.

"We can talk more about this on Monday, or we can just forget about it. It's okay." I squeeze his arm a little and he looks grateful. As he turns around and walks unsteadily through the kitchen door, I see her.

Birgitta is standing in the hall, watching me. Her thick lips are pinched together, her face is tense, her arms crossed over her heavy breasts. She gives me a knowing look, filled with a mixture of contempt and sympathy.

I am ashamed.

How much did she see? What does she think of me?

She comes closer and stands in the doorway. She looks at me again but says nothing.

"Well, so . . ." I say sheepishly, feeling my face burning.

I am ashamed because her husband was groping me?

Birgitta just looks at me. She says nothing but slowly raises her index finger toward me as if to reprimand a disobedient child, or point me out—a guilty person. Then she turns and goes out into the garden without a word.

Stefan loved diving. It had been his passion for more than a decade. When he wasn't out diving, he was planning his next diving trip with his equally obsessed friends. Great Barrier Reef, the Red Sea, South China Sea, the Gulf of Mexico. Stefan had been all over the world, but there were always new countries to visit, new seas to discover.

The first few years, I never went diving with him. He knew how afraid I was of the dark and he fully accepted that I wanted to avoid any situation that might lead me beyond the reach of light. Then he slowly started to broach the subject. "Maybe you can do a test dive, at thirty feet it's still light."

I started to seriously consider learning how to dive. This was right at the time I started working as a cognitive behavioral therapist, and the very heart of CBT is to expose yourself to your fears. It is the only way to move past them. So I decided to fulfill his wish.

I will never forget my first dive. It was on one of our long winter vacations. Stefan took special care to make sure he introduced me to his great passion under the most favorable circumstances. We went to the Maldives. As I stood on the warm white coral sand with the tank on my back, all my doubts vanished. The Indian Ocean gently received me as, unaccustomed to the heavy equipment, I carefully slid into the water.

The first things I registered were a feeling of weightlessness and the rays of the sun breaking through the surface, forming a moving pattern on the solid sand bottom. Everything was silent, except for a persistent clicking and the hissing and bubbling that my own breathing caused in the regulator. Stefan took my hand and together we swam out to the reef. He was attentive, helping me equalize the pressure as we started swimming deeper. Six feet became twelve, which became twenty-five. We floated along the wall of the reef. Surrounded by millions of fish in all the colors of the rainbow, I felt a stillness I had never experienced before, and I remember thinking that now, only now, do I understand Stefan.

I received my diving certification and started to accompany Stefan more and more often on his trips, both in Sweden and abroad. We dived in warm, salt, tropical seas, in the turbid waters of the Baltic, in old abandoned mines, in shipwrecks, and in forests of brownish-green kelp billowing along with the waves. As my diving improved, my fear of dark water gradually disappeared.

Then something happened that shouldn't have happened. We were diving outside Kungsbacka on the west coast of Sweden with Stefan's buddies Peppe and Malin. Stefan and I had just started our first dive when something frightened me and I was seized by panic.

It was dark, of course, a loathsome, dense, impenetrable darkness, massive as a concrete wall. The black water's chill penetrated through the seams of my wet suit. I remember an almost transparent shrimp swimming nonchalantly past my mask and vanishing into the darkness, like a space probe on its way into Nothing. Its small legs moved jerkily and made it look like a mobile on a string, the kind you hang over a baby's crib. Against my will, I felt my body getting stiffer, my heart beating faster, and the familiar cramp spreading in my body. I turned around to give Stefan the sign for ascent. I still had control over my body, but as I looked around I saw only more darkness. No Stefan. Instinctively, I groped around in the dark water, seeking the cold, hard steel surface of the tank or the rough neoprene.

The realization struck me in stages: Stefan wasn't here. I would have to get up to the surface by myself. I was alone in the darkness. The cramp in my chest was almost unbearable and I felt that I had to, *really* had to take off the mask because I was going to suffocate. I had to get out of this horrible darkness. I tried to think about sunlight. I closed my eyes and saw it before me, but it was too late. The damage was already done. My thoughts could no longer affect my panic-stricken, uncontrolled body.

I brought my hand toward my forehead and took hold of the upper edge of the mask and coaxed it carefully off as I spit out the regulator. The cold water that washed over my face felt liberating, and with surprise I heard a gurgling sound coming out of my throat as I rose uncontrollably toward the surface.

I was inconsolable that evening. I had violated the most fundamental safety rules of diving. Stefan sat on the edge of the bed and stroked my hair. He was worried and confused: How could I simply lose control like that? I know he never understood how I could lose control over my body so easily.

After all, his body always obeyed.

It took several years for me to get over this incident, to get past the panic-stricken feeling of total loss of control, surrounded by all the darkness, the cold. A prisoner in my own body.

It is yet another stunningly beautiful but oppressively stifling late-summer evening. The tall pines shade the house and it is pleasantly cool inside when I come home. I open all the windows and French windows anyway, call for Ziggy, and take the cat food out of the cupboard. He ought to be hungry, because he didn't eat anything yesterday and was out all last night and all day.

With a certain reluctance I go through the mail, but there is no gray envelope waiting for me this time. I pull on an old bleached-out bikini and take a quick swim. The sea has warmed up in the hot summer and it is a pleasure to swim, but today I keep it short. Instead, I spend the evening listening to David Bowie, drinking sour wine out of a box, skimming through research articles, and writing treatment plans. It is almost half past midnight when I set the articles aside, curl up on my side in bed, and almost immediately fall asleep.

I wake up in the middle of the night and it immediately strikes me that something is wrong. Before I've even opened my eyes, I know something has happened. It's as if the air is different somehow. It feels suffocating, pressed against my face and my body—it seems far too heavy and tactile to be air.

I look up. Close my eyes. Look.

There is no difference in what I see with my eyes open and closed: compact darkness. A velvety, hollow, black hell. My heart beats faster as I lean over the side of the bed and fumble for the flashlight on the floor. It's a solid one, made of sturdy black plastic and really big. Waterproof, it is presumably also suitable for white-water rafting, hiking, and bar fights. I always keep it by the side of the bed.

But not now.

All I can feel on the spruce floorboards are dust bunnies. The room is completely dark, which is unusual this time of year, when a little light will find its way in from outside. I can hear rain drumming against the Eternit roof and at a distance an ominous rumble. The stifling summer evening will now have its inevitable sequel in the form of a real summer storm. This is not unusual here where I live.

There is something special about thunder by the sea—I don't think it happens more often, but the sound seems amplified. There are no forests or buildings around it that can serve as a muffler. Instead, the rumbling of thunder rolls back and forth over the surface of the water like a bowling ball on a stone bench.

I try to turn on the bedside lamp. Nothing happens. Maybe a fuse has blown? After much hesitation, I force myself to sit up and tentatively set my feet on the worn wood floor.

I can't help but smile a little at myself. This is absurd, the situation is pathetic. A fuse blows and I become . . . incapacitated, irrational. I desperately search my memory for something to hang my thoughts on, a mental line to hold on to as I slowly lift myself off the bed. But the only thing that fills my awareness is the music I was listening to before I fell asleep.

Ground control to Major Tom

I shiver. An animal cries out in the distance and I feel a cold draft along my legs. Is a window open?

Take your protein pills and put your helmet on

The house is quiet. Too quiet. Slowly, I slip across the cold floorboards out of the bedroom. The only thing I hear is the rain and the waves regularly crashing against the rocks below the house, like a gigantic animal's heavy breathing.

Then.

A sharp pain flashes through my shinbone, spreads along my thigh all the way up to my groin. I double up. Another crash and something lands on my big toe with a dull thud. What is going on? There is a chair in the middle of the floor. Why is it here? I can't remember pulling it out. The chairs are always around the table in the kitchen. And now—my toe—what the hell *is* that? I bend over and investigate the object that fell on my toe.

It's the flashlight.

Ground control to Major Tom

I turn on the flashlight while I massage my shin, but nothing happens. Is it broken? Once again I feel the cold night air streaming toward me. Something is terribly wrong. And the whole time: the music in my head that won't go away.

Why is the chair in the middle of the floor? Why is the flashlight on the chair and not by my bed? I remind myself to stop drinking so much. Obviously, I must have moved the chair and for some strange reason put the flashlight on it. I just don't remember when and why. But this sort of thing happens to me sometimes. Once I fell asleep on the rocks and woke up in the middle of the night, ice-cold, covered with mosquito bites, my back unbelievably stiff. *In the dark.*

If I wasn't so afraid of the dark, it could have been a funny story, or possibly embarrassing. Another time, I left the freezer wide open after a late-night ice cream raid. All the food was ruined. That wasn't a funny story either, just expensive. No more wine this week, I tell myself, as I let go of my shin and get up unsteadily.

A slight queasiness forces me to stand still a moment. I don't know if it's due to the wine or the fear, but I can feel my heart pounding in my chest, inexhaustible and twitchy like a Duracell rabbit. Carefully, I start moving toward the hall, one foot tentatively in front of the other—I don't want to risk running into something again. Where is the fuse box? Distance and proportions become distorted in the dark, and although I have been in the cramped space that is my hall innumerable times, I can't find the familiar little metal box.

Sweat breaks out on my forehead, runs into my eyes making them burn, and I feel tears welling up. I grope with my hands along the bead board paneling that covers the walls. Why in the world did I stay in this dark house? Why didn't I move to the city? Like a normal person. No, I simply had to stay. Alone out in Stockholm's archipelago wasteland. I should have done as they said.

Like Aina said.

I can hear my own halting breath. Damn house. Damn dark shit hole.

How am I going to find it? Suddenly, the reassuringly cool metal of the fuse box is under my sweaty fingers. As a reminder that the only thing that is misplaced in this room is my own exaggerated reaction. I take a deep breath and concentrate on the fuses. They're the old-fashioned kind: gray with a loop that falls off when the fuse has blown. But it's totally dark, so it's impossible to determine if one of them is broken.

Suddenly, a flash of lightning illuminates the house with a ghostlike, blue-white glow. For a moment I can see the fuse box as clearly as day—the heavy metal frame, the rounded porcelain fuses, and the black Bakelite main breaker: It's switched to Off.

A thought starts to form in my mind, an insight that is growing gradually, like a diver in turbid water slowly rising toward the surface who perceives the light increasing in stages. *Has someone been here?* But before I have time to seriously think that through, I hear a creaking noise. The hall door is caught by the wind and blows wide open, filling the house with cold, damp night air just as the boom of thunder echoes over the sea.

The storm is near.

With shaking fingers, I force the small black Bakelite switch back up. The house is instantly filled with light. From the kitchen comes a sigh and a gurgling sound as the refrigerator starts up again. I sink down on the wood floor among old sneakers and rubber boots, and wipe my sweaty brow with the back of my hand. The floor feels cold and damp, and it takes a while before I realize that it is not my own sweat I am feeling on the shiny worn floorboards. That is when I see it, right inside the threshold, a wet puddle, bearing witness to someone's presence.

It's a footprint.

Date: August 28
Time: 3:00 p.m.
Place: Green Room, the practice
Patient: Sara Matteus

"I have to ask you something that maybe doesn't belong here," says Sara, looking hesitant.

It is fifty minutes into our session, and I am getting ready to wrap it up. Sara is dressed in a minimal tank top that makes her skinny body look even thinner. She is leaning forward in a way that makes her look like a sad, starving dog. She is holding a pair of sunglasses in her left hand and slowly strikes them against her bony thigh, lost in thought.

"Sure," I say, perhaps a little absentmindedly.

I'm finding it hard to concentrate and be attentive after the events of last night. I didn't get much sleep. After I fixed the power outage, I lay in bed in a sweaty, sleepless daze, twisting and turning until morning came. Not even a couple glasses of wine helped with the anxiety. When the alarm clock rang, I forced myself out of bed and had a painkiller for breakfast.

"It's about this guy . . . or man. Same difference . . ."

Sara pauses, gathers up her courage.

"He seems to like me, we talk about *everything,* we have *fun,* but . . . he doesn't want to have sex with me."

Sara switches to drumming her sunglasses against the Kleenex box on my little coffee table, as if to underscore the significance of her words. She looks distressed, and I guess that this is probably the first time she has run into this particular problem. In psychology-speak, Sara is what we call "sexually acting out." Others might call her loose, but for Sara this is not about sexual satisfaction. In reality, it's the insecure little girl inside her that is struggling to be acknowledged and appreciated.

"Has it been like that all along?" I ask in a friendly but neutral tone.

"At first I thought he wanted to wait until we knew each other better or something. I mean . . . I was almost, like . . . flattered. As if I were a *fine wine* or something, that should be saved."

Sara laughs for a moment and looks at me with an expression of feigned surprise.

"Then I slowly started to wonder if maybe he's impotent or something. It's not really all that unusual at his age," Sara says, as if she knows everything about the sexual problems of middle-aged men.

"But I think he wants to, though something is holding him back. I mean, I can tell he wants to, but he pulls back when it's about to happen. He gets almost . . . he gets almost *angry.* How can that make him angry?" she asks quietly, looking closely at me.

"I don't know," I reply tentatively. "There are so many reasons and I don't know your friend, of course. It could be anything from fear of not measuring up sexually—I mean, you're attractive and young and so on— to physical ailments or emotional blocks. What do you think? After all, you're the one who knows him best."

"I don't think anything." Sara shrugs, but I can tell from her facial expression, from her entire posture, in fact, that she is tormented by something. She shrugs again and looks me intently in the eyes.

"Okay, it's like this . . . it's like he's carrying a lot of . . . anger. As if he's really angry . . . inside, and it comes out when we start getting close, *physically close,* that is."

Sara's voice fades and she lets her head hang down toward her chest. She suddenly appears indescribably fragile. She curls up in the leather armchair like a little bird and wraps her arms around her knees.

She sits like that, silently, for a long time, and I let her be.

"Sara," I begin hesitantly, "have you thought about why it is so important to you that the two of you have sex?"

"Oh, my God!"

She lifts her head and looks at me as if I'm crazy. "My God," she repeats. "We've been seeing each other almost every day for at least a month. He sleeps at my place and he says he wants to live with me. *Hello!* Don't you think it's strange that he doesn't want to sleep with me?"

I don't answer, but I know she's right.

In the city, people don't look at each other when they walk by. You look down at the ground. That's just how it is. Maybe that was why she never saw me? But still, it was really strange. During the early summer, several times I came so close to her in line in Söderhallarna market that I could have easily put my hands around her little bird neck and squeezed. It would have been over in no time.

Once I touched her bony arm in line at the ATM. It was downy and warm from the sun. I pulled back my hand as if I had been burned and shivered with disgust. But she didn't see me, she only scratched her arm a little absentmindedly with her short, unpolished nails.

I started to feel invisible, like those pitiful down-and-out bastards who make their home in Medborgarplatsen. The ones no one looks at.

Drunks, crazies, young guys with swollen muscles and big tattoos are invisible. The whores, too, with their tormented, demanding stares, stick-thin thighs, worn-out veins, and hungry sex. I saw them looking and heard their voices inside me: "Wanna FUCK? I can help you: I see your pain. I see YOU."

When the invisible people show up in the subway or on the streets, ordinary people discreetly look away. The invisible people populate the parks of Stockholm, the underground labyrinths where the subway trains rush forth through the night, and the homeless shelters. They are the ones who ride the night bus from one end station to the other in an endless loop, never getting anywhere. They are the ones who beg for a meal at lunchtime among the customers at McDonald's.

And to her I was invisible, just like them. I was on the same level as any old alcoholic. Me, of all people!

One day, right before Midsummer, I nonchalantly stood in front of her on Götgatan, my stance wide, blocking her path.

But she only stared down at the street and made a determined half circle around me without even lifting her gaze.

It was then that I decided. She'd had her chance, her chance for atonement, and she blew it.

For that reason, I had to punish her.

It is late afternoon and I feel tired and listless. I know I was more distracted during my hour with Sara than is appropriate, by my standards, anyway, but the alternative would have been to cancel today's session, and I think that would have been worse for her.

Her boyfriend worries me. Who is he, and what does he really want with Sara? I know that her love life should not be at the center of our therapy, but still, I can't help being worried. At the same time, I'm starting to doubt my own intuition. How can I really assess anything rationally right now? I'm so shaken up and afraid that I see danger everywhere.

Threats.

I sigh heavily and try to think about other things. I can't let fear win.

I open the window in my office. Voices drift up from the market below. I toy with the idea of talking to Aina. Maybe I should accompany her to the art opening she's going to and stay the night in her little studio on Blekingegatan. We both have the day off tomorrow.

The thought of waking up in her tiny apartment is appealing. A little hungover, wake Aina up, and then go down to the 7-Eleven to get breakfast. An old routine. We've done it many times before. I get up and cross the small hallway, into Aina's office.

I find Aina sitting in the lotus position on the floor, talking on her cell phone. She sparkles and laughs loudly, which means there is a man on the other end. Although it's unclear which one. She looks up and sees me. As I start to back out of her office, she signals that I should stay put. With a couple short sentences she concludes the call and looks at me.

"Siri! Tell me about it!"

I am confused. I don't know what she wants to hear. "Tell you what?"

Aina simply smiles.

"You looked like you . . . well, like you wanted to share something," she says, and perhaps she is right. Sure, I would like to tell her what happened last night, but I can't. I can't bear to.

"I wanted to talk about the exhibition," I say instead.

"You're coming!"

Aina's smile is almost more radiant than the one she had on her lips during the phone conversation with the unknown man.

"Hot damn, that's great! Do you know how long it's been since we went out together? You have to stay over too, and then we can have breakfast in Helgalunden if the sun is out."

Aina's enthusiasm knows no bounds and it just sweeps me away. Wonderful Aina, with her ability to make other people feel chosen and special.

"By the way, that was Robert on the phone."

"Which Robert?"

"Ha ha, that's a good one," Aina says, giggling. "You know. Robert from the crayfish party. The one who plays guitar."

"I see, you're still together?"

Aina squirms as if my question had teeth.

"No, not exactly. But he wanted your number," she says with a broad smile.

"My number, why?"

Aina laughs at my confusion and puts her head to one side. "Why shouldn't he want your number? I guess you'll have to ask him when he calls."

Then she notices my expression and raises her accented eyebrows. With a certain worry in her voice she says, "But you look tired, how are you sleeping, my darling? You really ought to think about talking to someone. Or medication. Whichever you think is best."

"Aina," I interrupt her. "I didn't come to discuss . . . my mental health. I just came because I wanted to thank you for the invitation to that party you've been trying to convince me to go to for the last two weeks. You know . . . *the party.*"

"Sorry."

An apologetic smile.

"*The party,* right, cool! Are you done for the day?" She looks at me inquisitively. "Because then we can go buy a bottle of wine now."

We walk down Götgatan. Countless people are on the streets, many are in a hurry, carrying bags and packages. After a brief stop at the liquor store and the H&M at Ringen, we have a quick dinner at Aina's place consisting of Thai takeout with red wine. The combination is unorthodox, but it works.

We get changed, throw on something dressier, a little makeup, some product in our hair. For the first time in a long while I think I look good. Aina is radiantly beautiful in jeans and a blue silk camisole. Her long hair has been bleached by the sun and hangs like a light silk veil over her shoulders.

Siri and Aina. Aina who is tall and blond. Curvaceous. Happy. Always on the verge of laughing. Siri. Short and dark. Slender. A tomboy. Earnest. But of course, once you scratch the surface a little, the reality is not so simple. Aina is an amazingly capable therapist and serious through and through. Behind the sparkling smile and the blond hair lies a sharp intellect. She is easily misjudged, but anyone who tries to outshine Aina in academic discussions is not likely to attempt again.

The party is in a gallery in Östermalm. One of Aina's artist friends has finally been given the chance to show her work. There are whispers of breakthrough, and Malena, the artist, is making the rounds with bright red cheeks and eyes wide open. It looks like the whole situation seems unreal to her. Aina and I quickly lose sight of each other. She notices some acquaintances and I prefer to head over to the little bar where white wine is served in plastic cups and Japanese rice crackers in separate cups. Not too classy but efficient if you want to get drunk. And I want to.

I look around at the guests. It's the usual mix of acquaintances Aina likes to hang out with: artists, musicians, and unclassifiable cultural types. I don't really feel at home among these people. The whole thing is pretty pretentious; everyone is beautiful, confident, and just so. And yet I feel stimulated by being out among people. My lonely house feels far away and I'm distracted from my panic and fear.

The following morning is just as we had planned it. Hungover, we sit on a blanket in Helgalunden, drink Diet Coke, and watch the people around us: dog owners walking through the park, sunbathers lying spread out on the grass, a couple in love making out without embarrassment on the blanket beside us. I feel calmer than I have in a long time. The thought of going home is not frightening at all. We sit in the park and chat for several hours before I pack up my things and walk toward Slussen and the buses to Värmdö.

Date: August 30
Time: 2:00 p.m.
Place: Green Room, the practice
Patient: Peter Carlsson—assessment interview 2

It is time for Peter Carlsson's next appointment. This will be our second assessment interview, in which I know more about him and therefore have more opportunities to get him to open up about what's so important and what is making him look so hopelessly tormented in my Lamino chair. During the past week I had doubted whether Peter would show up for his second appointment. Sometimes it just seems too hard to come back; patients are ashamed and think they have revealed too much. Sometimes they're simply not comfortable with the therapist. But Peter is here. He sits dutifully and waits for me to begin. I can see that he is ill at ease. His face is bright red and he avoids eye contact. When we greeted each other in the waiting room, his hand felt sweaty and I could tell that he was embarrassed that I had discovered that he could not really control his bodily functions.

After a polite exchange of pleasantries, we take a look at the scales he filled out since his last visit. Then I ask him to tell me why he is seeking help right now. What just happened that made him finally try to get help for his symptoms, since he's had them for almost twenty years?

"Well, you see . . . I have a girlfriend. She is very important to me. I think this is the first time I've really been in love. I mean, *really* in love."

I nod encouragingly and indicate that he should continue.

"We met a few months ago and everything was starting off well, but I was still worried. I mean, I've had relationships before, but I've always broken them off after a short time. But with this woman I don't want . . . I mean I want to. I *want* something with her."

"So you've had relationships before, but you've broken them off, and now you've met a woman who matters to you, and you want it to work out. Did I understand you correctly?"

Peter Carlsson nods in silence, and I can see tears welling up in his eyes.

"Can you tell me why you broke off your previous relationships, and why you are worried that you will have to break this one off as well?"

"I have thoughts," he mumbles, "images inside my head. And they scare me."

"Can you describe these thoughts?"

"It's . . . so hard."

He looks tormented.

"Tell me about the last time this happened."

"Yesterday evening. It was yesterday evening. We had . . . something to eat and drank wine. She, my girlfriend, got tired and went to lie down. She was lying on the bed, asleep. And I could visualize how I . . . how I . . . I mean, how unbelievably easy it would be for me to put my hands around her neck . . . and just squeeze. I saw how vulnerable she was at that moment and how unbelievably easy it would be to . . . *injure* her."

"And how did those thoughts make you feel?"

"I don't know. At first they were almost . . . exciting."

Looking embarrassed, Peter Carlsson stares down at his shiny shoes, as if that was where the solution to his problems lay.

"But then I got really scared. What if I were to hurt her *for real?* After all, I . . . do love her."

He curls up in the chair and his body starts shaking. Tears are streaming down his cheeks and I make my usual gesture toward the box of Kleenex.

"And I assume that you've had these thoughts in previous relationships?"

He nods.

"Tell me more about it," I encourage him.

"I almost always have thoughts that I could hurt them. Like with the car, when I thought I could run someone over. But it's more "—he hesitates—"more like I might lose control. You know, that I might go . . . crazy. What if I go crazy and do something I can't control? Like with the car accident, which isn't about running someone over deliberately but that I hurt someone accidentally. It is more as if I lose control, do something insane, like you see on TV, you know, like the guy who cut his girlfriend up with an ax."

Peter is referring to a widely publicized criminal case.

"It's always been this way . . . for as long as I've had relationships. But it's gotten worse."

"In what way has it gotten worse?"

"I don't know. The thoughts have become more intrusive. They become images. Like little movies being played in my head. When I'm going to . . . when we're going to . . . when we *try* to have sex, it's like I see a movie in my head."

Peter hesitates. My sense is that, whatever he's about to tell me, it's not something he really wants to share.

"We start kissing, for example, or . . . well, you know. And I get aroused. But then, then come those horrible images, and I . . . I do everything I can to drive them away. Start reciting song lyrics to myself or multiplication tables or . . . but the images come anyway. Images of how we are making love. And she's lying there, defenseless. And trusting. She trusts me. First we make love normally and she enjoys it. She enjoys it and I enjoy it. But then . . . then . . . uhh . . . then something happens with the images. I see myself lifting my hands and laying them on her throat. And she looks at me and opens her mouth as if to say no, but no sound comes out. No sound at all! And I squeeze. She trembles and her back tenses but she can't do anything. She bends, arching upward, like a bow . . . Her eyes are big and black and I see her surprise and her terror. I squeeze the life out of her while I am still inside her, and when she stops breathing, only then do I come."

Peter Carlsson looks almost annihilated. He is still crying.

"How do these images make you feel, in retrospect?"

He doesn't answer, just runs his hands repeatedly up and down his suit-covered thighs in an almost spastic motion.

I wait for his answer.

"I'm so afraid. What if I were to actually lose control and do her harm? I do love her. These thoughts make me feel *loathsome,* like a damn *sex criminal.* I really don't want to hurt her."

"Do you enjoy these fantasies?"

I realize that the patient could perceive this question as provocative, but it is important for me to ask in order to understand what lies behind his thoughts. Is he a sexual sadist, or are these compulsive thoughts?

"Enjoy?"

Peter looks indignant.

"No, I *don't* enjoy them. I want to be rid of them. I wish they didn't exist. That's why I'm asking for help. To make them disappear. Don't you get it?"

"What do you do, if anything, to try and make them go away?"

"I've stopped watching the news and reading about lunatics and people who lose control and break down and kill people."

Peter stops himself. Silence fills the room.

"Anything else?"

"I stopped having sex. If I don't sleep with my girlfriend, the thoughts don't come in the same way. But . . . what woman wants a man who won't have sex with her?"

I weigh Peter's words. The images he talks about make me feel slightly nauseous, and while I'm not certain, I think that what he is describing are compulsive thoughts and nothing more. Intrusive, unwanted thoughts and images that give rise to strong anxiety. A fear of losing control and realizing the thoughts, which often leads to avoidance of what triggers them.

Often, different kinds of rituals appear, just like they did with Peter, in order to keep the thoughts at bay. But avoidance and rituals end up keeping the problem alive; they can perhaps even make it worse. My job is to help the patient stop these behaviors and learn to directly confront the painful, anxiety-producing thoughts. The treatment principle is that discomfort and fear are reduced when you stop trying to avoid specific thoughts and situations. It sounds simple, but it is extremely hard for the patient and demands a lot of courage as well as faith in the therapist. In this case, I still feel a certain indecision and decide I need guidance from a more experienced colleague.

I manage to calm Peter down by explaining what compulsive thoughts are, emphasizing that most likely his problem can be solved. We schedule another appointment, and when we part I think I see a light in his eyes.

Perhaps it is hope.

After Peter's session I walk over to the small kitchen. I am deeply affected by the conversation we just had. His problems are in some ways uncharted territory for me, and I don't really know how best to tackle his case. Sure, I've treated compulsion before, even sexual compulsion.

But this?

Does the fact that I am a woman make therapy more difficult? Perhaps I ought to refer him to Sven, but I need my patients—they're the ones who pay my salary.

Ziggy is gone. I can no longer deny this fact. I haven't seen his plump gray body for over a week. Of course he disappears sometimes, off on unknown adventures in the pine forest along the water, but never for this long. I've searched in the garden, by the pier, and in the woods between the house and the main road. I've inspected the treetops in case he's gotten himself stuck up there. I've set out bowls of his favorite food on the lawn and waited. I felt certain he would soon return, curl his soft body next to mine in bed and, unconcerned by my fretting, carry on his usual carefree cat life.

That's why this evening I am standing outside again, peering out over the little patch of grass in my yard that extends like a shaggy sun-bleached rug all the way to where the softly rounded, gray granite cliffs begin. Along the side of the shed, nettles grow yard-high. Every spring I tell myself I should dig them up, but of course I don't. Sometimes I find comfort in knowing that I am incapable of change; it gives me a sense of security in a world where nothing is constant and reliable. I embrace my own passivity and think, full of self-pity, that I can't be expected to just pick myself up and continue to live as if nothing happened, after the kind of slap in the face I received. It would be more or less like climbing out of a burning car wreck, brushing away the soot with a smile, and asking whether there's a good restaurant nearby.

I see it often in my work: how people develop mannerisms and some-times even outright damaging behaviors to shield themselves against life. I always force them to confront their fears. Subdue them. Dare to live in the present, for what it is. Even if it hurts. I know exactly how to do it, there are well-proven methods.

I'm just not able to do it myself.

The last rays of sun tinge the cliffs outside bright orange, and I shiver—still in my wet swimsuit after a swim—as I stand inside at the French windows, my hand on the glass.

A faint scratching noise interrupts my musings. As if a twig were scratching against my front door. A faint . . . scraping. As if a dozen fingernails were scratching weakly on a cloth.

My initial reaction is fear. It comes instinctively, without my consciously assessing the situation. Suddenly, all my senses are heightened: I can clearly see individual pinecones outlined against the orange sky, the faded seed heads of chervil at the edge of the lawn that resemble stylized fireworks against a backdrop of dense gray stone.

And the sound.

It's as if a child was writing on my door with a pencil. A tentative, dry scraping that comes and goes. Rhythmically. Like sprawling words formed by a small child's unsteady hands.

I walk slowly toward the hall, without a plan, simply trying to make my steps as quiet as possible. Halfway there it hits me: Ziggy, of course, it's Ziggy—he's come back! Maybe he's injured and weak, trying to get my attention.

I cover the last few yards in two long bounds, heave myself against the worn but massive oak door, and open it to the forest on the other side. The sun has gone down and only a faint grayish-blue sheen remains between the knotty pine trunks. Ferns, blueberry branches, and moss spread out before me, but I can't see Ziggy's round little cat form anywhere. I step tentatively out on the wooden steps.

"Ziggy!" My voice echoes thin and toneless in the summer evening.

But except for the far-off sound of a motorboat, everything is quiet. And then there's something else. The sound of something fragile snapping. Like twigs, small, thin twigs. I imagine Ziggy wandering confusedly among the ferns and moss-covered boulders. Injured and disoriented.

"Ziggy, come here, kitty!"

But there's no cat coming my way.

I go back inside and get my big flashlight from the bedroom and grip it firmly in my right hand as I carefully step outside again.

"Ziiiggy!"

The evening air is damp and filled with the saturated aroma of moldering plant parts and pine trees. I turn on the flashlight and aim it at the woods. The trunks of the pines cast irregular shadows that resemble grotesque elongated figures that fall time and again as I sweep the beam of light from left to right. A bat flies through the light with jerky movements.

"Ziggy! Come, buddy! Come to Mama!"

Slowly I walk among the pines at the edge of the forest. I am still barefoot, in my swimsuit. The pine needles stick in the soles of my feet, but it doesn't bother me. All I want is to find Ziggy.

I reach the clothesline. The sheets that I hung out to dry this morning reflect the strong light from the flashlight and I squint involuntarily.

"Ziggy!"

But no Ziggy appears.

In the corner of my eye I perceive a movement. The sheet farthest to the right flutters and I hear a muted snap. Then another twig snaps, a sturdier one this time. Much too big to have been broken by Ziggy's dainty, lithe feline body. It's the kind of twig that breaks only under a heavy weight. Only a large animal or a human being could have broken a branch like that. I know it's so. My entire body knows it's so.

My stomach clenches and my grip on the flashlight gets firmer. Suddenly I am aware of how I must look, standing there in only a swimming suit, the gigantic flashlight held out in front of me in my right hand like a crucifix, as if I believe it can keep whatever lies in the dark ahead away from me.

I stay standing stock-still for a moment, then I run back to the house and slam the door behind me. I collapse inside the door and with trembling fingers start picking out the needles from the soles of my feet.

Perhaps what is about to happen is caused by my fruitless search for Ziggy and the persistent feeling that someone was outside my house, someone saw me half naked and shivering as I looked for my cat among the pines, with a flashlight as my only weapon.

I feel depressed, afraid, and alone, and decide to console myself with the last bottle of rosé in the refrigerator. As it turns out, I drink more glasses than I thought I would, and when the bottle is empty I treat myself to a little red wine as well. I drift off into a restless, dreamless sleep lying on the lumpy, uncomfortable couch under a plaid blanket, with the stereo on way too loud. That's why I don't hear the phone ringing at first; it rings many times before I finally wake up and answer. The connection crackles and whistles, and I can hear only with difficulty what the gentle, androgynous voice is saying.

"I'm looking for Siri Bergman."

"This is she."

"Hi, I'm calling from the emergency room at Stockholm South Hospital . . ."

"Yes?"

"A friend of yours was admitted here this evening, Aina Davidsson . . ."

I can't seem to formulate a reasonable reaction to this. Is Aina at the hospital?

". . . and she would really like you to come. She was run over by a motorcyclist on Folkungagatan."

"Oh, my God, is she okay?"

The voice hesitates for a moment.

"Well . . . it's serious but not critical. She has a head injury that we're a little concerned about. If everything goes as planned, we will transfer her shortly up to the intensive care unit . . . So that we can keep an eye on her."

If everything goes as planned?

"We're taking good care of her, you don't need to worry, but as I said, she would really like you to come. Preferably as soon as possible."

My stomach is knotted with fear and hunger as I lean against the kitchen counter. Images of Aina's face flicker before my eyes. I pull a cereal box from the shelf and quickly stuff a couple fistfuls of muesli in my mouth and pour myself another glass of wine to wash it down. Two big gulps.

It's been so long since I last drove my car that I can barely find the car keys. I fumble with the ignition in the dark, and it takes me a while to turn on the headlights. I feel nauseous and dizzy, and a throbbing pain is growing stronger and stronger beneath my skull and between my eyes. It's as if an angry animal were desperately trying to escape from my head through my eye sockets. I am forced to hold on to the steering wheel so I don't fall out when I lean over to shut the car door. I know I shouldn't be driving, but Aina is my best friend and one thing is clear to me: I could not cope with losing her, too.

The night is dark, and the narrow, curvy road meanders treacherously through the quiet landscape. I am driving very slowly but still manage to end up twice with the front wheel on the grass at the side of the road.

As I approach Värmdö church, I notice a dark car behind me for the first time. It follows me through the city. But I don't give it any more thought.

Not then.

As I reach Grisslinge, I see blue lights. It is now obvious that the car behind me is the police and that they want something from me, so I pull over and roll down the window. A man approaches from behind, and against the background of flashing blue a young police officer is suddenly standing in front of me.

"Good evening, your driver's license please."

I fumble for my purse and realize I didn't bring it with me. I can see for myself how erratic and uncontrolled my movements are, so I place both hands on the steering wheel, squeeze it hard, take a deep breath, and look up again toward the policeman, who now has a wrinkle between his eyebrows.

"Uh, I'm really sorry, but I'm on my way to see a friend who's in the emergency room and . . . I'm afraid that I didn't . . . well, that I didn't bring my things."

I can hear how lame my excuse sounds, but the policeman's facial expression is inscrutable. If he is surprised or irritated, his face does not show what he is thinking.

"Okay, we would like you to take a Breathalyzer test. Have you done it before?"

"Yes . . . sure."

There's something about the overly serious expression on the young policeman's face. I can't help it; suddenly the whole situation seems so absurd I have to laugh.

I look up at the policeman and hope that my laughter will get him to see the humor in the situation, but he only looks self-consciously toward the police car. For some inexplicable reason this gesture provokes me even more, causing me to laugh even louder. I really try to subdue it, but before I can collect myself I double over in another uncontrollable laugh attack. My whole body cramps up in a convulsion of laughter and tears stream down my cheeks.

The policeman says nothing, only hands me the Breathalyzer and clears his throat.

I exhale red. Once. And once more.

Curtain.

I have to get out and follow the policeman to his car. I hope it's not too obvious that I am swaying, but when I see the meaningful look the younger policeman gives his partner as we approach his car, my stomach knots up.

There are two of them: a middle-aged, stocky man with reddish hair and a gap between his teeth, and the younger guy who is evidently called Amir. During the drive I desperately try to explain the seriousness of the situation: Aina's accident, the call from the hospital, the head injury, the intensive care unit. There is something indescribably humiliating about all this, as if I were trying to cover my shameful behavior by presenting a long, drawn-out excuse that is as embarrassing for me as it is for them.

They kindly explain that they can't release me, or drive me to the hospital, but promise to call the hospital from the station. I give them Aina's cell phone number, too.

Five minutes later I am overwhelmed with dizziness and nausea. In the meantime my headache has grown into an intense pain that drums under my eyebrows like dull thunder and I can feel cold sweat gathering between my breasts and traveling down toward my belly in small rivulets.

"Please stop . . ."

My voice is a feeble whisper, but both policemen hear it and from experience stop by the side of the road.

"Are you feeling sick? Do you have to throw up?"

"No, no, of course not," I say as I empty the contents of my stomach on the passenger seat.

When we arrive at the station, the redheaded policeman goes with me to a room that appears to be down in the basement. If he is upset or disgusted that I soiled his car, he doesn't show it. He looks like he's thinking about something completely different: dinner, the hockey game this weekend, or his ex-wife's new boyfriend. I assume he encounters *my type* several times a week, and that this is not something he is going to think about when his shift is over. A routine case. A drunk broad who decided to drive into the city from Värmdö even though she should have known better. A traffic hazard, perhaps also a human tragedy— but who cares?

I am instructed to blow a few more times into a larger Breathalyzer that is connected to a computer. Automatically, a form comes out with the evidence of my guilt.

They received a tip, he told me. Someone had seen me drink and then get into the car and had called them. And no, he can't tell me who it was. I wonder for a long time who it might be. There are no neighbors who live close enough to be able to see what I'm doing.

Later, I am left to sit in something that I assume is a cell, a drunk tank. It is a degrading, bare little windowless room with a PVC-coated mattress and a floor drain in one corner. They explained that I have to sober up in jail in accordance with the law on the custody of intoxicated persons. A broken fluorescent ceiling light blinks constantly and contributes to my sense of degradation and humiliation.

Without my being aware of it, tears start running down my cheeks. When did I lose control of my life? Here, at the police station? When I got into the car while intoxicated? When I chose to stay in my isolated house despite all my friends' protests? When I started imagining things were happening at night? When Stefan died?

How long have I been sitting here? Twenty minutes? An hour? I've lost all sense of time.

Suddenly the door opens and I stand up. When I see who is standing outside I am filled with both joy and confusion. How is this possible?

Aina looks completely healthy—there is no sign that she was just injured. She leans against the doorjamb, tilts her head to one side, and looks at me with an expression of concern.

Stefan and I were married in December. It was a simple ceremony at City Hall, with our closest friends and relatives. Stefan's mom and dad, my parents and sisters, Peppe and Malin, and their twins. Aina was there, of course, and Hanna, my oldest girlfriend, who lives in New York and works as a graphic designer. I remember that she was very pregnant at the time and constantly drying off the sweat from her red face with a flowery Marimekko scarf. Afterward we all went to the KB restaurant and had Christmas lunch. My off-white sixties-style woolen dress with oversized buttons from the thrift store fit snugly over my belly.

But was it possible?

Could I have been showing already?

I was in my seventeenth week when we got married, and my slender body still concealed the pregnancy well. Only Stefan and I knew.

Two weeks later, Stefan and I went to the maternity clinic in Gamla Stan to meet our midwife, Inger, and to undergo the mandatory ultrasound with one of the doctors.

We expected images of the baby to put up on the refrigerator, nervous minutes until the doctor would declare that everything looked good, information about growth and expected date of delivery. But as I was lying there on the bed with cold jelly spread over my stomach, I could see the doctor's worried expression. She didn't say anything, only furrowed her brow a little, put her head to one side, and gave Stefan a quick glance. Did she know he was a doctor?

I lay still and waited for her to find the missing finger, or suddenly see all the chambers of the heart clearly and declare that they looked fine. I let her move the transducer back and forth across my belly without my asking any questions or protesting; perhaps everything would be all right if I kept quiet and cooperated?

"I see . . ." she began and then fell silent.

"The fetus is normal-sized at this stage," she continued carefully. "Here is the spine," she indicated on the screen, and something that looked like a small string of pearls stood out white against the gray-black background. "Here is the pelvis." She made a gesture toward something that did not resemble a body part, or anything else, for that matter, as she twisted the transducer a little and pressed it hard against the side of my belly.

"Here is the bladder, there is fluid in it, which is normal, here are the kidneys . . ."

I felt my growing impatience. Couldn't she just say that everything was fine and spare us this uncertainty?

"Is everything as it should be?" I interrupted her, trying to keep my voice steady and calm.

She looked at me but did not answer immediately.

"Here is the head," she continued, and I could see a light-gray sphere outlined against the dark background on the screen.

She was silent for a long time and seemed to observe the head from various angles.

"I would like you to go to Stockholm South Hospital and do an extended ultrasound," she said as she turned toward us, lifting the transducer from my belly and taking a piece of paper from the little steel table beside the bed. With slow movements, she started wiping the cold jelly from my belly with a rough, unbleached paper napkin.

"What's wrong?" Stefan suddenly sounded angry.

"It's not certain that there *is* anything wrong, but . . . there are parts of the brain that I can't really see with my equipment."

The brain? I felt my eyes watering up. I don't cry easily, but the tension during the ultrasound combined with my raging hormones caused the tears to flow down my cheeks in a torrential stream.

The brain? Did our baby have a brain defect? Would it be handicapped? I thought about small children in wheelchairs, special transportation services, special schools, and apartments adapted for the disabled. I clenched my teeth so hard that I almost got a cramp and curled up into a little ball on the green plastic bed. Stefan leaned over me and whispered in my ear that everything would be fine.

The very same day we got the results from the second ultrasound at Stockholm South Hospital. The doctor was a middle-aged Arab. He seemed tired and worn-out but was very friendly and took time to fully explain the situation to us in accented Swedish.

"The fetus's brain is not normally developed," he said matter-of-factly. His gaze did not waver before our dismay and shock. We just sat there for a long time and let the words sink in.

"It's called anencephaly. The primary defect is actually absence of skull bone, which leads to the cerebral cortex not developing normally. With the ultrasound we can see the lack of a cranium and both hemispheres of the cerebrum."

Neither Stefan nor I could utter a word. We sat silently while the doctor carefully explained the significance of what he had just said.

"With this type of defect, the fetus cannot develop normally, and even if it were to survive until birth, the child would die soon thereafter. I am truly sorry, but I recommend that you terminate the pregnancy as soon as possible. You can schedule an appointment this week."

I was confused. The whole situation was absurd. The terminology the doctor used felt as though it was created to serve as a buffer between us and the truth. The child I was carrying was a *fetus*. He did not want us to kill it, but *the pregnancy should be terminated*. After that, a *normalization of my hormones would allow for a new conception within one to two months*.

That evening, Stefan and I quarreled for the first time in a long while.

"But what if he's wrong?" I cried. "What if the baby isn't injured and we killed it?"

"It's not a baby, and you make it sound like a murder. We are terminating a pregnancy that can't lead anywhere." Stefan's face was red with anger and something else.

Something much more frightening.

"But what if they are wrong? We have to . . . have to ask someone else to do an ultrasound. That's the least you can ask before they kill—"

"Shut up! No one is going to . . . *kill* anyone, okay? And . . . I saw it myself on the ultrasound."

"You're an orthopedist, damn it. What *the hell* do you know about fetal diagnostics? Everything that's not broken or twisted is . . . too . . . *advanced* for you."

"Even I could see that it didn't have a *brain*. Don't you get that, Siri? *It doesn't have a brain!*" Stefan sank exhausted on the couch and buried his head in his hands. His breathing had gotten heavier and I could hear subdued, drawn-out sobs.

I sat silently beside him, struck mute by my understanding at last of the term "anencephaly": no brain.

We requested another ultrasound before the abortion and got it without any questions. The previous diagnosis was confirmed by yet another understanding, amiable, but helpless doctor. "*There's nothing we can do in this kind of situation. You will be able to have a healthy baby later.*" He was wrong, of course.

Three days later the child was removed.

Aina is in my arms, alive to the highest possible degree. Her hair tickles my cheek. Her scent in my nose is sweet like honey. Above us, the blinking broken fluorescent light continues to throb. I hold her hard, almost desperately, like a life buoy.

"*Aina . . .*" My voice is a sob.

"What is going on with you? Are you okay?" Aina inspects me in a way I don't recognize; there's something dark in her gaze, a hint of irritation. I press her to me without saying anything, while tears run down my cheeks.

"What actually happened?" Aina asks, raising her eyebrows and squinting slightly.

"I thought you were dying," I squeak, taking hold of her arms, perhaps a trifle too brusquely because she backs off, pushes me away, friendly but determined.

"Listen, the police told me. But . . . I didn't have an accident. I was at yoga. I . . . really . . . don't understand any of this."

"But they called . . ." My voice breaks.

"Who called? Siri. *Who?*"

Then I understand. Carefully, I try to formulate what I think I know.

"Aina, someone lured me here. Someone is following me. Someone . . ."

I don't know what kind of reaction I had expected from her, but she just closes her eyes completely. As if to shut out the whole scene. She backs off a couple of steps and places her arms across her chest, indicating her distance.

"*Listen, Siri, you have to pull yourself together!* I completely understand your making up a story for the police. But . . . don't involve me in your drunken lies."

She pulls the door closed behind her and leaves.

Leaves me alone with the shame.

As I sit abandoned in the bare cell, I begin to understand what must have happened. Someone was watching me outside my house. Someone was there a long time, sitting on the rocks, looking through my windows, watching me as I went swimming in the bay.

He saw me looking for Ziggy in the woods, recognized my vulnerability. My drunkenness. Then this someone called, to lure me to the city. He knew I was going to take my car. Tipped off the police. And, most important of all, he must also be the one who sent me the photo and turned off the power. Maybe he also moved my flashlight that night. Now I am convinced that it's not just a matter of isolated, innocent incidents.

Someone out there in the darkness wishes me harm.

It is an oppressive, dusty late-summer afternoon as I jog down the stairs from the office to make one of my mandatory visits to Systembolaget in Söderhallarna. It has become a bit of a ritual; Fridays mean wine shopping. I never buy more than one box at a time. Sometimes I supplement it with a few bottles of good wine, in case I need to treat myself during the coming week. You see, the bottles are a reward. What the box is I don't really know. Calling it consolation would probably be a bit much; rather, it serves as a kind of cement, the very mortar that gets the days to stick together, regardless of how sharp and edgy they have been. It's like everything is evened out, flows together. Nothing sticks out. Life itself becomes smooth, level, and easier to navigate.

I would rather not think about the visit to the Värmdö jail. Not now. Instead, I think about the responsible use of alcohol, namely that it's okay to have a glass of wine with dinner on a Saturday evening. There's nothing wrong with that. It's completely adult behavior that I intend to adopt. Soon. Maybe this weekend.

The liquor store is full of people stocking up for the weekend. Young guys maneuvering shopping carts full of beer cases out of the store. Old ladies packing Rositan or Marinellan liquor with endless care in their wheeled shopping trolleys. Self-assured middle-aged men who leave the store with bags heavy with Amarone or Bordeaux.

I find a box of cheap French wine. Presumably sour and oxidized before I even open it, but at this price it's still quite a steal.

Then I freeze. Sure, it's cramped in the store, but the hand that I feel on my right thigh can scarcely have ended up there by chance. Since my arms are full of wine and my way forward is blocked by an elderly couple, I turn around to confront the person who thinks he knows me well enough to put his hand on me.

Matted red hair.

A beard that brings to mind pictures of my dad in the seventies.

A faded T-shirt and a guitar across his shoulder. He is standing so close I can smell his body odor: sun-warmed skin and sweat.

It's Robert. Aina's Robert. Although, not anymore—because as far as I know it's over between them.

I am so taken aback that the impertinence I had prepared got stuck in my throat. I just stare and back up a couple of steps instead. I don't want to get too close to him.

"Hey there!"

He looks happy and doesn't seem to realize that he just violated my personal space, that he isn't someone who can touch me like that.

"Hi."

"Thanks for the party! It was fun. Exciting colleagues you have," Robert says, grinning so broadly that had I wanted to, I could count all his fillings.

"Were you thinking of someone in particular, or are you just being generally disparaging?"

I'm not laughing. There's nothing funny in his comment. I don't understand the logic either: Does he think he'll win me over so that we can have a contemptible conversation at the expense of my colleagues?

"Listen, I was just trying . . . to be funny."

"I don't think you're funny," I say, and hear at once how hard the words sound. They fly out of me. Impossible to take back once they've been let loose. It wasn't my idea really to respond so harshly, but the fact is he frightened me when he snuck up behind me without saying anything.

He purses his lips and nods slowly, as if he just understood something important.

"Well, okay, then. I won't disturb you anymore."

I don't say anything, just watch him as he lumbers out of the place with the guitar over his shoulder. Slouching. Offended.

Only afterward does it strike me: How long had he been standing behind me? And how close? Close enough to hear my breathing?

Close enough to smell my scent?

SEPTEMBER

I lay her gently down into the water with all the self-control I can muster. An indescribable sorrow fills me, as unexpected as it is sudden. I wouldn't have believed I would feel anything. I didn't think I could feel anything anymore. Not for real. I thought my emotions were dead. Now I know that maybe something inside me is still alive, despite everything. I don't know if that's good or bad.

Slowly, I let go of the cold, smooth body. It slips between my fingers like a water animal in flight, sinks slowly but then floats upward again and remains hovering a few inches below the surface.

Weightless like a spacecraft hovering in the middle of nothing.

Sorrow is still heavy in my chest and now I know why: Justice is done, but I can never get my life back.

Once upon a time my life was perfect, like the pictures in the glossy, heavy pages of a homemaking magazine. Little things were important: snow tires, espresso machines, sunscreen, tax assessment notices, recorder lessons, vaccinations.

Then she took everything from me.

The ride home to Värmdö feels lovely. The thought of my little red house calms me, slowly releasing the band of tension that has wound itself tightly around my head during the long day at the office.

When I get off the bus, the sun has finally disappeared behind the clouds and a damp, hot wind sweeps over the cliffs. On the horizon, a massive wall of violet-blue clouds is gathering over the sea. I figure I should probably take my evening dip early, because it looks like rain.

As I balance my way across the flat rocks in front of my house, the first raindrop falls on my cheek. The sea feels warm and welcoming as I dive from the rounded swimming rock that Stefan and I used to call Lasse's Ass, after his stepfather. I swim straight across the bay toward the little crooked pier in front of my house.

That's when I see it: first, as a movement in the waves by the small stony beach to the right of the pier. As I swim closer, I see something lying in the water. I swim even closer. Curious but also a little worried. Last fall a dead seal washed up at that exact same place.

I climb up the other side of the pier because the sharp rocks on the right side make it far too risky.

Once I'm up on the tar-scented little pier, I finally see her. She is lying naked under the water, her fair hair drifting around her head like an aureole. Her eyes are open and her face rests almost peacefully against a large yellow-brown bushel of kelp. With every wave, her head heaves and her hair makes a billowing motion, like the seaweed wrapped around her body. Her mouth is open and her lips have taken on a blue color. Her arms are stretched above her head as if she were trying to reach something out there in the water. Her fists are half clenched, but I can still see traces of the green nail polish on her unnaturally pale, slender fingers. Her body is small and thin like a child's, but with the shape of a woman.

It is Sara Matteus.

How do you assess a person's life? Is there some kind of divine power that spreads suffering and misery equally among us all? That creates justice and balance out of chaos? A hard childhood, a difficult adolescence, illness and alienation? So much the better, for then comes success and a career, life-long love, money in the bank, and golden years in a circle of loving children and grandchildren.

I know this isn't true. Sara will never win the lottery, meet the right man, or use her difficult experiences to rehabilitate young girls gone astray. Her life was short and hard, and that thought consumes me, makes my hands tremble and my eyes tear up.

We are sitting in my living room. I'm on the couch, with my legs curled under me and the old tartan blanket wrapped around my body, while across from me on two kitchen chairs sit Sonja and Markus, police officers who seem to have an endless supply of patience, understanding, and sympathy. They listen patiently to my confused report, stuff pillows behind my back, offer coffee, and Markus kindly brings me the glass of wine I ask for instead.

I have told them everything I know. My story must be confusing: disorganized, incomplete, partial observations and memories. Piled on top of each other. Woven together. That I came home, took my usual evening dip, found Sara by the pier, and can't recall how I got into the house and dialed 911. That I then had a confused conversation with the officers in the first patrol car to arrive on the scene, as they cordoned off the area around my little pier with plastic tape.

How I became hysterical and cried against one policeman's shoulder while the other one, a young blond woman, called for the "duty desk" and something called the "MDA doctor."

I couldn't understand why anyone would call for a doctor when Sara was so obviously . . . dead.

"So, she was one of your patients," Sonja starts when she has supplied me with yet another glass of the sour wine from the box.

"Yes."

I try to answer the questions clearly and confidently, but my voice doesn't really hold up. It sounds hollow and weak.

"Why did Sara come to you? I mean, she must have had some kind of psychological problem?"

"Sara had a psychiatric diagnosis, borderline personality disorder, or emotionally unstable personality disorder, as some prefer to call it."

Sonja is the one asking the questions, she is clearly in charge. A dark, middle-aged, thin and sinewy woman with obvious authority. But there is something stressed about her manner. Her words come quickly—treacherous as streaming, shallow water in a flood. It looks harmless, but if you don't watch yourself you are going to be swept away.

She pushes a strand of shaggy dark hair behind one ear. I wonder what it's like to work with death. With evil. Misery. If it shows in her face, in the wrinkles on her forehead, in the hard lines around her mouth, in her way of clenching her fists so that the knuckles whiten as she fixes her gaze on me.

Markus makes a note. He is young, looks like he's twenty, but I assume he must be older. Blond, curly hair, a childishly plain, boyish face. Like a cherub. Light, clear blue eyes that watch me constantly. His body is compact, like an athlete. Sinewy, tan muscular arms, broad shoulders.

"I'm sure you know that the therapist-client privilege can be broken when a person is subject to a police investigation. And there will be an investigation now, because Sara is . . . dead." Sonja says the last word hesitantly, as if it is dangerous and must be pronounced with greater care and respect.

"I know," I answer.

Contrary to what most people think, therapist-client privilege also does not apply if a client discloses that he or she has committed a crime punishable by more than two years in prison. Only clergy have an absolute obligation to keep confidentiality.

"Tell me a little more about borderline personality disorder," she encourages me.

"Okay, I'm sure you already know this, but as I said, borderline is a kind of personality disorder. The typical borderline patient is a girl. She is emotionally unstable and sometimes self-destructive. Has unstable but extremely intense relationships, often acts out sexually, and is also sometimes prone to suicide. Although Sara really wasn't suicidal."

I realize that I sound like I'm spouting facts out of a psychiatric textbook and interrupt myself with a little more wine.

"And what does this all mean in practice?" Sonja asks, glancing at the watch on her slender wrist.

I briefly recount Sara's background. Everything from her foster home placement and the sexual assaults to her habit of cutting herself.

"Why do these girls cut themselves?" Markus asks in a melodic Norrland dialect.

It is the first time he speaks during our conversation, and I am fascinated by how light and gentle his voice is, just like his face.

"To subdue the anxiety, or maybe to get attention. Because they are filled with self-hatred. There are also those who maintain that cutting oneself has become somewhat fashionable. And not everyone who cuts herself has a borderline problem. These days you can learn how to cut yourself on the Internet. If one girl tries, her friend will try it too. But it's not the same thing as a borderline personality disorder . . ."

Markus nods. He doesn't look like a policeman, I think. He looks too young. On the other hand, I don't know what a real-life detective looks like. I've never been interrogated this way before. Because that is what they're doing, under the surface of empathy and kindness.

"So you were going to cure Sara from this borderline thing," Sonja says, examining me.

"No, not cure. Borderline personality disorder is not like the common cold. It's more about helping the patient find a functional behavior, to be able to put up with painful emotions. We worked on getting rid of her self-injuring. So she wouldn't cut herself," I explained. "I, we . . . tried together to make her life more . . . bearable."

Markus makes another note on his pad.

"And all your patients have this kind of"—he hesitates—"borderline problem?" He seems satisfied that he used the terminology correctly.

"No, no, it's fairly unusual. The majority of patients who come to me have anxiety disorders. They may be afraid of various things, spiders or blood and such. Some have social phobias; they become nervous in social situations. Others have panic attacks. I use something called cognitive behavior therapy. For simplicity's sake one might say that I don't try so much to figure out *why* people have problems, but rather I focus on *how* these problems can be solved. Usually we work with practical exercises. Say you're afraid of spiders, for example. Then you have to practice looking at spiders, then touching spiders, and so on. It's called exposure. Well, and I also have a number of depressed patients and some who have eating disorders."

Markus and Sonja nod as if depression and eating disorders are daily fare for them, which perhaps they are. What do I know about police work?

"So Sara wasn't normal?" Sonja asks, her head to one side.

"*Normal*? What is normal? No, she definitely was not normal based on psychiatric assessment criteria. But 'normal' is a relative term, not an absolute one. Isn't it? Every person that falls within two, three standard deviations from the median is normal by definition. That doesn't mean normal is better. Do you think all the great composers, authors, and artists were *normal*? Do you think *normal* people have carried civilization forward?"

I realize that I sound aggressive without really meaning to, but I am so desperately anxious to make sure that Sara will not be reduced to an antisocial, maladjusted mental case.

"Sara was talented and funny," I say almost inaudibly.

"I understand," says Markus, looking at me.

For a moment I feel confident that he actually does.

Suddenly we fall silent and look out over my property where crime scene technicians are still lumbering around. There are two bearded men in their midfifties in boots, uniform trousers, and tight T-shirts that fit snugly around their swelling, ball-like bellies. They are so alike they could be brothers, and they strongly remind me of a TV personality from my childhood who hosted a car program.

It has stopped raining, the sun has gone down, and darkness is starting to settle in. The familiar cramp is spreading in my chest.

"What was your relationship like with Sara? I mean, did you socialize privately?" Sonja continues.

"Never, we only met in therapy. But we liked each other," I add.

"Did Sara know where you live?"

"Absolutely not. We never give out our private contact information to patients, and I have an unlisted telephone number."

"Who paid for Sara's therapy? Based on what you've told us, I can't imagine she paid for it herself."

Sonja is right. Sara could never have been able to afford therapy on her own. Most of my patients are financially pretty well-off. A few get support from the county to go to therapy. There's a deep injustice in that. There are functioning forms of treatment, but only a small number of privileged people have access to them.

"Sara has a sympathetic social worker," I answer. "Her psychiatric out-patient contact thought she should take part in a project for borderline girls, to help them get certified therapy from specially trained psycho-therapists. But then they decided that Sara was functioning too well to be placed in the program. You see, she was not suicidal. Cutting herself wasn't enough. At Social Services they still thought that Sara should have the opportunity to receive therapy, so even if I don't have the same qualifications as the project therapists, she ended up with me. Social Services pays."

"Do you have any idea how she ended up in the water outside your pier?"

I shake my head mournfully and look at Sonja. Her gaze is inscrutable.

"Siri, I have to ask. Where were you between three and five o'clock this afternoon?"

I look at her with surprise.

"I never thought I would get a question like that. Between three and five," I search my memory. "I was in session with a patient, Anneli Malm."

"Do you have witnesses?"

I shrug. "My colleagues were there, Anneli too. Of course."

Suddenly I remember.

"I film the conversations with my patients. The time and date are registered automatically. Feel free to check my recordings."

Sonja nods, squirms in her chair, and brings the palms of her hands together in a gesture that I interpret means she has something important to say.

"Siri, are you certain that Sara was not suicidal?"

"Absolutely," I answer. "Besides, everything was going really well for her right now. She had stopped cutting herself and she had met that guy I told you about earlier . . ."

I fall silent. There is something unspoken between Sonja and Markus, some insight about Sara that they do not want to share with me, but I know it anyway. Sonja gives Markus a brief glance and takes a deep breath.

"There are things that indicate this may have been a suicide. There is much that indicates that Sara has . . ."

She hesitates, searching for a suitable way to put it, as if such a word might exist.

"There are signs that indicate that Sara did not drown in an accident."

"Such as what?"

"She had cuts on her arms."

"Sara always cuts her arms," I say, and think before I continue. "Were the wounds fatal in themselves?"

"I can't answer that. We have to wait for the coroner's report."

"The fact that she cut herself is nothing new in any case. That doesn't have to mean she committed suicide."

"Hmm. There's more. We found a suicide note. It was on the rocks next to her clothes."

"A suicide note?"

"Yes. I'm sorry I can't show it to you now, but in the letter she writes that you are . . ." Sonja hesitates again, glancing quickly at Markus.

"She writes," Sonja starts again, "that the therapy is one reason she has chosen to end her life."

"I don't understand . . ." My voice is just a whisper.

Markus gets up and sits tentatively beside me on the old lumpy couch. Suddenly he looks tired. Police-tired. Seen-too-much-misery tired. Despite his age. Carefully, he pulls the blanket up over my shoulders.

Sonja continues without further hesitation and without softening the truth. She speaks quickly. The words fire like machine-gun bullets through the room—unforeseeable and painful, impossible to defend against.

"She writes that her therapy made her realize how sick she is. That she can never be healthy and that she has harmed too many people. The fact is she writes quite a bit about your conversations, what you talked about in detail and when you met. She even gives the dates for certain conversations."

Sonja stops for a second and rubs her temples but seems to decide that I can bear to hear what comes next.

"She ends the letter by writing that she is taking her life out of consideration for her family and because she now understands that her life lacks meaning, and that she wants to thank you for helping her realize this."

Darkness.

Suddenly everything goes black. It takes awhile before I realize that I am crying and have burrowed my face deep in the blanket, blocking out all the light. In the distance I can hear Markus awkwardly ask whether there is anyone he can call, and I think I give him Aina's phone number.

She wants to thank me for helping her realize that her life lacks meaning. The words ring in my head as I lie on the couch and desperately clutch a pillow. I remember an article I read in the *Svenska Dagbladet* about subway drivers in Stockholm and how difficult it is for them with all the suicides who jump in front of trains. The toughest of all, the article said, was when the jumper makes eye contact with the driver, sometimes even smiles. As if creating a wordless understanding between the victim and the unwilling executioner.

She wants to thank me for helping her realize that her life lacks meaning.

Aina arrives. I can hear her speaking with Markus outside. They talk quietly and quickly, as if they don't want me to hear. Markus's voice is calm, Aina's shriller. Then I feel Aina's cheek against mine and she says that everything's going to be okay. I so desperately want to believe her.

No guilt.

No shame.

No regret.

But no real satisfaction either. Not the relief I had expected and perhaps hoped for. Only the aching sorrow in my chest.

But despite that, another step toward the goal, a piece of the puzzle in the grand plan I have so carefully orchestrated is accomplished.

I look around the little room that is mine. At the bare walls and the tasteful furniture. He is lying on the floor under the table. I imagine the roundness of the body under the old blanket I covered him with. On the table the books, complete with detailed instructions. It's crazy what you can find in the library.

I have laid out everything else that I require on the table. Set in a neat row on top of the plastic tablecloth. Plastic bottles, cans, tools—the shiny steel reflects the cold glow of the ceiling lamp.

I suspect this will not bring me the peace I am seeking either, but that no longer matters.

The plan has acquired a life of its own; it already replaced the final goal a long time ago.

My colleagues sit around the table in silence. Aina stares vacantly into the middle distance and Marianne lowers her eyes to her lap, nervously clenching her hands. Clenches and releases them, clenches and releases. It's like an incantation.

Sven takes my hand and looks me straight in the eyes.

"Siri, you *know* it wasn't your fault. Sara was sick. It happens to all of us sooner or later. Losing a patient isn't unusual."

There is no trace of flirty Sven in his eyes, only a safe, friendly, older colleague. And his gaze does not waver. Suddenly I feel infinitely grateful that he is here. I squeeze his dry, warm hand and try to smile back, but it doesn't work. I just can't tell him that this has happened to me once before. One time is no time—but two?

"Have another cookie," Marianne offers in vain. The lemon bars from the bakery on Folkungagatan remain on the plate.

"I'll see my patients as usual this week," I say, looking at Marianne with feigned calm, but it doesn't sound convincing. I can hear my voice quivering.

Marianne nods and looks hastily at Sven, as if seeking his approval, but Sven is looking doubtfully at me.

"Are you sure? You don't need to play the hero with us. Take some time off instead," Sven suggests.

"No. I really think the best thing for everyone right now is if I continue as usual."

I get up, go to the sink, and rinse my coffee cup to show that I have decided and try to look calm and collected as I set the cup in the dish drainer and turn back toward the table, leaning against the sink.

As if in response to an invisible signal, Marianne gets up, brushes the crumbs from her wide hips, and leaves the room. Only Aina, Sven, and I are left.

A rather uncomfortable silence follows. Aina looks at Sven and then down at the table. Sven clears his throat, rubs his palms against his rust-brown corduroy trousers, and looks at me.

"Listen, Siri, I don't want to beat around the bush: I think you drink too much. Aina told me about your DUI."

I open my eyes wide and glare at Aina, but she does not meet my gaze. She pushes the crumbs around on the little table with her finger instead. From left to right. From right to left.

"Siri, I know what I'm talking about. Many years ago, yes, long before I came here, I had the same problem myself. Sometimes I wasn't entirely sober when I went to work. Well, I mean, no one is saying that you're drunk at work, but—"

I interrupt him. "This is totally absurd. Damn it, I'm not an alcoholic and YOU ought to know that, Aina. YOU'RE the one who gets loaded every weekend. And screws everything and everyone. How did you get the brilliant idea, by the way, to spread this rumor here in the office? And you, Sven, if there's anyone who has problems with alcohol, it's you!"

"Siri," Sven says in a lowered voice, "it's in the nature of things for you to deny it. It's not strange either for you to try to justify your behavior to the police. And Aina told me out of pure concern for you. For your sake. And for the patients. Whatever, we both think it would be good if you took a break. To think through this thing about your drinking. To get over Sara's death. We can take your patients for a couple of weeks. Come on, it's not a big deal."

"NO," I yell far too shrill and loudly. "NO, I have to continue working. Don't you get it? That's just what this is all about. *He wants me to stop working.*"

Aina and Sven exchange worried glances when I mention the man who has no name. The man who perhaps doesn't exist. I can tell from their expressions that they are wondering whether I've gone completely crazy, or if, with a fool's stubbornness, I am simply refusing to let go of the lie they believe I have created as a protective shield.

Keep working.

There is so much that needs to be done, so many practical things that have to be arranged. Sara's relatives. I ought to ask the police whether they were informed and if they eventually want to talk to me. A broken family. I know that Sara was only sporadically in touch with her parents in recent years. They had divorced soon after she ran away from the foster home. Her dad moved to Malmö, where he quickly met a new woman and together they had two children. According to Sara, they were happily living in one of the nicer suburbs, and an older half sister, a failure with zigzag scars on her arms and legs, was not welcome to visit and jeopardize their marital bliss.

Sara's mother lives in a small apartment in Vällingby. Sara told me that she started drinking pretty seriously in recent years but has still managed to keep her job at an insurance company. I know her mom loaned Sara money now and then, but otherwise their visits had been rare, to say the least, with the exception of the failed attempt to celebrate Midsummer together.

At best, a therapist can help people. Help them feel better, get over difficult events, abandon destructive behaviors and ideas. But the first and most fundamental requirement of a therapist is to do no harm.

Shouldn't I have understood, shouldn't I have done something to stop her? Does my inability to foresee Sara's death make me a bad therapist? Does my lack of insight make me an accessory, an unwilling executioner? *She wants to thank me for helping her realize that her life lacks meaning.*

With a single rapid movement I sweep the cookie plate off the table. It crashes to the floor. At Sven's and Aina's feet, shards of porcelain are mixed with crushed pieces of lemon bars.

Date: September 6
Time: 1:00 p.m.
Place: Green Room, the practice
Patient: Charlotte Mimer

Charlotte clears her throat discreetly, and I realize I've been sitting in silence for far too long. She is expecting my comments regarding her entries, and I mumble something positive and laudatory. Because Charlotte truly has made progress. She has managed to retain control over her food and reduced the manic physical exercise she previously subjected her body to.

She is sitting with her slender, manicured hands clasped casually over the purse in her lap, but all I can see is Sara's skinny dead body slowly being rocked by the waves. Aina and Sven were right. I should take time off. All my energy goes into trying to be present for Charlotte, and yet I can't seem to muster any real engagement.

"I've been thinking," she says tentatively. "For the first time in my life I feel that I truly question how I'm perceived, how I'm treated."

Charlotte drums her fingernails against her purse.

"I'm proud that I've chosen to focus on my career. I'm proud of my competence. But I only function in my role as a woman. In line with the demands that are placed on women in our society."

Charlotte looks distressed, and it becomes clear to me that she has suddenly started to question things that she had previously simply rationalized away.

"I am the most qualified marketing manager at our company. I work incredibly hard. But even so, it's like it's not enough. My male colleagues have higher salaries and louder voices, and I'm sick and tired of always having to shout to make myself heard." She interrupts herself, and I see that she is blinking in rapid succession. Her throat is red again, which always happens when she is agitated, and her fingers are drumming faster and faster.

"I mean, it's like I've always thought that talk about glass ceilings and the old boys' clubs was nonsense. I've always thought it's only my performance that counts. And now I realize that I was . . . wrong. The guys overtake me, even though I accomplish more. They play golf with the boss and take saunas with the board and God knows what else."

Charlotte Mimer is angry. Her jaws are clenched and she squeezes her eyes shut as she talks. Her whole posture signals repressed rage. I have never seen her anger so clearly before. And I don't know what to say. I assume that she is right. What she is saying is true; women are marginalized. I even see it as a therapist. I see how the problems of young girls are trivialized and neglected. I see the lack of treatment homes for girls. How the schools' limited resources go toward keeping rowdy boys in line while girls are expected to manage on their own. They are expected to navigate a teenage existence so full of demands and contradictions they're almost doomed. . . . Again, I see Sara Matteus's pale face before me. If someone could have seen Sara earlier. If someone could have helped her when she was a little girl. That's why I simply nod encouragingly at Charlotte.

"The problem is, I don't know what I should do."

Charlotte suddenly looks tired.

"If I start bringing up these issues with my boss, I will be perceived as a troublemaker and can forget about advancing my career. Then I might as well go back to . . . the call center."

Her expression indicates that this would be a fate worse than death. Something she doesn't wish even on her worst enemy. My own expression must betray what I'm thinking, even though I am trained to mask my feelings and opinions, because Charlotte suddenly smiles.

"I know," she says. "There are worse things than working in a call center."

That statement is so absurd we both start laughing.

"But . . ." Charlotte hesitates again. "I mean, I know I ought to do something. I shouldn't just let this slide. I shouldn't . . ."

She seems to be bracing herself. Gathering the courage to formulate something out loud that she previously only dared to think.

"Sometimes it feels as if all this therapy has done me more harm than good."

Charlotte stares out the window as she says this, and I see that she doesn't want to look at me. Doesn't want to meet my eyes.

"Before, everything was okay. Not good, not at all, but it was okay. It was my life. I didn't reflect so damn much on whether it was good or bad, whether it was right or wrong. I just . . . just was. The way I was. Now I question everything. My work, my role at the company, my bosses, my femininity, my sexuality."

She sighs deeply, and I notice that the red patches on her neck are spreading down toward her modest neckline. Her forehead shines with tiny beads of sweat that form an almost invisible membrane over the fine-pored skin.

"And I feel so damn angry, too. Indignant. Almost all the time, actually. Angry and disappointed in myself for letting my life slide out of my hands. Angry at my colleagues. At Mom. At Dad. And at you. I feel so damn mad at you because you're the one who got this all started."

She looks at me for a long time in silence, and I try to decipher what I see in her eyes: Is it resignation, or something else? Perhaps it is years of suppressed rage bubbling up like dirty water from an overflowing drain.

It is evening. Summer has finally released its hold, and a light drizzle that a westerly wind is pushing out over the sea sweeps over Stockholm. I'm wrapped in a towel and staring out at the gray sea, sitting on the ugly, lumpy mustard-yellow couch in front of my big French windows. Aina is sitting next to me. We are silent. Our bathing suits are hanging to dry on the flaking white garden furniture outside.

Aina has been staying with me for a week now. I haven't forgotten that she talked to Sven about my life, but I have forgiven her. Now everything is back to normal. On the surface anyway.

She has come to my rescue, knowing how afraid I am of the dark. She also wants us to swim every day. I know she's worried that if we don't do this, I will never dare swim in the bay again. I do as she says but without enthusiasm.

The crime scene technicians and police cars are long gone and there is not a trace of what happened on the shore. Sara's death left no mark, I think, getting up and starting to turn on all the lights out of habit, because it's getting dark. Aina positions herself half naked on the rag rug and begins her evening yoga routine.

I am walking to the kitchen to get a glass of wine when suddenly there's a knock at the door. Who could it be at this hour? I put on Stefan's old navy blue terry-cloth bathrobe and tentatively go to the front door.

"Who is it?" I ask.

"It's Markus Stenberg, from the police," answers a gentle voice.

I pull on the sash at the waist and look back toward Aina, who understands and retreats to the bedroom to put something on. Slowly, I open the door and squint out into the semidarkness. Markus is standing in the rain. His hair is wet and from inside the house I can smell his damp wool sweater.

"I apologize for not calling first, but I would like to talk to you. May I come in?" He looks self-consciously at my bathrobe.

"Sure," I say, gesturing toward the living room. "Aina and I went swimming."

"May I sit down?" He points at the couch.

I nod and sit down cross-legged on the rug, because there aren't any armchairs and I don't want to sit down right next to him. Aina comes into the room and nods at Markus as she sits down beside me.

Markus clears his throat and looks slightly embarrassed at the sight of the two of us—half-naked women sitting on the floor.

"Sara did not commit suicide," he begins in his melodic Norrland accent, holding my gaze and running his hand through his short, curly hair.

"We received the medical examiner's preliminary report today. There was no water in her lungs, which means she ended up in the water when she was already dead. The cuts on her wrists also occurred postmortem. Besides, she was pumped full of sedatives. Benzodiazepines," he says gloomily. "And alcohol. The body also showed signs of strangulation. Sara was murdered."

I don't know what to say. Sara was murdered? Murder seems even more inconceivable than suicide. I want to say something but can't get the words out.

"But *who* would have murdered her?" Aina asks in my place.

Markus shrugs. "There are so many reasons to kill someone," he says, sounding exhausted.

The comment sounds misplaced coming from such a young man.

"You wouldn't believe me if I told you how little a human life is worth to some people. In any case, are you aware of someone who threatened Sara in some way?"

I shake my head. "Absolutely not!"

"Did she have any enemies? For example, any jealous ex-boyfriends?"

I shake my head again, slower this time, searching my memory for some clue as to why anyone would want to kill Sara, but I cannot remember anything important.

"She had a new boyfriend, an older man. Sara was confused by their relationship, he gave her lots of attention but didn't want to"—I pause and feel as though I am betraying Sara's confidence, but continue anyway—"he didn't want to have sex with her."

"Was she afraid of him? Did she feel threatened?"

"No, I think she just felt confused."

"Do you know who he is, what his name is?"

I try to remember whether Sara had mentioned a name, whether she said anything that might reveal her boyfriend's identity.

"I have no idea, you'll have to ask her friends. Maybe they know more than me."

Markus looks searchingly at me. He doesn't take his eyes off me.

"Could Sara's murder have anything . . . to do with you, Siri?"

"What do you mean?" I ask, baffled.

"In the suicide note, which we now must assume was written by someone other than Sara, there is quite a lot of criticism against you. Besides, Sara was found alongside your pier. One possibility, *among many,*" he emphasizes, "is that someone carried out the murder, at least in part, to get at you somehow."

He makes this last statement sound like a question.

I am speechless, struck mute by shock. That Sara died because someone wanted to harm me seems awful and is, if possible, even worse than the notion that Sara took her own life.

"But who would want to kill someone to get at *me?*"

Aina looks just as perplexed but says nothing.

"Think about it, Siri. Is there anyone who might want to hurt you?"

I try to think, but all I see is Sara's skinny dead body floating in the water beside the pier.

"No one," I say. "*No one* would want to hurt me."

Markus sighs and tries again. "Siri, has anything strange happened recently? Have you received any threatening telephone calls, have you been involved in an accident, a lovers' quarrel, trouble at work?"

Markus's voice fades when he notices my face.

"A number of things have happened," I say hesitantly.

I'm not sure whether I should mention the anonymous letter and come across as silly, but I decide it's best to bring it up.

"I got a strange letter," I say faintly, getting up to retrieve the gray envelope.

I hand it to Markus and sit down again. Aina looks at me questioningly while Markus calmly studies the envelope and photo.

"I'll keep this," he says, not revealing what he is thinking. "Anything else?"

"No, but I must admit that I've felt like I was being watched here at home during the summer."

"What do you mean, watched? Did you see anyone?"

I shake my head. "No, I guess it's more like a feeling." I look apologetically at Markus. "I'm sorry, I can't prove it."

In front of me I see the power switch and the wet footprint on the floor. I start to tell Markus in detail about my theories that someone was in the house while I was asleep. He looks skeptical, runs his hand through his shiny damp blond hair, but doesn't say anything to indicate he doesn't believe me. He changes the subject and returns to the letter.

"Who would send you such a letter?"

I remain silent a long while and stare out through my dark windows. The sea is no longer visible. At a distance I see something that must be navigation lights. I hear nothing aside from the wind, which seems to have increased in strength.

"I don't know. *No one.* Someone who wants to mess with me. Make me think I have a secret admirer . . ."

I pause. Privately, I have played with the thought that maybe Sven sent the photo to annoy me, but now the whole thing seems absurd.

"*No one,*" I answer again, more convinced this time.

Silence again. Nothing but the wind dancing in the crowns of the trees and the waves crashing against the cliffs can be heard. Aina looks at me. I can't read her expression, and I know she is going to demand an explanation as soon as Markus leaves. I want him to stay. I feel strangely attracted to him. The calm he seems to spread around him. His respectful attitude toward Sara. The fact that he listens to what I say, takes it seriously, and doesn't treat me like a complete idiot.

Aina clears her throat. "You ought to tell him, Siri. Tell him about . . . when the police caught you."

Markus looks at me but does not look particularly surprised.

"You mean the DUI," he says lightly.

"How do you know about that?" I am confused.

Markus shrugs. "It's my job to know that sort of thing."

"Okay, well, I got a call that evening. Someone called me and said that Aina was at Stockholm South Hospital and that I needed to come at once. I got in the car. Right away. I know it was stupid, but I really thought Aina was dying and there's no way to get a taxi out here."

"That's easy to confirm. We can check whether anyone called you that night and, if so, where the call came from."

He makes a note, gets up, and I assume he is about to leave, but he stops and turns toward Aina and me.

"Yes, one more thing. What kind of job did Sara have?"

"She was unemployed," I answer, without going into the details of her complicated arrangements with various employers.

"Apparently she wore rather expensive clothes."

"I think that guy she met gave her money."

"The guy whose name you don't know?"

"The guy whose name I don't know." I nod, looking out my dark windows again.

Markus has no more questions. We exchange a few pleasantries about how nice it is to live close to nature as I follow him to the door. Before he steps out into the dense darkness, he turns toward me one more time. For a brief moment I think he's about to caress my cheek. I close my eyes but no fingers touch my face and I am ashamed of imagining things about this guy, who is not only a policeman, but much too young for me. Ten years younger. At least.

Just a kid.

He takes out his card, turns it over, and jots down some numbers on the back.

"These are my numbers. On the back is my private cell number. You can call anytime. If you think of something or have anything to say that you think may add to the investigation. Anything at all. Anytime at all."

I take the card and put it in the pocket of the bathrobe. We remain standing close to each other, perhaps for a moment too long. Then we shake hands and Markus disappears out into the evening.

Aina is sitting on the rug, looking up at me.

"What was that letter? Why didn't you tell me?"

Tentatively, I start telling her about the letter. About the mysterious photo. About the power outage during the storm.

"Why, Siri? Why didn't you say anything?" she looks primarily confused—not accusing, as I'd feared.

I explain quietly my fear of making her fret too much. About the risk of wearing out my friends and the desire not to be a burden. To not be a burden to anyone.

"Siri, sometimes you are such a doofus!"

Aina moves closer to me and I place my head against her shoulder. For a long, long time we sit like that.

Outside, the evening has turned into night.

Date: September 14
Time: 2:00 p.m.
Place: Green Room, the practice
Patient: Peter Carlsson

Peter Carlsson and I have been talking for more than twenty minutes. We have devoted almost half the time to analyzing what triggers his compulsive thoughts about harming his girlfriend. He seems to be feeling better than the last time but is still tormented when he has to talk about the horrible things he doesn't actually want to do but still can't keep from imagining in detail.

His nervous expression and apologies are starting to get on my nerves. There's something that doesn't add up. I don't quite know what it is, but there's something strange about Peter. Fake. Sometimes I sense that his apologies are only empty phrases that he has memorized and repeats intermittently in order to put up with himself. That what is actually behind his dapper façade remains hidden, a secret.

"By the way," he says suddenly, in the middle of a graphic description of his rape fantasies. "I ran into Charlotte Mimer in the hall. I didn't know she came here. We worked together at Procter & Gamble."

I stop in midmotion and suddenly become guarded. I look at him. His expression is eager and open.

"Although perhaps you can't talk about your patients?"

"No, I can't."

He looks disappointed. "So you can't say whether Charlotte is your patient?"

"No."

Now I am mad at Peter, although I don't show it. Everybody knows about therapist-client privilege.

"Peter, I would like us to get back to what we were discussing earlier. You mentioned that sometimes you have thoughts relating to strangling?"

"Well, I don't always hold the woman around the throat, I mean, *in those images,*" Peter clarifies.

He says "hold around the throat" when he means strangling. I assume it makes things easier for him.

"It could also be that I am burning her with a cigarette. *Only in my thoughts, of course,*" he repeats, as if to indicate that this has nothing to do with reality.

"Or cut her wrists and drown her," I suddenly say, harshly.

"Uh . . . yes, exactly." Peter is baffled but also looks relieved, as if he couldn't have said it better himself.

"In principle it can be anything at all, anything that hurts . . ."

Suddenly I can't bear to listen anymore. I get up brusquely from my chair.

"You'll have to excuse me, Peter, but that's it for today."

Peter looks surprised, but there is something else in his eyes, too, something ugly. He looks *satisfied.* As if the fact that his therapist inter-rupted the session means that he has succeeded in proving to her that he is a monster.

I throw open the door, rush out of the room, and run into Marianne, who seems to have been standing right outside. If I didn't know better I would have thought she was eavesdropping. I try to explain the situation to her: I'm exhausted and Peter is behaving strangely. Can she help me?

"You'll have to think of some excuse," I say.

"Such as?" she asks vacantly, placing her hands on her round hips.

"Say I'm pregnant and have to throw up or something. Women get really sensitive when they're pregnant, don't they?"

Marianne stares at me in shock as I run toward the door.

"Cancel all appointments this afternoon," I add as I open the door to the stairwell and leave the office.

I wander aimlessly around the streets by Katarina Church. It is liberating to get out in the cool air. The clouds hang heavy over the church steeple, as if the weather wanted to mimic my emotions. I sit down on a bench in the cemetery and look out over the gravestones. For once I feel no remorse for how I behaved. Listening to Peter Carlsson's violent thoughts doesn't feel right. Not to me, not to him.

The image of Sara's dead face appears again. Sara. Who could have wanted to hurt her? Did someone kill her to get at me? The idea seems unlikely. I wonder about Markus's words: "a possibility" they are working on, one "among many." What other theories might the police have?

I ransack my memory, trying to remember what Sara told me. She had a history of substance abuse. I know she did drugs during the time she was homeless. Not large quantities or anything heavy, not according to her, anyway. Even so, the fact that she used drugs also means that she must have come into contact with any number of shady characters. Maybe there is someone from her past who wanted revenge over some old injustice. A debt? Unfinished business? Drug money? This whole chain of thought feels absurd and improbable. Why would someone take revenge on Sara now? After all these years. There is also the letter, the suicide note that isn't really a suicide note. The letter that Sara's murderer must have written. And whoever composed the letter knew about me. Knew that Sara was in therapy. Even knew what Sara and I talked about in detail. I know that most murders are committed by someone close to the victim and that it is unusual for the perpetrator to be a stranger. Who was close to Sara? There are several girlfriends she mentioned during our conversations. Linda and Nathalie. Broken young girls, just like Sara. I have a hard time imagining that either of them would have attacked her. I imagine that the murderer is a man, not only because murderers are most often men but also because the person Sara met recently is a man. A man who behaved strangely, to boot. I try to make a summary of sorts of everything I know about him.

He is older, but what does "older" mean? Sara was twenty-five. What did "older" mean to her? Thirty-five, like me? Or fifty-five, like her father? My impression was that we were talking about a man who is older than me.

He has plenty of money. Sara was showered with expensive designer clothing and other presents. But what does that really say? Stockholm is teeming with rich guys in their forties.

The main thing that sets this man apart is that for some reason he approached Sara, courted her, gained her confidence, but did not want to have sex with her. Why would a middle-aged man have this kind of a relationship with a young woman? Why? I can't answer. But I know it's not normal. I think about how worried I was when Sara first told me about the man she had met. My intuition that something wasn't right. I suddenly feel convinced that my intuition was correct. Something was wrong.

I search my memory to see if I can remember whether Sara mentioned how they met. She may have said something about this, but I can't remember. The video recordings of the therapy sessions, I think. I have to look at the videotapes. Maybe there are additional facts there, details I've forgotten. I decide to look through the tapes when the police, who borrowed them to make copies, give them back to me. And when I can bear to. Watching Sara curled up in the chair, talking about her life as she puffs on one of her endless cigarettes, seems impossible right now.

The room is bright, with white walls. In the corner is a well-kept Kinnarps desk with a shiny surface. There doesn't appear to be a speck of dust. On the bookshelves, also from Kinnarps, are Jofa binders arranged by color. I am sitting in a visitor's chair at a small table in what must be a designated area for questioning. It strikes me that the furniture and the arrangement of the room are not unlike my own. A room for work, a room for talk.

On the other side of the table are Sonja and Markus, the police officers on Sara's case. Unlike our previous conversation, this is clearly an interrogation. The tone is friendly but formal. There is not a trace of warm blankets or refills on glasses of wine. On the table in front of me is a mug filled with coffee-machine cappuccino that Markus made for me. "From our new coffee machine," he announced, not without irony in his voice.

It is Sonja who runs the meeting with her rapid, slightly nervous conversational style. Markus sits beside her, taking notes and interrupting now and then with a question.

"How much do you know about Sara's substance abuse?"

Informing me that the circumstances surrounding Sara's death are still unclear and that it is no longer a possibility that Sara committed suicide but that she was killed instead, Sonja steers the conversation to Sara's past.

"A little . . . not that much really. But you watched the tapes, right?"

"Well, yes, we've copied them and are in the process of looking through them. By the way, you can take the original tapes with you when you leave. In any event, we assume you must have talked with each other also when the camera wasn't on. Hence the question."

"Sara used drugs, and then she quit. On her own. Because she wanted to."

"Do you know that Sara has a record?"

"Yes, I know that she had been arrested for shoplifting, and maybe for possession, too?"

"And for handling stolen goods. We also know that she prostituted herself occasionally. Did you know about that too?"

For a moment I remain silent. That Sara had prostituted herself is news to me, and the information makes me feel sick. I can imagine how bad things must have gotten for Sara when she decided to sell her body and can only guess how much of it she must have repressed in order to even bear it.

I shake my head. "No, I didn't know that."

Somehow this is embarrassing. As if I ought to have known all of Sara's secrets, as if my ignorance on this matter makes me a bad therapist, underscoring my incompetence.

"No? So you don't know if she was still in touch with individuals from that period in her life?"

I shake my head.

Sonja sighs quietly.

"We still don't know whether Sara's death is connected to her past or if in some way it's connected to you. There are signs that indicate the crime may have been aimed against you."

I nod again. Markus had already explained this to me.

"And what is your relationship to drugs?"

"Drugs?" I repeat Sonja's question mechanically.

"I have no relationship to drugs. That is, not illegal drugs. Now and then I drink a glass of wine, but nothing more."

"You were recently taken in for a DUI? I'd say that sounds like more than a couple glasses of wine."

"That was a special situation, of course I never would drive under the influence otherwise, but as I already explained to your colleague . . ."

Sonja almost imperceptibly raises an eyebrow and looks briefly in Markus's direction. I suddenly have the feeling that Markus hasn't told Sonja about our conversation.

"Assistant Detective Stenberg may have already discussed this with you, but now I'd like to."

I am surprised by her sharp tone and notice that Markus looks embarrassed, shifting back and forth on his chair. I feel guilty for having put him in an awkward situation but also realize it's not my job to protect him.

"No, I do not use any illegal drugs. Never have. No, I don't usually drive drunk, but someone had called me and said that my best friend was dying. I got scared and was shocked and . . . I got in the car. Half-baked, stupid, idiotic, I know."

"The majority of people we bring in for DUIs have extremely good excuses for driving a car in a state of intoxication."

"Yes, but, as I've explained—"

"Your husband died in a diving accident?"

Sonja changes the subject yet again, and I feel confused and deceived. As if Sonja's other questions were only a maneuver, intended to bring me to this exact point. I suddenly realize that this is what happens to crime victims. Nothing is private anymore. Nothing can remain secret. Sara's life will be exposed in the slightest detail. I've heard people call it psychological autopsy. And my life will also be scrutinized. My secrets will be disrobed and exposed as well.

"That's correct."

"I've reviewed the report, it was done by our colleagues here at the Nacka police department."

"Yes, that's possible. I can't recall exactly . . ."

The investigation into Stefan's accident is unclear and vague to me. I know that it was done, I know that it concluded that his death was an accident.

That's all.

"Strange that your husband should die in a diving accident, and now one of your patients is found dead by what at first appears to be drowning, near your house."

Sonja's voice is neutral. Her face gives me no clues about what she's getting at, but I feel discomfort growing inside me, building up like a cumulus cloud on a hot summer day, and I'm suddenly afraid of throwing up in her tidy office. All over the Kinnarps furniture and the notepads.

"Where are you headed?"

My voice is a hoarse whisper, and even though I try to sound attentive, unaffected, I understand what Sonja is trying to provoke in me. Markus looks uncomfortable, avoids meeting my eyes, and I wonder what happened to the kind police officers who took care of me in such a gentle and considerate way just a few days ago.

"I'm only saying that this is a strange coincidence. A strange fluke. And police officers don't like flukes, you understand?" Sonja says, not letting me out of her sight.

"And?"

"And what do you have to say about that?"

"That I don't know what the hell you want from me. Do you think I murdered Sara? Or what?"

As soon as I have said the words, I know I have let myself fall into Sonja's trap. She looks at me, still with a deceptively neutral expression.

"Well, what do you have to say about that? Did you do it?"

Date: September 18
Time: 4:00 p.m.
Place: Green Room, the practice
Patient: Charlotte Mimer

I have moved Charlotte's scheduled appointment. I don't want her to risk running into a former colleague while she sits in her therapist's waiting room. In the meantime, I've also realized that I can't keep Peter Carlsson as a patient. I simply cannot listen to his fantasies any longer. In another situation, I could have maintained my professionalism. But given what's been going on in my life, it's impossible.

"I'm serious!"

Charlotte looks at me intensely and steadily. The new Charlotte. Changed. She is showing sides of her personality I have never seen before.

"I really think I'm going crazy. Insane. I have no control anymore. Do you understand? No control."

She strokes the leather Mulberry purse in her lap. I'm sure it's an original, unlike my own unused one that has been sitting in the closet ever since my parents gave it to me after their trip to Thailand last winter. Her nails are carefully manicured, her hands look small and neat. Her hair is perfect as usual, and it occurs to me that her hairstylist probably charges a higher hourly rate than I do.

"I'm going to end up like Aunt Dolly. Crazy."

"Aunt Dolly?"

"Oh, she's just an old relative. She went completely nuts. Started shoplifting with another old lady. Oh, my God, completely nuts. What if I end up like her?"

*   *   *

Charlotte's entire appearance signals perfection and control. Everything except the nervous stroking of her purse. That, and then the phrase she repeats over and over: *no control, no control.*

"Stop!"

I look at Charlotte. Imperatively. "You have to explain what happened. What is happening. Otherwise, I can't say whether you really are going crazy."

I smile carefully to show that, of course, I do not in fact believe that there's any way she is going crazy. She seems to understand my subtle signal, because she immediately appears to calm down. Her hands come to rest on the coffee-brown calfskin. She takes a deep breath and then slowly exhales.

"I did a strange thing. A damn strange thing."

The cuss word sounds alien and incongruous coming from Charlotte's mouth. It doesn't befit the preppy woman sitting in front of me. I nod to show that I'm listening and wait for her to continue.

"My boss. You know I've told you about my boss. That I was mad at him. That I couldn't talk with him about feeling passed over without sounding like a whiner—the kind who nags about discrimination and quotas instead of focusing on performance."

"I remember."

"Well, I . . ."

Charlotte stops herself and looks at me. She's trying to gauge whether I'll be able to take in the facts she's about to reveal.

"I hacked into his email."

"You hacked into his email?"

I repeat Charlotte's words slowly and immediately feel stupid and dense. What she is telling me seems like such foreign behavior for her that I have a hard time understanding her words.

"I hacked into his email. He was at a conference, some forum in Denver. I don't know what. I was working late and, well . . . it just happened."

"It just happened?"

Again I repeat her words and feel silly. I know we all do peculiar things when we are under stress, but what Charlotte is telling me is so baffling I don't really know how to react.

"Yes, it just happened. It was actually quite interesting. As it turns out, he is having an affair with one of the younger accountants, a girl who reports to him. So he's fucking a direct report. Rather clumsy. But even more stupid to keep that kind of evidence on your work account."

She smiles. A crooked, almost twisted smile, and for a moment I don't want to look at her. Something in her eyes frightens me.

"I thought about forwarding the email to his wife, but that would have been completely unhinged. I mean, I really would have to be crazy to do it. And I have no reason to harm him personally. You know that. I feel I've been wronged professionally, not personally. At any rate, in his in-box, I found an unread email from one of our biggest customers. An urgent one. It contained the draft of a contract and requested a quick reply. I knew he had been waiting for the draft. So . . . so I deleted it."

She laughs and shakes her head fervently, so that her brown hair twirls around her pretty face. For a moment, Charlotte looks so delighted that I get scared. A cold, clammy feeling suddenly spreads from my belly up my body. Who is this person sitting across from me? Who is this woman? But as quickly as the feeling started, it is gone, replaced by the therapist's clinically clear-sighted mind-set. Of course Charlotte feels like she's losing control. No, not losing it—letting it go. And it's about time.

Perhaps she senses what I am thinking. I notice that her features harden.

"I did say that I was going crazy. That I have no control over myself anymore. This is pure madness. It felt good in the moment. Right when I was doing it: Delete. Gone. But then came the anxiety. I packed up my things and ran from the office. I forced myself to go in the next day. Scared to death of the consequences of my behavior. And do you know what's ironic?"

I can't think of a good answer so I just shake my head.

"The mail server crashed the next day. All unopened mail was lost. So my trespassing went . . . unnoticed. I can't believe that I had such luck. And I can't understand how any of this could have happened at all. How I could do such a thing. It's just crazy. I have no control anymore, Siri!"

She looks away, her jaw clenched and a resigned, slightly absent look on her face. She is no longer focusing on me but is staring out

the window toward the twilight slowly settling down over Medborgarplatsen.

"Do you know what I saw on my way here?"

"No," I answer truthfully. How should I know?

"Well, there was a woman walking on Götgatan, she seemed about
my age. Talking on her cell phone, laughing. But . . . there was blood
running out of her nostril."

I am looking at Charlotte but don't know how to react to this.

"Well, I know it was just a nosebleed, but I couldn't help thinking—"

"What, Charlotte? What were you thinking?"

She rubs her palms together and looks down at the floor.

"I thought that's the way it is . . ."

"What do you mean?"

As she squirms in her chair like an eel, she seems reluctant to answer
my question.

"I mean . . . you're walking along, you're happy . . . maybe, or in any
case . . . content, you think everything's fine. But it's not."

I lean toward her, wanting to hear the rest.

"It's not fine. Not really. Somewhere, you're bleeding. Without knowing it. Maybe you have a tumor in your belly growing big as an orange
while you're walking around ignorant, grinning. Maybe right then your
husband is screwing your best friend . . . The point is . . ."

Charlotte swallows and I notice her lower lip trembling lightly.

"The point is . . . the point is, that's what life is. That you can never
count on anyone or anything. That everyone is basically . . . selfish. That
life itself is . . . *unpredictable.* And silly little me, I've been so damn naïve,
I only just realized this now."

Tears are running down her cheeks. She looks at me imploringly, her
voice is small and fragile when she speaks again.

"You have to tell me the truth, Siri. Am I going crazy?"

As I step into his office, Sven is twirling around on his beat-up office chair. With a little imagination, one might call it retro-trendy: IKEA, late seventies, the mustard-colored fabric hanging in long tatters down toward the floor, exposing the foam rubber stuffing, which swells like bloated dough through the tears in the fabric. He has taken his shoes off. I don't know why, but I hate when men do that. On the airplane, at the office, on the bus . . . their stinking socks, everywhere. Sven does not seem to notice my disapproving look. He makes a gesture toward the only chair in the room that isn't cluttered with notes, reports, and books.

"Siri, sit down."

His tone is friendly, but I can tell that he's had a long day; there may even be a hint of irritation as he removes his reading glasses and rubs his face.

"Damn, I should have tidied up . . . but . . ."

He pauses and observes me as I sit on the old wooden chair across from him.

"How are you doing, really? Can you sleep?"

All these questions: Am I sleeping? Am I drinking? How does it feel? Really?

"Thanks, everything is fine."

I can tell that he doesn't believe me, but who cares? That's not why I'm here.

"Listen, Sven . . ."

"Hmm."

He looks at me as he takes out his pipe and starts filling it. We had all agreed that he would not smoke in the office, but everyone knows that he does it secretly anyway. Sometimes you can smell it all the way in the stairwell. He has apparently decided that it doesn't matter if I see him smoking today. Maybe he feels his behavior is excused now that I am officially a drunk driver.

"Can you . . . can you take Peter Carlsson on as a patient?"

Sven shrugs and lights the pipe.

"Had enough?"

"Yes."

It's a relief that he understands me immediately and doesn't demand any further explanations. But of course he knows about Peter's problems from our weekly meetings.

"Yes, sure, I can do that. I see no immediate problems."

I am grateful, but I'm not sure how best to express it. It is also a little awkward to be alone with Sven for the first time since his unwelcome advances in my kitchen during the crayfish party.

"Something else."

I try to focus, to carefully formulate what I'm going to say. I want to address what happened at the party, to get it out of the way, but I am not sure how to begin.

"The crayfish party?" He waits for me to confirm.

I nod. "The crayfish party."

"Yes, it was really unfortunate that Birgitta had to see that."

I am shocked. Perhaps I had expected an apology. Or an excuse. But not a comment on his bad luck because his wife caught him while he was groping me. He makes it sound like his assault had been something we had both enjoyed. I wonder whether this really is how he remembers the encounter. If it justifies his behavior by making me an active participant.

"I see. So what did Birgitta have to say?" I ask sarcastically.

"Yes, yes, wouldn't you like to know, huh? You're all the same."

"What do you mean the same? Who?"

"Women. Are. The. Same. All women. Curious. Gossipy."

There is something dark in his eyes now. He blows a puff of smoke between us and reaches for his cell phone, signaling that our conversation is over.

I stand up, surprised at how uncomfortable I suddenly feel, surprised at how he has humiliated me. Has he?

I stand in the doorway for a moment, but he twirls a half turn, and with his back to me, enters a number on his phone.

Her house was like an aquarium at night. It lit up the whole bay from where it lay, nestled between the rocks. I looked at the house and the house looked back at me with its shining yellow, always indifferent eyes.

From my place on the ledge—still warm after the sunny day—I could follow every step she took, but she could not see me as she wandered from room to room with a large flashlight gripped firmly in one hand and a glass of wine in the other.

A few steps behind her came the other woman, her shaggy blond hair pulled back in a loose bun. One of her breasts almost slipped out of the tiny tank top she was wearing, and my stomach clenched. She turned slowly to face the window, and for a second I could see her straight on. She ran her tongue luxuriously over her upper lip and smiled, as if she could read my mind.

Now I was close, maybe two yards from the window. They were standing in the kitchen, scooping cat food into a bowl. Soon she would set the bowl out on the steps, hoping the cat would return. The next morning, she will bring the bowl back inside, with just as much food in it.

I slowly backed away and retreated to my simple campsite beyond the large, round rock. I lay quietly in my thin sleeping bag without falling asleep until the sun painted warm yellow streaks on the bare cliffs.

And suddenly she was with me again: Her glistening hair was present in the dew-covered leaves of the forest in the light of dawn.

Like reflections of the sun.

I caressed it with my gaze.

Her skin was present in the trunks of the slender chalk-white birch trees, shamelessly bent over by the autumn storms. And her blood was mine. At one time, we were one and the same, two incarnations of the same being, of the longing for life in itself.

Now there's only absence.

Everything I do, I do for Her. To bring justice where no justice exists, to give meaning to what is meaningless. This is all I can do. I know no other way. I never had a choice. This insight grants me consolation. It frees me from any guilt.

Aina and I are lying on Lasse's Ass, listening to the waves lapping against the big rock. The September sun is pleasantly warm, even if it takes two sweaters to sit outside and not feel cold. We are hungover and stuffed with aspirin. We had a late night. It's as if all the horrible things that have been afflicting me are compelling me to cling to superficial things. A safe, predictable place of refuge in my own chaotic life. That's why I spent the whole day yesterday flipping through old fashion magazines and reading endless features on hair removal, protein diets, and other meaningless articles. Aina and I ate an irresponsible amount of chips and, as usual, drank far too much wine.

We are slowly starting to get on each other's nerves. Even though she is my closest friend, I know that it'll soon be time for her to go home. My little house is starting to feel cramped and claustrophobic. So we decided that Aina will go back to her place today. Maybe my solitude isn't always self-imposed, but I appreciate it anyway. In the corner of my eye I notice Aina close her eyes and smirk.

"What are you thinking about?"

"I'm thinking about . . . Massoud." She laughs and continues slowly. "And . . . he has no clothes on!" She laughs again, louder this time.

"You *are* a slut," I answer primly.

"Nah, I've just taken on the sexual initiative."

Aina laughs as only she can, chortles, and stretches out on the rock like a cat.

She always has a new boyfriend. It's pointless for me to get to know them, since they are all quickly and mercilessly replaced by a new candidate within a week or two.

"Go for it, girl," I say, amused.

"What are you thinking about?" Aina wants to know, a more serious tone slipping into her voice.

"Have you ever wished you were someone else?"

"No, not really." Aina shrugs. "Have you? *Do you?*"

I hesitate. "Sometimes I wish I was a little more like you."

"Ach, cut it out. And what is it *exactly* that you would want to be? Dyslexic or slutty?"

"I wish I didn't take everything so seriously. That I was"—I search for the right words—"more easygoing, I guess."

Aina sits up on the rock and observes me in silence.

"Siri, dear Siri, I know that you don't like it when I say this, but because I'm your friend, and friends should speak the truth, I'll tell you anyway. You *really* ought to go to a therapist and talk about this!"

I sigh. My head feels too heavy to start a fight, so I answer, tired, "It's really not that bad. These days it gets dark by the time I come home from work and I get by anyway."

"I'm not referring to your fear of the dark, and I'm not talking about Sara Matteus. I'm talking about Stefan's death. You need to come to terms with it."

I tense up involuntarily and answer much too fast. "I'm over his death, *you're* the one who always brings it up."

"Only because you refuse to acknowledge what happened, which makes it impossible for you to move on."

"Acknowledge what? What in the hell do you *mean*? It was an accident. An *accident*." Somehow my voice sounds both shrill and feeble. I continue.

"A stupid, senseless accident. And you, more than anyone, ought to be able to respect that I don't want to . . . talk about this . . . anymore."

My body is shaking with rage as I turn around and climb down from the rock. Aina does not follow me. I hate her for it. She stays up there because she knows she's right.

Just biding her time.

Waiting for my confession.

It's eight o'clock on Sunday evening. I am standing alone in front of the French windows, looking out over the sea, which is still visible in the fading daylight. The temperature is in the upper forties and hard rain drums against the roof. I've taken my evening dip, been to the bathroom, and turned on all the lights in the house. Calm has settled over my little bay, but concern grows inside me. Is Sara's murderer—who knows the way to my house, where I swim each evening—out there in the darkness? I sit on the couch and take out my laptop. Might as well get a little work done. As soon as I've settled in, my cell phone starts ringing. Had I turned it on? It's my work cell, the number I give to my patients. Usually, I have it on only until 6:00 p.m. on weekdays, but for some reason it's on. I go to the hallway and retrieve it from my bag. Should I answer? Curiosity gets the better of me and I press the little green button.

"Yes, this is Siri Bergman."

"Siri?"

"Yes, this is Siri."

"Hi, this is Charlotte Mimer. Excuse me for calling so late on a Sunday, but I was at a sales conference in Helsinki and only just got home."

Charlotte sounds out of breath, as if there isn't enough air for all the words she wants to get out. But I hear something else in her voice, too. Something I don't recognize. Is it anger, is it fear?

"What happened, Charlotte?"

"Siri, I'm really sorry, I don't know how to say it, so I'll just come out with it. When I got home awhile ago I found a letter. I mean, I read a letter that arrived while I was away," she corrects herself, anxious as always to get the details exactly right.

"And?" I ask.

"It was about you. The letter was about you. It says that I should watch out for you, that your patients commit suicide and that you are . . . umm . . ."—Charlotte clears her throat—"unfit to be a therapist."

Her voice sounds distraught. She seems to be on the verge of tears.

Her voice becomes shrill. "Is that true?"

"Is *what* true, Charlotte?"

"Is it true that one of your patients took her life in your backyard? It says that you forced her into it. Is that . . . true?"

"Charlotte, can you get the letter and read it to me?"

I hear her sniffling on the other end of the line and I summon all my authority as Charlotte's therapist.

"Read me the letter," I say, more harshly than I intended.

"I have it right here."

"Read it!"

"Okay. Uh. 'I am writing to you in light of the fact that you are a patient of Siri Bergman. You don't know me, but nonetheless I feel that it is my duty to warn you about Siri. She is not only egocentric and incompetent, but she also constitutes a danger to her patients. Several of her patients have taken their lives per her direct orders. Sara Matteus was only twenty-five years old. Less than a month ago she drowned herself on Siri Bergman's property. For your own sake I hope you can find a new therapist, one you can trust and who has empathy and interest in your problems. A friend.'"

Silence.

"Is it true?"

"Is *what* true?"

"That your patients kill themselves."

Her voice suddenly sounds thin and fragile.

"Charlotte, listen very carefully now. First of all you must *not* throw that letter away, no matter what, okay?"

"Okay," she whispers.

"There is a sick individual who is stalking me and trying to destroy both my life and my career."

"So it's *not* true." She sounds relieved.

"Actually, one of my patients has died, yes."

"On your property?"

I hesitate before I answer. How did I end up in this situation? Why must I sit here and defend myself against false accusations? I sigh.

"She did die on my property, yes. But I had *absolutely* nothing to do with her death. She did not commit suicide, she was murdered."

"Murdered?" Charlotte chokes, as if she has something stuck in her throat. Her voice is a mere hiss. "*Murdered! On your property?*"

I can hear her now gasping for air.

"Charlotte," I begin, but I can only hear her gasping on the other end of the line.

"The person who wrote that letter murdered her? Is that what you mean? On your property? Murdered one of your patients . . ."

"It *could* be that way, yes."

"And now he has *my* address? A *madman?*"

A madman, a word that seldom escapes my lips. In my world, there is no such thing. You can be psychotic or depressive or manic, but never mad.

"Yes," I reply quietly, "a *madman*. Charlotte, I want you to come to the office tomorrow so we can talk this through. You're scheduled at your usual time on Monday, right?"

"I don't know," she says hesitantly.

"Promise me you'll come?"

"I can't, I'm sorry. I don't know if I dare. Maybe we should take a . . . break." She suddenly sounds serious and has recovered her professional, steady voice.

I don't answer, but I understand. She is scared and I can't blame her for that.

As soon as I hang up, I quickly reach up to the little shelf above the couch. I feel around among the dust bunnies and what I think are dead insects, and find what I'm looking for: a business card. My hands tremble as I wipe away the dust and walk over to the phone.

You can call whenever you want.

Markus arrives forty-five minutes later. He follows the same ritual as the first time we met: sits me down on the couch, puts pillows behind my back, and places the dirty old plaid blanket over me. I think this may be standard police procedure when someone is in shock.

"Do you want anything?" he asks.

"A glass of wine," I answer. "If you'll have one too," I add.

Markus disappears into the kitchen where I hear him open a bottle. He returns with the bottle and a glass.

"I'm working tonight," he says, gesturing toward the single glass.

I nod tiredly and close my eyes.

"Tell me," he says, and I recount the whole conversation I just had with Charlotte. Of course Markus wants to speak with Charlotte and see the letter. I promise to put him in contact with her.

Then I go on to tell him about the paralyzing sensation that overcomes me when I think about how many people around me seem to die. About my fear of what is out there in the dark. The words gush out of me, a story rushing like a stream of stale, foul-smelling water. As unpleasant as it is, it can't be stopped. But Markus isn't turned off by it. He just nods silently and stares out my black windows.

"Are you single? Or are you seeing someone?"

Maybe it's the alcohol—the question comes out of me unexpectedly. I regret it immediately—I feel like I'm crossing an important boundary, busting through into his private sphere. True, he has also asked me personal questions, but I assume that's just part of his job.

"No, there's no one special," he mumbles curtly, still looking away.

I can tell that I have made him self-conscious. He appears remarkably young and awkward tonight, sitting here on my ugly couch, dressed in a hoodie and jeans, and that's when I feel it. There is tension in the room. I stare at him for a moment. He avoids my gaze and clears his throat.

"Listen, Siri, is there really no one who would want to harm you?"

"No, I really can't think of a single person."

"And you haven't witnessed anything strange recently, aside from what we've talked about."

I shake my head.

"Who has access to your patient records?"

"All of us who work at the clinic, Aina, Marianne, Sven, and me."

"And the videotapes?"

"It's the same. Only my colleagues can access them."

"Could any of your coworkers be behind this?"

"Absolutely not," I answer quickly, too quickly perhaps.

Markus runs his hands over his damp jeans and looks searchingly at me.

"I think it's high time we set up some kind of protection for you. I will arrange for a patrol car to drive by a few times a day. I don't like you to be out here alone in this house, after all that's happened."

I don't know why, but my stomach turns at the thought of having uniformed police officers lurking in the bushes outside.

"Absolutely not. I don't want the police here. All I want is peace and quiet."

"Sometimes you don't have a choice, Siri. Sometimes you have to accept help. We can't force you, of course, but . . ."

I shake my head vehemently. "I don't need any help. And last thing I need is a bunch of cops snooping around here—Oh, I'm sorry, I didn't mean you . . ."

We both stop talking and look at each other in silence. With curiosity this time. There are small raindrops trapped in his fair eyebrows, and the backs of his hands are covered with soft sun-bleached hair that glistens in the light from the table lamp next to the couch. Outside, the rain is falling with constant force.

"I should probably go now."

"Can't you stay until I fall asleep? You can close the door behind you when you leave."

He nods and looks at me, amused.

I go quietly to my room and crawl into my big bed. When I wake up, it is morning and Markus is gone.

"For starters, I'd like to welcome you back."

Sonja's handshake is firm and her gaze direct. I am back in the tidy white office. Just like last time, the room is immaculate. I realize that I appreciate this. There are no teetering stacks of paper, no photographs, no paintings. Nothing that reveals anything about its occupants. The room is anonymous but somehow peaceful. I have always imagined interrogation rooms as shabby, cramped spaces with worn-out, rejected furniture cobbled together from all other departments in the public sector. Rooms with yellowing walls, locked windows, and a strong odor of stale cigarette smoke and sweat. A little like the smoking rooms at the psychiatric wards where I worked when I was a student. Maybe there are interrogation rooms that do look like that, how should I know?

"Well, once again we meet under slightly different circumstances. I realize that perhaps our previous conversation was painful, but I hope you understand that we have to do our job."

Sonja looks sincerely apologetic. I was not expecting such sympathy. Today we are meeting alone, without Markus. I find myself distracted, wondering where he is and what he is up to. My thoughts surprise me a little. Why should I care?

"There is further evidence that indicates that Sara's death was in some way directed at you. For this reason, I'd like you to think whether there is anyone who might want to harm you in some way."

"No. I still can't imagine who would be after me. Who would want to hurt me."

"In your work you must meet a lot of sick people. Isn't that so?"

"That depends on what you mean by 'sick.' I work in a private practice, most of the patients I see have a psychiatric problem, but at the same time are functional enough to work or support themselves in some way. They have actively sought private treatment for various reasons and usually pay for it themselves. But sure, if by sick you mean they've had a psychiatric diagnosis, then yes. But just because you have psychiatric problems doesn't mean you're crazy, not at all, in fact."

"So when is one crazy?"

Sonja looks at me attentively, as if she really wants to hear my own definition of what crazy is.

"Well, I guess that depends. According to the law, you are considered insane if you are a danger to yourself or others and if you cannot take responsibility for your actions. I don't see that kind of patient. Not because I don't want to, but because they require other forms of treatment. We simply don't have the right resources for that type of patient."

"You have never had any patients who took a special interest in you? Who were more curious than is normal?"

I let my thoughts wander to the various individuals I had treated throughout my career.

"Once, a male patient asked me out, but that was five years ago, and it wasn't so strange, really. The therapy was coming to an end and he asked me rather elegantly whether I wanted to go to an exhibition with him. I can't recall which one."

"And how did you respond?"

"I declined, of course. It's not ethical to date patients, either current or past."

"And how did he react?"

"If you're wondering whether he was offended or if I felt threatened or anything like that, you can forget it. He simply laughed and asked whether it would be unprofessional for me to go out with him. I told him that was the case, and that was that."

"What did you treat him for?"

"Dental phobia."

"Dental phobia?"

"He was afraid to go to the dentist. Nothing unusual. He was very ordinary. The treatment went well. He was satisfied. Nothing special."

"Perhaps we should speak with him anyway."

"I would really appreciate it if you didn't do that. I'm absolutely convinced he has nothing to do with this."

An almost imperceptible wrinkle appears on Sonja's forehead. I provoked her with my unwillingness to drag my old patients into the investigation.

"You don't want to break therapist-client privilege, right?"

"Exactly. My patients come to me to get treatment, and they know that our conversations are confidential. It's an important part of my professional role. I have no desire to subject them to police interrogation."

Sonja nods and I know that she is not going to insist, even if she would rather I cooperate more fully. She changes the subject.

"There are no individuals in your private life who could conceivably—how should I put this—be more interested in you than normal?"

"No. Nobody. I have no enemies. That's just absurd, do people really have enemies? I thought stuff like that only happened among criminals. And maybe among jealous exes."

"And you don't have any? A jealous ex, that is."

"My most recent ex is now the father of three, lives in Västerås, and works as an engineer. He was the one who broke up with me. We were twenty-two at the time. I find it hard to imagine he would want to harm me now."

I think about Johan. The boyfriend I met in high school and dated until the first year of college. The one my parents adored, who practiced driving with my dad and flirted with my sisters. He broke things off because he thought our relationship had gotten too serious. It's probably because it prevented him from taking on a bigger role in student activities. Or maybe he really thought that I was too serious. Too depressed. He could never understand why I chose to study psychology. He thought I should have gone to business school or become a doctor.

"But you have nothing against us contacting him, I hope? You weren't bound by any professional agreement there."

"Sure. I'll get you his address."

Sonja gets up from her chair and reaches for the only sheets of paper on the desk nearby.

"I'd also like you to look at this."

She holds out two pieces of paper. One is a handwritten letter and the other is a color copy of an envelope. The envelope has Charlotte Mimer's name and address on it.

"This is not the original; we sent it to the forensics lab. We would like you to take a look at the letter, to see if you recognize the handwriting, or the language, or anything at all."

I look at the brief note. The text agrees with what Charlotte read to me over the phone. The letter is printed in neat, clear letters. Without knowing why, I suddenly think of Charlotte's food diary entries. Though there is no resemblance between this and Charlotte's careful, beautiful personal handwriting, there is something that reminds me of her. Maybe it's the restrained style, or the methodically executed letters? Maybe it's the sense of control that permeates the text?

"Do you see anything that looks familiar? Does it remind you of anyone? Even the smallest detail is important."

I simply shake my head. Hesitantly, Sonja pushes a strand of dark-brown hair behind one ear. I note that she has three earrings in her earlobe, two pearls and a gold dolphin.

"You must understand that whoever wrote this letter, and whoever is . . . stalking you, has quite a bit of knowledge about you—your life, your habits, and your patients. What about your colleagues at the practice? How do you get along, really?"

The question does not come as a surprise. Yet it bothers me more than I could have imagined. The practice, my colleagues: Sven, Aina. Nothing in my life is private any longer. And everyone who surrounds me is potentially a liar.

I can't answer Sonja. I sit quietly, my gaze fixed on the little gold dolphin in her earlobe. The light catches it, and for a moment, it actually seems to move.

OCTOBER

I am sitting with Aina at Jerusalem Kebab on Götgatan. It's dark outside and Södermalm is swarmed with people on their way home from work. Young, trendy types are mixed with stressed-out parents pushing three-wheeled strollers and old folks leaning on dangerous-looking walkers. A group of young women in head scarves is laughing as they head toward Medborgarplatsen; perhaps they are on their way to the mosque.

As always, Aina stuffs an entire falafel into her mouth and I don't comment on her lousy table manners. Red sauce dribbles down her chin.

She leans toward me and whispers, "I think Sven may be involved."

"Oh, cut it out."

Even though my mouth is full of hummus and salad, I can't help but smile.

"No, I'm serious. Listen to me. He has access to the records. He knows where you live. He chases every single skirt and could very well be that guy Sara told you about. The one who *listened* to her so well, the one who *saw* her."

"And so why would Sven start strangling women, write hate letters, and trick me into a DUI?" I ask, shoveling more hummus onto my fork.

"Because he *hates* women!" Aina says triumphantly.

I raise my eyebrows, but she continues without paying attention to my reaction.

"His life has been full of personal failures caused by women. He was chased out of the university because he was seeing that girl. His wife is infinitely more successful than he is. And what is her main focus of work? Gender research! You can just imagine the lectures he is subjected to over dinner. Besides, his office is dominated by two little girls, *one of whom has rejected his sexual advances on a number of occasions.* Talk about feeling castrated."

"Aina, are you serious?" I am laughing out loud.

"Why not?" She acts offended and wipes her mouth with the back of her hand. In the corner of my eye I can see her wiping off the sauce on her worn jeans.

"Okay, it's a *theoretical* possibility," I admit.

For a brief moment, my thoughts turn to Peter Carlsson. He knew Charlotte Mimer from before, and he recently discovered that she was a patient of mine. Plus, his compulsive thoughts revolve around violence and sex. I've been thinking about Peter a lot over the past few weeks, tormenting myself by going over the three conversations I had with him, word by word. Could Peter be dangerous? For real? Could he be the one who killed Sara? Should I say anything to Aina, Sven, or the police? At the same time, I am well aware of the therapist-client privilege. And I can't go to the police and talk about Peter just because he has strange thoughts. That would be highly unethical. I have nothing more substantial than my paranoid fantasies and relentless concern to go on. Why would he want to kill Sara? Why would he want to harm me? As far as I know, he has no motive. I decide not to bring up my suspicions with Aina. It just seems unnecessary. After all, I'm the one who needs to keep her paranoia in check.

Not noticing my silence, Aina continues on a different track.

"Maybe it's Birgitta, I mean, maybe it's because she can't stand it when other women flirt with her husband."

I can tell Aina is very excited by this new idea.

"And she always acts so damn special. You saw how she reacted at the crayfish party when Robert talked back at her. And then she saw Sven pawing you."

"But why would she kill Sara? An iconic feminist on a murder spree? Oh, cut it out."

My patience is starting to wear thin. This game isn't fun anymore, and I don't want to speculate about who might have killed Sara. Sara is gone. Dead. Murdered. Sitting here, guessing who might be her murderer, feels shameful.

"Okay, then, maybe it's not very likely, but it's certainly possible."

Aina licks hummus from her fingers and continues.

"Or maybe Marianne. Maybe she's bitter and jealous of you . . . because you . . ."

Aina pauses and seems to be thinking.

"Because . . . I don't know. She was also a little sore at that crayfish party, when I tried to be nice to Christer."

"Sore? When you were only *trying to be nice* to Christer? Aina, sometimes you are just too much. You practically thrust your tits in his face. You think it's strange that she would get upset? And if so, then, damn it, *you're* the one she ought to be mad at. Not me. And certainly not Sara."

"He was strange, too," Aina continues, ignoring me. "Christer, that is. It's like he didn't seem . . ." Aina searches for words.

"I realize this may sound boastful, but most men usually react to me. In some way. Even if I don't rub my tits in their face. Okay, I know how narcissistic and superficial that sounds, but he was . . . cold in some way. There was no way to get through to him."

Now I'm about to explode.

"Aina, *for Christ's sake*! Stop it. Sara is dead! I don't like this conversation. We don't know whether her murder even has anything to do with me, and you're sitting here . . . making it into a party game. This isn't Clue. You just turned everyone around me into a suspect. Sven, Birgitta, Marianne, Christer . . . because *you* think they are strange. Don't you get it that none of these people have a reason to hate me? Sure, maybe they dislike me, but not hate. And what about you, then? You're strange, too."

I realize I've gone too far and fall silent.

"Forgive me," I mumble.

Aina is serious now, the giggly silliness is gone. I sigh heavily as I look down at my sticky, empty plate. After sitting in silence for a long time, Aina locks eyes with me before speaking.

"Forgive me. I was thoughtless. I was only trying to . . . I don't know."

She runs her hand through her hair before continuing.

"They've questioned everyone at the practice now, and made copies of all the videotapes with Sara. What else are the police doing? They don't seem to be getting anywhere."

"I went over it all with that police officer, Sonja, the one who is leading the investigation. There's also a prosecutor, someone she reports to, whom I haven't met yet. At any rate, there is a law about secrecy in preliminary investigations. You know, they can't talk about what they're doing. Not even to me. But she did mention that they had called all the contacts in Sara's cell phone and visited all her previous employers. Talked with all her neighbors. Her boyfriends. Her mother. Made a careful forensic investigation. I don't remember, but there were several things. I actually think they're doing a thorough job."

"But they don't seem to have any suspects. Just think if that person is still sneaking around in the bushes on Värmdö, watching you!"

Aina can tell from my face that this wasn't the right thing to say.

"Do you want me to stay with you?" she asks gently, placing a sticky hand on mine.

"I don't know how to say this," she continues, hesitantly, "but you mean so much to me. I can't stand the thought that anyone would want to hurt you. This whole thing is crazy. I'd be happy to come and live with you for a while again."

We go quiet. Her hand lies on mine, and she caresses my wrist lightly with her damp fingertips. Suddenly her closeness is too much for me to bear, as if she wants something I can't give her, and I worry that I am going to disappoint her as usual.

"That's not necessary," I say and gesture that I don't need company this evening.

I explain that I have lots to do. It's a lie, of course, and Aina knows it, but she simply nods silently and looks out into the night that has now settled over the throngs of people on Götgatan.

That night I dream about Stefan. He is sitting close to me on the edge of the bed and rests his damp head—his hair is full of seaweed and kelp—lightly against my belly.

"I miss you," I say, stroking him carefully over his cold back, but he does not answer. Instead he gets up and searches for something. He looks under the bed, in the closets, on the bookshelf, even under the rag rug on the floor.

"What are you looking for?" I ask.

"That's what's so weird," he answers, annoyed. "I've forgotten what I'm looking for." His light hair is sun bleached under the greenish-brown algae and his skin is tanned brown, but under his eyes are those dark rings he had at the end. When he could neither sleep nor eat and restlessly wandered around the house at night.

"I need something." He runs his hand through his hair with a confused expression on his face.

"Siri," he says quietly, looking desperate. "Can you help me look?"

"I will help you look," I reply.

Outside my window, Medborgarplatsen is deserted. The sky has taken on a saturated, deep blue color with turquoise undertones. Prussian blue, I think. Though I haven't painted in a long time, I still remember the names of colors. The façades of the buildings around Björn's Park are dark brown—red with a tinge of violet—*caput mortuum,* which means "dead head"—a color I love. In front of the Greek food cart I can see a few shivering Stockholmers lining up in the clear, chilly fall evening.

In my little green consultation room, everything is calm. From the CD player on the shelf above the desk Pink Floyd calls out: "*So, so you think you can tell, Heaven from Hell . . .*" I am not so sure I would be able to see the difference. Know that it was him, if one day he was standing in front of me.

I am the only one left at the office, even though it's just five o'clock. Everyone has gone home to their families, dogs, and TV shows. Aina has a date as usual. I simply have not been able to collect myself sufficiently enough to declare the day over, though I probably ought to go home, like a *normal* person.

I start packing my things absentmindedly, turn on my cell phone, which I had turned off during office hours, and grab my notepad and some old thumbed-through magazines I want to borrow from the reception desk. My cell phone beeps. I have three missed calls: all from Marianne. That's unusual; it's her day off. She never calls when she's out. I walk to the kitchen to get some coffee and call Marianne. She answers after a few rings.

"Siri, how nice of you to call back. Sorry for disturbing you, but we need to talk."

Typical Marianne: always apologizing, even when I'm the one calling her.

"Shoot," I say while I pour cold coffee into a cup and put it in the microwave. Silently, I curse Sven for never putting the coffeepot back on the hot plate.

"Siri, I need to see you."

"Well, I'm coming in at ten tomorrow, I'll—"

"This evening. I would much rather see you this evening."

She sounds out of breath and hoarser than usual. I can see her in front of me, as if she had just rushed up a stairway or run across a street and is now leaning forward from fatigue, resting her left hand on her curvy hip as she talks to me on her cell.

"I see, but couldn't we do it on the phone? I was actually about to go home. I'm the last one here."

Marianne clears her throat, and I hear voices in the background.

"It's . . . it's not such a good time to talk right now. My son is here. And his girlfriend. They've just come back from India. We're looking at pictures right now. Couldn't you stop by a little later? There's something I want to show you."

This is an unusual request. Marianne and I don't typically socialize privately.

"This is important. I wouldn't ask you otherwise," she adds in a low, urgent voice.

"Marianne," I say, and part of me wants to laugh.

Orderly, lucid, wonderful Marianne who always has a solution to every problem, who always is the calmest and most collected of all, the last to leave the office. Suddenly I don't recognize her. The hoarse, urgent voice, the impetuous manner, it's not like her.

"Is it a matter of life and death?"

I don't mean to sound flippant, it just comes out that way.

Marianne sighs. "Please, Siri, can you just stop by here?"

I hesitate for a moment. Marianne lives on Karlbergsvägen. However I look at it, it will be a detour.

"What time do you want me to come?"

"Come around seven. I'll run out and buy a few pastries so we can have coffee. And could you bring Sven's records that are on his desk? I didn't get everything done yesterday, I can try to get them done a little later this evening."

So Marianne is working nights for Sven? Anger rises in me. As far as I know, she has never worked nights for either me or Aina.

We hang up without saying anything further about what it is Marianne so desperately has to show me right away. I return to my office, turn on my computer, and work awhile longer.

Marianne's apartment is on the fourth floor of a grand fin-de-siècle building. I have been here only once before, when Aina, Marianne, and I went out to a bar in an attempt at sisterly solidarity. As I push the small brass button, the doorbell, I hear a muted vibration, but the door remains closed. Hesitantly, I place my ear against the cold, varnished oak surface and listen closely but hear only silence. No steps coming to meet me. I rub my cold hands against each other while backing up a few steps to look out the corridor window down at the street. Everything is still. The small, well-tended garden in front of the entrance is deserted, just like the neighboring yards. A pearl necklace of neat, small doormats in front of the clean buildings. Suddenly I sense a movement between the trees on the other side of the street. There! A man in a trench coat pushes a stroller and carries grocery bags as he hurries away in the darkness toward St. Eriksplan. I shake my head at my own imagination and ring Marianne's doorbell again, to no avail.

Nothing happens, not even when I bend down to call through the mail slot. I carefully pry open the brass flap of the little slot, just enough to glimpse the outlines of the carpet inside. It is dark. The smell of coffee mixed with Marianne's perfume seeps through the slot and out into the hallway. A faint voice murmurs monotonously from inside without paying attention to me. I assume the TV is on.

"Marianne? It's Siri. Are you there? *Marianne?*"

Carefully, I push down the handle and the door slides open without a sound. This worries me—it is not like Marianne to leave her front door unlocked.

I grope for the light switch in the hall, and suddenly the room is bathed in a soft yellow glow. Polished wood floors, a small rag rug on the floor, and a coatrack to the right. Mirrors cover the wall across from the door, and I am startled by my own frightened reflection. I enter quickly and shut the door behind me. It closes with a soft click.

"Marianne," I try again, as I enter the living room on the left.

It is cozy in a way my parents would appreciate. Curved chairs upholstered in Josef Frank material, an oversized bulky leather couch, thick, welcoming carpets on the floor, brass sconces on the walls, which are decorated with large, naïf paintings in strong colors, which I know Marianne has painted herself.

"Hello!"

A Discovery Channel program is playing on the TV in front of the window, the volume turned low. I reflect once again on how little I really know about Marianne; I would never have guessed that she would be interested in science or nature programs, or in the show playing right now, a program about crime. "*The woman never suspected that her own brother could be involved in such a horrific crime . . .*" a nasal voice intones in a British accent.

The room is empty. I move on to the kitchen, which is also quiet and dark. Massive oak doors, a Miele stove—Marianne must have come into some money after her recent divorce, I think. On the table is a pile of papers neatly packed in a transparent plastic folder with a yellow Post-it note that says BILLS—TO PAY. I suddenly feel ill at ease. Something is not right.

"Marianne?"

Still no answer. No Marianne. Only the nasal voice from the living room: "*As soon as the driver arrived he understood that something was terribly wrong . . .*"

I walk into her bedroom and hesitate in the doorway; my heart is pounding and the familiar feeling of impending catastrophe is spreading rapidly through my body like poison. I try to convince myself that this is just a normal visit with a dear colleague in her cozy apartment. Of course Marianne will show up at any moment—she wouldn't be in the bedroom. I take a deep breath as my fingers feel for the light switch.

". . . although the driver could see blood on the floor, Mary Jane was no-where to be found . . ."

The room is empty.

An enormous double bed with a quilted cover and way too many pillows stuffed into white, crocheted needlepoint coverings almost takes up the entire room. There are pictures of children and friends on the nightstand. I slowly walk over to the pictures and crouch to see them. Two little boys in bathing trunks laugh into the camera, and I can see that the smaller one's front teeth are missing. He is holding a beach ball under his skinny suntanned arm that says TEMPO on it.

Her sons, I think as I stand up with the uncomfortable feeling of having done something forbidden—like snooping in someone's medicine cabinet or purse. All this time, I've had a suffocating feeling that I'm being watched, as if I was sharing Marianne's apartment with *someone* who doesn't want to make his presence known. That I am being seen although I myself cannot see, like being in my lit-up house at night. I wipe the sweat from my forehead with a shaky hand.

". . . in the barn he finally found a trace of her . . ."

I return to the living room and sink down on the puffy leather couch. I remain sitting like that a long time without doing anything. Marianne is one of the most responsible people I know. I seriously cannot believe that she left her apartment after having invited me here. I start to think that she probably hasn't run out to buy cigarettes or pastries as I had hoped, or gone down to park her car in a better spot. What do you do when someone vanishes like this? I can't really call the police. How long do you have to wait before you know . . . before you know that someone has disappeared? A few hours? A whole day? A week?

On the table in front of me is a neat bundle of gold-embroidered fabric in all the colors of the rainbow—saris, I presume. Must be a present from her son and his girlfriend. Alongside it rests a large coffee cup, half empty, and I test it by resting my palm against it.

It is still hot.

". . . there was blood on the floor, inside the car, and . . ."

Suddenly I realize that I cannot stay in Marianne's apartment another minute. Without looking, I rush toward the hall and the door, prepared for anything. But no one blocks my way as I force the door open with all my weight and make my way out to the stairwell.

While I rush toward St. Eriksplan, I call Aina, who does not answer; the answering machine asks me courteously to leave my name and number. She is presumably at the bar now, that is, if they haven't left already and gone home. I shake my head and try Markus's cell phone. No answer there either, but I leave a message anyway, no matter how confused and incoherent it may sound.

I go down to the subway with a gnawing feeling that something horrible has happened this evening, and that I, in some way, am an accessory to it.

The next morning I arrive at the practice earlier than usual. The clump in my stomach has been replaced by nervous energy—I have to find out where Marianne is.

Aina meets me in the corridor with a broad smile.

"I don't want to know," I say, shaking my head.

"Are you sore?"

Aina looks surprised and hurt.

"Is Marianne here yet?"

"No. It's really strange—she hasn't come in and she hasn't called. It's not like her to just . . . just not show up."

I tell her about yesterday evening, and Aina's eyes open wide as they do when she is worried or scared. The corner of her eye twitches a little as she slowly takes hold of my arm.

"Have you called the police?"

"No, she'd only been gone half an hour or so."

"Why didn't you call Markus, or Christer?"

There is something accusatory in her voice.

"I don't have Christer's number. I don't even know his last name. I called Markus, but I couldn't get hold of him—*or you.*"

"Oh." Aina blushes slightly and lets go of my arm.

"As I said, I don't want to know. I'm much too worried about Marianne to hear about your escapades."

My voice is unnecessarily harsh. I know it's petty of me, but sometimes I just can't indulge Aina in the quick adventures she lives for. It's as if I wanted her to promise me that she will share my solitude.

"At the reception desk," Aina interrupts my train of thought.

"Reception desk?"

"The binder with emergency contact numbers. Don't you remember?"

I remember. Marianne, who had attended a class on the role of the secretary in crisis management, had collected names and numbers of our closest relatives "in case something happens."

I go around the reception desk and start searching among Marianne's neatly arranged, color-coded binders. Farthest down in a slender binder marked IMPORTANT PAPERS I find the sheet of numbers. By Marianne's name, Christer and both sons are listed as relatives. I take the phone and dial Christer's number. He answers at the first ring.

We are sitting in the cafeteria near the large foyer at South Hospital. An unending stream of people come and go around us. Nursing staff dressed in white walk with rapid, self-assured steps toward the counter, serve themselves the daily special, and continue to the cash register. Worried relatives sit in silence with a cup of coffee, looking straight ahead in a daze. Talkative senior citizens seem to have experienced the high point of the week with their hospital visit. An older woman carefully feeds a man who sits shaking in a wheelchair. My guess is that it is her husband who suffers from Parkinson's.

Christer sits across from me. His eyes are red rimmed and it is apparent that he hasn't gotten much sleep. He constantly rubs his hands together. I notice that the cuticles on his thumb and index finger are torn apart far down and that an ugly, inflamed red color is starting to spread there.

"A hit-and-run accident?"

I hear doubt in my voice.

"A hit-and-run accident," Christer confirms. "The police are quite certain. There are witnesses, too."

"What happened? I mean, I spoke with Marianne yesterday evening. She wanted me to stop by, but she wasn't there when I arrived."

"They think she ran down to pick something up at the 7-Eleven. She was there right before the accident. A bunch of kids who were sitting nearby eating cinnamon rolls saw her. She was just going back home, you know. Took a shortcut across Odengatan. There was a red light, and she had no reflectors on. I think she found that sort of thing was . . . unnecessary."

Christer interrupts himself and I can see the tears well up in his eyes again.

"A car came, probably driving too fast, and didn't have a chance to stop. Not a chance."

Christer shakes his head and starts working on the cuticle of his middle finger, slowly pulling away a long piece of skin so that the flesh is exposed. He doesn't seem to feel the pain.

"There were witnesses," he repeats. "They saw that she flew through the air. Several . . . several yards, they say."

He sounds strangely practical and collected, but I have met people in shock before and know that he probably still can't fully grasp the consequences of what has happened. Near us, the man with Parkinson's starts weeping loudly. His wife looks around apologetically, gets up, and starts pushing his wheelchair. They quickly disappear through the exit.

"And yes, the car kept going. Maybe it was someone who was drunk, or didn't have a driver's license, or who just got scared. But he ran away. No one was able to get the license plate number."

"So how is Marianne doing?"

"She has head injuries. They gave her, what's it called, an MRI. Apparently they didn't see any bleeding, but the brain is swollen. That's why she's still unconscious."

"So she's going to be all right?"

"It's more serious than it sounds. They have to reduce the swelling. If they don't, she may have lasting brain injuries, or, in the worst case, die. I've been up with her. She's lying there like she's tied up, with tubes and IVs and all kinds of contraptions."

Christer sighs and his eyes begin to shine again.

"I should have been there. I should have gone shopping for her. I don't get why she suddenly had to go out in the darkness and . . . without reflectors. She didn't have any reflectors. I was at a business dinner. I was sitting there having scallops in wine sauce, then the police called me on my cell phone. It's too terrible. I was eating scallops, did I say that? In wine sauce. And she . . . she . . ."

Christer clenches his jaws and I can't help but take his hand. Squeeze it lightly.

"I am so sorry," I murmur.

"I'm glad you came." Christer looks up at me. "Thank you, Siri," he whispers, squeezing my hand back.

I pull myself together and try to find the right words without seeming intrusive.

"Do you know what Marianne wanted to talk about with me?"

Christer turns to me, and his red-rimmed eyes wander as if he can't understand this irrelevant question.

"No idea. Does it still matter now?"

I shake my head slowly and lightly squeeze his hand again.

"No, it doesn't matter anymore."

Sometimes I think about my last days with Stefan. The spring of 2005 was difficult. A splinter of uncertainty had wedged its way into our relationship, an insight that chafed at me. The unpredictability of life? Maybe that was the problem. My body had regained its normal boyish shape. The slight swelling of my belly, so well concealed to everyone except Stefan and me, was gone. I was empty again.

We had moved into the cottage on Värmdö. Maybe that could be our project now. A substitute for the child that never came. In the beginning everything was fine. We worked on the renovation together from morning to evening. We could be silent for days on end, lost in deep concentration, and forget mealtimes as we worked, two sweaty bodies, side by side. There were only brief exchanges:

"Do you have the level?"

Then silence.

Then Stefan started to become increasingly passive. I think he took the loss of the child harder than I did. He withdrew from me and others more and more. His daily runs got longer and longer.

"It can't be good for your body to run five miles every day," I said to him, but he didn't answer.

He withdrew into himself and would not let me or anyone else in. At work, he seemed to function well, but more and more often he came home exhausted and went straight from the door to bed, where he then lay awake with eyes shut tight until I came to lie down beside him. I crept up behind him, closer, always closer, and fell asleep tormented by the feeling I had deserted him, because I knew he couldn't sleep.

Morning. Stefan continued to lie quietly with his eyes shut tight, but I knew he was awake. My hand sought his—he pulled back. My cheek searched for the soft support that was his shoulder—no comfort.

"Stefan, how are you, really?"

"Fine."

"Really . . . ?"

"It's okay. I don't want to talk about it."

"I *know* it's not okay. You're not sleeping like you should, you're losing weight, and you've gotten . . . completely . . . so damn . . . *passive*. You sit on that couch for days on end. It's like living with a dead person."

Looking down at our newly sanded floor, Stefan only shrugged. I saw no sign of emotion in his face that could have given me some clue as to what he felt or thought. His gaze was expressionless and directed at the wall behind me.

"*I* think you're depressed. I mean, it's not so strange, is it, after what we've been through? I see that kind of thing every day, and you must, too, in your job? I really think you have to do something about this, for your sake and for mine, but . . . mostly for *our* sake. It doesn't feel as though we can . . . talk to each other anymore. I could give you the name of a good therapist, or you can talk to a colleague about getting some antidepressants prescribed. I don't know—"

"*Shut up!*"

Stefan interrupted me with a shout. He suddenly jumped out of bed and I could see spit spraying from his mouth as he continued.

"I *hate* it when you analyze me. I don't need to see a damn psychologist or take any happy pills. The only thing I need is to be *left alone*. Can you get that through your overanalyzing little psychologist brain? I need a break from *you* and your *damn concern*. Your cloying curiosity and your worry. Leave. Me. Alone."

I glimpsed a type of madness in Stefan's face, I couldn't recognize him, but the feeling was gone as quickly as it came.

"You know nothing about my problems, *nothing*. First this thing with the child . . . and then my job."

"Your job?"

I couldn't understand a thing. Stefan had always loved his work.

"I see patients with spinal cord damage every day. And I'm the one who has to tell them they're never going to walk again. I'm the one who has to talk to their loved ones, explain to the girlfriend that they will never be able to have a normal sex life again, never have children in a normal way, explain how the catheter functions, talk about physical therapy."

"But Stefan, why didn't you say anything—"

"*Shut up.* Leave me alone. I want you to leave me *alone.* I want to wake up one morning *without* being judged by your searching gaze, *without* hearing the concern in your voice. I want to wake up *without you!*"

Stefan sank down on the floor in front of me, like a rag doll or a deflated balloon. He remained sitting on the rug in a peculiar position that resembled one of Aina's yoga poses, with his forehead pressing against the floor. I could see his shoulders shaking in the semidarkness. Carefully, I sat down beside him and took his hand. It was cold and damp.

"Stefan, do you realize you're sick?"

He didn't answer, just shook, producing strange noises that sounded like drawn-out sobs, like crying in slow motion.

"Stefan. You have to get help. This is like any other illness."

He nodded slowly between sobs.

"Do you want the number of one of my colleagues?"

"Noooo!" The word sounded like a howl, and suddenly I was afraid. Afraid of my inability to help him, of my shortcomings, and of the unpredictability of life.

"Promise me you'll get medication?"

He nodded. "I promise."

I remember that summer with painful acuity. It's as if every aroma, every nuance, and every incident had etched itself in my memory and left an impression I will always carry with me. Like an insight that will not leave me alone. An understanding of my own boundless imperfection.

Stefan procured himself some medication. I saw it on the bathroom shelf. Citalopram. He took it obediently and even just a few weeks later I thought I could sense an improvement. Finally he could sleep, read his mail, get the newspaper, go grocery shopping, and take initiative.

Was he fully restored?

Hardly.

In June I was really, really happy for the first time in months. Stefan seemed better and Aina and I had opened the practice together with Sven. The summer was stunningly beautiful. Outside our window, the dog roses blended with the giant leaves of the morning glory. The wild jasmine was in bloom, enveloping the house in an overpowering, slightly stifling aroma. The evenings on the rocks were long and light blue. Even the summer darkness seemed welcoming and friendly.

Stefan had started diving again. Maybe it was logical that it would happen when he was diving. Maybe he would have wanted it that way, if he could have chosen?

I remember that the morning was lovely, calm, and slightly chilly. We had breakfast on the wooden steps outside the cottage, like we always did, my bare feet on his. Silence. No worries yet. I drank from his coffee cup as usual, and we had hardtack with caviar paste. Out on the sea, a sailboat was trying to cross eastward, in vain. Stefan commented that the sailors would have to use their engines today if they didn't want to get stuck there, bobbing in the flat sea.

The day's diving trip was to Vindö, Abborrkroken. I had dived there myself, a massive rock wall that descended 150 feet or more straight down into the water.

I read the culture section of the newspaper while Stefan packed his equipment in the car and got ready. A quick kiss, and a wave from the car as he drove off. Maybe I am remembering wrong, but he looked happier than he had in a long time.

I spent the day working. We were in the process of hiring a receptionist and I had to read all the applications carefully, because I am hopelessly particular in such matters. Time passed so quickly that I forgot to have lunch and noticed with surprise that it was starting to get dark when I heard a car drive up behind the cottage.

I put on my red clogs and went out into the cool summer evening to meet Stefan. But there, in the twilight under the pines, stood Peppe and another man I had never seen before. They stood motionless next to the clothesline that ran between the shed and the small bent pine we had christened "the gnarly one." They looked so funny, like monuments, that I almost laughed. I smiled as I walked up to greet them but stopped when I saw Peppe's eyes. *That's* when I understood.

To this day, no one knows exactly what happened to Stefan. He was found at a depth of over fifty yards. The technical investigation showed that his equipment was in perfect shape. He had plenty of air left, and the autopsy did not indicate any physical problems that might explain the sudden accident. His death remains a mystery. Sure, everyone has theories: fear, lack of fear, contempt for death, death wish, lack of practice, carelessness as a result of long experience and routine, loss of orientation in the darkness, suicide, murder, mysterious illnesses and cramps, just to name a few. I didn't want to think about *how* it happened; it was hard enough to be confronted with *that* it happened.

The first month after his death, Stefan was with me every night. If I listened carefully I could hear his breathing. Sometimes I sensed his body beside mine as I drifted in and out of half sleep. In the morning, the room was filled with his scent. When four weeks had passed, he left me for good.

This, I cannot forgive.

Markus is sitting silently across from me with a teacup resting in his large hand. Around us, the restaurant is empty; the lunch rush ebbed out long ago.

We are at the Blå Porten restaurant. Markus had suggested we meet here because he had an earlier errand on Djurgården. I feel inexplicably foreign in this part of the city, marked by its strange mixture of rich Stockholmers, the cultural elite, and tourists. In the courtyard outside the window, green garden furniture is stacked up along the walls and the rain falling to the ground forms small, muddy rivers that slowly but surely flood the stone-paved courtyard. There is not a person in sight.

"So, I wanted to talk to you about a few things."

Markus takes a small black notebook out of his pocket.

"We checked your calls that evening when the police caught you for . . ." He doesn't say the word but instead looks embarrassed, pauses, and flips the pages in his notebook.

"Someone called you fifteen minutes before you were stopped, but the call came from a prepaid cell phone and we can't trace it to a user."

"But then you must believe me, right?"

Markus doesn't reply but nods slowly and takes something out of the black backpack that I remember from our previous meetings.

"Sure, I believe you. It's obviously the same person who killed Sara, wrote to Charlotte, and sent the photo to you. But . . . the problem for you is that none of this matters when a DUI is involved. There was no doubt that you were driving while intoxicated. Whether or not anyone lured you into taking the car."

Markus is still looking down at his papers as he says this. As if he wants to spare me the humiliation. As if that would suffice.

"You know, that really doesn't matter. Just . . . just so long as you believe me. And that Aina and Sven believe me."

My voice is no longer composed. It gets shrill and much too loud, and a couple of old ladies who have just walked in look worriedly in our direction. I bury my head in my hands and feel the tears burning behind my eyelids.

"I'm sorry. I just don't know if I can take this any longer. I'm starting to believe you were right."

"Right about what?"

"About this . . . crazy . . . guy. Right that he really is after *me*."

"Of course he is."

Markus takes my hand and looks at me steadily with his pale blue eyes, without being bothered by my breakdown. No longer embarrassed, he is present and empathetic to the highest degree. I am reminded of the fact that I like people who dare to be physical—*men* who dare to be physical.

"There's something else. What happened to Marianne—"

"Marianne? What does she have to do with this?"

"Maybe she knew something," Markus says, inspecting me across the table as he pulls on the loose threads of his frayed jeans.

"Now I really don't get it. What does Marianne's accident have to do with this?"

"If it really was an accident." Markus hesitates a moment. "We've been in contact with the Norrmalm police, who investigated what happened, and there is a witness who claims that someone pushed her out into the street. And since Marianne had set up a meeting with you, we think maybe she wanted to talk to you about something important. About Sara."

"About Sara? Why about Sara?"

"That's what we have to find out. We think it all fits together. What happened to Marianne is part of our investigation now."

Markus roots in his bag again and takes out a plastic folder with a yellow Post-it note saying BILLS—TO PAY on it.

"I've seen *that* before," I say, running my hand over the smooth plastic. "It was on Marianne's kitchen table that evening. Why do you have it?"

Markus doesn't answer. Instead he runs his hand through his blond hair, which is still wet from the rain, takes the bundle of papers out of the folder, and pushes them slowly across the table, toward me.

"*Case notes?*"

"Yes, but not just any case notes. These are copies of your notes about Sara Matteus. Someone wrote their own notes on the copies. Look at this . . ."

Markus leafs through to a page where there are long sentences written in blue ink.

"May I?"

Not waiting for his permission, I reach over and turn the bundle of papers toward me so I can read.

"This is Sven's handwriting," I say, feeling my stomach clench. Why did he have copies of Sara's case notes?

I try to decipher his scrawled handwriting, but as usual it is almost impossible to comprehend. ". . . *would not necessarily mean . . . problem with authority . . . self-aware.*" Sven's comments say nothing and cannot explain why he had the records.

"Do you read each other's case notes?"

"Sometimes."

I blow my nose loudly in a red napkin that was already lying crumpled and damp on the table when we arrived, unconcerned that I am mixing my bodily fluids with some other customer's.

"Sometimes we help each other out with a patient, or maybe someone needs to look up a record to make a case study. Sven does some teaching on the side and writes scientific articles and that sort of thing."

"About Sara?"

I shrug.

"And if Sven borrowed the notes, why were they at home with Marianne?"

I shake my head. I don't know what to say.

"There's something else."

"What do you mean?" I look up at Markus.

He takes a bite of a lavender cookie and points at the pile of papers without saying anything. I notice traces of white paint on his fingers. Maybe he was painting over the weekend? It strikes me that I know nothing about how he lives when he's not working. I have a sudden desire to touch the specks of paint and ask him about it. I long to feel the rough, dry palm of his hand in mine. So near, and yet so far away. Instead, I leaf obediently through the bundle of case notes.

Something falls out of the pile and lands on my lap. Carefully, I pick it up. It is a black-and-white photograph of a young girl, taken with—it must be acknowledged—a certain degree of artistry. She is heavily made up. Her eyes are framed by layer upon layer of black kohl. Her hair falls in soft strands, her gaze is provocative, and her mouth is perhaps smiling a little, it is hard to say. She is lying on her back on what appears to be a flat rock, her torso naked, with one hand resting between her breasts. It looks like she is holding something. A pendant, maybe? There is something vulnerable about her whole appearance, something childish in spite of her provocative pose.

"Sara," I say faintly.

"Do you have any idea why Marianne had a photo of Sara?"

I slowly shake my head.

"Have you seen this picture before?"

"No. Never. It's . . ."

I can't finish the sentence, because something ties up my throat. Markus looks at me in silence. Then he nods curtly, as if he knows exactly what I mean.

"Vulnerable, she looks so horribly vulnerable. In the midst of all the provocation," he says, coaxing the photo carefully out of my hands, gently turning it over so that it lies upside down on the table between us. As if to show Sara some respect.

Outside, the rain falls with unabated force.

So it's here, the day I have dreaded for the past week. I run my hand nervously through my hair and rustle aimlessly through the piles of papers on the desk in front of me. Aina's face appears in the doorway. Without making a sound she mouths, "*She's here now.*" I stand up and go to the door to welcome her. She had called and asked for an appointment. I could hardly refuse.

"Hello, welcome. Please sit down." I gesture toward the armchair.

Kerstin Matteus nods and sits down with noticeable exertion on the edge of the seat. She is in her fifties and considerably overweight. She avoids making eye contact with me—back and forth her eyes flutter, looking out across the room and down at the floor, just never at me. Used and worn, her clothes look cheap and appear too tight for her massive body. Her top has a low neckline and I notice that her sun-leathered, wrinkled breasts are squeezed into a bra that is far too small. The dark parting in her hair betrays a bleach job that is growing out. She holds firmly on to a black handbag with big bare patches where the smooth synthetic plastic has flaked. I cannot see any apparent likenesses between her and Sara. How this gigantic woman can be the mother of slender, delicate Sara is beyond me. But then again, she probably didn't take pills for several years, which usually efficiently eliminates all forms of subcutaneous fat.

Suddenly I feel self-conscious. What do you say to a woman who has just lost her child? And does it matter that the child was not five, but twenty-five, and on her way down in a society that was no longer able to take responsibility, no longer able to care about her? A broken person with lousy genes and a difficult childhood. I don't think any of this matters; the pain is bound to be the same.

I clear my throat and look down at my desk.

"Kerstin," I begin carefully. "I am so, so sorry about what happened to Sara. Is there anything I can do to help you? Perhaps you have some questions about . . . about Sara's final days. We did see each other quite a bit and she was really making progress."

I briefly report on the treatment and Sara's progress.

"She was feeling much, much better and had stopped cutting herself. I think she had even met someone, someone she cared about. She talked a bit about you, too, Kerstin. I know she loved you very, very much, even though there were times over the years when you didn't get along."

"Who could possibly have wanted to kill my little Sara?"

She speaks slowly and calmly in a voice that is hoarse and raw from years of smoking, but also with sorrow. Kerstin looks up at my green walls and then over at the window that faces Medborgarplatsen. I don't know if she really expects me to answer her question.

"Well, I'm not with the police. I only know what Sara and I discussed here at the office."

"How can someone do such a thing to another human being?"

Her gaze is still avoiding mine, but in her voice I sense resolve. As if she wants to get to the bottom of something important.

"It must have been an evil person, no?"

For the first time during our conversation she looks up at me, and I nod slowly, incapable of answering her question. *An evil person.* Obviously.

"I don't know," she says, and her eyes fill with tears.

"I don't know . . . how I will cope with this." Her voice becomes shrill and she leans forward, supporting herself with both hands on the little coffee table between our two armchairs. Her head slowly sinks down until her forehead rests against the tablecloth and I notice light red creases in her neck protruding from the back of her sweater. Her weeping is clearly audible now. It is that uncomfortable, uncontrolled kind of weeping. The kind that makes people recoil in terror, the kind that causes tears, saliva, and snot to run in floods. Hopeless, defenseless, unrestrained weeping.

I know it all too well.

"Here," I say, offering her my box of tissues, as if a few Kleenex could alleviate her sorrow.

She doesn't react.

I crouch down carefully before her and softly stroke her coarse, bleached hair. A faint but unmistakable odor of mints mixed with alcohol reaches me in puffs when she sighs.

"It . . . hurts . . . so . . . much."

Every word is an effort.

"I know," I say.

"Does . . . it . . . ever . . . go away?"

"No," I reply. "It never goes away—but eventually, it stops hurting so bad."

Vijay Kumar opens the door with a broad smile. He looks the same as always, with his black mustache and white teeth, and we give each other a warm hug.

How many years has it been? Ten? Is that even possible? Vijay was in grad school with Aina and me. We were always together when we were students. After graduation he stayed at Stockholm University to get a doctorate in psychology. His dissertation was titled "A Comparative Study of Applied Methodologies for Inductive and Deductive Criminal Profiling." I have to admit I never got around to reading it, even though he had several articles based on it published in, for one, the *Journal of Forensic Psychiatry & Psychology.*

"Siri, my dear."

Vijay holds both my hands in his, the way he used to when we hung out in school. Suddenly this public display of affection embarrasses me and I gesture toward Markus.

"Vijay, this is Markus, the policeman I told you about. You spoke on the phone, right?"

"Yes, I was the one who sent you the pictures," Markus says, shaking hands with Vijay.

We follow Vijay's gangly form down the narrow corridor in the Department of Psychology. He is wearing worn jeans and a flower-print shirt. Apparently, as a newly tenured professor, you can wear whatever you want.

His office is small. Books cover the walls from floor to ceiling. Where he ran out of shelves, they are stacked in piles, forming massive, leaning, unsteady towers. It is mostly psychological professional literature, but there are also some books about art and design. I know that Vijay is interested in art. He told me once in confidence that he collects Swedish and Danish constructivists. I remember foolishly nodding as if I knew what a constructivist was and promised not to reveal this secret to anyone. "The Baertling," he had whispered, "that one alone is worth half a million."

In the window, I see a photograph of a blond man in sailing attire standing on a pier. It's Olle, Vijay's Olle. I had forgotten to ask if they were still together when I had called, or perhaps I didn't dare ask. Ten years is a long time, a lot can happen.

Vijay turns off his phone to avoid interruptions and turns toward me.

"So, Siri, darling. From what I understand, you have a serious problem hanging around your neck."

"You think?" I ask.

"Well, that's my understanding anyway," says Vijay, taking out a thick plastic folder with photos and papers.

I glimpse Sara's soft, dead body between his hairy hands. He catches my gaze and carefully closes the folder and sets it on the desk between us.

"First and foremost, I want you to be aware that my remarks are informal in nature. A solid investigation would require considerably more time."

He spreads his arms apologetically and stands up.

"Do you want coffee?"

Without waiting for an answer, he turns on the phone and calls someone to order three cups of coffee.

"Yes, bring milk and sugar. And those snacks with pieces of chocolate in them, you know . . . exactly, chocolate chip cookies."

I imagine the woman at the other end of the line taking Vijay's order—it always seems to be women who do that sort of thing.

"I've gone through the material: Sara's patient records, the pictures from the murder scene—excuse me, the place where the body was found—and the police report."

"So, what do you think?"

Markus looks at Vijay in anticipation.

"Well, profiling is not an exact science. I, or one of my colleagues, cannot exactly describe your suspect. We can only make general statements based on statistically established facts from similar crimes. For example, I can say with ninety-five percent certainty that your perpetrator is a man, because the majority of violent crimes are committed by men. And then, the condition of the crime scene and the nature of the crime indicate that you are dealing with a well-organized, structured individual."

"How do you know that?"

I can sense a slight skepticism in Markus's voice—the same hesitation I felt when I suggested we visit Vijay in the first place. But Vijay doesn't seem to notice; he is used to arguing for his case.

"The crime scene was neat. The perpetrator left no evidence, beyond what he had planned to leave, that is to say, the farewell letter. We usually distinguish between two main groups of perpetrators with this type of crime. There are the disorganized, impulsive ones who literally beat someone to death in the heat of the moment or happen to kill someone when a robbery goes wrong. As a rule, they don't plan the deed in advance, and they often leave lots of physical evidence, like cigarette butts, fingerprints, fibers, body fluids, and so on. Then we have the well-organized, structured ones who plan their deed a long time in advance. These are considerably less common. In this group of perpetrators, there are many different types, everything from sexual sadists to psychopaths. Because they leave behind less evidence and are, well, smarter, you might well say, they are often more difficult to link to the crime."

"So what does this type of murderer look like?" I ask.

"Hmm, if you're speaking in general terms, and not referring specifically to a very organized murderer, as in your case, he is most often young, around twenty to twenty-five, has low socioeconomic status, is unmarried, and is often a substance abuser. He has recently experienced an emotional loss, for example, his girlfriend left him. It is also common that there are several criminals in the immediate family, such as siblings or parents. The typical murderer also often has a long criminal career behind him, despite his young age. It could be anything, but he often has a criminal record. And then there are other, earlier problems, such as pyromania, problems in school, and that sort of thing. Also common. Many have psychiatric problems, like paranoia, depression, or schizophrenia. There are female murderers, too, of course. Studies indicate they have a different background. Often they come from dysfunctional families and have been subjected to assault, although that can apply to men as well."

Vijay's voice has taken on a lecturing tone and it is clear that he is talking about his favorite subject. I know he can continue his lecture endlessly if no one intervenes. I clear my throat to get his attention. Vijay looks at me and smiles wryly. He has understood my message.

"But in this case, not many of the ordinary descriptions apply. This murder has not been performed by a—"

There is a knock at the door and Vijay gets up to open it. A middle-aged woman wearing sturdy boots and a thick moss-green cardigan looks in tentatively.

"Coffee?" she inquires.

Of course, I think, but say nothing. Vijay's words about sexual sadists and psychopaths are gnawing at my insides. *Evil people.* Wasn't that what Kerstin Matteus said?

"So, based on what you know about this perpetrator—our guy—*who is he?*"

Markus leans forward toward Vijay with renewed curiosity.

"I would guess a middle-aged man, highly educated and able to function successfully in social situations. The farewell letter is well written and lacks misspellings and that sort of thing. It indicates a socially adapted individual. The crime seems well planned and the crime scene—excuse me, the place where the body was found—lacks physical traces. This indicates that he is intelligent and can plan in advance. Then he seems to have the capacity to emotionally shield himself from the victim, that is, he is a coldhearted bastard. The victim is only a chess piece in his game, a person he can do without. He is *a man with a mission.* Based on what you have told me about what happened after the murder, I believe the crime is not aimed at Sara, but at you, Siri."

Vijay looks at me searchingly.

"No," I say and answer the question he hasn't asked. "No one would want to harm me in that way."

"That's what you think," Vijay says cheerfully, popping a cookie in his mouth.

"When you figure out who the perpetrator is, I think the motive is going to be personal, very personal. Someone you offended or whose toes you stepped on earlier in your life. Someone who feels that you have treated him unjustly. *A perceived injustice.*"

"What do you mean?" I ask uncertainly.

"I mean that even though you can't immediately think of anyone who hates you enough to kill, you will understand his motive when the whole picture becomes clear to you. Remember that the injustice that may have caused this is simply a *perceived* injustice. A normal, healthy person perhaps would not think you had done anything wrong. Or at least would not be prepared to kill because of it. It may be someone you rejected sexually or someone who feels wronged by you in some other way. Perhaps a patient who thinks you're incompetent? Someone who is easily offended."

"How can you be so sure it's personal?" I ask.

"As I said in the beginning, you can never be one hundred percent certain in this job. But there is a lot that indicates that the crime is aimed at you. For example, the body was found on your property, below the pier, where you swim every day. Right?"

I nod.

"Besides, this so-called farewell letter is nothing but a long finger pointed right at you. Sara's finger, from the other side. And then the other letter to, what was her name? The anorexic, excuse me, the bulimic."

I study Vijay in silence. He doesn't know everything. I haven't told him about the DUI. It's just too embarrassing.

"I'd like to know," I begin, "if this person hates me enough to kill, why not attack me directly? Kill me?"

"Ahh, *that* is an interesting question," Vijay replies, smiling broadly.

He brings his index fingers together and leans back pensively in his chair.

"I think he wants you to suffer. The way he thinks he has suffered. He wants to see you shamed, deprived of all dignity, your position taken away from you. If he had killed you right off, he wouldn't have achieved that, would he?"

"And now?" My voice is only a whisper.

"Yes, the risk is probably pretty great that the situation will escalate. He didn't achieve what he wanted with Sara's murder. I would be careful, Siri, *very careful,* if I were you."

I sit, speechless, incapable of uttering anything as silence settles in the room. Through the small window I can see students, or perhaps teachers—it's hard to tell the difference these days—leaning against the wall, smoking. A guy in a knit cap comes toward the small group of smokers. His T-shirt says INSTANT ASSHOLE—JUST ADD ALCOHOL. Students, I decide.

"Do I know him?"

"It's possible. In any case, I'm pretty sure that you have some kind of relationship or connection to him."

"How do you know that?"

"The letter contains information that not just anyone could have about you. Furthermore, the crime is extremely personal per se. It's you, your person, he wants to get at."

"Could he be a colleague of mine?"

Vijay shrugs. "I assume it's a possibility."

He must see how discouraged we feel, because he says, "Don't lose hope now. Try to think, Siri, who could want to harm you? Combine that knowledge with what you know that I'm not aware of, that is, who could have had the opportunity to carry out the crime and have access to the information that it required. There, you have your perpetrator."

"Vijay, what should I do?"

My voice fades away.

"I'm afraid you'll have to ask Markus that."

I look at Markus, but his gaze is lost in the distance, out the window and over toward the horizon.

We leave the office and walk back toward our car. Vijay accompanies us.

"Vijay, tell me, how do you cope with . . . all this? The death, all the evil you see?"

"Well, now, I don't think about it in terms of good and evil. Besides, people would murder and torment each other just as much even if I didn't exist. It doesn't go away just because you close your eyes. As I see it, maybe I can make a difference. Maybe I can discover something that leads to a criminal being arrested, that prevents him or her from committing more crimes. That protects an innocent person. That's enough for me. If I've saved one person, I'm satisfied."

Vijay pauses and lights a cigarette.

"But I must admit it's hard to talk with victims' relatives. It gets under my skin, the realization of how . . . how fragile life is."

He suddenly looks older, huddled up against the wind, with the cigarette in his hand. Deep creases run from his nose down toward the corners of his mouth. His mustache has streaks of gray in it and his shirt is a little tight around his belly. Why didn't I notice before? Taken out of his context, the liberal academic environment, Vijay suddenly appears lost, like any man taking his first steps toward middle age. I feel a sudden tenderness for him as we say good-bye. This time the hug is longer and more intimate. I burrow my nose down in his flower-print shirt and take in the aroma of aftershave, cigarette smoke, and sweat.

"Take care of her," Vijay says slowly, looking at Markus for a moment before he turns and goes back into the massive red-brown brick building.

Date: October 12
Time: 4:00 p.m.
Place: Green Room, the clinic
Patient: Charlotte Mimer

"Bloody hell!"

Charlotte is rocking back and forth, her slender arms around her knees, which are drawn up on the chair. Her hair is unwashed and plastered against her cheeks soaked with tears. Her glasses, which she doesn't usually wear, are so fogged up I can't see her eyes, and the obligatory suit has been replaced by a gray tracksuit.

Although she was the one who wanted to end therapy, she called yesterday and asked to come back because she was feeling so bad. We booked her for an emergency appointment today.

"What happened?"

I lean toward her, pushing the box of Kleenex to her side of the table. She nods and hesitantly takes a tissue. The cold light of the fluorescent bulb and the room's green walls are reflected in her pale face. She looks sick and haggard, cowering in my armchair.

"I told my boss straight to his face. That I knew he was screwing Sanna. That I thought he was a pathetic creep. That he ought to be happy that such a young, smart girl wants to sleep with him even though he is such a loser. I quit my job. Did I already say that?"

Charlotte takes off her glasses and rubs away the steam as she looks searchingly at me, as if I had the solution to her problems at my fingertips. But all I can do is nod encouragingly to get her to continue talking.

Through the wall I can hear Sven, who has kitchen duty this week, unloading the little dishwasher. All the silverware is being tossed resolutely with a clattering thud into a drawer, even though Aina and I are always nagging him to sort them properly.

"Did I say that I quit my job?"

I nod at her. She is still frenetically rubbing her eyeglasses against her speckled-gray sweatpants, as if trying to remove an invisible but intolerable stain.

I take a deep breath before speaking. "I think it's best if you tell me what happened from the beginning. When did this happen?"

Charlotte blows her nose noisily in a paper tissue, and sets it on the table before she resumes rocking back and forth on the chair.

"It was . . . uh . . . the day before yesterday. We had a performance review, that is, *he* had a performance review with me."

Charlotte grimaces and the tears rise again. I lean over and gently stroke her arm.

"Take your time. It's okay."

She shakes her head. "It's *not* okay. I don't have a job anymore."

These words are just a whisper.

"Wait a moment. Let's take it from the beginning. You had a performance review."

"*He* had a performance review. *With me.*"

Charlotte, as usual, is careful to get the details correct, even in her distress. She sighs, slowly and dejectedly shaking her head. When she continues she speaks deliberately, with exaggerated clarity, articulating every word as if I were a child.

Or perhaps simply not very clever.

"And. He. Said. A. Lot. Of. Shit. That. Doesn't. Make. Sense."

"Like what?"

"That I wasn't sufficiently proactive. That I have to learn to take ownership of my area of responsibility in a more proactive way. Uhh . . . There's no point in explaining. You wouldn't understand anyway . . ."

I feel a sting of irritation at being dismissed by my patient but let it pass without comment.

"He said I had to develop my leadership skills. That I wasn't ready yet for a promotion. In brief: a lot of bullshit. It doesn't make sense. It's so unfair. I've given up . . . everything. And then that pretentious piece of shit stands there and criticizes me for no reason at all. When he himself . . . Although he himself . . ."

Charlotte sobs, unable to finish her sentence.

"Although he himself what? Tell me, Charlotte."

Charlotte hesitates and massages her calf with one hand while she wipes away tears and blows her nose with the other.

"Although he himself is a horny loser who is screwing a subordinate, even though it's against all the rules."

"So what did you do?"

"I already told you. I said to him that I knew what he was doing. What I thought about it. And now I don't have a job."

"Did he fire you?"

"Of course he didn't. I quit."

"But . . . but why? It's not your fault that he made a mistake."

My hand is still resting against the rough cotton of her hoodie. Now and then, I press Charlotte's arm consolingly.

"I couldn't stay there after I said those things to him," says Charlotte, shaking her head again, making damp, brown strands of hair dance around her face.

"But really, think about it, Charlotte, he's the one who has done wrong. And just because you pointed that out—even if you were too direct—why does this mean that *you* have to give notice?"

"I know . . . I'm just a hopeless case . . ."

Now Charlotte is crying loudly, her face buried against her knees, emitting little sounds like a captured animal. I stroke her arm again and glance up at the clock: ten minutes left, time to wrap up.

"That's not what I meant, Charlotte. I'm just saying that you didn't do anything wrong."

"That doesn't matter anymore." Charlotte's voice is flat and nasal.

"Listen, I think that . . . perhaps it's useful for you to actually allow yourself to lose control sometimes. You know, so much in your life is about control."

Charlotte instantly freezes and in one second she turns into a block of ice.

"I don't have a JOB. Don't you get what I'm saying? And it's *your* fault. You witch!"

I abruptly let go of her arm and stand up. Surprised at my own reaction, I am suddenly not sure who she is, this sobbing, red-faced woman in a tracksuit, sitting in front of me. Perhaps there is something about her I've missed. Perhaps I've opened a door to something dark and forbidden.

Charlotte jumps out of her chair and rushes toward me.

"Forgive me, I don't know what got into me. *Forgive me. Forgive me.*"

She throws her thin but surprisingly strong arms around me and hugs me tight, real tight. As if I were her last straw. Maybe I am?

Her cheek is wet against my throat and I feel her breath on my neck. We remain standing there like a couple in a dance, frozen in midstep, in time and space.

It's dark outside and I can see our image mirrored in the black window. I see the fragile child in Charlotte, see the sinewy, tree-climbing arms, the apple-picking arms, that are squeezing my body, but I also see something else in her eyes. Something that makes the hairs on my neck stand up.

Suddenly, with a surprisingly controlled, soft voice, Charlotte says, "Siri . . . am I going crazy?"

I see him every day at the practice, at the coffeemaker, by the copy machine, in the reception area. His gray-streaked hair and mandatory corduroy jacket—he seems to have one in every color. Sometimes I meet his gaze and cannot keep from wondering whether he can see it in my eyes.

The fear.

Sven, Aina, and I move around the clinic like a group of strangers. All painfully aware that nothing can return to the way it was before.

We don't talk about what happened to Marianne and what has been happening to me. In order to stick together, to cope with the practice, the patients, and everything else, we have to keep silent. Not mention what we are all thinking. It's simply too dangerous to talk about.

The emptiness Marianne has left behind is almost tangible. Her scent in the restroom, the neat little notes in my calendar. *"Anneli Asplund 12:00—remember to bring the needles!"* Her clothes in the small closet: pink crocheted sweaters, flowered scarves, all hanging on the padded clothes hangers in impeccable order. On the hanger at the far right is a little blue cloth bag filled with lavender. For the scent. So tidy, such focus on small details, so very Marianne.

I have a strong desire to see her, to hold her hand for a while. But Marianne cannot have visitors. She is still lying unconscious at the hospital. "No point visiting yet," the nurse said when I called.

And at the practice, we continue our nervous avoidance, our worried dance through consultation rooms and corridors, our hands filled with papers and coffee cups, as if this makes us appear focused and professional.

Aina and I have talked about Sven. Neither of us really suspects him of being involved in Sara's murder. Neither of us ever saw him even talk with Sara. But neither I nor Aina can ignore the facts. Sven is one of a few people who knew enough about Sara's therapy to be able to credibly forge her farewell letter, with all its references to my conversations with her. He knows where I live and even that I am in the habit of swimming every day between the rocks and the pier. He knows that Charlotte Mimer is my patient and has access to her address. Sven might very well have been able to send her the letter that warned her about me. But, most serious of all, there are his handwritten notes on Sara's records in Marianne's kitchen. And the photo. The photo of Sara on the cliffs. Did Sven take that, too?

I know that the police have questioned him. Many times. Markus does not want to go into what they have concluded but hints that it isn't much. "It's like interrogating a pinecone," he said. "He sits there staring down at his damn Birkenstocks and doesn't say a thing, I mean literally NOTHING of value." Markus hints that even if they have no evidence against Sven, there are gaps in his alibi. Hours when he can't explain where he was, when no one can remember whether they saw him, not even Birgitta, despite Sven's claims that they were together.

Sven is a lot of things, but a murderer? But who could it be otherwise? Peter Carlsson? Could he be Sara's secret friend? Could Sara have perceived him as middle aged? Nothing seems to add up. Peter has a set of psychological problems that perhaps makes him suspicious in this case, and he knows that Charlotte Mimer is my patient. But that's where the similarities between him and the murderer end. He can't possibly know where I live. Nor can he know about Sara's and my conversations. Unless he was Sara's secret boyfriend and she confided everything we talked about to him, but that doesn't seem likely—the references in the farewell letter are far too accurate. The person who wrote that knew exactly what we had talked about and when. Dates and times, it's all there.

Besides, and this worries me more than anything else, what motive would Peter Carlsson have, or Sven? Vijay had said *a perceived injustice.* I have, as far as I can recall, never met Peter before in my life. And Sven? Does he hate me because I am a successful woman? Do I personify what hobbled his career and made him stagnate at a little practice on Söder? *A woman hater,* married to one of the world's most prominent researchers in gender studies? *An evil person?* I can't believe it.

I think about the voice on the phone that evening when the police caught me; I try to remember what it sounded like. It didn't sound familiar. It definitely didn't sound like Sven. Or Peter.

That leaves Aina and Marianne. Not even in all my most paranoid moments could I imagine that Aina or Marianne is involved in this. But who else has the knowledge? The knowledge of my conversations with Sara, information about where I live, Charlotte's address? Who knows about my swims by the old crooked pier?

I am getting nowhere and it makes me insanely frustrated. There must be something . . . something I've forgotten. One crucial detail.

I try to analyze the problem from another angle: the motive. *The perceived injustice.* Is there some rejected lover, some passed-over colleague, or offended patient that I have repressed in my past? No matter how hard I try to remember, I can't think of anyone. And then there is another problem, of course. Even if there was a person who, for some reason, wants to take revenge, how could he have access to all the information he needed to carry out the crime? Patient records, addresses . . . Another dead end.

Perhaps there is someone else who has access to the office and our patient records and notes. I made a list of all the outsiders who have been on the premises in the past six months and submitted it to Markus. It was depressingly short, consisting of only the cleaning company and the IT guy.

The cleaning company is a Greek family. I know them all personally and they clean during office hours, which makes it unlikely that they would be able to smuggle patient records out of the office. The computer technician's name is Ronny and he is from Örkelljunga. I have only spoken with him on the phone and I have a very, very hard time believing he could be involved. I'm not even sure our patient records were in the office when he was last here.

This uncertainty creates a vacuum. A waiting period.

Calm before the storm.

Out of nowhere, he was suddenly standing there with his silly little dog on a leash. He was in his midthirties. Neatly dressed, everything he wore was from the best brands, discreet, and with style. Even though darkness had already started to settle over the bay, I could see how freshly scrubbed and together he looked, like a Christmas pig with plump, rosy cheeks and a round belly that bulged out over the black jeans. He probably had a wife who was fattening him up and two snot-nosed kids up in one of those vulgar McMansions a little farther east on the bay.

"Um, excuse me, sorry, I didn't mean to disturb," the man began in a painfully nasal voice, "but . . ." He held back the little spotted dog who was growling, his ears drawn back and showing his teeth. "I was just wondering . . . I mean, I've seen you several times here on the cliffs when I was out walking with my dog. Do you live around here or something?"

The man's question sounded like an accusation. I did not reply but instead sat up in the sleeping bag I had laid down under a pine tree by the edge of the cliffs for the evening.

"Do you live in the house down there . . . ? Because . . . uh . . . as far as I know a single woman lives there. Or . . . ?"

The man's voice petered out, he was noticeably nervous now. He stood there balancing on his toes, raising himself up and down with small, jerky motions. If he were smart, he would have left at this point, back into the darkness, disappearing forever, but he stood there sheepishly on the trail as if he was expecting some kind of reward for his behavior.

"Does she know you're sleeping here?"

I climbed out of the sleeping bag without answering and reached for the blue backpack I always have with me.

"All I'm saying is . . . even if you don't have anywhere else to go, this isn't the best . . ."

I rooted around in my backpack among ropes, plastic bags, and masking *tape until I found it. My field knife has a broad, sharp blade of shiny-blue steel and is serrated along one side. With a practiced, imperceptible movement I hid it up my sleeve, stood up, and started slowly walking toward the self-righteous man with the silly little dog. The morality police on an evening walk.*

"This is not a camping site," the man explained emphatically, as if he was trying to convince himself of what he had just said.

"And I'm not a camper," I replied, and with two quick leaps I was upon him, and he instinctively grabbed on to the tree behind him, as if seeking support.

As a result, he was now perfectly positioned between the tree and my field knife.

With a single motion I slit open his protruding belly, from the navel to the sternum. Something foul smelling and organic seeped out with a sigh as the man fell to the ground without a word, his back still resting against the large pine behind him.

I tugged at the leash and pulled the growling little dog toward me to silence it. But the cut that wounded the dog in the neck also freed its collar, and with a stifled, wheezing bark, it disappeared into the night.

It is evening. Outside my cottage, solid darkness has set in and I can hear the autumn winds chasing across the cliffs. All the lights are on and my big flashlight is always within reach, to be safe. I am curled up on my couch. There's an empty plate on the table, still sticky from ketchup and food scraps, and in my hand I have my obligatory wineglass.

Ziggy's food bowl remains empty by the front door. I have decided not to put food out this evening, because I understand now he is not coming back, even if I sometimes think I hear the sound of his soft paws at night.

The floor is covered with videotapes from my patient sessions, all dated and marked in Marianne's neat handwriting. I rub my eyes. I'm trying to find a clue here. Is it even possible? Is there anything in all these conversations, in these hundreds of hours that might explain what is happening? A word, an unconscious gesture, or a revealing look?

I fast-forward to one of my conversations with Peter. Arms wave spastically at double speed. His head jumps up and down. He is constantly adjusting his tie. People's tics become so obvious when you play them at double velocity. I stop the tape.

I feel faint. Peter's face is frozen in a grimace on the flickering TV screen. His eyes are vacant. *An evil person?* I take a gulp of wine to calm myself and fast-forward a little farther.

> *"How do these images make you feel, in retrospect?"*
> *"I'm so afraid. What if I were to actually lose control and do her harm? I do love her. These thoughts make me feel* loathesome, *like a damn* sex *criminal. I really don't want to hurt her."*
> *"Do you enjoy these fantasies?"*
> *"Enjoy them? No, I don't* enjoy *them. I want to be rid of them. I wish they didn't exist. That's why I'm asking for help. To make them disappear."*

"What do you do, if anything, to try to make them go away?"

"I stopped having sex. If I don't sleep with my girlfriend, the thoughts don't come in the same way. But . . . what woman wants to be with a man who won't have sex with her?"

I am reminded of Sara and how her new man didn't want to sleep with her. How much the absence of physical intimacy confused her and made her feel inadequate. For someone who understood a woman's worth as her ability to attract men, the consequences are crystal-clear: She's not woman enough.

I sink to my knees among the videotapes, searching for the conversation with Sara that touches on this particular subject. My hands are uncertain and I know that once again I've had a little too much wine this evening. It takes me a few minutes to find the right tape.

"It could be anything, from fear of not measuring up sexually, I mean, you're attractive and young and so on, to physical ailments and emotional blocks. What do you think? After all, you're the one who knows him best."

"I don't think anything. Okay, it's like this . . . it's like he's carrying a lot of . . . anger. As if he's really angry . . . inside, and it comes out when we start getting close, physically close, that is."

I rewind a little. Sara moves jerkily backward in the consultation room and takes an extinguished cigarette from the ashtray and brings it to her mouth.

"But I think he wants to, though something is holding him back. I mean, I can tell he wants to, but he pulls back when it's about to happen. He gets almost . . . he gets almost angry. How can that make him angry?"

I rewind again and force Sara to pick up the extinguished cigarette once more.

"He gets almost . . . he gets almost angry. *How can that make him angry?"*

I stop the tape and Sara freezes as she walks across the room—for a moment it looks like she is hovering above the floor. Like an angel. A nicotine-dependent angel with blond ringlets and scarred forearms.

Why would Sara's efforts at seduction provoke this guy to the degree that it made him angry? Why does a middle-aged man buy expensive gifts for a young woman and then get angry when she wants to get close to him? What type of relationship is he looking for? An older man, a younger woman—almost still a girl—platonic love, gifts, father and daughter. Could it be that simple? Was he looking for someone who could be his daughter?

Suddenly, I remember something Sara said in one of our last conversations. I dig around again among the videotapes on the floor until I find it. I insert the tape and fast-forward several minutes. Sara looks unusually neat. A black top hangs loose on her thin upper body, and there are no holes or patches on her jeans. She has no makeup on and her hair is in a ponytail. She looks considerably younger than twenty-five. Sure, I think, she could pass as someone's teenage daughter.

"He likes it when I open them. Meaning, he wants to watch as I take off the wrapping paper and all that—because the gifts are always nicely wrapped, with gold ribbon and that kind of thing. Yesterday I got one of those down vests, you know, with leather on the outside."

"It doesn't make you uncomfortable when he gives you so many things?"

"Why should it?"

"Well, for example, because maybe he wants something from you in return."

"Like what?"

"Well, what do you think?"

"At any rate, not . . ." (Sara mumbles something inaudibly.)

"What did you say?"

"At any rate not sex! He doesn't want me . . . " (Sara sniffs.)

"Here." (I hand Sara the tissues.)

"He doesn't want me and he says it's because I remind him too much of someone . . ."

"Of who, Sara?"

"I don't know, his daughter maybe."

"Does he have a daughter?"

"He doesn't want to talk about it. He refuses to talk about her."

"But he says that you remind him of someone? Of her?"

"Hmm."

I pause and close my eyes. So Sara's boyfriend and presumably also her murderer is a middle-aged dad with a grudge against me and an in at the office? And the reason he avoids physical intimacy with Sara is that she reminds him too much of his daughter. That's just what he wants, to get close to her in the same way a parent does. Loving her like his child. All her attempts at seduction are therefore refused with disgust. Who is this man? Obviously a disturbed person, but still intelligent enough to conceal his intentions and lead what appears to be normal life. I look at the clock. Ten forty-five. Too late to call Vijay.

Then I hear it—a gurgling, growling sound and then a dull thud, coming from outside. I'm not scared; I'm simply surprised, as it doesn't sound like a human noise. Still, my legs barely hold as I slowly try to stand up and peer out through the black windows toward the sea.

The darkness out there is as impenetrable as a concrete wall. The room is bathed in a bright light that effectively prevents me from seeing what's outside. Quickly, I reach for the light switch and squeeze my eyes shut. I've done it a hundred times before, but I still don't like it. I turn off the lights and slowly accustom my eyes to the darkness. The outlines of the room emerge, summoned at first from memory rather than seen.

There! A shadow is moving outside my window. I see it clearly—the silhouette of a person disappearing in the faded rosebushes. I don't need to see more. With a quick movement, I turn the lights back on.

Someone was in my garden, right outside my house. A man? Maybe he had even pressed his face against the window and watched me as I sat on the floor with my eyes glued to the TV. Perhaps he was looking at Sara?

The thought makes me sick to my stomach.

I wait a long time before I carefully crack open the patio door to look out. The waves and the wind are all I can hear. The raw chill in the night air feels like a damp breath against my body. The sky is black and I can discern neither trees nor cliffs, only the faint glistening in the sea.

The light from the living room illuminates a little patch of grass in front of the house and glistens on what at first I think is a piece of black plastic but then realize is a dark, wet spot. I let go of the door, which immediately blows wide open in the wind, and go carefully down the cold wooden steps toward the grass.

Crouching, I bring my hand toward the spot and think I must be mistaken when I sense heat radiate up from the ground. But when I look more carefully, I can see a fine steam rising—wet, slippery, like light fog on a summer morning. I touch the spot gingerly and look at my fingers.

It is blood.

Markus does the same things he always does when I call him over in the middle of the night. He wraps me up carefully in the blanket, brews strong coffee, and makes the necessary phone calls. In this case, he sends for technicians to investigate the blood.

I don't say much. A chill has spread inside me that no blankets or hot drinks can relieve. It is as if I only just realized that someone actually wants to hurt me. What have I done to cause all this? What is my guilt, and how can it be atoned for? When and where did this chain of events begin? And, most important of all, how can I stop it? Because I no longer doubt that there is more to this story and an ending that I'm not sure I want to see.

A perceived injustice. Let he who is without guilt cast the first stone. Am I that, without guilt? Who bears the guilt that Sara's life was so difficult? Who bears the guilt for her death? Her family, herself, society, the murderer—*an evil person*—or maybe me? And how can I be sure that I am completely without guilt, just because I never wanted to hurt her? *It's just like with Stefan,* is all I can think. I fall asleep on the couch with the blanket pulled all the way up to my nose and the untouched coffee cup abandoned on the table.

"Time to wake up yet?" Markus looks contented, sitting there on my couch in a hoodie and jeans.

"What time is it?"

"Ten thirty. I thought you needed to sleep. The technicians were here, worked for three hours, had coffee in your kitchen, and went home."

"I'm sorry I—"

"You don't need to apologize. It was animal blood, by the way, not human blood."

"What kind of animal?"

"They don't know yet, but I imagine it was an injured animal you heard out there last night."

"But I did see someone."

"Yes, I know, but it's incredibly easy to see wrong. You were afraid. It was dark. Maybe it was a deer."

"A deer?"

"Yes, or a badger. There are a lot of badgers here. May have been a badger that was hit by a car—"

"But nobody drives by here," I interrupt him, annoyed.

"Either way, I wouldn't worry too much about it."

Markus goes to the kitchen and starts looking around in the cupboards. I can see his blond hair through the doorway. Outside, the sun is shining. It is a lovely day and the little bay is framed by fall leaves that have changed to every color from lemon-yellow to ocher and reddish-brown. The sea lies peacefully.

"Don't you have *anything* to eat?"

"There's a little bread in the freezer. Maybe some cheese, too, I'm not sure."

"There's not a thing here. What do you actually live on?"

"We have to talk."

"Sure," says Markus as he continues to dig around in my kitchen. I'm not completely comfortable with him snooping around in my cupboards and drawers, so I raise my voice a little.

"I mean *really* talk. I found things in the videotapes yesterday that I think are important."

Markus comes out of the kitchen, a pepper and two apples in his hand.

"Tell me," he says, sitting beside me on the couch.

And I tell him. That Sara's boyfriend was possibly looking for a father-daughter relationship, or happened to end up in one. About the segment where Sara suggests that he has a child, a daughter who resembles her. Markus listens attentively. He and his colleagues have watched all the tapes but had not noticed this in particular, he says.

Finally, I also share my thoughts about guilt, that I wonder if I am guilty, directly or indirectly, in what happened to Sara and Marianne. I don't mention Stefan. It's still too hard to talk about.

I expected him to dismiss my concerns and say that it's obviously not my fault, but instead he simply shrugs and looks out the window.

"I guess we're in the same boat."

"You and me?"

"Everyone. All people," he explains, biting into one of the apples. "Everything we do. All the actions we take without being able to foresee the consequences. All the complicated connections between events, relationships between people. You pull on a thread at one end, and someone drops down dead on the other. It's not anyone's fault—or maybe it's everyone's? But to me, the *intent* is more important than the *cause*. The cause is mechanical, the intent has a direction, a force of its own."

I take the other apple from his hand and bite off a piece without saying anything. His comment surprises me. In some way, I hadn't expected him to deliver such a well-reasoned, well-formulated insight. Somehow I had assumed that he was less sophisticated.

Banal.

A man who doesn't require a user's manual. A man whose reactions to any situation in life can be foreseen. And fended off, if necessary.

"Whatever," says Markus, looking at me, his eyes red from the night's work.

"There's one thing I'm still wondering about. Marianne, she's still unconscious. I need to ask you and your associates about her in order to form a better picture of who she is and how she lives. What did she do in her free time, for example?"

"I don't really know. Isn't that strange? You see someone every day, and even so, you never get to know her. Not really."

"Happens all the time."

"I think the one who knew Marianne best was Christer, her boyfriend."

"What do you know about him?"

"Not very much. Marianne describes him as friendly and, well . . ."

supportive. He has certainly been a big help to her in her career, or whatever you want to call it. Listens to her and understands her and so on. I think he is, or was, in finance."

"Yes, he said that. What is your impression of him?"

"Well, I don't know. It's not like I know him very well. I've only met him a few times. But he seems intelligent and . . . sensitive, maybe. He seems to take an interest in several things—music, art. Smart enough not to seem pretentious, even if he is . . . uh, you know."

Markus doesn't answer. He just bites into the apple again and looks out over the sea.

That night I dream about Stefan again. I feel his presence strongly, his scent is with me in my nostrils, his skin just out of reach of my hands, but he isn't there. Sweaty and in a panic, as if I have a fever, I rush around the cottage and on the property to find him. I raise the thorny branches of the rosebushes, heavy with dark violet buds ready to burst open. I wander among the pine trees, stumble in the thicket, and fall. The damp, soft hair-cap moss gently catches my body.

On the rocks, I stop and look out over the sea, which has a peculiar coppery color. When I turn my gaze toward the sky, I realize that it has given the sea its color; brown-red and ominous, it presses down over the bay. I walk down to my crooked, tarred little pier and hesitantly take a few steps out onto the brittle boards, already aware of what I will find: Stefan resting peacefully on his back in the glistening copper water. A bunch of seaweed forms a soft, billowing pillow whose fringes caress his cheeks like a thousand gentle fingers.

"I miss you," I say. "It's always the same. I miss you and you aren't here."

Stefan's thin blue-white eyelids look like they are made of rice paper. They flutter; he opens his eyes and looks right at me.

"But, Siri dear, do you still not understand? Don't you get why I had to go?"

I'm thinking about talking to Sven. Markus has warned me against this; he doesn't want me talking to anyone the police have questioned. He would prefer that I move in with Aina and take a sick leave. "Get out of the game," was how he put it. But instead I'm back at the office, walking down the corridor toward the room we call the Yellow Room.

Sven's room.

He is sitting with his back to the door. A rust-brown corduroy jacket is tossed over his chair. His desk is covered with stacks of professional journals, notepads, and loose sheets of paper, which I recognize as case files that shouldn't be there. Coffee cups, ashtrays, and apple cores are balanced on top of everything. Sven is a good therapist but a lousy administrator. In Marianne's absence, his office and case files have devolved into chaos.

"Sven, do you have a moment?"

Sven swings around on his chair, and from his eyes I can tell that he is surprised; perhaps my presence frightens him.

"Of course, sit down."

He makes a gesture toward the visitor's chair, which is full of papers and folders. For a minute I lose patience with him and his mess. Maybe Marianne had nothing against picking up after him, but neither Aina nor I have any intention of doing it.

"And where is it exactly you suggest I sit?"

It wasn't my purpose, but I can hear the harshness and sarcasm in my voice. Sven leaps up out of the chair.

"I'm so sorry."

As he clears the folders and papers, I notice that his hands are shaking. Some sheets of paper fly to the floor and end up under the bookshelf. Finally he seems to give up. He places all the papers in a big pile on the floor, sinks down in his chair, and takes out cigarettes. It occurs to me that I actually prefer them to his pipe. I sit across from him and look directly at him. How can it be possible? Self-assured, shrewd Sven reduced to a chain-smoking bundle of nerves.

"We have to talk," I say.

"I suppose we do."

"Sven," I begin hesitantly, "you are one of a few people who had access to Charlotte's address, Sara's case records—"

Sven interrupts me with a desperate tone of voice. I notice that his hands, yellow from the nicotine, are still shaking as he speaks.

"Siri, you have to trust me. I *absolutely* did not sneak into your garden at night, I didn't send a letter to Charlotte Mimer or . . . or kill Sara Matteus. How can you even think . . . I can understand . . . I can understand how it might look from the outside, but *good Lord,* how long have we known each other? Do you seriously think I'm involved in . . . in all this?"

I sigh heavily and look up at Sven. Fear fills his eyes as he looks at me across his small desk.

"No, I can't seriously believe you are involved. Or rather, I don't know what to believe anymore. Can you please explain one thing to me, Sven: How come your handwriting was in Sara's case files? Which were in Marianne's kitchen to boot?"

Sven furrows his brow and hesitates for a moment.

"I borrowed Sara's file a couple of months ago. I wanted to use it for that article I'm working on, you know, the one about self-injuring behavior in young women. I made copies of a few pages and, sure, I made notes on them. There's nothing strange about that. Or is there? What I don't understand is how my papers ended up at Marianne's."

"And the photo?"

Sven shakes his head and suddenly looks profoundly sad.

"I had never seen it before the police showed it to me. There was something terribly sad about that picture. Don't you think?"

He shrugs, as if to underline that he really has nothing to do with it.

"You have to believe me, Siri. I don't know what else to say. My life has become hell. The police have interrogated me *and my wife.* They've called my friends to ask them what kind of person I am. I can tell from their eyes that they think I'm lying. What do you do when someone has decided you're a liar? How do you convince them you're innocent? Where do you turn when you run out of arguments? How can I convince *you*?"

"By being honest."

"I am being honest."

"Where were you when Sara died? Birgitta said you weren't at home."

Sven sighs deeply and buries his head in his hands, mumbling something at the floor.

"At home. I was at home. With Birgitta."

"But . . . ?"

"I don't know!"

Sven suddenly leaps up from his chair and starts pacing back and forth nervously across the room, the lit cigarette still in his hand. He looks at me with a resigned, almost desperate expression. His eyes wide, his gaze fixed on me the entire time. His whole body is quivering with nervous energy and I can see patches of sweat spreading under his armpits.

"I don't know why. I can't understand it. Why she won't give me an alibi. She's lying to the police. Why, Siri? Why? Can you give me a single reason?"

I think I can, easily, but I say nothing. Instead, I observe Sven in silence.

"Twenty-three years. My goodness, we've been married for twenty-three years. And then she does this. I don't understand it."

"You don't suppose maybe Birgitta could be upset about your . . . affairs with other women," I attempt.

Sven looks at me with something like fury in his eyes. He is almost screaming, and small drops of saliva are hitting me in the face as he leans forward.

"Damn it, Siri. That has nothing to do with you. There must be some things that can remain private in this awful story. It has nothing to do with you. It's private."

Sven straightens up and remains standing a few feet away from me. He seems calmer now that he's been able to take out his anger on me. He still has a little self-esteem left.

Integrity.

And, of course, he's right, I have nothing to do with his affairs. Without saying a word, he puts out the cigarette in an apple core, grabs his corduroy jacket, and leaves the room.

I didn't expect it to be so heavy.

After I finally caught and killed the little runaway dog outside her house, I carefully wrapped both the man and the dog in the black plastic bags I always have on hand. The bags weren't long enough to cover the whole body, not even when I forced it into a fetal position, so I had to overlap the bags. I slipped two over the man's head, which reached his hips, and slipped two more bags over his feet and legs. That covered him up to the waist. The dog had to lie by his feet. There was more room down there. Then I sealed the package with many rounds of light-brown packing tape—at the seam and around the waist, throat, and ankles.

The plan was simple.

Now I only needed to drag the package a few hundred yards along the trail to the small natural harbor where a few small boats are moored by the abandoned pier. I would row out and dump the body, wrapped in an anchor chain, at a safe distance from the shore. But I had underestimated the exertion that was required to pull a grown man so far. Several times, I sank down to my knees from exhaustion, a claustrophobic feeling welling in my chest. This always happens when my air passages tighten and refuse to let air pass. I breathed in puffs from my inhaler and worried that, for the first time, everything had not gone as planned.

I had made a mistake and risked everything.

It's a good year for mushrooms. All through the fall, the forest around my cottage has been filled with brown, stately porcini, slippery Jacks, and orange birch boletes that looked like spilled oranges in the hair-cap moss under the clothesline.

I am sitting on the wooden step outside my French windows with a basket between my knees, cleaning chanterelles. Aina is standing in front of the shed, chopping wood. She has taken off her thick sweater and through her thin cotton top I can see her sinewy, muscular body and large breasts as she cuts the damp wood with powerful, exact movements. I never would have thought that Aina could chop wood, but once again she surprised me. As if she could hear what I was thinking, she grins broadly and puts the ax down in the grass next to the woodpile, dries the sweat from her forehead, and walks over to me. I tell her she should put the ax in the shed, but Aina only smiles.

"I'll do it later, princess."

I tell her that I would rather she did it right away because I know that otherwise it won't happen at all. But Aina only shrugs and smiles.

"I promise to do it, but first I want to go for a swim."

She pulls off her top, trousers, and panties, throws them in the grass beside me and runs toward the rocks. Reluctantly, I set aside the mushrooms and follow her to the water. A swim doesn't appeal to me today. The temperature has fallen well below fifty, the sky is solid gray, and a northerly wind rushes over the sea, adorning the waves with small, white, foaming crests. But after standing there on the rocks, looking out over the dark water, watching the yellow-brown kelp and the fall leaves that have gathered in the water, and hearing the gulls circling curiously above us, I slowly undress and move carefully to the far end of the rock ledge.

Aina lets out a howl as she throws herself from the rocks down into the ice-cold water, making me wince. We hardly spoke to each other today. We've let the silence fill the morning, the forest's sounds speak for us: the persistent knocking of the woodpecker for larvae in the bark of a tall spruce, the branches snapping under our rubber boots, and the buzzing of insects impossible to see with the naked eye.

Aina lands with a terrific splash several yards below, producing a cascade of small, painfully cold water drops that reach my frozen feet. I hesitate a few seconds and then dive in.

Frigid water surrounds my body as I quickly swim across the small bay toward the pier, grasp the rotting wood—slippery and smooth from seaweed and water plants—and catch my breath. My fingers, stiff with cold, lose their grip and I swim in toward shore, toward the warmth of the cottage and Aina, who is already waiting, wrapped up in the plaid blanket.

Afterward, we eat thick slices of rye bread with chanterelles sautéed in butter and drink hot chocolate. Once again, I remind Aina about carrying the wood into the shed and putting away the ax, but she just squirms and mumbles something about doing it later.

Outside my cottage, twilight is falling over the sea as the wind picks up.

NOVEMBER

We are sitting in my living room, Aina, Vijay, and I. It's dark outside, and one of the first real fall storms rages over Stockholm. Branches whip against the window in my bedroom. I've lit the small cast-iron stove in a corner of the living room. Three moving boxes sit in front of the windows, packed with the bare essentials. I have finally given up and am trying to find a temporary place to live until Sara's murderer is arrested.

My friends are pleased with my decision. I, on the other hand, feel a little like a child who has unwillingly capitulated to her parents' unremitting arguments. There is a part of me that wants to rebel against all this. Against everyone who thinks that *I* am the one who should change *my* life. Against the faceless man who has finally succeeded in getting me out of here.

We are giggling, eating popcorn and mezze that I bought at Söderhallarna, and drinking red wine. Since I have guests, I bought several bottles of really good Chianti. Everything is laid out on the rug. But there is a serious undertone to the apparent cheerfulness. We are meeting to talk about what happened, because we hope that Vijay will be able to help us.

Aina lights a cigarette. I can tell she is tipsy, both by the way she is moving and the fact that she is smoking.

"So, Vijay, what do we know about this guy?" asks Aina, drawing on her cigarette.

"We have to distinguish between what we *know* and what we *believe* . . . What we know is that the murderer has detailed knowledge of your office and your patients, and he knows where you live, Siri. And where Charlotte Mimer lives. What we believe is that he is a middle-aged man, that he is the same person as Sara's boyfriend, that he is mentally disturbed and for some reason wants to harm you. Further, we think he had some kind of father-daughter relationship to Sara, or wanted to, that he has a daughter of his own who in some way reminded him of Sara. He is intelligent, well-spoken, and organized. Also . . . Marianne was probably on his trail and maybe he was the one who made sure she couldn't tell you what she knew."

"A coldhearted bastard, you had said, Vijay. Do you remember?"

"Hmm, he sees all of us as pawns in his game. He sacrificed Sara to get at you, Siri."

Vijay stops talking, and we remain sitting silently on the rug in the living room. I can hear the waves breaking against the cliffs outside and the wind rushing over the islands. The storm is here, I think. I close my eyes for a moment and then ask the question that has bothered me for a long time.

"*An evil person?* Is that what he is?"

I look searchingly at Vijay.

"I don't believe such a thing exists. Evil people, that is. I think there are *evil actions,* carried out by broken people. And I think he's broken, that he suffers."

"So you think it's forgivable, that he killed an innocent person like Sara?"

"That's not what I said. I only said that I don't think anyone is born evil."

"Can't you become evil?"

"You can become the sort of person who commits evil actions."

"And even then, you're still not evil?"

"Not necessarily. Uh, listen, you can ask a priest about that, or maybe a philosopher. I'm a scientist."

Vijay takes out his tobacco, starts rolling himself a cigarette, and continues.

"Let me try to explain what I mean. Let's say we have an individual with really lousy prospects for the future. Do you know the theories about the possible consequences of injuries to the brain's frontal lobe?"

Aina and I both nod. The frontal lobe is a sensitive area, considered by many researchers to be the center of what in layman's terms we call ethics and morality.

"Let's assume that such an individual is subjected to a disadvantaged upbringing, without opportunities to create strong, lasting bonds with his parents, perhaps in combination with abuse, sexual or some other kind. The risk is that this person will develop what we usually call antisocial personality disorder. It's often already noticeable in childhood. Bed-wetting, cruelty to animals, and pyromania are usually clear, early signs. That's not to say that bed wetters or people who are cruel to animals are psychopaths, far from it. But some of them are. I wouldn't want to say that those individuals are *evil people*. I mean, evil implies they've made some kind of active choice, doesn't it? Chosen to be evil."

"But you think this is that kind of . . . injured individual?"

"Yes, absolutely."

"There's something I've been wondering about. Could it be a woman?"

Vijay twirls the wineglass between his fingers and takes a sip.

"In theory, yes. But in practice it's not very likely. Almost all these kinds of criminals are men. Why? Were you thinking of someone in particular?"

I shake my head. "No, but think about what happened last week. You know, when I saw someone outside my window and then found that puddle of blood. Do you think it was him, and in that case, what could have been his objective?"

Vijay takes a grape-leaf dolma and stuffs the whole thing in his mouth.

"Hmm, yes, I think it was him. What kind of blood was it, by the way? Did they figure it out yet?"

"A dog's. Markus thinks it must have been a dog that got hit by a car, lost its way, and ended up on my property. But . . . it's pretty damn far to the nearest road."

"Hmm." Vijay scratches his mustache and looks at Aina, who in the meantime has curled up on the couch and fallen asleep. "Hmm," he repeats, "I think it was him. I really think so."

"Why?"

"I can't really say. It's just . . . too much of a coincidence. I don't believe in chance. Not in this case. Maybe he wanted to scare you?"

"That may be it. So what do you think I should do?"

"Exactly what you're doing. Move. Stop thinking about him and let the police do their job."

"I just have to find somewhere to live . . ."

"Siri, I've said it before, and I'll say it again. Move in with your parents, or with Aina. You can't hang around here waiting to find the perfect apartment. Hello, this is Stockholm. I don't like the idea of your living out here all by yourself. Let's find this sick guy first."

Vijay's dark gaze holds mine.

"I mean it, Siri."

I nod, and the cold, clammy feeling I've come to know so well spreads inside me. My life: a constant struggle to overcome fear, to retain some kind of normalcy.

"Cheers!" I say, raising my wineglass to Vijay.

Later, I am on my knees in front of the toilet, vomiting what looks like raspberries—a disgusting mixture of red wine and popcorn. I don't know if it's the alcohol or the fear that is making me sick.

I wipe the sweat from my forehead. My hand is shaking so violently that I can hardly guide my movements. I realize that my life is no longer mine alone.

It is morning. A raw, cold, gray-blue November morning. Dark violet clouds are gathering on the horizon, but the wind has died down. Yellow and rust-brown leaves from the rosebushes and apple trees cover the little overgrown patch of grass that separates my cottage from the cliffs. Vijay is still sleeping on the couch and Aina in my bed. I can hear her muffled snoring.

I have wrapped myself in an orange wool blanket to keep the cold out. I walk slowly over to the window. My head aches a little, but I know I have only myself to blame. The remnants of our dinner are on the floor: popcorn, hummus, avocado halves, a few half-eaten dolmas, and cigarette butts. A little red wine has spilled and left a purplish stain on the wood floor to the right of the rug. Everything is quiet. I look down at my watch: quarter past nine.

When I open the door to the patio, the cold air rushes toward me, making its way relentlessly to my skin. I wrap the blanket around me tighter and go out to sit on the steps.

On the hill above Lasse's Ass, I see a group of large black crows. It looks like they are squabbling about something edible in the bushes, but it's impossible to see what it might be. I get up and go toward the rock. The grass is damp and cold under my feet. I can feel, more than see, that there was a frost during the night. There is a kind of stiffness in the blades of grass, a crunching that hints at the approaching winter.

By the time I arrive up on the rock, the birds have flown away. Everything seems to be in perfect order. The sea is lead gray, heavy, and calm at my feet. The bare branches of the trees are outlined starkly against the sky. Slowly, I fold up the blanket and set it on the rock, take off my panties and T-shirt, and with small, hesitant steps walk the last bit out onto the ledge. There, on the cold rock, where the yellow-green lichen spreads out below my feet, peace finally comes over me again. On the surface, yellow leaves are floating in the foamy water. After a few seconds' hesitation, I dive in and swim with regular movements out toward my little crooked black pier.

Somehow I know that this is my last swim in the bay this year.

Date: November 15
Time: 4:00 p.m.
Place: Green Room, the practice
Patient: Charlotte Mimer

"Yes, I feel better today, Siri. I am so ashamed of my behavior last time. I don't know what . . . what happened. I've become so incredibly . . . *unstable* recently."

Charlotte smiles carefully at me—not a happy smile but an apologetic, self-deprecating gesture. Though she is evidently ashamed of her behavior during our last session, she does appear to be feeling better today. She is wearing the same tracksuit as last time, but she is a completely different person. Her hair glistens, newly washed, and she is sitting straight, her legs modestly crossed and her hands folded in her lap.

The old Charlotte is back.

"Don't think about it anymore. In here, you don't need to be under control. In here, you can allow yourself to lose control. One might say that here, you can confront your loss of control and all the difficult emotions that come with it. Do you understand?"

"Hmm."

Charlotte is squirming a little in the chair but doesn't say anything.

"Try to look at it this way: Control is central to you, you do everything you can to retain control. In every situation."

"Control over food?"

"Sure, control over food, but in the end it's your own feelings you are trying to control. By not eating, by exercising manically, by always being in a good mood. And so on. *I* think it's a healthy sign that you spoke up with your boss."

Charlotte laughs a hoarse, joyless laugh and inspects her well-manicured nails.

"Well, that worked out really well. I've now been to the unemployment office. With all the other welfare cases. It was a . . . hmm . . . new experience."

"Is that how you see it? I mean, that whoever is unemployed is a welfare case?"

Charlotte squirms, aware that she expressed herself in a politically incorrect way. The familiar redness spreads over her neck.

"Well, I don't know. Maybe. *Some* are, in any case."

"Charlotte, I'm not judging what you say, I'm only trying to understand why it is so hard for you to accept that you are someone who needs to go to the unemployment office."

"Because it means that I've failed, at least in regard to my career."

"And what would happen if you had indeed failed? Why would that be so terrible?"

"I don't know."

"Think about it. What would you think, for example, if one of your friends had to go to the unemployment office? Would you think he had failed?"

"Of course not!" Charlotte answers immediately, looking me in the eyes.

"So then you have . . . stricter rules for yourself than for others?"

"I guess so . . ."

I try to summarize what Charlotte has just said and clarify my view of her situation. Her description of her fear of failure is typical of many high-performing individuals who are under a lot of pressure.

"So could we say that you have developed a strategy to avoid feeling like a failure, and that strategy is to maintain control—in every situation?"

"I suppose so. But wouldn't you want it too?" Charlotte whispers, her face ashen.

"Do I want to maintain control?"

Charlotte nods and looks at me seriously, her eyes like large, dark marbles.

"Well, of course a certain degree of control is both necessary and desirable, but it is . . . a means. Not an end in itself."

Charlotte does not seem to be listening; she is no longer looking at me. Instead her gaze is fixed on the lithograph hanging above my little table. It depicts a woman riding a butterfly, an image that Aina considers far too psychodynamic for our offices. But I like it anyway, so I leave it there despite her protests. And when children visit, they are usually captivated by it.

"How does it feel to lose control, Siri? How does it feel when someone else controls your life?"

"What do you mean?" I ask, and at the same time I realize I know exactly what she means. I know how important it is for me to maintain control over my life. And how it feels to lose it, when it slips between your fingers like a wet bar of soap.

Charlotte stares at me intensely and slowly nods.

"Exactly," she says quietly.

After Stefan's death, I was paralyzed. I was incapable of arranging the funeral or his inheritance. Mom and Dad had to help me, and they were happy to do it. No one questioned why I spent days, even weeks in bed. Mom brought me meals on the little red IKEA tray they had given me as a birthday present a few years earlier. Cabbage rolls, meatballs, and cod with egg sauce—real comfort food. Dad opened the mail, made sure that bills were paid, and told everyone who needed to be told about Stefan's death. I lay there unmoving, unreachable, and inconsolable between the damp sheets. I didn't shower for weeks, which meant I could smell my own pungent body odor as I turned in bed, but that didn't bother me. It was as if I were sitting next to myself, observing my sorrow from a distance.

I do not have many memories of the funeral, aside from the fact that it was held at the Forest Cemetery and that the chapel was covered with a beautiful beige mosaic. I also remember what the minister looked like. I actually think I remember how everything looked, but not what was said or what happened.

When Mom and Dad finally left me in peace, Aina moved in. In the beginning, she did everything for me—cooked, washed my hair, and shoveled snow so the car could make it up to the cottage—but after a while, I'm not sure how long, we fell into a wordless daily routine. A collaboration in which we divided up the household chores. A couple of months passed and suddenly there it was, the day I felt that I had to make my way back into the world. I explained to Aina that I wanted to start working again, and the only thing she said was, "So I guess we'll drive in together tomorrow morning?"

After that, my daily routine regained some semblance of normalcy. Nothing was the same anymore, but nevertheless it appeared to be like it always was. I went to work every day, saw my patients, and spent evenings writing case notes, reading, or chatting with Aina. The weekends were painfully long but could be survived by dividing them up into brief, manageable portions: reading, two hours; grocery shopping, fifty minutes; washing the car, forty-five minutes; peeling potatoes, twenty minutes; and so on. The trick was never to be without something to do, never to let my thoughts wander.

Despite everyone's protests, I chose to stay in Stefan's and my little house by the water. Secretly, I harbored a vague plan, the general idea of which was that once I felt strong enough I would sit myself down and seriously assess whether it was good for me to stay in that house. Obviously, that day never came. Winter turned to spring, and when the sun melted the last of the snow and the snowdrops sought their way up through the leaves I never got around to raking last year, I felt a quiet joy that I had decided to stay. This was my home, and nothing could make me leave.

How wrong I was.

It is Friday evening and I'm at the ICA supermarket. Around me, people are occupied with routine grocery shopping. An older woman fills her shopping cart to the brim with everything she needs for the weekend, and a man in his thirties races with his little daughter through the aisles. Bad, jazzy Christmas music is everywhere, and Advent candleholders and stars are already being sold in one corner of the store. I feel alone and shut out from this sense of community. I know that Stockholm is full of single-person households, that I am not the only thirty-five-year-old who does not have a family to go home to. But right now, that's no consolation. I wish I were someone else, anyone, just not Siri Bergman. Maybe the girl who is choking with laughter as her dad tickles her, maybe the young woman with an Eastern European name behind the deli counter.

Anyone, just not the person I am.

It's not only the solitude that eats away at me, it's also the fact that someone is threatening me. At night it takes me a long time to fall asleep, because first I have to methodically go over all the facts, all the suspects. I ransack my past, but I can't contemplate someone who would want to play with me so cruelly. Sometimes I have fantasies that I am responsible for something horrible, that I unconsciously committed a crime and that innocent people had to suffer because of me. Am I being punished for some atrocity I committed without my being aware of it?

I think about Sara and the guilt weighs heavily on me. If only she had gone to a different therapist, to a different practice, or to Aina, then maybe she would still be alive. But Sara is dead because she was my patient. It's my fault. And there is nothing I can do that will change that.

As a psychotherapist, you work toward change and improvement. I think that what made me want to become a psychologist in the first place was that simple: to help people. I was inspired by the notion that I could help make a difference in a person's life. Not heal or make whole, but make a difference. It sounds presumptuous now. And I really did make a difference in Sara's life. She's dead. She's gone. She no longer exists.

And I'm guilty.

My cell phone rings, and I'm embarrassed to discover that I'm just standing there, frozen in front of shelves full of milk cartons, effectively preventing people from getting past. I back away to take the call. When I see Markus's name on the display I briefly feel a gentle flutter in my stomach. A feeling that passes so quickly that I'm not sure I even really felt it.

"This is Siri."

"Hi, Siri, it's Markus. I have the night off and, well, since your refrigerator was so empty and I'm a pretty good cook, I thought that maybe I could invite you to dinner? You know, a real dinner. I can come to your place and cook, I mean, if you'd like."

My spontaneous reaction is delight. Another person in the house. Someone cooking dinner. A man who doesn't mind cooking at my stove. I answer yes without really thinking. We agree on a time and hang up. I put back the two cans of tomato soup in my basket and walk toward the exit.

Markus rings the doorbell at seven thirty. I've cleaned things up a bit and even run the vacuum cleaner once around the house. I've made an effort with my clothes and general appearance, for once. A skirt and tight top instead of jeans and a knit sweater.

I am nervous and happy, and have a bad conscience. Markus remains standing on the steps and I can tell that he is surprised, that he is taking it all in. Suddenly I feel overcome by insecurity. What if I misunderstood the whole situation? But Markus smiles and walks past me through the hall and into the kitchen. I pad after him in my stockinged feet. Masses of groceries are lined up on the kitchen counter as well as two bottles of wine.

"I'll cook. It will be a surprise. You can set the table in the meantime. And pour some wine."

Markus looks happy as I open a bottle of red wine and pour two glasses. It's a strange feeling. This is not an interrogation, not a questioning, not a conversation. This is a date. A real date. As I set the table, we talk about Vijay and Olle. Markus is curious about their relationship and whether Vijay is Hindu and how his culture views homosexuality. This is something I really can't answer.

When dinner is ready, I sit at the table while Markus serves. He made saltimbocca with sage sauce, and my whole kitchen smells of spices. Once again he has baffled me, challenged my prejudices: I never would have thought that he could cook—really cook.

We sit across from each other, and when our eyes meet it is as if they cling to each other. We act relaxed around each other but are also nervous, and perhaps a little self-conscious.

"Why did you become a policeman?"

Markus looks surprised at the question, as if being a policeman were an obvious choice.

"I became a policeman because I wanted to drive fast and catch crooks," he says, grinning.

"Is it that simple?"

"Well, I was really young when I got into the police academy. I had thought about studying criminology and law at university, but . . . I went to the academy instead. I wanted to try it out for real. And I had clear principles and ideas about what was right and wrong. Good and evil."

Markus looks fervent, as if it is important for him to convey to me what led him to this decision.

"And . . . do you still have your principles? Do you still know what good and evil mean?"

"I've been a policeman a few years now, so of course my thoughts and opinions have changed. I know that the world is not black and white. That people are not solely evil or good. And that even good people commit evil actions."

Markus looks weary, and I think about what his day-to-day must be like.

"How do you cope?"

"How do *you* cope, Siri? You're a psychotherapist. Every day you see people who suffer and who have already survived God knows what kind of misery. But you cope, don't you? And I cope. I cope because I have a life outside my work. Because I know that life consists of more than violence and death. And I cope because I know I'm doing the right thing. I'm a good policeman. I do a good job."

Markus falls silent and looks at me as if seeking confirmation for what he just said. I nod slowly, because I think that somehow I understand what he means, where he's coming from.

I watch him sitting there across from me at the lopsided kitchen table, and suddenly I imagine his smooth, pale face approaching mine, him leaning forward to kiss me lightly on the lips with his well-formed, lovely mouth. His soft lips pressing against mine. The thought comes out of nowhere and I look at him, his blond hair and blue eyes, his Ramones T-shirt. For a moment, I think about it, that he is wearing this T-shirt even though he is too young to really remember the band.

Much too young.

I know this to be true, but I don't want to think about it.

Our eyes meet and once again we stare intensely at each other. Markus reaches across the table, his hand touching mine. His fingertips graze the back of my hand and I think about Stefan and how infinitely painful it is to lose the one you love. Will I dare take the chance to love again and risk the pain of a loss anew?

"Why did you come here, Markus? What do you want from me?"

Markus looks self-conscious. Embarrassed. But I know that I must hear the answer.

"I came here because there's something about you, Siri. Something that moves me. This means that I think about you more than I ought to. This means that I want to be with you."

He falls silent and looks down at our intertwined hands.

"It's not so simple," I answer. "Us. The investigation. We shouldn't—"

The words line up in my mouth, but it's as if I can't get myself to actually say them out loud.

"I know, but . . . I can't, don't want to . . . worry about that."

He looks serious and I know that he means what he says. The music has stopped and the only sound now is the branches banging against the living room window. I get up from my chair and go around the table without releasing his hand. As he takes me in his arms, I wonder what has held us back for so long.

Later, when his sweaty body is on top of mine, I have other thoughts. Darker thoughts. I think that I deserve this young body, the solid muscles on his back and buttocks and the unwavering energy. I deserve his desire, his convulsive breathing in my ear, and his attention. My life has been so miserable the last few years that I deserve him, like a hardworking laborer deserves his pay or an athlete his medal.

It's early morning, and the bedroom is filled with a warm dawn light, different from the cold, blue-black morning rays that usually seep in through the curtains. Without looking out the window, I know that it has snowed. Only snow can make late-autumn dawn change colors this way. The house is completely quiet. Markus is lying beside me. He is breathing almost soundlessly and he is motionless. I can make out his face in the gossamer light. Where the pillow has pressed against his pale cheeks, light-pink lines run across his face. He looks so calm, so different, almost like a child.

My room is transformed. I have lived here alone for more than a year. No one has slept in my bed with me. This was the room that shared my memories of Stefan. Now there is another man here, sleeping in my bed.

Markus is so unlike Stefan, a completely different man, but not necessarily the wrong one. There was a time when I thought I could never love anyone again. That my love was used up and I had no more to give. I thought that my feelings had died with Stefan, scattered in the memorial grove along with his ashes.

We take a walk around the bay. Big snowflakes continue to fall silently around us. The bay lies open, the water is still and black. The trees are covered in white snow. It is beautiful but fleeting. Presumably, the snow will melt by tomorrow. I walk in silence because I don't know what to say. I think about Sara and the fact that her death brought Markus into my life. Is it allowed to build happiness on the death of another? I know the thought is irrational, but it's there anyway. Can anything good come out of these horrible events—*may* anything good come out of them? Markus seems to pick up on my thoughts and looks questioningly at me. I decide not to say anything and he accepts it.

I wonder how we would appear to an observer: a couple in love, hand in hand, going for a walk in the snow. Suddenly I feel a strong sense of unease, as if someone really is watching us, and start looking around for signs of someone secretly following in our footsteps. Naturally, Markus notices my mood shift; still, I am surprised by his question.

"Do you feel it, too?"

His gaze traces the outlines of the trees.

"Yes. Someone's here."

My answer comes instantly, and now I am sure that I am right. I have no idea what makes me feel so certain, but nature no longer seems untouched out here. Maybe it is the blackbirds that suddenly fly up between the trees over by my house. Maybe it's the silence that suddenly seems less compact. I feel ill at ease.

"Shall we head back?"

I squeeze Markus's hand and feel pressure in response. It is almost a half-mile walk back to the house, and the trail is slippery with snow. It takes longer than usual. We walk as quickly as we can; without speaking we help each other over roots and patches of ice.

When we come to the clearing where my house is, we slow down. My eyes scan the house, which appears to have winter clothes on, a summer house with a warm white comforter on the roof. Thin, white smoke coils from the chimney and light is beaming from all the windows. Of course all the lights are on, even though it's just a gray November day. The whole picture looks like an idyllic fairy tale.

As we stand there quietly observing the scene I suddenly see it: On the wooden steps in front of the French doors is a small, curled-up gray figure. It takes a few seconds before I realize what I am looking at.

"It's Ziggy."

I rush ahead to welcome my long-lost cat, but Markus grabs my arm and carefully pulls me back.

"Stay where you are. There are footprints around the house. We don't want to disturb them. I have to call the technicians."

He already has his cell phone in his hand.

"Who cares about footprints? My cat has come back."

"Siri, don't go—"

But it's too late. I don't listen to him. I run toward Ziggy, who seems to be peacefully looking out at the garden from his spot on the steps.

Only when I get really close do I sense something wrong. Ziggy sits unnaturally still, not reacting when I call to him. When I finally reach him and carefully extend my hand to stroke his back, I am surprised by how completely stiff he is. No, not just stiff, but *hard*. He falls over with a hollow thud, like a piece of wood falling to the ground, and remains in the same fixed position.

Then I understand.

He is stuffed.

Someone has stuffed my cat.

I can't sleep at all that night, or the following nights either. The thought of Ziggy, of the fate he met, keeps me awake, and I ask myself again and again how anyone could do such a thing to a poor innocent animal.

I have finally given up the battle to stay in my house. Not even I can deny the simple truth any longer. It is dangerous for me to be here, someone is seriously after me. The whole thing is so incredibly obvious and I no longer understand why I tried to deny it.

Aina has arranged an apartment for me. A friend of hers was invited to be a guest researcher at an Italian university for six months, and his studio on Hantverkargatan is now vacant. Empty. At my disposal.

The apartment is small and spartan, but functional. Still, it is not my home. It is a place where I can stay until the police arrest the man they are hunting. If they catch him. I have secretly started to doubt they ever will. I am no longer certain about anything. I cannot remember my life as it was before. Before Sara died. Before my pet was transformed into a museum piece, before Marianne was in a coma and my lawn was covered with blood. It feels as if it's always been this way, as if I have always been threatened. The sensation is so familiar that it has come to define me. I am Siri. I am hunted. Threatened.

Persecuted.

I still haven't told my parents or sisters anything. There is no law that says adult children have to inform their parents of every single thing. Maybe I have a moral obligation to tell them what is happening, but I can't cope with their suffocating concern right now.

Even more guilt to bear.

It's my fault if they worry.

Instead, Markus comes to pick me up, with my bag and three boxes, and helps me settle in.

The apartment has a furnished hall, with a desk and a chair. The walls are covered with shelves filled with books on intellectual history and philosophy. There is a living room with a 1930s-style couch with slender wooden arms and a small round table. A tiny TV, a sleeping alcove with a bed so narrow I can't see how anyone can sleep in it. And more books. In the kitchen there's a table with two chairs. As a hint at the approaching holiday season, someone hung up a Christmas star in the living room window. Once again I think that this is not my home. It is a refuge. An extremely temporary refuge.

From the day we found Ziggy, Markus seems to be constantly by my side. I am unaccustomed to his nearness. But also grateful. Carefully and hesitantly, we are trying to find the balance between the circumstances that brought us together and what we feel for each other.

It is nighttime. A raw, cold, damp rainy night. But darkness never really manages to overwhelm the city, not the way it does in my cottage. It is never fully night here, just a different kind of daytime in which artificial light keeps the darkness at bay.

Markus has come to help me assemble a shelf. It's not that I can't assemble it myself, but there are no tools in the apartment. Even though Markus has been here for several hours, we haven't started on the shelf yet. Instead, we ate the leftovers of yesterday's take-out pizza, drank sour Italian wine, and made love in the narrow, uncomfortable sleeping alcove.

It bothers me that nothing in the apartment is mine, that everything is on loan. Even the sheets we are lying on—now damp and pushed together in a tangled pile at the foot of the bed—are on loan.

The window facing Hantverkargatan is open, and blasts of brisk air race around our naked legs like invisible hairy nocturnal animals. Markus's hand is on my neck, slowly stroking my short hair as he looks out over the dingy little room with an empty gaze.

I have to bite my tongue not to ask the question that I imagine women always ask. But I decide that I really don't care what he's thinking. The moment is enough. I want to rest in this perfect moment and not tear apart the fragile silence to demand some kind of affirmation.

And why fish for proof of his affection? I myself don't know what this is, the fragile but irresistibly enticing attraction that exists between us. Is it love, or are we only borrowing each other's bodies to fill all those black holes we feel inside?

Somewhere in the distance I hear sirens. They seem to wake Markus from his reverie. He pulls himself up to rest on his elbow and looks at me as if he only just realized that I was lying beside him, kissing first one eyelid, then the other.

Tenderly.

"You know, you ought to let us protect you. Even if you've moved, you still need protection."

I exhale a deep sigh of irritation and something else. It bothers me that he doesn't respect my decision and that he still thinks he knows what I need better than I do. That he, so young and with such little experience of life, thinks I am in need.

"We've already had this conversation. I don't want the police around here. One cop is enough."

"Very funny." Markus sounds offended and removes his hand from my neck. "Don't you understand what kind of risk you're exposing yourself to?"

Slowly I sit up, pull on my panties, and wrap the blanket tightly around my shoulders. I'm freezing.

"Listen to me. If I let him—or her—limit my life to that degree, then he has already won."

"I'm sorry if I seem dense, I really don't get how you can see this as a defeat. Managing risks . . . just shows how strong you really are."

"Great, perfect. Then I guess we've proved that that's just what I'm not—strong, that is. Because if I'm not up to having cops around . . . then I'm weak."

"Forgive me, Siri, but now you're really being difficult. All I want to do is help you."

"And you think that this is the right thing to do?"

I hear my voice getting shrill.

"Yes, that's why I'm saying this. Because I know it's the right thing."

"And since when are you so sure what the right thing is?"

Now I am being mean. I feel it permeating my whole body, this desire to put him in his place.

"What do you mean by that?" Markus asks, as he climbs out of bed and starts getting dressed.

"What I mean is, do you think, for example, that it's right to sleep with me? What do you think Sonja would say if she saw you now?"

Markus grins stupidly, his mouth half open, which only fuels my anger.

"How ethical is it to sleep with a witness? During an ongoing investigation?"

"Cut it out. Since when was it punishable to screw?"

"Shall we call Sonja and ask? I can—"

"You are completely nuts," Markus interrupts me, kicking a pillow that had fallen to the floor. The pillow hits my wineglass a few yards away and it breaks with a clatter, but Markus doesn't seem to notice.

"I didn't ask to take care of you, Siri!"

"Since when are you the one who's taking care of me? I'm probably almost old enough to be your mother."

"Which clearly doesn't stop you from behaving like a little brat."

Markus is yelling now, and it strikes me that I've never actually seen him angry before. In some sick way I am enjoying it. It's so physical. There's something attractive about his fury. Something almost sexual. I really must be nuts.

"You can put your stupid shelf together yourself."

Markus storms out of the apartment and leaves me alone, still in the ridiculously small bed.

I lean back and look out through the window at the dirty gray nonday, the neon night. I decide that this is not love. This is therapy for my body. An urge that must be satisfied.

Nothing more.

I dream about Stefan again. He is tanned and strong and happy as only he could be. But something is wrong. He is lying very close beside me in bed, and I feel his breath against my cheek coming in cold, damp thrusts. I don't meet his eyes because I realize I have betrayed him. Another man has been in my bed, another man's hands have caressed my body. It is a betrayal worse than death, a treachery that cannot be forgiven, I realize that. But Stefan only laughs and pulls me closer and closer until my nose is buried in his armpit and I am filled with his scent; he smells of mud, seaweed, and grass. I run my hand over his back, which is strong and only slightly damp, which is strange since he was lying in the water for so long.

He lifts me up with his strong arms as he turns on his back so that he can lay me down on his belly. My head comes to rest against his cold, damp right shoulder. I run my hand through his wet hair and absent-mindedly pluck remnants of seaweed and leaves from it. Stefan kisses me carefully on the cheek and declares that he is happier than he has been in a long time. "*Much, much happier than I've been in a long time.*" He says that things were so bad for him, but that everything is going to be fine now.

I wake up with a pain in my chest that is so strong I can hardly breathe. I know immediately what it is: guilt.

I am forced to sit up and concentrate on breathing so as not to lose control over my pain and sorrow. It's so hard to lose him, so hard to let him go. I can't have him, but I can't be without him.

How long can I live like this?

It's dark outside, even though it's only three o'clock in the afternoon. I am back in the offices of the police in Nacka. Sonja has called me in for further questioning. Instead of her office, we sit in a light room with pale green walls, furnished only with four chairs and a slightly higher table. A modern fluorescent light fixture hangs from the ceiling. In one corner there is a video camera on a tripod. I am alone, facing the camera. Sonja sits in the chair in front of me, and Markus is at an angle behind her. It is a strange situation. Markus and I have been so intimate, and now here we are trying to appear unperturbed by each other's presence. Sonja is not aware of what has happened between us. Markus knows he ought to tell her, but he also knows that if he does, he is going to be removed from the case and he doesn't want that. He doesn't want to discuss this with me and asks only that I respect his decision. He also thinks that it won't affect his work negatively. Quite the opposite.

I have decided not to get mixed up in this, although I sincerely doubt that it's a good idea for him to still be on the case. He is no longer neutral; I assume the legal term is "exceptionable." But I still don't say anything. Perhaps I do want him to remain on my case; this makes my connection to everything that is happening tighter, I find out more from him than I would otherwise.

"Welcome again, Siri. My office is occupied today, so we'll have to sit here, even though this is not an official interrogation."

Sonja looks weary. A strand of dark hair streaked with gray hangs over her face. I wonder how many cases she is working on at the same time.

"I can imagine that you are shaken by what happened."

Sonja is referring to Ziggy. I nod to confirm. I can't bear to tell her exactly how upset I was after the macabre discovery. I am still surprised by the sadism behind such an act. Who wants to play me this way? And why?

"I want you to accept certain safety precautions, meaning a security alarm and a special cell phone linked directly to us. It's simply unacceptable that you don't already have some form of protection."

"Markus and I have already talked about this."

I notice Markus's grimace too late. He doesn't want me to talk about our having had more contact with each other on our own.

"Really?" Sonja looks surprised. She raises one heavily painted eyebrow and inspects me in silence.

"Yes, in connection with . . . the cat, I mean. Markus came out to the house then. I called . . ."

Sonja waves her hand impatiently, as if she thinks I'm drawing out the conversation in order to delay the issue.

"At any rate, we can't let you stay in the house right now. I must ask you to move out for a while."

"I've already moved."

"That's news to me, *good news*. Nevertheless, I think that you—given the circumstances—need additional protection."

"I don't want to be monitored by a police officer."

"We don't have the resources for that kind of protection."

Suddenly Sonja smiles sarcastically. A crooked, tired smile.

"If you are going to be monitored by someone, then it would be a security guard. We don't have enough police officers to keep an eye on all potential crime victims. Maybe we can have a patrol car drive past your house at a scheduled time each day, but if you've moved anyway that's hardly necessary. I was thinking more about a phone that allows you to quickly make direct contact with the police. And a security alarm for your apartment."

I think about the implications of her plan. Being able to reach the police quickly would be a relief, of course. Even though I don't want surveillance day and night, I can no longer deny that I am afraid. Perhaps a direct phone would make me feel more at ease. I nod and mumble something to the effect that it would be okay.

"Good. A colleague is going to help you with this. Presumably Stenberg."

Sonja nods at Markus, who also nods. He is going to see to it that I am protected from all danger. My gaze settles on his hands. *Those hands.* He looks at me and I suddenly realize that he knows what I'm thinking about: his hands, and what they know. What they have done with me. With my body.

My cheeks feel hot and I lower my gaze, incapable of looking at Markus anymore. I try to find a neutral subject of conversation.

"What's going on with the investigation?"

"We are looking into a number of different leads, but we don't want to get locked into anything, as you surely understand."

Sonja again looks weary.

"And what does that mean? That you don't know anything?"

My voice is getting thin and sharp. I feel strangely angry. It's their job to capture the bad guys. The criminals. This is a fundamental fact that has been in my consciousness from an early age. The police capture villains and protect the weak. In the countless number of books, comics, and movies that accompanied me throughout my childhood, the pattern was always the same.

As it turns out, reality is very different. The police cannot capture the person stalking me. And the police cannot protect me either. Which is partly connected with the fact that I am not letting them protect me. But perhaps the real reason these interrogations and the surveillance seem so meaningless goes deeper than that. I feel resigned and hopeless in a way that is difficult to explain. I've never had so little control over my own life before. There is only one way forward, and someone else has staked it out in advance for me. I have a strange feeling that my fate is sealed, that like in a Greek tragedy I am heading toward my own downfall, and that nothing I can do will keep me from ending up that way. Rationally, it's clear to me that this thinking is unrealistic and pessimistic, but I don't have the strength to get these ominous thoughts out of my head.

"We're doing everything we can, Siri."

Sonja looks at me sympathetically and I am suddenly ashamed. Of course, I understand that the police are doing what they can. Sonja already told me about all the people they've interviewed, how they dug deep into Sara's past, looking through all my videotapes in pursuit of leads, all the technical evidence. But if I myself can't figure out who might feel such hatred toward me, how can the police have any idea?

"We questioned all your colleagues a number of times, as you are probably aware."

I nod.

"We are investigating any other violent crime we can think of that might be connected to the threats made to you."

Once again I nod.

"We have also contacted the national Perpetrator Profile unit. We told them that your case is a priority and that you are in danger. The individual we are seeking is already guilty of murder. We know he did not act on impulse. He is capable of executing his premeditated actions. This is no ordinary murder investigation."

Sonja falls silent and I can tell that she thinks she has said too much.

"But I must ask you once again to think about any individuals in your circle who may want to harm you. However far-fetched it may seem."

I was ready—as ready as I ever would be—as I stood outside her house with my blue backpack in my hand.

But.

She wasn't there. Actually, I had already suspected it, as I had carefully approached the cottage through the dense forest and saw . . . or more likely it was what I didn't see that made me understand: no brightly lit windows, no half-empty wineglasses on the kitchen table. Not a movement. Not a sound.

She had gone underground. I had foreseen that this might happen, and it really didn't change anything, because I knew how to find her and get her to return. Everything was predetermined. Now I only needed to pull on a couple threads to set events in motion, nudge fate in the right direction.

I turned around and started walking back toward the main road. It was time to visit another one of Siri's twisted patients.

Darkness.

Life has taught me a few things about darkness. About the blackness that penetrates your very soul when you least expect it. Like discovering that your rubber boots are leaking halfway through the swamp. The same cold, clammy feeling.

Sometimes I sense it in my patients.

Perceive it.

Sometimes it's enough to crack open the door and the darkness seeps out. But normally you can't tell. You look at the people around you. They seem normal, do normal things, and live their extremely ordinary lives. It is hard to conceive just how much darkness can fit inside someone.

Hard to grasp.

It's even harder, of course, to imagine that a friend or a colleague could be filled by it. Controlled by the darkness.

I can't believe it.

I look into Markus's eyes across the table. Try to process what he is saying. Take it in. That it is probably someone I know. Someone who has a connection to the practice.

We are sitting at a little vegetarian restaurant on Fjällgatan. I would never have guessed that he liked this kind of food, but he is happily digging into the marinated chickpeas and tofu stir-fry.

Around us, the lunch rush is starting to thin out. A woman in her fifties wearing a white tunic with batik print and chunky silver jewelry looks around for her lunch mate, lost. I think absentmindedly that she looks like a psychologist.

To my right, a young woman with a baby is speaking agitatedly with the staff.

"He has to eat something too, surely you must understand."

The black-haired, pierced waitress looks uncomfortable and talks quickly, in a low voice.

"But we can't warm up meat products in our microwave. Not even baby food."

"And why not, can you give me one good reason?" the young mother counters.

"Because it will make a smell in the microwave and—"

"I'm sorry, but that's bullshit. But you know what, it doesn't matter. I've lost my appetite anyway."

I watch the woman get up, the baby on her hip, pack the jar of baby food in the big diaper bag she had hung on the chair, and quickly walk out of the restaurant.

Markus raises an eyebrow and looks at me.

"So are you for or against it?"

"For or against what?" I ask in return.

"Meat."

"Meat." I have to laugh. "For or against . . . I don't know. It's good."

Then we are suddenly serious again. Markus spears chunks of carrot with his fork, but instead of bringing the food up to his mouth he sets it down on his plate, looks at me, and takes my hand. He looks serious and I wonder what he's about to tell me.

"You know, the puddle of blood in your garden, the dog blood? The same night that happened, a guy from Värmdö disappeared with his dog. He was going to take a short walk before dinner but never came back to his girlfriend and their child. No one has seen him since. He lived a few miles away from you. At the beginning, they didn't connect his disappearance with Sara's murder. The guy had debts and was also unfaithful to his girlfriend. There were reasons to believe he was hiding voluntarily. But there may be a connection. Maybe he saw something that evening. Or someone. Maybe he saw too much . . ."

I shake my head and close my eyes, thinking I can't bear to hear more, but Markus takes a firm hold of both my wrists, as if bracing me for what comes next.

"There's more. That afternoon, when we found your cat. The technicians found footprints in the snow, made by a man's size ten and a half shoe. Worn sole. Some kind of sneaker, but it was impossible to determine the brand. In any case, it was a man's footprint. Apparently, they can calculate how much the person weighs, more or less. Don't ask me to explain how. They're guessing we are dealing with someone who weighs about one sixty to one seventy pounds. If we consider the shoe size and assume the man has a normal weight, that means he is between five ten and six feet tall."

"You don't know anything else?"

I feel disappointed and led on.

"Wait a moment." Markus interrupts me. "We know that the man was snooping around on your property and that for a certain period of time stood in the same spot, by those tall trees down by the water. Presumably he hid down there and was spying on us."

"So he was there. He was there, watching us?"

The recollection of how I felt we were being observed is unsettling.

Markus nods. "He was there. Or someone was there, and most likely it was him. We also have traces of car tires. And this is interesting. It's a special type of snow tire that isn't used on very many cars—actually, they're almost only used on newer Volvo models. And we also have a witness."

"You have *what*?"

"Someone saw a black car, probably a Volvo Cross Country, driving down the main road at a relatively high speed. The timing fits and the witness is credible."

"Who is the witness?"

"You know I can't give you that type of information. Damn it, I shouldn't even be telling you this much . . ."

Markus stops himself abruptly and wearily shakes his head.

I realize I have gone too far. Markus has already crossed a number of boundaries to inform me, and I know I shouldn't ask for more. Instead, I nod, indicating that he is right.

"Sonja is right," he says suddenly, picking at his vegetables.

"Right about what?"

Markus doesn't answer, just continues to pick at his food. He does that sometimes, I've observed. He closes up, doesn't answer my questions. I almost get angry.

"Right about what?" I repeat.

Markus sighs and draws his hand through his hair.

"She's right that I'm not . . . impartial anymore."

"What do you mean? Why did she say that? You haven't told her about us, have you?"

My question is feather-light and careful, but nevertheless it has an edge. I know that I sound accusing. Markus nods slowly and fixes me with his eyes.

"I've talked to Sonja, yes," he says, sucking in air to confirm, in the typical Norrland manner.

It's an innocent statement, but I know what it means.

"I'm going to be removed from the investigation."

I glare at Markus sitting across from me in his usual hoodie. I refrain from reminding him that I had warned him about this, but anger is growing inside me, spreading to every cell. This also means that our relationship, or whatever you want to call it, is official. But Markus doesn't seem to notice my reaction.

"It's okay. I'm not getting fired or anything. Sonja transferred me to an assault case. A teen gang in Tumba stole a thirteen-year-old's cell phone and twenty-five bucks and kicked his head in."

I shake my head, incapable of verbalizing my fury.

"I don't know . . ."

"What?"

"Maybe it's okay for you, but I'm not sure this is . . . good."

The fact is, I don't think what Markus just told me is okay at all. It feels as if he is taking things for granted. Taking me for granted. As if we were a couple. As if I were his. Completely.

"What do you mean?" Markus looks confused.

I withdraw my hand from his.

"I don't want to talk about it anymore. Can we talk about something else?"

I can tell that Markus is offended. He leans back in his chair and crosses his arms over his chest.

"I can't figure you out, Siri," he says.

I laugh curtly. A misplaced, loud laugh that cuts through the air.

"Well, join the club."

Markus is not amused. He looks demonstratively out the window. Takes in the marvelous view. His jaw clenched, he looks out toward Skeppsbron, enveloped in damp gray November mist.

And I am staring down at the chickpeas, as if that would help.

Then he looks back at me. There's something different in his eyes now. Something harder. I know that I've hurt him, disappointed him. I don't understand why I always have to mess things up. Why it has to be so hard. He would be better off without me.

I am a burden to him, too.

I am sitting in the kitchen at the office. Aina has temporarily stepped into Marianne's shoes and decorated the room with an electric candlestick and red aromatic candles that smell like spruce and currants. There's an amaryllis in the window that won't bloom for another few weeks. The practice seems to have entered a new order, and we are getting used to the empty reception desk. Though we all look hopefully at Marianne's place when we arrive in the morning, we know she isn't there, that she remains in a coma at South Hospital.

Her absence is tangible. In a small working group, every individual becomes very visible. But we still don't talk about it. We have slowly become accustomed to her absence. We sent flowers to the hospital but are waiting to visit her, and the reception desk and the file cabinet are more or less as she had left them.

In no way does Sven show how he feels about everything that has happened, about all the police interrogations. I wonder what he is thinking as he walks up the steps to work every day. How does it feel for him to meet Aina's and my eyes across the kitchen table? Is he looking around for a new workplace? Our practice seems to be dissolving at the edges, like a sugar cube in hot tea. What was once a pleasant, warm office, enhanced by the feeling of being your own boss, now feels uncertain and diffuse.

I hear the front door open and I know that Aina has returned from an exhibit. She glides into the kitchen with glowing red cheeks and static blond hair, bringing in with her a wave of cold air and crystal-clear frost. With a sweeping motion she tosses a brown paper bag onto the table.

"Fresh-baked cinnamon rolls from the coffee shop. Have one!"

I just shake my head. I'm not in the mood to stuff myself with pastries.

She looks at me, curious. "How's the apartment working out?"

"It's fine, thanks. You know that I really am very grateful—"

"Cut it out," she interrupts me. "You know that if I had my way you would have moved out of that damn house a long, long time ago—when Stefan died. I never understood why you chose to stay there. And the way things are now, well . . . it's the least I can do."

She tears open the paper bag and takes out an enormous cinnamon roll that she bites into at the same time as she wriggles out of her coat and throws it over one chair, sinking down in another. She looks tired. Inevitably, our relationship has also been affected by the events of the fall. Aina was there for me, an attentive listener through it all. She even found me an apartment.. She never asks for anything in return, but I know that I disappoint her. She's irritated when I don't listen to what she says. Her good advice seems to run off my back.

"Any news on the investigation?" Aina asks, her mouth full of cinnamon roll.

"Not much . . . Actually, there is something. The technicians found footprints from the person who killed Ziggy. From a man. And then there was a witness who saw a black Volvo that same day."

"A black Volvo?"

Aina stops chewing, leaving her mouth slightly open, and I can see the half-mashed, saliva-drenched piece of pastry.

"A Volvo Cross Country? Like the car your dad has?"

I nod and wonder how she knows that.

"I know who has a black Cross Country. In fact I'm quite certain, because I almost ran into his car in the parking garage."

A little piece of pastry drops out of her open mouth and lands on the table.

"Who?"

Aina wipes around her mouth with the back of her hand and says in a low voice, leaning toward me, as if she were sharing a secret.

"Peter Carlsson has a black Cross Country."

Vijay leans forward in the biting wind, his thin coat fluttering behind him like a tattered sail. We've left his office at the department and are now walking along Brunnsviken toward Haga Park. It is a beautiful day. For the first time in two weeks, the sun is shining. The sky is light blue and thin, veil-like clouds are quickly moving north. The only disturbance is the powerful gusts of wind that almost make us fall down on the narrow path. The snow has melted away and left smooth, wet patches of ice behind. I lose my balance for a moment and Vijay takes hold of my arm.

"Be careful, Siri!"

His reaction sounds so ominous that I start laughing. He has told me to be careful on so many occasions recently that it feels like they are all flowing together. This time I can actually do as he says. I concentrate on where I set my feet.

I told Vijay about Peter Carlsson. Not using specifics, I sheathed his story in veils of mist, changed facts and details so that he will not be recognizable. I am still tormented by the thought of breaching confidentiality and hurting an already vulnerable man. I cannot say anything to the police without having more to go on, but at the same time, I cannot get rid of my fear that it just may be Peter—I can't get his descriptions of violence and death out of my head. My fear has escalated after what Aina said about Peter's car. I feel like a gigantic wave has washed over me, making me lose composure and control. And for that reason, I have to talk with Vijay.

"What do you think, Vijay?"

He throws up his arms and I am close to losing my balance again.

"What do we know about the man we're looking for?"

Vijay's question is rhetorical and I let him continue.

"We think he is middle aged, well educated, has plenty of money. He is well organized. Easily offended. And very, very driven. He is a man with a mission."

Vijay stares out over the dark-blue water of Brunnsviken, where the waves are topped with foam. He looks resolute and worried, but I don't know what is really bothering him.

"We also think he had some kind of nonsexual relationship with Sara. For some reason, he chose not to be intimate with her. The patient you told me about actually doesn't match the pattern. He does not seem to have any personal connection to you. It is hard to find a tenable motive. True, he has some knowledge about the practice and he knows at least one of your patients personally. But what really makes me hesitate is the complexity of his problems. A man with the type of compulsive thoughts you describe is not really credible as the perpetrator, assuming he's not manipulating you during your sessions. To my ears, it just sounds like compulsive thoughts. His fear is that he might lose control and for some reason start doing crazy things that he really doesn't want to do at all. More or less like new mothers who hide all the medicines and hazardous things in the house because they get compulsive thoughts about harming their babies. He's afraid of harming what he holds dear. But you've already thought about all this, right?"

Vijay turns to me and I nod in response. Of course this is something I have already thought about. I think about the conversations Sven and I had about Peter Carlsson at the end of August. That feels like ages ago.

"So," Vijay continues, "the alternative is that this man has simply faked his symptoms. That he thought up this whole story to scare you. And to get close to you. That he gets a kick out of being able to trick you. People with this type of personality disorder enjoy feeling intellectually superior. And the man who killed Sara harbors a strong, exaggerated hatred toward you. A hatred so great that he doesn't hesitate to hurt others to get at you. He killed Sara Matteus. He . . . stuffed your cat . . . that is *horribly* sick. Deceiving you would be yet another way of humiliating you. Of getting at you."

I close my eyes and see Peter Carlsson's face before me. His blue eyes and combed hair, his manicured nails, the silk tie. I remember him as a very unhappy man. His suffering felt genuine, his shame and his tears, but also his eagerness when I hit the mark with my questions. I cannot believe that Peter Carlsson is Sara's murderer. As if Vijay can read my mind, he continues.

"You can't know, Siri. It is impossible for you to know for sure. I've met murderers who were part of search parties looking for missing children they themselves had killed. Perpetrators who fooled experienced police officers. You just can't know for sure."

"But what should I do?"

My question remains hanging in the air between us.

Vijay says nothing at first, but then turns toward me. "Have you talked to Markus about this?"

"Markus has been removed from the investigation."

I look away to avoid Vijay's eyes. I wait for a comment or a question, but he remains silent. Instead, I feel his hand stroking my coat sleeve. Vijay understands that this is not the time to ask questions.

"Maybe you should talk to him anyway. Even if he isn't working on this case, he's still a policeman. You are still talking to him, aren't you?"

I nod to confirm that I am—more than ever before.

"What do we really know about Sven? About why he had to resign and all that," I ask quietly, without looking up at Vijay.

I had considered bringing up this subject with him earlier. He works at the university, socializes in academic circles, and ought to know more about the inside gossip than Aina or I do.

Vijay seems baffled. "Sven? Sven Widelius?"

"Is it true that he was kicked out of the university?"

"Oh, *that* old story." Vijay grins and lights a cigarette. "Sure, he got kicked out. He had an affair with a student, a psychology major. It probably wouldn't have been any big deal if he wasn't also her supervisor for her thesis. Besides, there was a rumor going around that the girl wasn't stable."

"Not stable?"

"Depressed, vulnerable. I don't know, people say a lot of crap."

"What happened?"

"Someone tattled to the department chair. I don't know who, I guess no one really knows. There was speculation that it could have been one of the girl's classmates. The whole thing was hushed up. Sven got severance pay, stopped doing research, and started devoting himself entirely to his private practice. The girl disappeared, I don't know what happened to her."

Vijay stops talking and looks pensive.

"Although this is something you should already know, Siri. At least in part."

"Me? How so?"

"You were students together, she was in your study group. Anna Svensson."

"Anna Svensson?"

I remember a shy girl who joined our study group at the end of the eighth semester and with whom I tried to strike up a conversation a couple of times, but we never really got to know each other.

"I didn't know her, and I don't remember any gossip about her either. I was busy writing my thesis during those final semesters."

"You're probably right," Vijay answers. "There wasn't any gossip back then. What I know I only found out later. And from the faculty, not the students. At any rate, Sven took it really hard. Birgitta was close to leaving him, and his career was in ruins. He had his sights set on a position as professor in clinical psychology. Why are you asking me about this?"

I don't know how to answer. I don't want to suggest that I sometimes have thoughts about Sven and the remote possibility that he might be involved in all this. I realize that this would sound more paranoid than is permissible.

"He just seems down. I thought maybe he was dissatisfied about something, his marriage or his career or . . . you know . . ."

"Yes, I know."

Vijay coughs and changes the subject. "So you're still working at the practice as usual?"

"Sure, but less than before. Why?"

"Have you moved out of your cottage?"

"Yes, yes. I've moved. After that thing with Ziggy . . . I wasn't up to staying." I can tell my voice sounds small and thin, like a child's.

"But I'm thinking about moving back as soon as I can."

Vijay is silent and cowers in the wind, takes a deep inhale, and flicks away the cigarette butt. Then he shoves his hands deep into his coat pockets and looks at me for a long time before he continues.

"I don't think you've realized what a risk you're exposing yourself to. This guy is serious, Siri. He's dangerous. I don't think he only wants to harm you, only wants you to suffer. I think he wants to kill you."

He falls silent and looks at me again. Slowly and with emphasis he repeats the last sentence.

"I think he wants to kill you."

DECEMBER

It is evening and the office is empty. I have stayed behind to take care of various administrative tasks that have been piling up. At least this is what I told Aina and Sven. My real plan is to go through Sven's patient case notes about Peter Carlsson. I know this is unethical, possibly even a violation of confidentiality, but I have to know.

I sit at the reception desk with the paper copies of the case notes spread out in front of me, like a game of solitaire. Unlike me, Sven seldom records conversations on tape. I don't really think he has anything against filming his sessions, but I suspect the procedure is a bit too time-consuming and detailed to suit him. Sven is careless and disorganized and doesn't want to work more than necessary on administrative tasks. On the other hand, he is a brilliant clinician, and I hope that some of this will be reflected in his notes.

Despite my conviction that I am doing the right thing, I can't bring myself to start reading. Vijay's words have frightened me more than I want to admit. Vijay is a level-headed man. There is nothing theatrical or emotional about him. During all the years I have known him, I have never seen him agitated before, until today. I realize that he is right. I have to be more careful. My decision to stay in the house so long suddenly seems incomprehensible. How could I have been so stupid? It's as if I wanted to avoid acknowledging that I really was being threatened. That I really *am* being threatened. I take the topmost papers from the pile and start reading.

The first note contains a few short lines about Peter Carlsson's change of therapist and the circumstances of that change. Then there are case notes from two additional sessions neatly written out.

Date: September 17
Time: 3:00 p.m.
Patient: Peter Carlsson

Reason for contact: Patient comes to the practice for an initial assessment interview with the undersigned. For further description of the circumstances around transfer from the patient's former therapist, Siri Bergman, see the previous note.

Current: Patient is a thirty-eight-year-old man who comes to the office due to sexual compulsive thoughts with sadistic components. Has never had any previous contact of a psychological/psychiatric nature. He says that he is very bothered by these thoughts and explains that they basically affect all aspects of his everyday life. He experiences them as very frightening, giving rise to strong anxiety. Pat. explains that these thoughts started in his late teens, at the time he was in his first sexual relationship with a woman. Already early in the relationship intrusive thoughts occurred about harming his girlfriend. He tried then to actively dismiss these thoughts but states that this was not particularly effective. Pat. decided to break off the relationship out of fear that he would harm his girlfriend. He has thereafter avoided relationships with women out of fear that the compulsive thoughts would return and eventually lead to his actually harming someone. During the spring, however, pat. met a woman. He says that he is very much in love with her but that he is incapable of approaching her sexually out of fear that he will harm her. He describes their relationship as warm and loving. His girlfriend insists, however, that the couple should also have a sexual relationship. Pat. has told his girlfriend that he has problems with his sexuality and promised to seek help. He has not told her the true nature of his problems. Pat. emphasizes that he is not an aggressive man and that he has never harmed anyone deliberately. He completely denies that these thoughts are pleasurable for him.

His wish is now to get help so that these intrusive thoughts go away.

Background: Pat. grew up in Huddinge in south Stockholm. He grew up in a tight-knit family, the oldest of three siblings. He has two younger sisters. His father worked as an attorney at a government agency and his mother was a housewife. During the latter part of pat.'s upbringing, his mother started working outside the home as a medical secretary. Pat. describes his childhood as ordinary. He thinks that he was a calm, nice boy but that sometimes he had a tendency to worry. According to him, his father was troubled for many years with recurring depression. Otherwise, there is no history of psychiatric problems in the family.

Social: Patient is currently living alone. He works in a commercial bank. He describes his career as successful. He has a good relationship with his family and states that he is very close to his sisters. He also has several good friends with whom he often spends time.

Mental status: Good formal and emotional contact. Completely oriented. Pat. appears somewhat depressed. To the direct question, he denies suicidal thoughts but admits that he has felt resigned and meaningless. Pat. becomes noticeably upset when describing the contents of his compulsive thoughts.

Assessment: Thirty-eight-year-old man with sexually tinged compulsive thoughts. There does not seem to be any component of pleasure in these thoughts, and it is most probable that this is a less common form of compulsion syndrome. Additional assessment interviews are necessary, however. The undersigned will inform pat. that additional conversations are required before a decision about treatment can be made. In addition, pat. is informed that medical treatment may be effective with this type of problem.

Next visit on September 26 at 3:00 p.m.

I stop reading. The report hasn't given me any new information. If Peter Carlsson's motive is to manipulate, then it's not strange that his story doesn't change when he talks to Sven. And if the thoughts he is seeking treatment for really do exist, then he will obviously tell the same story. There is only one more case note left.

Date: September 25

Note: Pat. calls today at undersigned's office hours. He says he has decided to end the sessions, as he has contacted a psychiatrist for medication that he thinks is a more effective form of treatment for him. Pat. is invited to a conversation with the undersigned to talk this through, but he declines. We hereby conclude our contact.

So Peter has terminated his therapy with Sven. I wonder what this means. Presumably, nothing at all. Perhaps he simply had enough of Sven. I sit with the notes in my hand and inspect them again to see if I missed any details. I read the first note again: *Pat. grew up in Huddinge in south Stockholm.*

Suddenly I feel cold inside. A sensation that spreads in my body and makes me put the case record down. I also grew up in Huddinge. But Huddinge is big. This may very well be a coincidence. I check Peter's year of birth: 1969. The same as my older sister. I glance over at my cell phone lying next to me on the desk. I hesitate before entering my sister's number. She answers right away.

"Siri! How nice to hear from you. I heard from Mom and Dad that you might not be coming home for Christmas. Why not? It would be fun. Can't you come for a day anyway? Is everything okay? Are you feeling okay?"

Sofia's questions come at a rapid tempo, like relentless air rifle shots: not lethal but they sting when you get hit by them. In the background, I hear her two children squabbling about who gets to sit in the corner of the couch, and her husband's gentle voice trying to mediate.

"I don't have time to talk about that right now, Sofia, just listen."

"But—"

"Just listen!"

"Okay, okay." She sounds offended.

"Do you remember a Peter Carlsson, from your class, or your grade maybe?"

"Huh? What are you talking about?"

"Peter Carlsson. Tall, slim, good-looking guy. Though I don't know what he looked like back then, of course."

"When?"

"In school. In Huddinge."

Sofia is silent, and I guess that she is thinking about it. In the background there's a thud, followed by a shrill scream and prolonged crying.

"There was a Peter Carlsson in my class in middle school. He lived really close to us. In a house close to Långsjön. But tall and good-looking . . . well, I don't know. He was a little . . . special. Always fiddling with his keys. He was afraid he'd lose them and counted them over and over every day. A case for you maybe." She giggles before I hear her roar at the children.

"*Now you shut up.* Mommy is having an *important* conversation."

I think for a moment. I can't remember this Peter, but it sounds like it could be "my" Peter.

"But his younger sisters," Sofia continues, "they would have been your age. Petra and Pernilla. Who the hell calls their kids Peter, Petra, and Pernilla?"

"How can anyone call their kids Sofia, Susanne, and Siri?" I answer.

I don't expect an answer to my rhetorical question. Instead, my thoughts are racing. In my mind, I am back in the long, narrow corridors of elementary school. An image develops of a girl with crutches making her way with difficulty through the crowded hallways. Outside each classroom stands a cluster of kids, waiting to be let in. The girl makes an effort not to accidentally bump into anyone. Her gaze is fixed on the end of the corridor. She pretends she does not see or hear the other children. Just continues straight ahead. When she passes the group I am standing in, my best friend, Carolina, sticks out her leg. The girl does not see it and falls against the hard, dirty stone floor. She manages to break her fall with her hands, placing her palms into a puddle of something. "Oh, I'm sorry," Carolina says falsely. "I *really* didn't see you."

The others grin. I laugh audibly. With great effort the girl gets up and continues wordlessly on her way.

Crutch-Petra.

Petra Carlsson.

Cars are moving slowly south along Götgatan in the thick snowfall. It is rush hour, and pedestrians are huddling and walking quickly and determinedly toward the subway stairs. The cold and damp are seeping inside my wool coat. I am dressed too lightly, but I haven't been able to go out to my abandoned cottage to get warmer winter clothes. I still have a hard time accepting that I have been forced to flee my home, even though I feel safer in the little studio apartment on Kungsholmen island.

I have started working a little more—no new patients, just the old ones. This is for the sake of continuity, I tell myself; the patients' feeling of continuity, that is. The truth is probably also, at least in part, that I can't stand sitting alone for days on end in the gloomy little apartment on Hantverkargatan.

Something strange has happened over time. I have stopped planning farther ahead than a week or two. It feels as if time, my time, slowly but surely is approaching an unavoidable conclusion. I am not going to be able to escape the person who wishes me harm. Living this way, threatened and hunted, has made me feel more resigned than I would have thought possible. I no longer think that I can get away, and I see no opportunity to strike back. I feel stuck, fossilized. Only when I'm with Markus do I feel small, cautious rays of hope.

I turn off from Götgatan and jog along the tall buildings on Blekingegatan until I arrive at the Pelican. Inside the pub it is soothingly warm and dry. The buzz of the customers rises toward the high ceiling and the air is saturated with the scents of food.

Markus is waiting for me, leafing through a magazine. For a brief moment, I cannot resist the temptation to watch him from a distance, while he still doesn't see me. I take in his image. Register how his one hand plays with the snuffbox sitting beside him. How his hair is almost plastered on his temples from the dampness outside. There is something about his posture that makes me sense that he is frustrated. Even though he is busy with the magazine, he reveals his impatience and restlessness by being constantly in motion.

I walk over to his table and he jumps up to greet me. He envelops me in a long, warm embrace that brings us close again. We drink our beers and talk about this and that for a long time. Giggle. Behave like teenagers. I forgave him long ago for having told Sonja about us. And he has forgiven me for being relentlessly pedantic and exhausting.

Markus kisses my hands and runs his tongue over my knuckles, as he looks at me with a grin. It's such an intimate gesture that I feel embarrassed; instinctively I withdraw my hands, wipe them on my blouse as if to brush away invisible crumbs.

"I have to talk with you."

"Start talking." Markus grins again, taking hold of my damp hand, pulling it to him.

"It's about . . . it's about a patient."

I look around to make sure no one in our vicinity is watching us or showing any interest in what we're talking about. I am going to violate therapist-client confidentiality. It's bad enough to tell Markus; everyone in the Pelican doesn't need to hear. A couple in their fifties sits at the table next to us. Both are wearing name tags and are having an animated discussion in what sounds like Dutch. They seem totally uninterested in us. On the other side, a noisy group of guys seems to be talking about a concert they are on their way to. They don't appear to take any notice of us either.

"Okay, I'm listening."

I have Markus's full attention. I start slowly, telling him about Peter Carlsson and our three conversations. I tell him about his fears and fantasies about violence, sex, and death. Markus's expression wavers between curiosity, surprise, and something that resembles suspicion.

"He sounds totally nuts."

"He isn't necessarily nuts at all."

Without being fully aware of it, I find myself defending Peter Carlsson and describe the mechanisms behind obsessive-compulsive disorder. What appears to be crazy often isn't. On the contrary, individuals with obsessive-compulsive disorder are often the last ones who would really harm anyone.

"If that's the case, then why are you telling me this?"

"Because of the car," I answer quietly. "He drives a Volvo Cross Country. And because his sister was in my class in elementary school."

"His sister?"

"Petra." I look down at the table. "She was sick. She had a leg injury, after a cancer operation, I think. We . . . we teased her."

"Who's we?"

"The girls in my class. My best friend Carolina was the worst, but I wasn't that much better myself." I put my head in my hands and try to get rid of all the images that have tormented me since I realized the connection among Peter, his sister, and me.

Markus sits in silence. He is clearly trying to process and analyze what I have just told him. He needs to assess the weight of my story.

"Are you afraid of him?"

Markus's question is clear and concrete.

"I'm terrified of him."

My admission surprises even me. For the first time I have admitted to myself just how scared I am of this man.

"Okay, give me his information. I'll make sure Sonja checks him out."

I give Markus a slip of paper with Peter's full name, address, and personal identity number on it. We sit in silence and look at each other. It is hard to recreate the mood we were in before we started this serious conversation. Markus hesitantly strokes my cheek. Then he waves a waitress over and orders two more beers.

"Have you thought about Christmas?" he asks, abruptly changing subject.

"Christmas?"

"Christmas. Five days from now. What are you going to do?"

I imagine sitting with my parents, sisters, brothers-in-law, and nieces and nephews in Mom and Dad's brick house in Huddinge. It's impossible. I don't want to go. I can't.

"I just want to stay home." The answer came out quickly, before I had time to remember that I don't have a home right now.

"You can't stay at *home,* Siri."

Markus sounds as if he's losing patience with me, as he drums the snuffbox lightly against the table.

"I can stay in the apartment."

The thought of Christmas Eve alone in the little studio apartment on Kungsholmen does not feel all that terrible. I don't really care about Christmas anyway. I can watch TV shows and drink red wine.

"I have to work, so I can't be with you."

Markus looks worried, which annoys me. I don't need a nanny. I have lived alone for over a year, spent a Christmas without Stefan, and don't need to be taken care of the way Markus thinks I do.

I shake my head. "It's okay. I'll manage."

"Have you talked to your mom and dad?" He looks doubtful.

"Yes, of course I've talked to them, but we aren't going to celebrate Christmas together. We send Christmas presents to each other. That's enough."

His concern is touching, but it also provokes me. Markus picks up on my feeling. Perhaps it's his keen perception that makes me feel so strongly about him.

"Sorry, I don't mean to pry, I'm just wondering: Have you even *told* them what has happened?"

"It's complicated . . ."

"Maybe I'm dense, but how is it complicated? A crazy murderer is after you and you don't even tell your family because of some sort of misdirected consideration? If I were you—"

"Yes, but you aren't! Stop treating me like a child."

I don't mean to shout, but without realizing it, I have stood up and raised my voice loud enough to stop the conversations at the tables around us. "Bitch," I hear one of the tipsy regulars mumble from a table near the bar.

Without saying a word, I grab my coat and bag and rush toward the exit. "Merry Christmas," another drunk says, just as I open the door and disappear into the darkness.

He lived on Narvavägen, right next to Oscar's pastry shop. Breaking in was ridiculously easy. All I needed to do was wait in the street until an old lady with an overweight, limping poodle came out through the main door. I ran and held the door open for her. She smiled gratefully and with small, uncertain steps disappeared down Strandvägen.

The next challenge was his front door. I had brought tools and quickly got to work. It took less than three minutes to get the flimsy door open. And I didn't even have to try too hard.

Inside, the apartment was in semidarkness, but I still recognized the silhouettes of designer furniture: Jacobsen, Aalto, Lissoni. The guy had taste. There were also expensive electronics everywhere. Otherwise, the place was almost clinically free of personality. If I hadn't known that someone lived here, I would have thought the apartment was uninhabited.

I found his home office, which had a desk with three black-and-white lithographs above it, a chair, and a bookshelf. Carefully, I pulled out the chair and climbed on it so that I could inspect the bookshelf. This was the perfect place. Easily accessible for someone looking for something but a spot not immediately visible when you entered the room. I decided to leave the book there.

Then I sat down at the computer, took out the list of sites, and got to work. It was easier than I had expected. Much easier.

Aina calls it cleaning up.

She gathers all the handwritten patient records, a few invoices, and a letter from the tax authorities into a heap on her desk. In the process, an old packet of gum gets swept up as well.

"There, I'm just going to put this in the safe," she says, walking out to the reception desk, the stack of papers under her arm.

I sigh. I don't have the energy to raise the issue of her carelessness. I decide to let it rest. Aina comes back and sinks into her office chair, leans back, and looks up at the ceiling.

"I'm so damn tired today. You know. Three depressed patients in a row. You almost start having suicidal thoughts yourself. What if they're right? What if life really is meaningless? What if they've cracked the code, seen the truth, unlike the rest of us?"

Aina grins, takes a ChapStick out of her desk drawer, and starts moisturizing her plump lips.

I look down at my wrinkled linen skirt and hesitate. "Listen . . ."

"Hmm. What?"

Aina is still rubbing balm on her lips.

"Sven."

"Sven what?"

"What do you think about Sven?"

The room goes silent. Aina nods slowly and looks absently out the window.

"What do I think about Sven," she repeats slowly, emphasizing every word.

She looks at me with her clear blue eyes.

"You know, I really don't think it's him anymore. I think Birgitta is angry at him. Because he made a pass at you. And at others. It's her revenge, that's all, not giving him an alibi."

"So you don't think he . . . uh, is offended because I rejected him and so on?"

I try to sound like I'm joking, but I can hear that my voice sounds fragile. And I know that it could break at the slightest provocation.

"Offended? No. I think it's more like it whets his appetite to be rejected. Sven is, well . . ."

Aina trails off and seems to be thinking about something. She is still holding the ChapStick in her right hand, drumming it lightly against the desk.

"It's like Sven is turned on *exactly because you aren't interested.* Do you understand? Once you've given in, he's not interested anymore."

It takes me a few seconds to take in the full meaning of Aina's words. I look at her sitting there behind her white desk.

And I can tell that she sees that I finally understand.

Her neck blushes red like a tidal wave. She looks down at the floor.

"Shit, Siri. It was only one time. It just happened, you know." Aina's voice fades away.

I feel a growing sense of despair. Aina and Sven. Sven and Aina. My best friend and my colleague. My best friend and Sara's murderer?

"Damn it, Aina."

I don't mean to shout, but the words had to come out, couldn't be stopped. Too late now.

"Oh, don't act like such a prude, Siri. It didn't mean anything. And it doesn't change anything, does it? Really?"

Aina looks me directly in the eye. Her voice is hard. There is no guilt, no shame in her voice, and she doesn't look away as she gets up and throws the ChapStick on her desk.

Then, taking her time, she saunters nonchalantly out of the room.

Date: December 20
Time: 4:00 p.m.
Place: Green Room, the practice
Patient: Charlotte Mimer—final session

It is time for Charlotte's final session, something I always try to do with my patients, regardless of how the therapy has gone. It's important, both for me and for them.

"Maintenance?" she asks, looking up at me.

"We psychologists call it that. It refers to the methods used to maintain the healthy behavior that has been learned during therapy and prevent someone from regressing into unhealthy behavior or trains of thought. In your case, it's important for you to continue keeping your food diary and recording all the emotions that surface in connection with eating. Pay particular attention to any tendencies toward emotional eating: consolation, anxiety relief through avoiding food or vomiting, and so on. Well, you know all that."

Charlotte nods slowly and tilts her head to one side. She always does this when she is thinking about something. At the corner of her mouth, I see a hint of a smile. I don't know if she thinks I sound funny or if she's simply happy about her progress and the fact that her therapy will now be over.

"So I'm . . . healthy now?"

"Healthy or sick . . . it's hard to label it. We can at least agree that your behavior and your emotions about food and eating were *not* healthy when we first met. Now you're feeling well, food and eating play normal roles in your life, occupy an appropriate portion of your awareness, of your time. And even if you had an experience of total loss of control in connection with quitting your job, you managed that, too. Didn't you?

You are at least as healthy as anyone else, if you see what I mean. And, perhaps most important of all, you now have the tools to keep you from falling back into compulsive behavior and thought patterns; it's just a matter of using them."

I wait for an answer, but there is none. Charlotte's gaze has drifted away. It has wandered out the window and on toward the pale-gray December twilight that slowly envelops Medborgarplatsen. I can see a streak of gray above the temples and in the parting of her well-brushed hair. She has no makeup on today and, despite the gray hair, she looks young. The pearls around her neck signal class and something else, perhaps a conservative attitude, or maybe this is simply how one must look in her industry, an accessory as obvious as a man's tie. I don't know the codes in her world; I cannot decipher the signals.

"If you look back, Charlotte, do you think the treatment has worked as you had hoped it would?"

Her gaze is still fixed on some invisible point beyond Björn's Park, but I can see that she is starting to come back. Slowly, she gathers herself and brushes her hand over her black wool skirt with a slow, precise motion.

"It was easier than I thought. *The eating part itself* was easier than I thought," she corrects herself, suddenly looking right at me. I understand what she is referring to.

"And if the eating part was easier, what was harder?"

"That's hard to explain."

Charlotte raises her hands as if to indicate an invisible object in the air in front of her, as if her hands can help her define what she cannot verbalize.

"It's like this," she begins tentatively. "If we're going to be honest, and in here we should be . . ."

She laughs and makes a sweeping gesture through the room, from the window to the box of Kleenex on the table.

"I'm really a pretty square person."

I shake my head and open my mouth to protest, but she raises her hand to silence me.

"Yes, of course, I'm a square. Capable. Obedient. For just those reasons, I think this type of therapy has worked so well for *me*. A program to follow, exercises to be done. It suits my disposition, you know. It *was . . . easy.* The hard thing was . . . losing control. For the first time in my life, I didn't know who I was. The hard thing was that when you are as sick as I was, it's like the illness becomes a part of you. You could perhaps say that you *become* the illness. It becomes the mask through which you see the world."

"Your persona?"

"My what?" Charlotte looks at me, perplexed.

"Nothing. Do continue."

"Well, I mean that even if it, the illness I mean, is hidden from others, you yourself still know. And when it goes away it's like there's nothing left. There's a . . . hole, you don't know who you are. But you have to fill that hole, that vacuum has to be filled with something else. You have to create a new *Self.* It's been hard. And I think that's what made me . . . That's when I started behaving incongruously. Does that sound strange?"

"Not at all. I would say that you are describing an extremely normal reaction in these kinds of cases—even if it takes many different expressions. How do you feel now?"

"Do you mean, have I filled the hole?"

"Have you?"

"No. But I've started to accept it. Maybe it's not really a hole, maybe it's just an imagined vacuum. Like the hollowness that arises when you remove a tumor or a sick part of your body. *A phantom hole* . . . And I no longer believe I'm going crazy. On the contrary, sometimes it feels like I've never been as sane as I am now."

Charlotte smiles and for a moment looks completely calm.

"But I'm going to be honest . . ."

". . . and in here you should be . . ."

Charlotte smiles and I can tell that she is grateful that I am being playful.

"It was probably not just what happened to your patient that made me break off the treatment. I felt that I was losing control and it was uncomfortable for me to continue. It was easy for me to change my behavior. To change my eating habits. But changing the idea of who you are . . . that's really hard. I've been thinking quite a bit over the fall . . ."

"And?"

"And it feels like I can only take one change at a time. Not force anything. Sometimes I actually miss it."

"The eating disorder?"

"Of course I don't miss being sick, but I can feel a sort of . . . emptiness, a sense of being lost. I feel that hollowness and it gnaws at me a little. Then there is another issue too: I no longer have any excuse not to take hold of my life. New job, you know. Love . . . or lack of love. I get completely exhausted when I think about everything I still have to do."

I think for a moment.

"Work and love. Love and work: The goal of therapy."

"What do you mean?"

"Freud said that, he called work and love the goal of therapy."

"I'm not big on Freud."

I smile at Charlotte.

"Just take one step at a time. And listen . . ."

"Hmm."

"You can call me whenever you want."

We both sit in silence for a while, looking out the window. It has gotten so dark that I can see my own tired reflection in the windowpane. I get up and move over to the window. Slowly, I rest my forehead against the cold, smooth glass so that my breath forms two damp patches under my nose. On the square below, business is in progress as usual. The market sellers are offering straw goats and pigs, door wreaths of spruce branches decorated with red apples and other ornaments. Christmas is approaching inexorably.

"Are you okay?"

Charlotte sounds sincerely worried. I stretch and turn toward her.

"Absolutely, I was just thinking . . . it's almost Christmas."

"Uh, and?"

Charlotte looks confused; a wrinkle has formed between her eyebrows. I try to smooth over my odd behavior.

"What will you be doing for Christmas?"

"Well, I'll see my dad and work a bit. Write dutifully in the food diary. And then I'm actually going on a date."

"On a date, how nice."

"Hmm. Don't know if I've told you this, but I met a guy at that watercolor class I took at the Folk University. You know, on Götgatsbacken. We've gone out a few times, I assume it's too soon to say anything yet . . . but it feels good."

Suddenly, I am struck by an inexplicable concern. My stomach knots up and I move my gaze from the crowd on Medborgarplatsen to Charlotte's calm, well-groomed figure. She looks perplexed and I realize she can sense my concern.

We say good-bye. It is always sad when patients finish. Sometimes it's as if I forget why they are really here, that they are paying for my time, for my services. That they actually don't just want to see me.

"Take care of yourself," says Charlotte, giving me a light hug; it is as if she embraces me without touching me. An ethereal being through and through.

"And listen"—she tilts her head to one side—"good luck with that . . . person who's following you."

She looks at me for a long time.

"Uh, they'll probably arrest him soon," I say, because I don't want her to worry.

A smile flashes on Charlotte's face but disappears as quickly as it came and is replaced by a curl at the corner of her mouth that makes her look a little . . . condescending. As if she feels sorry for me and despises me at the same time. She opens her mouth, hesitates, and then says something that surprises me.

"And how do you know it's a he?"

She says this in a light, gentle tone, making it sound as if she is commenting on a new car or rattling off the ingredients for a recipe. There is absolutely nothing charged in her tone of voice, and nevertheless my hair stands on end. She turns and quickly leaves the room.

It is the day before Christmas Eve. For a week now, the temperature has been well below freezing and has transformed Götgatspuckeln into a gigantic glistening tongue of ice that pedestrians must move across with careful, tentative steps. A light snowfall buries the city under a dangerously beautiful, temporary white carpet that dampens all sounds. My collar catches the snowflakes, and as my body heat transforms them into droplets of water, the moisture makes its way farther toward my neck and down between my shoulder blades in small rivulets. My hands have turned into two stiff, unmoving clumps that I constantly have to massage to keep them from going numb. It is the price I pay for my own stinginess; paying hundreds of kronor for new gloves when I already have several pairs back at the house does not seem reasonable.

In the stores, Christmas shopping is at its peak. Expensive goods change hands while I silently pass outside the display windows. At the lamp store, blinking multicolor Christmas lighting shares the space with bright elves who bow in time to some inaudible Christmas song. And everywhere, there is resolute expectation in the eyes of everyone I encounter. They do not radiate joy or excitement but rather a kind of strained decisiveness as they move purposefully between the stores, forming small lines and sometimes large streams. Streams of consumers, I think.

Inside the café, a damp warmth strikes me. She is already waiting for me at the table in the back, by the window. Her cheeks are glowing red and I take a deep breath in her golden-yellow hair when we embrace. It smells of honey. Aina takes hold of my frozen hands and looks at me in mock horror.

"You're ice-cold! Don't you have any mittens?"

I shake my head and smile, as if mittens were a worldly problem that does not directly concern me.

We've met to exchange Christmas presents, a tradition we have kept up for years. It's never anything expensive, just small but thoughtful presents: a book, a CD that carries a certain meaning, or maybe a concert ticket.

Aina twirls her honey-hair and hands me a small, hard package wrapped in what looks like green tinfoil. I accept it in silence. The package cannot be opened until tomorrow—that is our agreement. At exactly ten o'clock in the evening, we call each other and politely say thank you for the gift, whatever it may be.

I hand her my present. It, too, is a hard package wrapped in colorful gift paper and a lilac ribbon. Aina looks delighted as she takes it. Her sweater has slipped down over one shoulder, revealing a red bra strap. She laughs out loud when she sees my critical look.

"Don't be such a prude, Siri. Maybe you need something a little revealing, too."

I don't know if it's the heat inside the café or her comment, or perhaps just that I cannot digest the fact that Sven and Aina had an affair, but suddenly I feel my face getting hot. I get up and free myself from the wet weight of my coat before I sink down again on the chair.

"So how's it going with Mr. Policeman?"

I answer truthfully that it's just fine, thanks, but that there are certain details in our relationship I have a hard time accepting.

"I'm not comfortable with the role I'm stuck in. He's the strong one and I'm the weak one; he's the hero and I'm the victim. Whenever we get together, it ends with me starting to cry for one reason or other. And he consoles me, of course. And then I get angry with him, even though it's not his fault. It's so"—I search for the right word—"*banal,* you see? That's not me, *you* know that, don't you? Besides"—I hesitate—"sometimes I think he . . . takes me for granted. I mean, I don't even know if I want to be with anyone. But he, he seems to think we're a—"

"A what?"

"A . . . couple." I purse my lips and my voice gets small as I say the dangerous words. I almost don't want to say it.

Aina shrugs. "Do you know what I think?"

She licks the sugar residue from the giant pastry she had just eaten off her fingers.

"Sure, spread your wisdom . . ."

She doesn't look at me directly, doesn't pick up on my sarcasm, but I decide not to make a scene. Not this time, too. I already succeeded in ruining my last date with Markus before Christmas.

"I think that you never, I mean *never*, would have been interested in him if he wasn't a policeman and you a victim. I mean, good Lord, how old is he? Does he even have an education?"

"What a damn snob you are. Does that even matter?"

"Siri, I don't think you get it. I only want what's best for you. But you're so . . . fragile. People can exploit you."

Damn Aina. Damn Aina and her well-intentioned, condescending interpretations of reality. Of my life. I look at her sitting there with her eyes wide open and a worried expression. She senses my indignation and tries to lighten the mood.

"Oh, if you want to have fun . . . I mean, I won't prevent you. Go ahead and see inspector . . . baton. Inspector Orgasm."

Aina grins.

I can't help it. Suddenly I have a giggle attack that just won't end. We double over with laughter.

Our good-bye hug is warm and long. Once again, I take in the sweet honey aroma of her hair. I get sugar crystals on my cheek. Her hands are strong and warm as she grasps me around the shoulders and looks me deep in the eyes.

"So we'll talk tomorrow at ten. Promise that you'll come over if you're bored. You're welcome anytime, you know that. I don't get why you want to celebrate Christmas Eve in a studio on Kungsholmen."

This last sentence she says in a mumble, almost inaudibly. I watch her as she disappears down Götgatsbacken in the twilight. She alternately jumps and jogs off into the darkness, a grown-up Pippi Longstocking in a red bra.

The last thing I see is her bright red scarf and red mittens that are eventually also swallowed up by the darkness. It's time to go home now. Soon it will be dark.

Much too dark.

Markus's phone call comes right before midnight. I am lying in bed, reading. Every corner of the apartment is lit up and the flashlight on my nightstand is surrounded by empty wineglasses.

"We've arrested him. It's over, Siri."

"What?" is all I can get out.

"They brought in Peter Carlsson today. Do you know what they found on his coffee table?"

"What are you talking about? The police arrested Peter?"

It's as if my thoughts are on fast-forward. I have a hard time understanding what Markus is trying to tell me. Slowly I manage to put the words together. Formulate a sentence. The police have arrested Peter.

"The photo, the photo of Sara Matteus. You know, the one you found with Marianne? It was at Peter's, or more precisely, a similar one was on his coffee table."

"What photo?"

"Siri, the photo of Sara on the rock. You know, when she was topless."

The photo of Sara. I think of her eyes in that picture. Her vulnerability. Anger boils inside me. Anger and sorrow over Sara's death.

"Do you know for sure that it's him?"

Markus sounds calm and reassuring when he answers. "Why else would he have the photo?"

"I don't know. What has he said?"

"He claims he doesn't know how it got there, that it wasn't there in the morning. Does he really think we'll believe him? There were more things, too. They found a book about how to stuff animals up on his bookshelf. A little hard to explain, that. And a lot of links to sick websites about serial killers and torture on his computer. Besides, he has a prior record, for possession, five years ago."

"Narcotics possession? But what does that have to do with this?"

"Listen, Siri, I've seen this so many times before. It all begins with finding one thing that doesn't add up. A white lie, a note on his criminal record. Then you start to unravel and it never ends. Besides, he fell apart immediately, he said that he was a bad person and a bunch of other crap."

"What exactly did he say?"

"I don't know. I wasn't there, of course. I was . . . taken off the case. This is what I heard. I thought you'd want to know right away. Thought you would have a more peaceful Christmas."

I still don't fully understand everything Markus is saying. Images of Sara, curled up in my chair with a cigarette in her hand, come to me. But there's also the image of a shapeless stranger who is chasing me. Observing me. Who wishes me harm. An image that suddenly has a face: Peter Carlsson. I am not prepared for my own reaction. Don't understand at first what is happening. I have a hard time getting air. I take a deep breath. Then comes a sound. I know that it is coming from me, but I can't seem to do anything to stop it. It starts as a muffled moan and then turns into loud sobbing. It is as if I am watching myself from outside. I see the weeping, hear the loud sniffling. But I feel nothing at first. Then an almost unfamiliar feeling spreads inside me.

It is relief.

I have made a decision: I will celebrate Christmas in my own house. The logic is simple. Peter Carlsson is sitting in a cell somewhere and no one requires my presence today.

My gloveless, frozen fingers suffer under the weight of the grocery bag I am carrying along Munkbron toward Slussen and the Värmdö buses. The low morning sun paints Stockholm in a light golden shimmer and the snow crunches under my boots. It is cold today, really cold. This morning, the thermometer outside my kitchen showed five degrees.

Bus 438 is full to the brim of families with children and grandparents celebrating Christmas. Bags full of gifts are crammed into every conceivable corner, bags that will be taken home in a few hours, full of crap that no one really needs. In my bag, there is only one gift; flashing green, it rests like a jewel on top of a hunk of cheese and a pack of crackers.

I think about Peter Carlsson all the time. It's impossible to see through a person. You can't tell from the outside whether someone has performed evil actions or had evil thoughts. If a person has decided to conceal or withhold parts of himself, it is extremely difficult to see through the lies and discover the omitted truth. I'm a psychologist, not a mind reader. I remember Vijay's words: "You can't know, Siri. It is impossible for you to know for sure." Once Peter Carlsson decided to trick me, there was nothing to prevent him from succeeding.

I shake my head and shudder slightly, despite the oppressive heat on the bus. Maybe I can spend the evening looking through the video recordings of my conversations with him. All the tapes are still locked up in my safe out in the cottage. Maybe if I see them again I will understand. Understand evil.

As I walk from the bus to the cottage, my thin, worn boots sink down through the snow crust, wetting my ankles. The sun is shining through the pine and spruce, and I can see that the path ahead of me is pristine.

Surrounded by the sounds of the forest and with my nose filled by the cold, odorless air, I stop for a second when I catch sight of the cottage and the water in the bay, which is covered by ice and snow. This is something I had never seen before at this time of year.

The house is resting peacefully between the snow-covered rocks. Not a movement is visible. No tracks in the snow to give away the animals' secret trails.

When I come up to the door, I have to try several times before the key finally slides into the old-fashioned lock. My frozen fingers are that stiff.

Inside, the air is lukewarm and dense with dust and humidity. I set the supermarket bag down on the floor and go from room to room, turning on the radiators and checking that all the lights work.

In the kitchen, the fridge and freezer are on, but moldy vegetables and spoiled milk betray my hasty departure. I pour out the gelatinous clump of milk in the sink and slowly start emptying the fridge of its contents. I lift up a bottle of Amarone from the bottom shelf in the kitchen. I want to indulge myself with something more than the usual red from a box. It is Christmas Eve, after all. It is Christmas Eve and I am at home in my cottage. The relief of returning is almost physical. My body feels light and warm. I realize how much I missed my home. It is paradoxical that I can feel so safe here, when everyone else perceives me as so vulnerable. Perhaps it is Stefan. He is in all the rooms in the house, tangibly present in the gently sanded moldings and carefully painted walls. I find a glass and a corkscrew and serve myself the strong red wine, raise the glass toward my reflection in the windowpane, and take a sip. A delicious, smooth warmth spreads in my body like rings on water.

I am home.

Wineglass in hand, I take out my cell phone and start making the calls that are expected of me. I talk with my sisters, their children, and Mom and Dad, wish them all a merry Christmas, explain again that Aina would be all alone if I didn't spend Christmas with her. I don't have a bad conscience about lying to my parents. They never understood my need for solitude, much less now. I think about how easy it is for me to get them to believe me, as if they desperately want what I say to be true. They say that of course Aina is welcome at their home in Huddinge, but I am quick to explain that Aina probably needs a little peace and quiet right now. Christmas can be a difficult time if you're at odds with those close to you, a sentiment my mom agrees with. She wishes us a pleasant Christmas Eve, reminds me to watch the classic Christmas cartoons on TV, and says good-bye. I can sense that Mom is grateful that Aina is with me and suspect that she really thinks I'm the one who needs calm, peace, and human closeness of the unconditional variety. My thoughts from the bus return—about how hard it is to see through someone who doesn't want to be exposed. I pour myself another glass of wine and cut a thick slice of cheese. It's time to look at the videos.

Peter's face fills the screen before me. Nervous and unhappy, he glances across the table toward me, my back to the camera. Dark-gray suit, blue-striped tie, nothing that sticks out, only well-tailored elegance from head to toe. For a second, he looks right into the camera and the look in his eyes resembles that of a wild animal. There is something there that makes me think he wants to escape from the office, tear off his suit, throw away the blue-striped tie, and take to the woods. I press Pause and think a little about my own initial reaction to the news. Maybe it is due to the contrast between his well-groomed, civilized exterior and his words, which reflect another side of him, a side that is about impulse and compulsion, that reeks of sweat and animals.

> "I get thoughts, images inside my head. And they scare me."
> "Can you describe these thoughts?"
> "It's . . . so hard."

I stop the tape again and Peter's body freezes in a peculiar position, half turned away, half leaning forward with both hands in front of his face. He is desperate and disconsolate. He feels completely alone and exposed in my green consultation room with its bland paintings and the little table where I sit, almost like a life buoy with the box of Kleenex available for meek consolation.

You have to trust your own eyes, your intuition, and your combined experience, Stefan always said, and he was a brilliant clinician. If I were to dare trust my own senses, they would tell me that Peter Carlsson could not have killed Sara, that he could not have injured Marianne or staged a plot against me. Peter is not a murderer; he is only an ordinary half-nutty, neurotic person. He is one of the many who have to gather courage to hold their lives together, to give structure to their days and nights. One of the many helpless people who have to take life one moment at a time and, in that way, force time to move ahead and give it a direction. Someone like me.

I close my eyes and run my hand across the videotapes that are spread out on the floor beside me. Here they are, all the compulsive thoughts, all the anxiety, all the tears. Here is Sara's slender body dressed in black, her scarred arms, green nails, and signature cigarette. Here is Charlotte's pearl necklace and dress suits, and her well-articulated, patient answers to my intrusive questions. Here is the man with big muscles and a beard who drives a Harley-Davidson but is afraid of ants ("and other small creatures with a lot of spindly legs"). Here is the mother who hid all the knives and scissors in the garden shed, because she had compulsive thoughts about cutting her son's eyes. Here is the corporate executive who was compelled to count to a hundred every time he went up a staircase, who always went sideways through doors and needed to park his car in a spot whose number was evenly divisible by three. All these people—no stranger than me, not crazy or evil—just trying to hold the seams together around their inner abyss. People who cautiously maneuver around catastrophe every day.

I prepare my Christmas dinner carefully. I turn on the oven, cut bread into thin slices to cover with chèvre and honey, take out the store-bought dolmas and the hummus. I turn on the CD player and let the music of Belle & Sebastian fill my cottage. Outside, it is starting to get dark. The bay is sleeping under its shimmering deep blanket of snow. The pines around the rocks are a black outline against the darkening sky. I am glad I came out here.

I don't belong in the city.

By the time the velvety darkness of Christmas Eve completely envelops my cottage, I have long turned on every lamp, lit up every corner, and filled the table with candles. I lie on my bed and look at the black windows, which reflect the contours of the room like a mirror. The flashlight is in my hand. The wine has made me sleepy. I close my eyes and let my body release.

I dream that I am celebrating Christmas with Stefan. The floor is covered with packages of various sizes and colors. Stefan is busy in the kitchen and I arrange the packages in a long row. A colorful snake of presents winds from the living room all the way into the bedroom. I can clearly smell the aroma of the ham that Stefan is baking in the oven from the bedroom, as I bend over the row of presents. When I open my eyes, the scent of ham remains, and I can hear a faint scraping sound from the kitchen.

At once, I know that something is wrong, but I have a hard time working up the usual fear. The whole thing is too absurd. Has someone come to cook ham for me in the middle of the night?

I fumble for my cell phone to check the time but notice that it is out of power. Slowly, I get up on unsteady legs, still a little tipsy, and go out to the kitchen.

I am so taken aback by the golden-brown ham baking in the oven that I don't see him at first.

"Hi, Siri."

There he stands, leaning against the window in a relaxed, laid-back pose that makes his gangly body look even taller than it is. He is the same as always: the reddish-brown hair, the regular features, the slender body. His mouth is broad and he smiles a little, stroking his goatee lightly as he inspects me.

It's Christer. Marianne's Christer.

"Take a seat! I've made dinner."

His tone is neutral and friendly, but I don't dare say no. Slowly, I walk over to the kitchen table on legs that struggle to support me and sink down on one of the gray wood chairs. I glance at the wall clock: one thirty.

"I thought about making some meatballs, too. They seem to fit. But I have to admit I'm not big on cooking, so I bought some at the store."

Christer smiles at me and goes to the stove and busies himself with the meatballs and something else I can't recognize. My insides are in turmoil—what does he want from me? In the middle of the night.

Christmas Eve night.

An unpleasant feeling is growing stronger and soon becomes a certainty. Something is terribly wrong with Christer. I should—no, I must—get out of here before . . . well, before *what*?

It strikes me that I ought to try to talk to him, figure out his intentions and, if possible, find an escape route, but my throat is tied up and my mouth is dry. I fold my hands under the table to keep them from shaking.

"How many meatballs would you like?"

The question is strangely friendly and his expression reveals nothing about his intentions.

"These are *real* meatballs, no bread crumbs and crap like that for filler, just one hundred percent ground beef and spices. Maybe egg, too—I don't really know. Do you have to use egg?"

"What do you want from me?"

It is no more than a whisper, but I am certain that he hears me. He looks at me but does not answer. In the frying pan, the butter has started to sizzle, and he adds the meatballs one by one in silence.

"Here, you can open the wine." He hands me a bottle of red wine and an opener.

"You do like red wine, don't you?"

My fingers are numb as I take the bottle. I look at it as if I don't understand what it is and rest it on my lap.

"What do you want?" I repeat, my voice steadier now.

"I am Christer Andersson. Good Lord, you still don't get it do you, Siri?"

I look confused at his gangly figure as he stirs the meatballs at my stove. I still cannot fully take in this improbable appearance in my kitchen, and the wine I drank earlier makes me lethargic. So Christer is standing in my kitchen at one thirty on Christmas morning, frying meatballs. And I think—no, I *know*—that he is Sara's murderer.

I shake my head in response to his question: *No, I still don't get it.*

Christer sighs and turns toward me, a spatula in his hand.

"I'm Jenny's dad. Jenny Andersson's dad."

The bottle slips from my grasp and splinters on the floor, wine splashes over my feet, but I feel nothing as I sit petrified on the chair. *He is Jenny's dad.*

Long red hair, fingers constantly drumming against her thighs in time with inaudible melodies, milky-white skin covered with freckles, a skinny girl's body dressed in jeans and a tight sweater with a leather strap around her neck.

Jenny Andersson—my patient who committed suicide. Her father found her with slashed wrists under an apple tree in the yard. And here he is now in my kitchen, frying meatballs. Suddenly, everything is painfully clear to me. He is avenging his daughter's death. In his eyes, I am the guilty one.

"Is it starting to come back now? I guess maybe she was just one of many patients, one in the crowd. It's not so easy to remember them all, perhaps?" He grins, but there is pain in his voice.

"Of course I remember Jenny," I whisper, rubbing my shaking hands against each other under the table, above the Bordeaux-colored stain growing into a lake. On the blood-colored surface I can see my own reflection. Leaning forward, I huddle on the chair as if to instinctively signal physical submissiveness and thereby appease Christer's wrath.

"So you also understand why I'm here? You killed my daughter with your carelessness and your incompetence."

"Christer, I did not kill your daughter. Just as—"

Swoosh. The blow comes without warning and strikes me in the face. I can feel something warm running down my cheek, but I feel no pain, only shock and despair.

"Now you shut up, you damn psycho whore. You killed her. Do you get that? You KILLED her."

Christer's voice rises to a howl. He turns toward me and with a single sweeping motion he throws the cast-iron pan against the wall so that the meatballs fly across the room.

He is standing close to me. I can hear his breathing, which is strangely rattling, almost asthmatic. And the odor, the odor of his body. He smells of acrid sweat, like an animal. He sinks down in the chair across from me and remains sitting with his head buried in his hands, rocking slowly back and forth as he produces a whistling noise. It takes awhile before I realize that he really does have asthma.

"You killed her," he mumbles, out of breath.

We sit in silence across from each other. The only sound in the room is the sizzling, bubbling noise from the ham in the oven and the ticking of the clock on the kitchen wall. Despite my groggy state, I realize that I have to get him to talk, I have to establish contact with him, make a bridge into his confused awareness, reach his rational self. Surely, he must have one?

"Sara . . ." I begin hesitantly.

Christer sobs, wipes his forehead and straightens up.

"Yes . . . Sara," he says, in a quiet but strangely calm voice. He seems to think a moment as he sits among the glass splinters, spilled red wine, and spoiled meatballs.

"Yes, poor, stupid Sara. Say what you want, but she is better off where she is now. Really nice-looking girl. actually, if you ignore her ravaged appearance, but, to be honest, she was totally nuts. Or, what do you think, Ms. Psychologist? Carving your arms with knives? Why does someone do that?"

"You killed her?"

"Whatever, she was dead long before I met her. I did her a favor."

Christer leans across the kitchen table toward me and looks at me, no, he *stares,* with strangely steel-gray eyes that remind me of lead shot or metal buttons or the small, shiny bodies of silverfish as they helplessly try to crawl away from my dishrag on the bathroom floor. He reaches out and strokes my cheek, and I notice that his palm is colored red by my blood.

"Damn it, Siri, I'm sorry it turned out this way. What should I say, so much time has passed . . . such a long time since I started following you, then I started discovering things about you . . . so I've almost started to think I know you. I've almost started to *like* you. Do you understand? I know what you have for dinner, what you look like naked, that you drink too much, and that you're having sex with that pathetic cop. Does that turn you on? Younger guys? Is that your thing? Do you want to feel superior? *Is that why you became a therapist?*"

I look right into his button eyes but say nothing. I am afraid of provoking him further, but he takes no notice of me and continues his tirade.

"You took my life from me. Do you know that?"

I still say nothing, let him talk. Explain. His voice is quiet as he continues, almost a whisper.

"My life was . . . *perfect.* I don't think you can understand. Everything we had. Our life. When you killed Jenny, you didn't just take her away from me, you took *my whole life.* Katarina, my wife, couldn't deal with it . . . she left me. Met a new guy. A bloody gynecologist, *would you believe it?* A gynecologist is screwing my wife these days . . . *Damn it.* I got fired, the company bought me out. My friends withdrew, thought I'd gotten strange. It was so damn humiliating. And it was all your fault. But you were never punished, your life just continued. *As if nothing had happened.* That's not right, I think you understand that."

Christer looks at me with an empty gaze and continues. His voice is stronger now and his hands are no longer trembling. He suddenly looks determined.

"And now here we are in the end, although I didn't want it to be this way. At the end of the road, so to speak." Using a blue-striped dish towel, he wipes my blood from his hand with a look of distaste.

His movements are jerky. With manic determination he rubs his hand as if to get rid of every trace of me from his body. There is growing desperation in my chest; I have to get a conversation started with him. Before he feels forced to act, to do something rash.

"I think I deserve an answer to certain questions. I can understand . . . your feelings, but I still have to know what happened."

Christer shrugs and looks at me indifferently.

"What do you want to know?"

"How did you meet Sara?"

"I've been following you a long time, Siri, longer than you think. And Sara, well, I found her through Marianne."

"Through Marianne?"

"I knew that Marianne worked for you, so I picked her up at a bar. It was pathetically easy, by the way. It was a long time since anyone had paid her any attention, I guess."

He seems to think a moment, carefully brushes away a few crumbs from his shirt and scratches his red hair.

"I had no particular intentions with her. At the time, that is. Mostly I wanted to hear more about you, find out if you were still sabotaging people's lives. And then . . . time passed. I got to know you through Marianne, in a way. And she was more than happy to tell me *everything* about her job. Sometimes I also followed you in the city—stood behind you at Söderhallarna, touched your hair as I went past you on the escalator, held open the door when you were going into the parking garage— but you never noticed. Once, I actually handed you your bag when you dropped it outside that disgusting place on Götgatan—what's it called? Gröne Jägaren, that's it. But *you never saw me*. It was as if I was *completely invisible* to you. Sometimes, I sat on the rocks outside here and kept you company while you knocked back wine like a damn alcoholic. And then, that thing with turning on all the lights . . . Listen, seriously speaking, it's pretty pathetic that you're afraid of the dark. You work with people's fears. Or at least, that was how Marianne put it."

He falls silent and looks searchingly at me, as if he is curious about me for the first time during our strange conversation.

"And then . . ." I ask in a whisper.

"The rest was no problem. Marianne had access to the case records and the patients' addresses. Sometimes, she brought your notes home to write up a clean copy. I've read every damn patient record on Sara. Besides, Marianne talked about her quite often. I think she felt sorry for her, but goodness, she felt sorry for everyone! Stray dogs, children in the Third World, whales, and God knows what else. She felt compassion for the whole damn world."

"Why Sara?"

Christer shrugs and crushes a meatball with his shoe.

"Why not? Marianne always thought you cared about her a lot for some reason. That you worked so hard to rehabilitate her. I just got curious. It wasn't a . . . plan to start with, it kind of . . . developed. It took on a life of its own. Until I took control, decided to guide developments in the direction I wanted."

He suddenly looks triumphant, like a naughty boy. A disobedient little boy with dead, gray button eyes. I think about Vijay's words, of his description of a middle-aged man, well established in society. Why didn't Vijay say how I should talk to him, how to get him to stop, what buttons to push?

"Sara told me everything about your therapy, and what she didn't tell me was in the records Marianne brought home. So it was easy . . . easy to write the suicide note, easy to get hold of Charlotte Mimer's address. And sure, I was the one who planted the photo and the book about taxidermy on Peter Carlsson. I thought about tipping off the cops about him as well, but they got there first, you might say . . ."

"And the blood on my lawn? The dog?"

"That was a mistake. I was forced. Forced to silence them."

"What do you mean, silence?"

Christer pinches his lips together and refuses to answer.

"I really don't understand . . . Don't you realize that you've destroyed the lives of a lot of innocent people?"

"Do you think I enjoyed it, or something?"

Christer yells hoarsely. "*I was forced to do it. For her sake . . . Forced to see that justice was done. That was the only way, the only way to get . . . some kind of peace.*"

He lowers his voice to a whisper. "It wasn't a *pleasure*. Maybe I enjoyed that thing with the DUI. More like a practical joke. Don't you think?"

"But Marianne? Was that you? Did you have anything to do with her accident?"

Christer sighs and for a moment buries his head in his hands.

"She thought she was so damn smart, she thought she had figured out how it all hung together. Found all my papers about Sara. She wanted to see you . . . to tell you about me. I couldn't let her do that . . ."

Christer pauses and looks at me.

"I didn't want to hurt Marianne. She's good, she took care of me, actually."

He falls silent for a brief moment and suddenly looks sad.

"But you realize how this has to end, don't you? There is *one* type of justice, and that's the kind you administer yourself."

He holds out his hands, which still carry traces of my blood, as if to show that they are what will administer this justice. In my belly, the seed of terror is growing to a glowing ball. He intends to kill me, that's obvious, that's what justice means for him.

My death is his justice.

And I will soon have no more questions to ask, no circumstances that must be clarified, no pretexts for maintaining the conversation. How great is the probability that someone will come here at this time of night? Markus is working. Aina is celebrating with her mother. Everyone thinks I'm sleeping safely in the apartment on Kungsholmen with the lights on. That Sara's murderer is sitting locked in a cell at the Kronoberg jail. My escape routes are limited. From the kitchen, I can reach the living room, and through that, my bedroom. There is a door to the bedroom, but it doesn't have a lock. Perhaps there's a way to block it.

"It's probably done now," I say, nodding toward the oven, where a thin, black film of burnt bread crumbs and mustard is starting to form on the ham and an odor of burnt meat has started to seep out.

Christer looks confused but gets up anyway, turns toward the oven, and picks up the oven mitt to take out the ham.

This is my chance, the best I am going to get. As Christer opens the oven and takes hold of the roasting pan, I get up, give him a forceful shove in the back, and run. It is not a particularly well-thought-out plan. I rush through the living room toward the bedroom. Behind me, I can hear Christer yell something, but it is as if my brain cannot understand the words, cannot decode their meaning.

I shut the bedroom door with a slam so forceful that a candleholder on the shelf above the bed falls down. It is caught gently by the comforter, as I press all of my weight against the door and inspect the few pieces of furniture in the room. The only thing that has weight and size to speak of is the bed. I bend forward and try to pull the bed from its place by the wall over toward the door, blocking it with my body at the same time.

BANG!

Christer crashes against the door with his entire weight and I am unable to keep it completely closed. The door opens an inch or two and he manages to push his foot into the crack before I regain control and push back.

"Bloody psychologist whore. Let me in!"

Christer's yelling rings in my ears. He is close now, so close that I can smell his intermittent breath and hear the whistling sound from his cramped air passages through the crack in the door.

"Let me in, otherwise I'll KILL you."

But I know it's just the opposite. If he comes in, then he will kill me. It would be easy, as easy as a dog crushing a small rodent with a single crunching bite. I am so small, so thin. I can't resist him physically, which he obviously knows, and I don't think I can outwit him either. So I do the only thing I can: press back with all my strength so that his foot is crushed by the door. Christer screams, and for a moment the pressure from the other side of the door ceases.

My fingers are sweating so much I have a hard time bracing effectively against the door. I slide and slip on the smooth floor. I take a chance and wipe one palm against my pant leg for a moment. Then, *BANG!* With terrifying force, Christer forces the door open—he must have taken a running start from out in the living room—throwing me backward against the bed, which is only halfway pulled away from the wall. I lie there like a cockroach on my back, helpless, without an escape route.

Christer comes slowly toward me. He is grimacing with pain and massaging his shoulder.

Then he is on top of me.

Quite calmly, he straddles my waist, and with a quick move he locks my arms with his knees. He is breathing heavily. And the odor, Christer's odor, that unpleasant, acrid stench of sweat, suddenly envelops me. I feel nauseated. Perhaps it's his weight against my abdomen, perhaps the stench, but I turn my head to the side and throw up on one of the blue pillows. I feel the warm vomit as it makes its way down along my neck toward my back.

"Oh, shit," says Christer, looking away in disgust.

It strikes me that he probably can't stand bodily fluids. Blood, sperm, vomit. He moves down along my thin body until he is sitting on my thighs, at a safe distance from the vomit.

"Oh, shit," he repeats, looking at his hands as if to check whether he has gotten dirty.

"You know I wasn't the one who killed Jenny, don't you?"

I don't know why I say that. I simply feel incredibly tired. I can't bear to lie any longer. I want to put an end to this torture.

His eyes watch me and he squeezes harder with his knees so that my arms ache from my elbows to my wrists from the pressure.

"I wasn't the one who killed Jenny, Christer. It was you. Your need to control and your overprotective ways suffocated her. Can't you see?"

"Shut up!"

The blow comes quickly and unexpectedly. It hits me right across the cheek, but it doesn't hurt. There is something slack and uninvolved about it. Like a slap doled out to a child for the sake of appearances by a parent.

"Shut up," he repeats, quieter this time.

He leans forward, and for a moment I think he intends to kiss me, but he lays his head against my chest and I can tell that he is crying.

"I never meant to do her any harm."

Christer continues his monologue, with words drowned in sobbing and inaudible grunting. For a second, he releases the iron grip he has on me with his knees. His body is shaking in convulsions of sobs.

Christer's pain is so strong, so physical. For a moment I believe that it is being transmitted through his body and moving on to me in soft streams. I think again about Stefan, how inconceivable it is that he is gone. I think about the grinding, gnawing sorrow that will not let go. And I understand Christer. In the middle of my nightmare, lying on my back in my bedroom with Christer's head against my chest and my sweater damp with vomit, red wine, and his tears, a sudden wave of sympathy comes over me. I know how it feels to lose someone you love, and how painful it is when there is no answer for the reason why.

"I'm sorry."

I look up at Christer, try to catch his eyes.

"It was unforgivable of me to say that. Of course it wasn't your fault that Jenny died."

Christer raises his head to look at me. His eyes are red rimmed, and snot and tears are mixed on his unshaven cheeks. He looks doubtful. Skeptical, but at the same time desperate enough to choose to take what little consolation I can offer.

Absolution.

"When Stefan, my husband, died, I became empty. I couldn't believe that he was gone. I still can't believe it. I can't accept it. I often think he's still here. That he is right behind me. I console myself with the illusion that he's just out shopping, or at work, or taking his car to the garage. I simply can't understand that I will never get to be with him again. I see him sometimes, at a distance. Glimpse him on the bus, or in the crowds on Götgatan. Sometimes when I wake up I can feel his warmth in the bed, and for a brief moment I feel his body next to mine. Then I remember the truth and he disappears, the warmth disappears."

Christer nods. He knows what I mean. Suddenly we are united, two grieving, solitary people, left behind.

"Jenny, she was my child, do you understand? *My child.* She changed so much in my life. Before Jenny, life was meaningless. She gave me meaning and warmth and a faith that some of the little that was good in me would endure. After her, after Jenny, life was less than meaningless. Nothing was left. Nothing *is* left. Until I started following you, Siri. You actually gave me meaning again. The idea that you would have to pay for Jenny gave me purpose. Peace."

We are both silent. United in a sudden, involuntary intimacy, his hands around my arms, like a lover. From the kitchen, I can hear the ticking of the clock, and the odor of burnt ham encircles us.

"Tell me about Jenny. What was she like?"

My question comes spontaneously. I had seen Jenny only as a patient, sitting in the visitor's chair, drumming her long slender fingers. I wonder who she was as a child, the two-year-old, the schoolgirl, the teenager.

"Jenny was—"

Christer hesitates, thinks for a moment and seems to wonder what words he should use.

"Jenny was different. She wasn't like the other kids in school. She was raw, vulnerable. She cared about everyone—I guess you would call her empathetic. I remember she cried when she watched cartoons when she was little. It was that show, what's it called, with the cat and mouse. First she felt sorry for the mouse that was chased, then she felt sorry for the cat that got a beating. When her guinea pig died, she cried for weeks and wouldn't get out of bed."

Again he seems to think, as he conjures up the image of his dead daughter.

"She was worried about me and Katarina, that something would happen to us, that we would be in a car accident or get sick. She wanted to keep us from driving. In school, the other kids quickly discovered that she was easily frightened and anxious."

He shakes his head and closes his eyes. For a moment he seems to be overwhelmed by painful memories.

"They tormented her, you know. Those stupid brats scared her, teased her. She was different and she wasn't allowed to be. But I showed them what was what. I invited the kids over for Jenny's birthday, and their parents made sure that they came. Those ass kissers wanted to stay on our good side. Katarina played games with them. Jenny was happy, suddenly all these children were nice to her. Her antagonists became friends, for a little while."

I am listening, fascinated; it's as if Christer is filling in the gaps I have in my image of Jenny. I see satisfaction in his face and wonder what will come next.

"Then Jenny fell down and hurt herself. Katarina went off with her, to put on a bandage and console her. I was alone with the kids. At that time I hunted, everything imaginable: small game, moose . . . whatever. I took out one of my hunting rifles and showed them. I loaded it, opened the window, and shot at one of our apple trees. A whole branch came loose. The kids just gaped; they thought it was great, of course. Then I told them that the same thing would happen to their little brains if they ever bothered Jenny again. They would be shot to pieces. And I let them understand that it was best if they kept quiet about this, so their parents wouldn't know what their little angels were up to. Then Katarina came back—she had heard the shot and wondered what the hell I was up to. I told her I was only showing the kids my rifle and she said I was out of my mind before taking it and putting it back in the gun cabinet. We never talked about it again. But after that, Jenny was left alone. She was lonely, but they stopped tormenting her. Some of the girls even tried to be nice."

He shakes his head, as if the knowledge of how wicked small children can be to each other is too much for him.

"She was talented, too. Musical. She played piano and violin even when she was really little. And she was so loving, but vulnerable. I tried to protect her, you know."

He looks intensely into my eyes again. "I really tried to protect her, you understand?"

I nod slowly. I think I understand.

"Christer, I think Jenny really wanted to die."

He looks at me without an expression.

"Jenny was one of the most unhappy people I've ever met. It was as if all her emotions were heightened, amplified. As if she was living inside them, instead of the other way around. She felt so much pain. She would sit in my chair and shake with anxiety. And I felt so hopeless. I truly wanted to help her. I wanted her to make it, to step outside and be like everyone else, enjoy life and laugh. Perhaps get a boyfriend. Simply be a young girl. You know . . ."

Christer nods. He still says nothing, but his breathing is becoming more and more labored. That faint whistling sound with each exhalation.

"She had tried everything, all the medications on the market, all the therapists, hospitals, treatment homes. Nothing could ease the anxiety and the pain. Nothing helped. She didn't want to live any longer. At the beginning, I blamed myself, but I slowly came to realize that none of us can stop a person who has already decided."

Words fall out of me like stones. And the cramp in my abdomen suddenly relaxes a little, as if it actually is a physical burden I am ridding myself of.

Christer still says nothing, only observes me, his face close to mine. The warm light from my bed lamp with the yellow shade makes his already reddish skin glow.

"When . . . does it . . . go away?" he whispers, noticeably struggling with his asthma.

"I don't know," is all I get out.

The weight of Christer's body has made my legs fall asleep and my arms ache.

"I don't know when it goes away, but I do know one thing: You blame yourself, you feel guilt. Unnecessarily. When Stefan died, I also thought that it was my fault, that I should have been able to prevent it. *But you can't stop someone who has decided.*"

Suddenly, I notice that Christer's facial expression has changed and I realize that I've forgotten that the man I am talking to is a murderer.

Someone who doesn't think and function like me. Someone who actually has decided—to kill me.

For a brief moment I thought we could connect, but now I understand that I've made a mistake. He looks at me with his blank, dead eyes.

"I. Feel. No. Guilt." He pronounces each word with difficulty.

"I feel. No guilt. Because the guilt. Is not mine. You. Killed her."

And suddenly I know that it is meaningless to try to make Christer see reason. It's like walking round and round on very thin, brittle spring ice, knowing the whole time that it is going to break. Sooner or later I will say something that provokes him and he will decide that the game, our little conversation, is over. That it is time for me to die.

I must get away from here now. It is my last chance.

And just then he moves his weight away from me for an instant, and I tear myself loose from his gangly but strong body and run out of the bedroom on my numb legs. I have only one alternative—I look toward the dark window and the dense darkness beyond the pane—I must go outside, into the darkness.

I can hear his yelling behind me as I fumble with the lock to open the front door. It slides up with a click, and the black, cold, dense night air immediately envelops me. Even though I am literally being hunted by a crazed murderer, I hesitate instinctively for a fraction of a second before I rush out into the darkness; my life is being threatened and still I am considering staying in the lit corridor of the cottage—my fear of the dark is that strong.

I run toward the pier in stockinged feet. I search in vain for footing on the ground. The cold bites into my skin and I slip again and again before I reach the shed.

He has caught up with me.

His hand grabs my arm, and with a yell he throws me back toward the cottage, heaves my whole body against the red wall. I can feel myself break, something in my jaw gives way and my mouth is filled with gravel and blood. He presses one knee down between my shoulder blades, takes hold of my hair, and starts banging my hand against the wall, over and over again. Blood is running from my mouth. It trickles down into the snow and forms a red pool that grows alarmingly fast. I see that what I thought was gravel in my mouth is actually teeth.

My teeth.

And the whole time, Christer is emitting a howling sound, uttering a bestial roar that sounds like nothing I've ever heard before. Then suddenly he stops and I can hear it again, that whistling, hissing. He falls to his knees and supports himself with his hands in the snow, all while his cramped air passages give off rattling sounds. He falls to his side, against the pile of wood that should have been chopped before the snow came.

And then I feel it there in my hand, the ax that Aina left by the woodpile in the fall, the one she never got around to putting back in the shed. It is frozen solid in the ground and covered with snow. With strength I did not know I had, I manage to tear it loose. And although everything passes in a few seconds, I have time to think as I stand there with the ax in my hand: *Have I become an evil person? Or only someone who commits evil deeds?* I could cut him on the leg and injure him enough to only neutralize him. But I don't want to.

I want to kill the bastard.

A feeling of intoxication fills me despite my injuries, or perhaps because of them. I raise the ax, and with a cry I drive it into the back of his head so that it is buried in his red hair.

After a short time, the whistling and hissing of his breathing has stopped.

So I am back at the house. My beautiful white house.

A gentle light filters through the stained lead glass in the bedroom window. It falls and falls down toward me where I lie on our wide bed.

Next to me she is asleep, my child: Jenny. She is lying on her stomach with her chubby legs drawn up under her body and her little diapered bottom raised in the air like an exclamation point. The thin red hair rests sweaty against the pillow and her pacifier moves now and then, rhythmically.

Carefully, carefully I creep as close to her as I can without waking her.

Now. I breathe in her aroma, the aroma of my baby. It is warm and round and smells a little sour from old milk.

I am so happy.

Silence.

I can no longer feel the biting cold. The man who once was someone's father, the man who murdered Sara and fried meatballs in my kitchen, now lies quietly in the snow, his head resting in a pool of steaming blood. I vomit blood—or is it red wine?—onto the wall of the shed and sink to my knees. Slowly, I crawl through the snow toward the pier. Every movement is laborious, and I notice that I am leaving sticky traces of blood behind me in the snow.

So weak, I'm not able to make my way into the cottage. Crawling on all fours, I slide a few yards out onto the ice. I dig my fingers into the snow and try in vain to pull myself forward. My body feels numb and my jaw no longer hurts. For the first time that night, my head suddenly feels clear—it is only my body that is no longer able to function.

I lie on my back and look up at the sky. It is the most beautiful sky I have ever seen. Millions of stars glisten in all the colors of the rainbow against the saturated black background, and the snow does not feel cold and hard anymore but soft and welcoming. I think about a poem Stefan wrote to me on a wrinkled piece of paper what feels like a hundred years ago, about how darkness is necessary for the stars to be visible, and suddenly I realize that darkness does not frighten me anymore, it embraces me gently, soundlessly, and infinitely.

It could be so idyllic.

From my soft bed on the ice I can see my cottage surrounded by snow-covered wilderness. All the windows shine invitingly, and despite the dense darkness, I can make out a thin thread of smoke rising from the chimney up toward the clear Christmas night. Not a trace of the violent struggle that just played out outside the house is visible, there's not a sound—only a faint clicking noise from the ice under this aching body that no longer feels like it's mine.

Much later, it starts snowing. Large flakes float soundlessly, covering my face. I glide in and out of a drowsy sleep, and it is then, when the snow comes, that I sense him lying down beside me. Stefan rests his chin against my neck and wraps his arm around my waist. We say nothing, only look silently at the stars and at the falling snow.

It smells like honey.

I feel a warm body next to me and, although I haven't yet opened my eyes, I know who it is. I take a deep breath, fill my lungs with the aroma of honey, and look. The room is white, I see the metal bed and the egg-yellow latticed blanket of the county hospital on top of me. Aina's hair tickles my nose. She must have noticed that I've woken up, because she turns toward me and strokes my cheek. I try to speak, but some kind of bracket—or cast—around my jaw makes it impossible.

"Shh. Don't talk. I found you frozen solid on the ice, princess. You were supposed to call at ten o'clock and thank me for the present, weren't you? When you didn't call I got worried. Finally I drove to the apartment, and when you weren't there I knew right away where you had gone."

Aina looks sad.

"I should have known what you intended to do. That you can never be trusted, you hopeless person. It's over now anyway. He's dead as a doornail. Markus and your parents are on their way here. I've chased away the other police officers for the moment."

Then she sees my eyes resting on the red roses stuffed into a small vase on the crooked nightstand and nods silently, stroking my hair.

"They're from Markus. He made me buy them."

Now she lies down again, close beside me on the roomy hospital bed, and I feel her damp breath against my throat as she rests her head against mine. I don't want to talk at all, just lie quietly with my nose in Aina's yellow honey hair.

EPILOGUE

"I know we haven't always been that close," I start, then hesitate a moment and rub my hand against my jaw, which still aches and locks sometimes.

I am searching for the right words, and when I think I have found them I continue.

"Maybe we're too different to be really close friends—you know, different goals in life, different experiences and ways of approaching people. I know I haven't always shown you the appreciation you deserved, that sometimes I've been irritated for no reason and even barked at you on some occasions. *Good Lord,* that was really stupid and unprofessional of me. But you should know that if there is anything I have always felt for you, it's respect. Respect for the work you've done, always meticulously, on time and without errors. Respect for your consideration and sympathy. Respect for the life you've lived, with everything that child rearing, separations, and striving for independence must involve."

I think a moment and study the white room before me with a sink and a steel chair as the only furnishings.

"Well, I have to admit that sometimes I thought you favored Sven. You know, his patient notes were always transcribed first, his calls were the most important to make, and his office was cleaned every day, even though that wasn't even part of your job description. But all that is so long ago now. When these kinds of things happen you reevaluate your life a little, don't you? Focus on what's important, let go of all the old stuff and . . . how shall I put it . . . see the good in your fellow human beings. You want to thank them because they've been there for you. It's that way for me, anyway. And I guess that's why I came here. To thank you for all the help and . . . maybe to say I'm sorry you didn't always get the appreciation you deserved."

I get up and look at Marianne, still unconscious on the hospital bed with her mouth half open, her chin resting slackly against her chest. If I didn't know it was Marianne I wouldn't recognize her, she is that changed. The curly, blond hair has grown out long and dark, her skin looks thin and paperlike now, a tube has been inserted in one nostril, and there's some kind of monitor on her index finger that looks like a clothespin and spreads a reddish glow on her hand.

I get up slowly and leave the room, without turning back.

A few months after Stefan's funeral I was alone in our house, without Aina by my side, no longer under my family's watchful eyes. It was a gray day. The hazy, dirty light that flooded the room gave it a worn, pale appearance that made it look like the summer cottage it really was. A temporary residence. At any rate, a completely hopeless project, from a practical point of view.

I had the vague notion of cleaning up his things—throwing away what was no longer needed, sorting through what would be given away, and saving what might be useful sometime in the future—but that proved to be harder than I thought. His newly ironed shirts and jeans were hanging in a row in our common closet. Why throw away perfectly usable clothes? Who could I give them to? I decided to leave the clothes untouched for the time being.

I moved on to the desk. It was still in the same state as the day Stefan died. No one had touched the worn desktop or blown the dust from the pile of papers stacked neatly in the far right corner. I ran my fingers over the rough surface, creating deep tracks in the dust. Resolutely, I went out to the kitchen and got a damp cloth, carefully moved the stack of papers to the floor, and started wiping the desk with long, sweeping motions.

The drawers were full of neatly organized stacks of paper. Carefully, I removed the contents of the top drawer and set it on the now clean, damp surface of the desk. Balance statements from the student financial aid office, bills, and tax documents were sorted in the pile. On each piece of paper there was a note: TO BE PAID or FOR TAX RETURN. I shook my head. It was not like Stefan to be so pedantic and tidy. The next stack, labeled IMPORTANT PAPERS, was also inexplicably well organized. Insurance policies, the contract of sale for the house, account statements from the bank—all of our life and household together recorded in a stack of papers.

I fiddled aimlessly with the documents, looked at the numbers that showed what we owned without seeing or understanding their significance. It was so good that everything was here, it would make things much easier for Dad, who was going to take care of all these financial matters, I mused, before my train of thought was interrupted by something else: a sinking concern, a fleeting feeling. Like a wrong note in a well-composed piece of music, barely audible but still perceptible. There was something that didn't add up here. Stefan was never this neat. I had devoted a considerable portion of our years together to keeping track of his papers and things.

I opened the bottom drawer. It contained only one piece of paper. A thin, crinkled, handwritten note with grease stains on it—it almost looked like wax paper—carefully folded down the middle and addressed "To Siri." The dim room suddenly felt stuffy, and I got up to open one of the French doors. The cold, raw air filled my lungs and I heard the screeching of the gulls, intrusive and sharp as I supported myself against the doorframe.

With fumbling, shaking fingers I unfolded the paper. It was a poem.

Don't be afraid of darkness,
for in darkness rests the light.
We see no stars or planets
without the dark of night.
The darkness of the pupil
is in the iris round,
for all light's fearful longing
has darkness at its ground.
Don't be afraid of darkness,
for in it rests the light.
Don't be afraid of darkness;
it holds the heart of light.

Date: May 15
Time: 3:00 p.m.
Place: Karlaplan Psychology Clinic
Therapist for treatment: Maryvonne von Arndtstadt
Patient: Siri Bergman—assessment interview

"Welcome, Siri. I know you're a psychologist, so I assume you are already familiar with how an assessment interview works. So I suggest we skip the formalities and that you tell me why you are here."

"I'm here because I have an unprocessed trauma that I would benefit from talking about."

"In your past?"

"My husband took his life a couple of years ago, or at least I *think* he took his life. I have always preferred to think of it as an accident. And there is no real evidence that has confirmed that it was suicide."

"That's not completely unheard of where suicide is concerned."

"I know. But recently events . . . outside my control have forced me to reassess what happened, forced me to realize that it probably was a suicide."

"Tell me."

Turn the page to read the first chapters from the next novel in the bestselling series by Camilla Grebe and Åsa Träff.

MORE BITTER THAN DEATH

Camilla Grebe and Åsa Träff

Translated by Tara Chace

Available from Simon & Schuster Summer 2013

Trade Paperback ISBN: 978-0-85720-949-8
Ebook ISBN: 978-0-85720-951-1

I find something more bitter than death:
the woman who is a net,
whose heart is like a snare,
and whose hands are fetters.
He who pleases God will escape her,
but the sinner she will ensnare.
—Ecclesiastes 7:26

GUSTAVSBERG, A SUBURB OF STOCKHOLM, OCTOBER 22, AFTERNOON

Everything looks different from below.

The massive legs of the enormous dining table, the oak tabletop with the distinct grain and the chalk drawing underneath—the one Mama hasn't discovered yet. The tablecloth draping down around her in heavy, creamy white folds.

Mama also looks different from below.

Cautiously she sticks her head out of her tent, glances over at her mother as she stands at the stove pushing down the spaghetti that's poking out of the big, gray pot like pick-up sticks with one hand as she smokes with the other.

There's a snapping sound as the spaghetti breaks under the fork's pressure.

Mama's worn jeans are hanging so far down over her rear end that she can see the tattoo on her backside and those pink panties.

From below Mama's bottom looks enormous, and she wonders if she should say so. Mama is always wondering if her bottom looks big or small. And she often forces Henrik to answer that question even though he doesn't want to. He'd rather watch the horses that are running around and around on TV while he drinks his beer.

It's called a hobby.

Mama puts her cigarette out in her coffee cup, picks up a little spaghetti that wound up next to the pot with those long fingernails, and stuffs it in her mouth as if it was candy. It crunches as she chews.

She picks up a piece of blue chalk and starts carefully coloring in what's going to be the sky. The drawing already has a house, their house, with a red car out front, the one they're going to buy when Mama gets another job. Through the window, the weak gray light of the fall afternoon filters into the kitchen, painting the room in a depressing, dark palette, but in her tent it's dark in a cozy way. Only a dim light seeps in, enough for her to see the paper resting on the floor in front of her and make out a hint of the colors of the chalk.

A steady stream of music from the radio, interspersed with ad breaks. Ads are when they talk, that much she has understood. Ads are when Henrik goes and pees out all the beer he's been drinking. Ads are also when Mama goes out and smokes on the balcony, but when Henrik's not home she smokes everywhere. Even when there isn't an ad.

The knocking is gentle and considerate, as if maybe it wasn't someone knocking but just absentmindedly drumming lightly on the wood as he or she passed the door to the apartment.

She sees her mother light another cigarette, leaning over the sink, seeming to hesitate.

Then the knocking becomes pounding.

Thump, thump, thump.

And there's no longer any doubt that someone is standing outside the door, someone who wants in. Someone who's in a hurry.

"I'm coming," Mama yells and slowly walks over to the door with her cigarette in her hand. As if she had all the time in the world. And Tilde knows that's so, because Henrik has to learn to wait. Everything can't always happen at once, can't always be on his terms. Mama's told him as much.

She finds a light yellow piece of chalk she thinks will make a good sun and starts drawing a circle with sweeping, round motions. The paper crumples a little and when she holds it down with her other hand a small tear starts up in the right–hand corner. A crack in the perfect world she is so carefully creating. She hesitates: Start over again or keep going?

Thump, thump, thump.

Henrik seems angrier than usual. Then there's the sound of the safety chain sliding off and Mama opens the door.

She looks through her pieces of chalk, which resemble grayish brown sticks in the darkness under the kitchen table. As if she were sitting in the woods under a spruce tree playing with real sticks. She wonders what that would feel like; she's never been to the woods. Just to the playground downtown and there aren't any trees there, just thorny bushes with small, small orange-red berries that the other kids say are poisonous.

She finds the gray chalk. She will draw a big, dark cloud. One swollen with rain and hail in its belly, one that scares the grownups.

From out in the hallway she hears indignant voices and more pounding. Muffled thuds on the floor, as if something was falling over and over again. And she thinks that she wishes sometime they would quit fighting. Or that Mama could throw out those yellow beer cans, the ones that make Henrik grumpy and irritated and tired.

She leans down to the floor so she can peek out from under the tablecloth. They're screaming now and something is wrong. The voices don't sound familiar. Henrik doesn't sound the way he usually does.

The hallway is cloaked in darkness.

She can sense bodies moving there, but can't see what's happening.

Then: a roar.

Someone, she now sees it's her mother, falls forward headlong onto the kitchen floor. She lands flat on her stomach with her face down, and she can see a red pool growing where her mother's head is resting. Mama's hands grab hold of the rug as if she wants to cling to it and she tries to crawl back into the main room at the same time as something small, shiny, and glimmering gold rolls into the kitchen from the hallway.

Someone, the man, is swearing out in the hallway. His voice is gloomy and sort of rough. Then footsteps enter the kitchen. A figure bends over, catches the little object.

She doesn't dare stick her head out to see who it is, but she sees the black boots and dark trouser legs that stop next to her mother's head, hesitate for a second and then kick her, over and over again in the face. Until her whole face seems to come loose, like a mask from a doll and red and pink goo gushes out in a puddle on the rug in front of her. The black boots are also covered with the goo that slowly drips down onto the floor, like melting ice cream.

It gets quiet, except for the music still coming from the radio and she wonders how it can be possible for the music to just keep going and going, as if nothing had happened, even though Mama is lying there on the kitchen floor like a pile of dirty laundry in a sea of blood that's growing by the second.

Mama's breaths are drawn out and wheezing. As if she had just inhaled water by mistake.

Then she watches how her mother is dragged out into the hallway, inch by inch. She's still clutching tightly to the little kitchen rug and it goes along with her, out into the dark hallway.

The only thing left on the cream-colored linoleum floor is the sea of blood and the pink goo.

She hesitates for a second, but then continues coloring in the gray storm cloud.

STOCKHOLM, TWO MONTHS EARLIER

Vijay's office. An infinitely large desk, and yet every last corner of the desktop is covered with paper. I wonder how he can ever find what he needs among all these thousands of papers, folders, and journals.

His laptop is perched on top of a stack of what looks like essays. A super-thin Mac. Vijay has always been a Mac person. Next to that, a cup of coffee and a banana peel. A tin of chewing tobacco is half hidden under a memo from the department chair.

"Did you start chewing tobacco?"

Aina gives Vijay an incredulous look and contorts her face in disgust.

"Hm . . . I was forced to. Olle objected to the cigarettes, but he puts up with the chewing tobacco."

Vijay smiles and Aina shakes her head in sympathy.

"Too bad. And here I was thinking we ought to grab a cup of coffee and take a smoke break in that biting wind out there, relive old memories and that sort of thing."

All three of us laugh, remembering for a second how we used to stand together in the pouring rain, snow, or broiling sun, season in and season out. Sharing cigarettes and coffee. Back then when life was less complicated. Or maybe it just seemed that way, back in those days.

I observe Vijay. The black hair, now with gray at the temples. The bushy mustache, a wrinkled blue-and-white-striped cotton shirt. He doesn't look like a professor, but maybe that's how you'd describe the Professor Look: the lack of any common style denominator. What do I know anyway? I don't know that many professors. But however little Vijay looks like a professor, I can't deny the fact that he's aged, just like Aina and me. We're older, maybe wiser, maybe just more tired and mildly surprised that life didn't turn out like we had thought, back then.

"It's not like I'd be hard to convince. Maybe we can go out and have a smoke anyway. Olle's at a conference in Reykjavik so it's not like he'll know." Vijay picks up his tobacco tin and starts absentmindedly picking at the label. "But," he continues, "that's not why I asked you to come . . . to discuss my nicotine habit, I mean."

Aina and I nod. We know that Vijay asked us here to discuss an assignment and we're grateful for it. Psychotherapists suffer just like everyone else from economic downturns and the offer of a long-term contract from a publicly funded institution is most welcome.

"So, it has to do with a research project in which we're going to study how effective self-help groups are for women who have been victims of abuse. The target group is women who are at risk of developing posttraumatic stress disorder, but who for whatever reason don't want to receive traditional treatment. The project is a collaboration between the municipality of Värmdö and Stockholm University."

Vijay has stepped into his professional persona. His eyes gleam and his cheeks are flushed pink. He is passionate about his work, doesn't view it as a job, a source of income, but rather as a lifestyle and perhaps also something that gives his life meaning. Plus, he can't deny that it does wonders for his ego, being the most knowledgeable, the expert. He often appears in the press, where he comments on various crimes and their presumed causes. It would be easy to psychoanalyze him, to believe that his satisfaction depends on his need for revenge. The put-upon immigrant, marginalized both because of his ethnic origin and his sexual orientation. Although that is far from the truth. Vijay's parents are well-to-do academics who came to Sweden on research grants and then stayed. Being gay was never an issue for his family. There were three other brothers who were providing his parents with all the grandchildren their hearts desired. Vijay may have been seen as eccentric, but he was also quite successful.

"Where do we come in, if this has to do with self-help therapy?" Aina interrupts Vijay's pontificating and he's forced to pause, something he isn't that fond of doing.

"I'm getting to that, if you'll just bear with me."

He stops talking, opens his tobacco tin, stuffs a snuff pouch under his lip, and then proceeds.

"The idea is for you guys to run the pilot study. Test the manual, take a peek at the psychoeducational portions, see if anything needs to be added or removed."

"Psychoeducation and self-help, that doesn't sound like CBT," I say, lost in thought. Aina is looking doubtful and Vijay is smiling placidly.

"It isn't CBT, not strictly speaking. But that doesn't mean it can't be effective. You guys know that there is far more demand for trained psychotherapists with a CBT approach than there are psychotherapists. This is one way of allowing more people to participate in different interventions that we know are effective for posttraumatic stress disorder and trauma, we simply want to make this type of approach available at a lower cost. Besides, there's a point to self-help groups, especially for people who have been victims. It gives them a sense of . . . of being in control, maybe. Empowerment. Well . . . you know."

"Empowerment?"

Aina still looks skeptical and glances over at me, looking for a sign, a signal of how I feel about this whole thing.

"How is it structured?"

I'm curious and want to hear more about how they expect the treatment to work.

"Eight sessions, two hours each. Every session will start with an instructional portion, reactions to trauma, men's violence against women, information about common symptoms of posttraumatic stress disorder, topics like that. After that there will be a less structured portion, the women can talk about their own experiences and listen to the others' stories. The group leader's role is to lead the conversation. Make sure that everyone gets a chance to talk and that no one becomes too dominant. After that, the leader will give a homework assignment, maybe asking the women to think about how their life changed after the traumatic event or come up with new goals for how they want things to be in the future. What they lost and what they think they could re-create, re-conquer perhaps. And then how they're going to do it. You'll receive a detailed manual, but you're free to depart from it. You evaluate the sessions together afterwards and offer opinions on the contents. Everything will be documented. It's important to remember that this is a self-help group, so the level has to be just right—it should have substance and be able to help them but it can't be too complicated. It's not psychotherapy, and the program won't be run by psychotherapists; the group facilitators will be women who suffered violence at the hands of men themselves. . . ."

Vijay interrupts himself and suddenly looks embarrassed. I know what he's thinking and what he's about to say.

"I, um, Siri . . . I'm not asking you to do this because you're a victim, but quite simply because you're a hell of a good psychologist and psychotherapist. You and Aina, you're good. Damn good."

"But the fact that I was the victim of violence in addition to being a psychologist and a therapist, maybe that doesn't hurt?"

I study Vijay, watch him weighing the various alternatives. I know him well enough that I have some idea what he's thinking. Tell it like it is or smooth it over? Pretend like nothing happened and that I'm the same person I was before or concede that what happened, the fact that another person tried to kill me, actually changed who I am?

"Does it bother you?" he asks.

He looks vulnerable and anxious. I contemplate his question, whether it bothers me that Vijay thinks that my personal history makes me better suited than someone else to do this job. And I realize it doesn't. My personal experiences are still with me, but they don't hurt anymore. It's no longer an open wound. I think I actually have control over my reactions and my ability to relate to what happened.

"No, it doesn't bother me."